IT WAS ALWAYS YOU

ERIKA KELLY

IT WAS ALWAYS YOU
Erika Kelly

ISBN-13: 978-0-9985177-9-7

Cover design by Melissa Panio-Petersen
Formatting by Serendipity Formatting
Editing by Kristy deBoer

Praise for The Calamity Falls series

KEEP ON LOVING YOU

"I adored this book! It is exactly what I love in a second-chance romance. The characters are so vibrant and real, I was rooting for them with every page." —*USA Today* Bestseller Devney Perry

"*KEEP ON LOVING YOU* is such a fun and sexy second-chance romance that I didn't want it to end. Their connection is a swoony blend of tender first love and sizzling heat, and Erika Kelly delivers a highly entertaining and sigh-worthy romance that shouldn't be missed."
—Mary Dube, USA Today

WE BELONG TOGETHER

"I loved every sweet, heart-wrenching, crazy, mixed-up minute of this book. It was an emotional journey from the first chapter to the last. This is Erika Kelly at her best, and this is a not-to-be-missed book!" —Sharon Slick Reads, Guilty Pleasures Book Reviews

"Erika Kelly damn near pulled my heart from my chest with Delilah and Will's story. It's so well-written that you feel everything. My heart got tugged so hard! I honestly cried at a few moments in the book. I fell all the way in love with "Wooby." It's hard not to, really." —Ree Cee's Books

THE VERY THOUGHT OF YOU

"Wow, THE VERY THOUGHT OF YOU was simply OUTSTANDING! This second chance, friends to lovers romance is enchanting and entertaining." —Spellbound Stories

"I just finished this story, and I want to start all over again. Or maybe at the start of series. To once again feel the events, the emotions, that brought these amazing characters together. To hear the banter and the arguments, the sorrow, the loss and the happiness that brought a family together and closer." —Nerdy, Dirty, and Flirty

JUST THE WAY YOU ARE

"An alpha cowboy and a smart, sassy princess collide in JUST THE WAY YOU ARE in Erika Kelly's latest, and it was fabulous! I was cheering for Brodie and Rosalina with every page. If you love stories with heart, steam, and plenty of swoon, don't miss this one!" —USA Today Bestselling Author J.H. Croix

"With the Calamity Falls series, Kelly doesn't shy away from charming. She captivates with delectable characters that wrap themselves around a heart. From the first hello to the final goodbye, Rosalina and Brodie are a match made out of the unpredictable, but the sweetest kind of heaven. JUST THE WAY YOU ARE is the perfect example of why I am hooked on this series. SWOONWORTHY READ!" —Hopeless Romantic Book Reviews

IT WAS ALWAYS YOU

"This book was full of every emotion you could ever feel. Gigi and Cassian proved you can conquer anything with true love." —Cat's Guilty Pleasure

"I could not put this book down! Erika Kelly always delivers a great love story and never disappoints! I recommend this book for romance lovers looking to get lost in a great love story." —Reading in Pajamas

CAN'T HELP FALLING IN LOVE

"I love everything about this emotional and sexy, second chance story. Erika Kelly writes a story that makes me feel like I'm right there with the two main characters, Beckett and Coco. It is a slow burn, passionate story with lots of underlying tension. I not only enjoyed this story, but I found it impossible to put down." —Cocktails and Books

"I loved everything about this book. I loved all the characters, from Beckett, 'I don't believe in love,' to single mom, small business-owning, closed-off Coco, to a fairy-believing five-year-old who will steal your heart! I cannot gush enough about how spectacular I thought this book was." – Bookcase and Coffee

WHOLE LOTTA LOVE

"BRILLIANT! This book was incredible, I could not put this book down, that is how good Lu and Xander's story was. I fell in love with these two characters instantly." – Harlequin Junkie

"Whole Lotta Love was absolutely perfect! You will instantly love this couple and their journey to find happiness!" – Just Love Books

YOU'RE STILL THE ONE

"Griffin and Stella really are soulmates. They bring out the best of each other, and when they're together, everything is better. Their world is better with the love they feel for each other. And I think they made my world better a bit, too." – Jersey Girl's Bookshelf

"WOW! WOW! WOW! Welcome to all the feels! I ADORED Stella and Griffin's story. I was completely lost in this book and didn't want to put it down. I FELT everything, and I can't tell you how much I loved it." – Books According to Abby

Titles by Erika Kelly

Sign up for my newsletter to read the EXCLUSIVE novella for my readers only! You'll get two chapters a month of this super sexy, fun romance! #rockstarromance #teenidolturnedboyfriend Also, get PLANES, TRAINS, AND HEAD OVER HEELS for FREE! I hope you'll come hang out with me on Facebook, Twitter, Instagram, Goodreads, and Pinterest or in my private reader group.

This book is dedicated to Amy Patrick, the kindest, most generous person I know. I'm lucky to call you my friend.

Acknowledgments

- To Superman: thank you for loving me, making me laugh, and listening to my stories every single day of my life.
- To Sharon: thank you for believing in me so fiercely.
- To Kristy deBoer: thank you for always making my books better.
- To Melissa: I am so grateful for everything you do, especially keeping me calm!
- To Erica: thank you for always being there for me and for your bottomless well of patience.
- To the romance writing community: I couldn't do this without the bloggers and reviewers like Obsessed with Romance, Guilty Pleasures Book Reviews, About that Story, Reading in Pajamas, Zoe Forward, Shirin's Book Blog and Reviews, Reads and Reviews, and Isha Coleman—to name just a few; and my friends in writer groups like the Dreamweavers, the DND Authors, Indie AF, and my Plotstormer girls.

Chapter One

CASSIAN ELLIS'S PHONE RATTLED IN THE CUPHOLDER. One hand gripping the steering wheel, he nabbed it and swiped his thumb across the screen.

Brennan: *She's down for it.*

Anxiety burst in his chest. Propping his knee to control the wheel, he shot back a text.

Cassian: *Leave her alone. I'm serious.*

Nobody touched Gigi Cavanaugh.

Nobody.

His eyes flicked back to the road just in time to spot the coyote in front of his truck. Slamming on the brake, he jolted forward, tires squealing as he came to a stop a foot in front of the terrified animal. Headlights gleamed in its stunned eyes.

"Dammit." Heart thundering, he tossed his phone onto the passenger seat.

He'd almost killed an animal.

He never texted while driving. Never. *You're losing your shit.*

He'd been away from Gigi all week, and he couldn't

stand it.

She's not my girlfriend.

She'll never be my girlfriend.

He knew that, but still. The idea that Brennan—that any of his teammates—would try to hook up with her made him crazy.

But that's not fair.

I can't have her—but they can.

He honked, and the coyote bolted into the sagebrush meadow. Accelerating, he turned down Blossom Road to find cars parked haphazardly all over the snow-crusted cul-de-sac. Impatient to see her, he drove his truck up the side of a hill, jammed on the emergency brake, and jumped out.

Damn, it's cold. His breath came out in quick, white puffs.

He jogged toward the house, snow crunching under his feet. Bass from the loud music shattered the brittle air.

The moment he opened the door, the noise and heat hit him. The place was crawling with people. It looked like everyone in his senior class had shown up.

"Dude." A teammate saw him and rushed over. Others followed, surrounding him. *Jesus, not now.* Someone shoved a plastic cup of beer at him, but Cassian waved it off, too focused on getting to Gigi.

"Congratulations, dude," a girl said.

"Monumental achievement," one of the guys said.

"Come on." One of the team's wide receivers tried to drag him deeper into the room. "Shots to celebrate."

"Hang on." Something about his tone caused their smiles to freeze. "I'll catch up with you in a minute." He shoved out of the circle.

Where is she? He was so amped, he felt like he could

hurl his truck off a ravine.

What if she'd had too much to drink, and Brennan took advantage of that?

Okay, first of all, Gigi wouldn't let anyone take advantage of her. But, secondly, Brennan wasn't a bad guy.

That's not the point, is it?

The point is…what if Gigi wants to date Brennan?

What if Cassian had to spend the last six months of high school watching her have a boyfriend?

For nearly four years they'd been pretty much inseparable. He'd never had to see her with another guy.

We're friends. Nothing more.

Her dad made sure of that.

Not finding her, he wove his way through the crowd into the game room. A group played beer pong on a pool table. Several people gathered around the fireplace, listening to someone play guitar.

Gigi.

His heart about exploded at the sight of her. Eyes closed, cheeks rosy from the roaring flames, she was beautiful—the most spirited, strong, positive person he knew.

And talented—not only could she sing, but she wrote songs that blew everyone away. For years, she'd performed at school functions—she was a rock star in the making.

Beside her, Brennan sat too close. Cassian wanted to shout at him to give her some space. But he didn't need to do anything, because when his teammate tried to cup the back of her neck, Gigi shrugged him off.

He smiled. Yeah, she had no interest in his cornerback.

Draining his red Solo cup, Brennan threaded his fingers through her silky, dark hair. Cassian's body went on high alert. She'd made herself clear—why wasn't the guy listening?

He wouldn't embarrass Gigi by making a scene, so he shot off a text.

Cassian: **Back off, man. Let her play**.

But Brennan wasn't looking at his phone. He had his mouth right up against Gigi's ear. Jolting to her feet, she jerked the guitar out in front of her like a shield. Brennan snaked a finger through the belt loop of her jeans and yanked. The moment she toppled onto his lap, she scrambled to get up, but Brennan wrapped an arm around her stomach and held her in place.

Cassian charged across the room. In one motion, he pried his teammate's arm off her and pulled Gigi away.

She whipped around and kicked Brennan in the shin. "What's the matter with you?"

"Ow. What? I was just playin'." Brennan slurred his words.

Barely hanging onto his self-control, Cassian leaned in. "Soon as we get back to school after winter break, I'm going to get the entire offensive line to show you what it's like to feel overpowered, got it?"

"Yeah, man. It's cool. We're cool."

He turned back to Gigi, who was shaken. "Come on."

The buzz of conversation and laughter only fueled his agitation. *I've got to get out of here.* He wanted to be alone with her in the quiet of his truck and drive, but it was December in Calamity. Their small, Wild West town, sandwiched between the Teton and the Gros Ventres Mountain Ranges, was bitter cold this time of year and blanketed in snow.

She tugged on his hand, head tilting toward the staircase. *Let's find a quiet room.*

Christ, no. He couldn't take her to one of the bedrooms. Not only would it give their classmates the wrong impression of them, but…he only had so much restraint. He forged ahead.

She tugged the back of his flannel shirt, pulling him into a small alcove. "Hey, I'm okay. Everything's fine."

"He's an asshole."

"He's harmless." Gently, she set her guitar against the wall, and then she gazed up at him with a sweet smile, amber eyes sparkling with excitement. "Tell me how it went."

A cartoon meme popped into his brain, a field of flowers bursting into bloom all at once. His spirits soared. Affection for her consumed him, disabling his ability to speak.

She beamed at him with so much pride. "I'm so happy for you."

He could only nod.

She smacked his arm. *Come on.* "Was it the coolest thing in the world?"

He wanted to be in their treehouse, sprawled side-by-side on the mattress, so he could tell her everything on his mind. He had so much turmoil, and she was the only one who could sort through all the crap and get everything to line up.

When he didn't respond, her brow furrowed. "I wish I could've been there, but at least my dad was." She gave him an encouraging smile. "Tell me everything."

"Not much to say." What she didn't know—what he couldn't tell her—was that he'd wanted her there while he'd signed his letter of intent.

He always wanted her with him.

He didn't need anybody but her.

I love you. With everything in me, I fucking love you.

He'd known it the moment he'd laid eyes on her his

5

third day of school at Calamity High. It'd been like smacking his funny bone. It had reverberated throughout his entire body, leaving him shaky and hyperaware of his senses—the smell of too many bodies in the hallway, the buzz of conversation, the taste of the tart apple he'd grabbed on his way out the door.

And, yesterday, he'd signed a contract that would separate them. He didn't know what life would look like without seeing her every day. Didn't want to.

"My dad sent pictures of you in your blazer with the pen in your hand. He captured the big moment, right when you signed." Her forehead creased. "Hey, what's going on? Are you okay?"

When she stroked his biceps, static electricity made the hairs on his arm snap to attention. This girl—with her plump, raspberry lips, amber eyes that probed and *always* found him worthy...She owned his whole heart. "I'm good." *I just missed you.*

And I realized I'm not completely myself unless I'm with you.

And the idea of going to college without her made it feel like his wheels were spinning out, kicking out gravel and dust. *Chaos.*

"What were the other recruits like?" Her eyes went wide with impatience.

He gave himself a mental shake. *I have her now. For six more months.* "It was in the Athletic Office."

A Beyoncé song came on, and even more people crowded the make-shift dance floor. People hollered and sang along with "All the Single Ladies." When someone stumbled into them, Cassian shifted to block Gigi from the crowd.

Boxing her in against the wall, his arms on either side

6

of her head, he leaned in so she could hear him. "There're twenty-three prospects but only five of us signed early." He didn't want to talk about the details, but he could see she wanted more. "The press was there, and there was a lot of talk about how we're the best recruiting class the Big Ten has seen since two-thousand-and-seven."

"That's so great." She scanned his features, obviously concerned. "Are you not sure about Michigan?" Thanks to the dry, mountain climate, she always wore Chapstick. It must've worn off, because she kept licking her lips, that pink tongue tracing the seam of her mouth.

"No, I am. It's good. I just…" He wanted to shove his hands into her thick, dark hair, scrape it back to see all of her. He needed to finally ease this constant ache from not being allowed to touch her. "The coach was talking me up. Best throwing arm he's seen in a generation…how my speed's pretty good for a guy my size…but then, at the end, after we'd all signed, he came up to me and said, 'Don't fuck this up. Don't get in an accident or do any stupid shit. That arm's mine now.'"

She nodded, like she understood. "He psyched you out."

"Injury's always on my mind. If anything goes wrong…"

"Hey." She set her hand on his shoulder. "If anything goes wrong, you're still at one of the top schools in the country. You'll get a great education and have a career."

"Yeah, but see, those are just words. You know I can't do anything but football. From the time I moved here, I've been on one track."

Frustration flashed across her features. "No, I don't know that. You're as smart as you are athletic. Look, I have a feeling this is about my dad, and you have to know that, unless you get a girl pregnant, flunk out of school, or become a giant, egotistical jerk, you can't let him down. He's really proud of you, Cassian, and he'll be the first to say you did this on your own. It was your work ethic, your natural ability, and your coachability. All he did was guide you. I know he's told you, but you have to believe him when he says you've made him very, very proud."

He blinked back the sting in his eyes. He owed her dad everything. The retired quarterback had plucked Cassian out of detention the first week of freshman year and spent countless hours turning Cassian into a great ball player. Tyler Cavanaugh had seen something in him, and there wasn't a chance he'd let the man down.

Gigi could say whatever she wanted, but her dad expected Cassian to play professionally. Cassian wanted it, too, of course. But…it was a hell of a lot of pressure.

She licked her lips, gazing up at him with those soft, imploring eyes. "You're not that self-destructive kid anymore. You turned yourself around. I think…I think sometimes you misunderstand. He doesn't need you to have his career. He just needs you to be a good man and live your best life."

My best life is with you. He knew that down to his bones. Everyone thought it was Tyler who'd changed him —and to a degree it was. He respected Tyler more than any other man alive. But it was Gigi who made him want to be a better man.

For her, he'd wanted to be cleaner. Nicer. Smarter. Not a chance would he have shown up at her house with a shitty report card or smelling like ass.

Gigi nudged him. "You know that, right? My dad cares more about you getting on the right path in life than having you follow in his footsteps."

"Yeah, sure."

Laughing, she smacked his arm. "Don't humor me. Tell me what you're thinking."

This is what I love about her. She makes me face my shit. He swiped a thumb across his lower lip. "Look, I owe your dad everything. I wouldn't be the quarterback of our team, and I sure as hell wouldn't be playing for a Big Ten school if he hadn't stepped in. And I'm…" How did he explain it without sounding weak?

"Scared."

Just hearing the word out loud calmed him. Knowing she understood made him chill out. "Hell, yeah, I'm scared. I'm terrified. How many hometown heroes choke in college? It's easy to be great in *Wyoming*, but it's a whole other level at a school like Michigan. And, even if I can handle myself on the field, I still have to perform in classes. And…" The thing that really messed him up. "I'm not like the other guys. Most of them started football when they were four. I didn't start until I was fourteen. That's late. I don't know that I have what it takes to make it to the pros. Everyone's going to be looking at me, comparing me to all the other QBs. I—"

She held up a hand. "Stop. Listen to me, your coach has been recruiting guys for over twenty years. He flew you out to do drills with his team—he's seen you in action. He knows what he's got in you." Those earnest eyes begged him to hear her. "I think, on some level, you're working so hard to earn your keep. It's not just with my dad. You do it with your aunt and uncle, too."

After his parents died when he was fourteen, he'd gone to live with his uncle's family in Calamity. For the first two years, he hadn't made it easy on them.

"But you have to realize…they all love you like a son."

He didn't know about that. Still, his hand went to his chest, to ease the ache in his heart.

"You're worthy just as you are."

The ache swelled so big it made it hard to take a full breath. This girl…she was the only person in the world who saw him right down to his bones.

And accepted him all the way.

None of the self-discipline he'd marshalled to get recruited by the top team in the nation compared to what it took for him to keep his hands off her.

To keep from kissing her.

"I'm so happy for you. You've earned this. Can you even imagine how many times my dad's going to fly out there to see your games? He should probably buy a condo near campus." The plea in her eyes hit him harder than her grin. *She needs me to be happy about this.*

Her best friend, Ashton, stumbled into them, laughing. "I'm stealing her for one second." Grabbing Gigi's wrist, she dragged her away.

Cassian leaned against the wall, closing his eyes. Gigi didn't know the price Cassian had paid for her dad's mentoring.

And she never would.

Last year, Tyler had found them in their tree house. Well, it wasn't literally in a tree. He and Gigi had constructed a make-shift cottage in the woods on her parent's property. They'd put up sheets of plywood, covered the space in tarps. Inside, they'd strung solar-powered lights and outfitted it with a mattress, bedding, and orange crates to store their supplies.

Cassian would never forget Tyler's expression when he'd discovered them. He'd gone rigid. Later, he'd pulled Cassian aside and said, "I want to help you. I want to get you all the way to the NFL. I'm doing it because I get you. I *was* you, but I have one requirement. You have to keep your hands off my daughter. She's got big plans, and the talent to realize them—but only if you give her the chance."

What could he say to that? *No, I love her, and if that means making her career secondary to mine, you bet I'm going for it?*

He'd never told her dad the truth. That it wasn't a crush. *It's not* hormones. *She's not a notch on my bed post.*

She's my heart. My soul.

No, he'd just promised to never touch the man's daughter.

And now, here they were, at that dreaded turning point.

College.

They'd applied to all the same schools, but that didn't mean any of them were right for Gigi. Everyone knew she belonged in a music program. She was going to be a star one day, and Cassian wouldn't hold her back. If she chose Julliard or Berklee, he'd celebrate with her.

Gigi came back, shaking her head. "She's wasted and looking for trouble. I can't even deal with her when she's like this." She turned him away from the manic dancing. "So, listen. I've applied to Michigan's School of Music." Her eyes glittered with excitement. "If I get in, I'm going there."

And here it is. Exactly what her dad didn't want to happen.

She looked so confident and happy, like, *This is it, we can finally be together.* And this…this is what made it so damn hard to keep his hands off her.

Because—miracle of all fucking miracles—he was

pretty sure Gigi Cavanaugh loved him, too. And she wanted him to tell her they could be together in college.

But he couldn't do that.

What kind of man would I be to take everything Tyler's given me and then screw him over like that?

All her joy sputtered out, turned into uncertainty. "Don't you want me to go school with you?"

"Yes." He said it in a growly whisper. His skin went hot, and his pulse kicked up. "But you're too talented, Gigi. The situation should be reversed. You should go to the best music program in the country, and I should play ball wherever you are."

Her features softened with hope and love. Danger pricked at the back of his neck.

She searched his eyes, and he didn't know what they revealed. He was sweating, his breathing growing erratic.

"I want things to be different in college, Cassian. I want…us to be together. I want that so much."

Trust Gigi to put it out there, to be honest and real. She didn't hide from anything.

And then, out of nowhere, she got up on her toes and kissed him.

The world exploded into brilliant colors. Need clamped down so hard his muscles ached. He licked inside her mouth, and she leaned into him. Desire burned wild and out of control.

He finally had her in his arms, her plump breasts pressed against his chest, her hand fisting in his hair. Her scent—exotic flowers, that hint of herbal shampoo—seeped into his bloodstream, triggering a primal roar of possession. His tongue did a slow dance with hers, lighting him up at the forbidden taste—mint, lemon soda—and he fucking wanted her more than he'd ever wanted anything.

Shit. Fuck.

You can't do this.

He pushed her away. His disloyalty to the man who'd made him into a star athlete disgusted him. His body waged war against his brain—desperate to have her back in his arms, yet knowing he'd never forgive himself if she compromised her dreams.

Her eyes went wide, scared. Her trembling hand covered her mouth, and her pulse throbbed in her throat. "What…why did you do that?"

Shudders wracked his body. Still, he forced a smirk. "Come on. You know I don't see you like that."

Hurt, anger, confusion fought for dominance on her beautiful features. Tears glistened. "Don't…don't do that. I'm not talking about now. I'm talking about next September."

But you're kissing me now.

And I can't resist you.

I can't.

"We're just friends, Gigi. Who cares where we go to school?" *Stop talking.*

Her expression…Jesus, she was killing him.

No, you're *killing* her.

Get out of here.

Just go.

He turned and took in the mass of bodies dancing and grinding on each other.

She pulled on his arm. "I know what you're doing. My dad told you to keep your hands off me, right? That day he found us in the tree house? Everything changed after that." She wasn't hurt anymore. She was fierce. "What did he say to you?"

He couldn't betray the man who'd flown across the

country to watch him sign his letter of intent. Like shutting down his computer, he felt his system going offline. One cell after another going black.

"Tell me." She got a fist full of his shirt and yanked it. "It's my life, too. I deserve to know what he said."

By force of will, he made his legs start moving. He walked away from her, deeper into the crowd, where everyone reeked of booze and weed. He needed to get out of there.

He felt dangerous. Like if she touched him one more time he'd finally give in and haul her up those stairs.

Fill all the emptiness inside him with her love.

Because that's what he needed. More than football, more than a career, more than anything on this earth, he needed to be with Gigi.

She reached for him. "Dammit, Cassian—"

He wrenched his arm out of her hold. "Stop touching me."

Her eyes filled with horror.

"I'm not attracted to you, okay?" He pushed deeper into the crowd and reached for the nearest body. The girl whipped around, her eyes lighting up when she saw it was him, their school's winning quarterback.

Oh, fuck. It's Ashton. She went from surprised to excited…to straight-up vixen. She shimmied with the music, swinging her hips side to side, as she made her way down his body and back up again. She kept dancing, a little awkward because she was so wasted, but there was no denying how happy she was to seduce him.

He felt Gigi watching him—of course he did. They were connected—deep down, irrevocably, their souls were made of the same fabric—and when he turned to her, he was surprised to find her worried.

Not crushed but worried.

You're not going to do this, are you?

Because you can't take this back. You know that, right?

But he couldn't play this out anymore. It was killing him, loving a woman he couldn't have. Spending every free moment with her but not being able to touch her. And, anyways, her dad had called it. Gigi would go to the wrong school just to be with him. He couldn't do that to her.

So, he reached for her best friend's ass and brought her up against him. And then…he kissed her.

The clash of lips, the foul taste of beer, the sickly sweet scent of perfume…everything was wrong. His body rebelled, shook with the offense of erasing Gigi's taste with someone else's.

Tilting his head, he forced himself to watch the destruction.

He'd seen Gigi experience every emotion under the sun. Joy when she got a standing ovation after a performance, contentment when they lay on their backs, feet braced against the orange crates in their tree house, talking about whatever was on their minds. Sorrow when her dog never came home, and outrage when her sister had broken her favorite guitar.

Everything except this one. Her devastation burned like acid on his heart.

He couldn't take it. He just couldn't. So, he reached for Ashton's hand and led her up the stairs.

Only this time he didn't look to see Gigi's reaction.

It didn't matter. It was done.

He'd pushed her away for good.

Chapter Two

Bottles littered the tables surrounding the hotel's pool. From Cassian Ellis's vantage point on the tiered middle deck, he could see two couples making out on some chaise lounges and another going at it so hard they kept knocking a potted plant against the wall.

It wasn't even midnight, and some of the guys looked bored, so he shouted down to the terrace below. "Turn it up."

Big Sean's "Bezerk" blasted, and he lifted himself onto the ledge before letting out a warrior cry.

A crowd gathered below, egging him on, clapping and whistling. A few guys came running up the stairs to join him.

With a shout, he cannonballed into the deep end of the pool. When he popped out of the water, he found others had joined him. Frothy waves of water crashed against the sides and splashed onto the concrete. People started jumping in, laughing and flicking water at each other. *Good.*

The song abruptly switched to Nelly's "Hot in

Herre," and then Amie Clover, the woman who ran his football camp, dashed across the patio and leapt onto the diving board. He'd never seen her so blitzed. *What're you doing, Amie?* In a tiny black bikini, she started swaying her hips, running her hands along her body and…

Oh, hell. She was going to strip for his teammates.

Their reactions would have been hilarious, the way one guy after another stopped messing around, jaws going slack, to watch the action. But, not only did she run his football camp for underprivileged kids, she was also a Mavericks cheerleader. He didn't want some hotel staffer whipping out his cell phone and grabbing shots of her stripping in front of the team.

Her job meant the world to her.

Dazzled, the guys called out, urging her on. She drank up the attention, using her toned body and trained muscles to seduce and entice. But then she grabbed her large breasts and gave them a shake.

This isn't good.

Hoisting himself out of the pool, he headed for the sound system, water dripping off his body. Instead of embarrassing her, he'd just change the song.

Except…*shit.* She reached behind her neck. She was about to take her top off.

Should he stop her? She was an adult, and she could do whatever she wanted with that banging body she loved to show off. He just wasn't sure how she'd feel tomorrow morning, knowing she'd stripped in front of the guys she worked with year-round.

The ties dropped, dangling. Fortunately, the swimsuit was wet, so the fabric still clung to her breasts. When her hands went to the ties at her back, Cassian jogged over to the diving board and jumped on it. Just as she flung her top into the pool, he blocked her from the guys.

"Hey." She gazed up at him, accusation in her eyes. When she tried to shove him, she lost her balance.

Cassian looped an arm around her back, catching her. "In four days, you're going to be bossing these guys around. You sure you want them to see you naked?"

She flicked a glance over his shoulder. "I'm just having fun."

"As you should. I just don't want either of us to jeopardize our careers." His coach was sick of all the bad press Cassian generated. If shots got out of a naked cheerleader at one of his parties, he'd hear about it.

He didn't need trouble.

He also didn't want her topless body up against his. He was very careful about the message he sent to women. If there was any chance he'd have to see them again or work with them in any capacity, he didn't hook up. At all. Ever. He never wanted to give a woman the wrong impression.

But just as he released her, her knees buckled, so he scooped her up and climbed off the diving board. His closest friend Dean "Mad Dog" Maddox stood nearby. "Toss me a towel."

Handing him one, Dean came up close. "She okay?"

Cassian nodded, wrapping Amie up before setting her down.

She gave him a soft grin. "You're a good guy, Cassian."

Tell that to the press that liked to have a field day with his reputation. "Let's get you some clothes." He grabbed someone's big T-shirt and handed it to her.

"Time to shut the party down," he said to Dean. "We

made it through the whole vacation scandal-free. Let's not press our luck."

Flashlights lit up the pool area in broad sweeps. Cassian whipped around to find police spreading out across the patio. A big, burly officer shined a light right at his chest.

"Cassian Ellis?"

"Yes, sir."

"Is this your party?"

Oh, fuck.

Gigi Cavanaugh shut off the mic so the recording engineer couldn't hear her and turned to her bandmates. "You guys, this isn't working. Let's just do what they want, okay? Play it as it's written."

At this point, no one seemed to care that the record label was running out of patience. They'd outgrown the band, and each wanted to put her own imprint on the songs.

"What's written sucks," the drummer said.

Gigi got it—she really did. "Yeah, well, our platinum records say differently." She tried for a smile, but she just wanted to finish this third and final album of their contract.

"I'm hardly changing anything." The bass player sounded like a belligerent teenager. "Besides, you know my riffs are better."

Gigi glanced through the window to find the producer watching. *This looks so bad, fighting in front of him.* She poked her head out of the sound booth. "Would you mind giving us a few minutes?"

"Christ." He threw off his headphones and shoved back his wheeled chair.

She led the way out. Two of her bandmates collapsed into the chairs the producer and sound engineer had just vacated, and one flipped the lid of the cooler and fished out a seltzer.

All brusque energy, their producer whirled on them at the door. "You've got two minutes to pull yourselves together." He let his eyelids fall closed for a moment, trying to calm himself. "We're out of time. You understand that, right? You get that if we don't finish this album, you're not only killing your reputation, but you're killing *mine*."

"Yes," Gigi said. "We get it. We'll do better." She gave him an encouraging smile, but he wasn't buying it. She didn't blame him. The moment he and the sound engineer walked out, she turned to her bandmates. "Guys, nothing's changed since they first signed us. They write the songs, and we play them. And, literally, as soon as this album's done, we're free to go off and pursue our own things."

"We're *artists*." Tanya, the youngest in the group at twenty-four, had changed the most over their eight years together. She'd gone from an eager and malleable sixteen-year-old to a Patti Smith wanna-be. "We're supposed to put our stamp on the songs."

"Well, that's the thing. We're *not* supposed to do that." It seemed insane that Gigi had to explain this to them yet again. "We have to meet our contractual obligations."

"But we're making it sound better," the bass player said. "We don't need to embarrass ourselves with this bubblegum crap anymore."

"If it's so embarrassing, you shouldn't have signed the second contract." Their first record had gone platinum, and they'd toured the world with it. So, of course, Gigi had re-upped when the label had offered a two-record deal. And, yeah, it was embarrassing. But it was a stepping stone. "And that *crap* not only made us rich, but it gave us tremendous fame. It's given us a platform." Fear bit into her jugular. She didn't believe a word of it. She was a Lollipop. She'd have to fight like hell to reinvent herself. It wouldn't be easy, but she couldn't wait to get out there and start trying.

But, to do that, she needed to meet the terms of the contract.

"Fine. Whatever." Tanya headed to the door. "Let's just finish it."

"Wait," Gigi said. "Don't let them back in until we all agree to play the music as it's written."

"This is so stupid," the keyboard player said. "I'm not even changing anything. I'm just giving the songs more of an edge. That's all."

"But our label doesn't want edge," Gigi said. They'd signed with the Hallmark Channel's version of record companies. "There's no wiggle room here. Okay?" She looked at the others.

"Fine," Tanya said.

"Whatever," the bass player said.

"Great. I'll get Harry."

"Let me go to the bathroom first," the bass player said.

Gigi wanted to say, *Oh, no, you don't. You are* not *getting high.* But, just as the woman reached for the door, it swung open.

In strode the owner of Clean Beatz, followed by the producer and sound engineer. Their grim expressions made her stomach plummet.

Gigi flipped on a big grin. "Hey, guys. We just took a break, and we're ready to get back to work."

In her pink and white-striped cardigan, the owner, Dale Hopkins, looked deceptively sweet, like a TV mom from a Sixties comedy show.

"Ladies, have a seat." Dale's tone invited no argument. She tapped her knuckles on the recording mixer, as she waited for everyone to find a place to sit. "You guys knocked it out of the park on that first album. The second one was a little tougher, but we did it. We created something we can be proud of. But this third album isn't working, and I'm not okay with that."

"We know, and we've just had a conversation," Gigi said. "We're all on the same page now."

"I don't know why you always have to speak for us," Tanya said. "You're not the leader."

Gigi shot her a look that said, *Not now.*

"We hired you for one specific reason." Dale ignored them both. "And that's to perform the songs we've given you. It was an opportunity any aspiring musician would be grateful for."

Was? Did she just say *was?* "We *are* grateful, and we're going to play the music just as you want," Gigi said.

"Really?" Dale said. "Because I've heard the tracks." She gave Gigi an accusing look. "You've rewritten the lyrics."

Heat flooded her. She hadn't thought anyone would notice. "No, no. I tweaked them a little, that's all." She hadn't changed the meaning of the songs…she'd just…

She'd wanted to make the songs better. Less embarrassing.

And now she just felt stupid. She'd berated the others for doing exactly the same thing. For some reason, she'd thought Dale would appreciate the better wording.

Dale turned to the other women. "In addition to recording the songs you've been given, you had one other requirement, and that was to have faultless reputations."

She dropped a gossip magazine on the mixing console. A collage of images covered the centerfold spread. A topless woman stood on a yacht. In some, an older man had his arms around her. The woman was young, slender, black hair...

A sickening feeling took hold.

"I didn't know he was married," the keyboard player said.

Oh, God. This isn't happening.

Dale's razor-cut silver bob shook with anger. "You had the world at your fingertips, and you took it all for granted. I'm deeply disappointed in your behavior."

Gigi had no idea how to salvage this situation. Drugs, adultery... Even if she could get her bandmates to finish the record, she couldn't fix their bad behavior. It was a clear breach of contract.

"Dale, I'm so grateful—"

The label owner gave her a pointed look. "If you were grateful, you wouldn't have changed the lyrics. Ladies, if I didn't have a tour booked, if I didn't have marketing ready to go and outlets waiting to get their hands on the merchandise, I would release all of you and walk away. But I *do* have commitments. And this album *is* going to drop. It's just going to be late, because..." She cut a hard look to the bass player. "You're going to rehab."

Everyone sucked in a breath. *Shit just got real.*

"And, while she's away," Dale continued. "I expect the rest of you to spend your time doing good work in the community. Whatever that means to you, I want to see you in the news for your philanthropy and not for your escapades on yachts. When Jess gets out, we're going to finish this album, and then I'm going to be done with you." With that, she strode out of the room.

They all looked to their producer, though Gigi didn't know why. There was nothing left to say.

"You've got the next thirty days to make yourselves look like the sweet, cheerful musicians she paid you to be when she formed this band," he said. "Or, I can promise you, you'll have a tough time finding work in this industry again."

From his fourth-floor window in the boutique hotel in Aspen, Colorado, Cassian looked down at the paparazzi swarming like bees on the sidewalk.

How the hell had this happened? He thought he'd covered all the bases.

Luckily, the police had let him go last night. It was nothing more than a noise complaint, since they hadn't destroyed any property.

But a photo had hit the press.

And it was bad.

Damn. "I did everything I could. Rented out the hotel, hired security."

"Had to be someone on the staff." Dean rubbed his fingers together. "Easy money."

"Yeah." Cassian glanced at his friend. "You want to pull a runner? Go down the freight elevator and out the back door? I could have a car waiting for us." He'd meant it as a joke, but it sure sounded good.

"Don't even think about it." Dean came up beside him and peered down to the street. His other teammates had flown out that morning, so Cassian appreciated that his former college roommate and closest friend had stayed with him. "Coach is on his way."

"If he's leaving his compound to fly across the country to talk to me, I'm pretty sure I don't want to hear what he has to say."

"You didn't do anything wrong, and I'm here to tell him that."

"Thanks, man." Cassian swatted his shoulder blade. "Except you're the one I'm supposed to be having threesomes with."

"Now, when I actually have a woman I care about, you pull me into this shit?" But his friend said it with an easy tone.

Dean's girlfriend, the princess of a European principality, might not appreciate the bad press, but she wouldn't doubt Dean. No one would ever question Dean Maddox's integrity. He was just that kind of guy.

"I've talked to the manager," Dean said. "He's going to look at the security footage." He pulled his phone out of his back pocket and started typing. Finding the damning article, he handed it over. "The angle of the shot gives us an idea which room it was taken from."

Cassian scanned the headline.

Has Ellis's Linebacker been Receiving More than a Football from his QB?

A photograph captured him holding a topless Amie, both of them huddled close to Dean. It absolutely looked like the three of them were about to hook up. Given the angle, it had to have been taken from one of the rooms overlooking the pool.

Cassian gave the phone back. "I want to know who had those rooms."

"That's the thing." Dean rubbed his jaw. "Our block of rooms was on the opposite side of the hotel. Amie used two of the ones overlooking the pool to store booze, shit like that. So, they were unlocked. Anyone could've gotten in them."

"You think it was one of the guys?" The betrayal sliced him wide open. Six years ago, Cassian had been drafted to replace the league's most beloved quarterback. *Tough act to follow.* That first season, the fans had actually booed when he'd jogged onto the field. It had taken a championship ring to win them over.

His teammates had taken a little longer, but after a couple years of treating them to extravagant vacations and parties, he'd won their loyalty, too. Or he'd thought he had.

If one of them had taken this shot and leaked it…that would suck.

"Why?" Dean asked. "What would be in it for them?"

"Well, for Zach, my position." His backup quarterback had an attitude towards him. A Heisman trophy winner, Zach Dimitri thought he was God's gift to football. He was good—obviously, or the Mavericks wouldn't have drafted him—but he still had plenty to learn. He just didn't realize it.

"What about Amie?"

He let that sit for a minute. She'd been on the *NFL*

Cheerleaders reality TV show for three seasons before being kicked off. He knew she wanted to get back on, and what better way than being involved with football players?

"Doesn't make much sense." When she'd gotten cut, Cassian had hired her to run his camp. She was damn good at it. Organized, efficient, and great with the kids. "It's a big risk. If she's caught dating a player, she's off the squad. No squad, no TV show. And I'd obviously fire her, so then what would she have?"

"True."

"And she's got a serious boyfriend."

A knock on the door set Cassian's heart racing. Sick with worry, he wanted nothing more than his coach's respect—his team's respect—and yet he kept winding up in the tabloids.

When Dean started for the door, Cassian tapped his shoulder. *I got it.*

My problem to deal with. But, on the other side, instead of Coach, he found a dejected Amie. "Hey." She wheeled her suitcase in. "I'm so sorry. I can't believe I did this."

Dean's body went hard. "Did what?"

She glanced up at him, confused. "Got so drunk that I stripped in front of the guys?" She gave a pleading look to Cassian. "I don't know what I was thinking. I never drink like that."

True. She didn't. "Hey, you're entitled to let loose any way you want. The whole point of renting out the hotel was so we wouldn't have this problem."

Eyes glittering with unshed tears, she stepped into his arms. "You're the best."

Always careful not to mislead, he gently pushed her back. "Have you heard from Steve?"

Tears spilled down her cheeks, and she swiped them away with a thumb. "No. He's not speaking to me. He asked me not to go on this trip. Said it's one thing to run the camp, but to party with the guys is totally crossing the line. He said, 'Reverse the situation. What if I went on a trip with a bunch of women from my office? How would you feel about that?' I'm like, this is my job. I work with these guys. I would never jeopardize my job by sleeping with one of them." She tipped her head back and groaned. "I'm never getting that drunk again."

"Coach is going to be here any minute," Dean said. "Best if you're not around."

Her eyes went wide. "Do you think I'll get fired?"

"It's possible," Dean said.

"If it comes to that," Cassian said. "We'll fight for you. Your contract says you can't date a player. There's nothing wrong with hanging out with us."

She nodded. "I promise I won't get drunk during camp. I'm not going to let you down."

"You never have," Cassian said.

She gave him a sad smile before walking out the door.

"I don't think it was her." Cassian jammed his hands in his pockets. "It was either Zach or someone who works for the hotel."

A hard knock sent a sting of adrenaline through him. This time, Dean opened it. "Coach."

The energy in the room went electric as the big, burly man powered into the suite with a sour expression. Coach Dan Hathaway, a former college wide receiver, gave a chin nod to Dean. "Give us a minute."

His friend glanced at Cassian, assessing him, before heading out.

Cut him off at the pass. "I'm sorry you had to fly all the way out here, but—"

"No." Coach cast a glance down at his bright, white sneakers and shook his head, the palm of his hand rasping against his day-old scruff. "I'm talking." He sighed, all weary and put-out. "You're young, you're having fun. I get that."

Strangely, those words gave Cassian a jolt. *Young and fun.*

He didn't feel young. And fun?

Am *I having fun?* He'd honestly never thought about it before. His life played in fast-forward mode. He was either training or playing or entertaining his guys.

"But you're the leader of this team." His expression went hard. "And you're embarrassing the franchise."

The words shot his knees out from under him. The blow left him staggering. An *embarrassment?* Jesus, that was the opposite of what he wanted.

He wanted to make Coach proud.

Even worse, what did Tyler Cavanaugh think? Did he regret wasting time on some party animal like Cassian Ellis?

It hurt to breathe.

But then…*hang on a second.* What had he done wrong? "My guys give up six weeks in their off-season to coach at my camp. These trips are my way of thanking them for helping me out. And I did everything I could to ensure our privacy." He started to get a little pissed off. "But, also—and I shouldn't have to say this because my sex life is nobody's business—I didn't have a threesome." He couldn't jeopardize Amie's position on the squad, so he had to be careful what he revealed about last night. Coach didn't need to know she'd been stripping for the guys.

"Amie almost fell off the diving board, and I caught her. Dean handed me a towel. That's it."

"You think I flew across the country to talk about a *party*? I'm running a football team here. And, while you're on my roster, I expect you to represent that damn team. You're in the news all the time—and not for your plays or your throwing arm or the way you lead on the turf, but for being the *Bad Boy Quarterback*." Hands on hips, he watched Cassian for a moment, that barrel chest pumping hard. "This is going to stop."

"Yeah, okay." What could he say? Coach was right. "I'll find out who took the picture. I'll get to the bottom of this."

"That's not…I don't care who took the damn picture." He lifted his arms in exasperation and let them drop to his sides. "You don't get it. Starting now, I don't want you in the news for anything other than your plays and your good deeds in the community."

"Well, that's a problem, because I don't want to exploit my camp. And, no matter what you see in the tabloids, I don't do anything reckless." He could see Coach's growing frustration. But he didn't know what the man expected him to do. The last scandal involved a model screaming at him on the sidewalk outside a restaurant. He'd had no control over that. After spending a total of two hours with her a year ago, they'd gone their separate ways. They'd never exchanged numbers. There had been zero expectations.

How could I have prevented a scene like that?

"Do you know what turned Tyler Cavanaugh's career around?"

"There's nothing wrong with my career." He'd been the

first quarterback in two decades to get the Mavericks to the Super Bowl.

"There's nothing wrong…" Coach pinched the bridge of his nose. "Right now, I could be in my shorts, toes in the sand, listening to my grandkids playing, but no. I'm babysitting the captain of the offense." He blew out a breath. "I'm going to ask again, and this time answer directly. Do you know what turned Tyler Cavanaugh around?"

Of course he did. "His wife." His mentor had undermined his potential by partying. Drugs, booze, women. And then he'd met Joss Montalbano, a super model in the Eighties, and he'd quit screwing around and started breaking records.

Coach held up a thick finger. "Yes, but it was one question she asked that changed his life. They met working on a set, some endorsement they were doing together. I think it was Adidas. He used every trick in the book to get her to go out with him, and she refused. Wanted nothing to do with him. On the last day of filming, the cast and crew went out to dinner, and he sat down next to her, thinking he could charm his way into her pants. Instead, she asked him what he wanted out of life, and he said, 'I've got a great life. What more could I ask for?' And she said, 'So all you want out of life is to be the joke of the NFL?'"

The comment pierced his brain like a spike—rendering him senseless. It took a moment to fully process the message.

Coach thinks I'm a joke?

Sure, stories popped up all the time about him being a playboy, living the high life with his extravagant gifts and trips. But, for fuck's sake, he never got drunk, never did drugs. He'd seen the pictures of Tyler, sloppy, stumbling, passed out.

I'm not like that. "I don't do drugs, and I rarely drink. I lead a clean life."

"But that's not your reputation. Do you understand that? The public doesn't see you eating vegetables and lifting weights and taking the offense on team-building events. They don't see the way you live the game, analyzing tape and discussing strategy. They see you partying and having threesomes and dating models." Coach scratched the back of his head with a beefy hand. "The point is, that one question hit Tyler hard. He'd never seen himself like that. He thought he was living the dream. I'll never forget the day he came to me, sober for the first time in…I don't know how long, and he asked me, 'Am I the joke of the NFL?' And I said, 'Pretty much.' He said, 'Why? I'm a damn good player.' And I told him the truth. He was the player people saw drunk and surrounded by women. When the media talked about him, it wasn't about his plays or his stats, it was about his exploits. And now, twenty years later, I'm saying the same damn thing to you."

Cassian had been in detention when Tyler Cavanaugh had walked into the classroom. Calamity had a lot of celebrities, and Cassian had known this guy was one of them, but he didn't care. When he was fourteen, football didn't mean shit to him. He'd been stabbing holes into the desktop with a pen, vaguely aware of Tyler whispering to the teacher, when he heard, "Cassian?"

He'd looked up sharply. *Me?* What the hell did Tyler Cavanaugh want with him? He'd gotten up, taking his time zipping his backpack—really drawing it out, like a true jerk. He'd never forget the screech his desk had made on the Linoleum floor.

But, mostly, he'd never forget following Tyler out of the room, into the empty hallway, and having the man turn to him and say, "You want to be the asshole who sits in detention or you want to be the quarterback of this school's football team?"

It wasn't the *quarterback* part of the sentence. It was the *asshole* part. Up until that moment, he'd been lost without his parents, pissed at having to live with an aunt and uncle and five cousins he barely knew, and filled with anger that he had to share a bedroom with a kid determined to make his life a living hell.

He'd seen himself as the cool rebel. But, right then, this big legend of a man calling him an asshole? It made all his sarcastic cracks in class, his whole loner persona, seem immature and lame. Especially when he held it up against the image of him on the school's football team.

And now it's happening all over again. He wasn't Cassian Ellis, top quarterback in the league. He was a joke.

"I'm going to ask you a question, and I want you to give it some thought," Coach said. "What's your goal?"

He jumped to answer. "I—" But his jaw snapped shut. Because he'd been about to say he wanted to be a great quarterback, but he knew that wasn't what his coach meant. He didn't mean something vague. He meant something specific.

Cassian had nothing. Because he'd never thought that far ahead. Now that he'd made it over all the hurdles—making the high school team, getting recruited to a Big Ten school, getting drafted—he devoted all his energy to making it to the play-offs.

And the continuous quest to win over the fans and his teammates.

"Yeah, I thought so. Give it some thought and get back to me. Your answer matters. In the meantime, cut the shit out. Let me tell you the difference between you and Ben. He didn't give them strippers and yachts. He gave them leadership. He didn't treat them to parties with coke and booze. You want to know why? Because we don't win games when we're loaded. Everything with Ben was about the game. He had good relationships with his teammates —but they were teammates, not buddies. They respected him because he led by example."

He gave Coach a terse nod. "Okay." He'd tone it down. Work harder to stay out of the press.

In any event, he was grateful Coach had only come out to lecture him. It might be embarrassing, but it wasn't the end of the world. "I'm sorry you had to come all the way out here, and I'll make sure to stay out of trouble in the press—"

Again, he held up a finger. "Because if you don't…I'm going to have to trade you."

Cassian's world went dark. Lights out, silent. Cold.

Yeah, he'd had a rough start with this team, but he'd worked his ass off to earn his place with them.

They were his family.

But then, underneath the fear, pulsed anger. "Traded? For what?" He really wanted to tell Coach the truth about what happened last night, but it could cost Amie her job. She'd already gotten kicked off the TV show that meant so much to her. "I wasn't drunk. My teammates weren't out of control. We didn't trash hotel rooms…"

But Coach gave him a hard look. "This comes from the top. Chuck's talking to me about the moral turpitude

34

clause in your contract. If you don't clean up your image, he wants you traded."

"I have never violated my contracted in any way. I've done nothing immoral."

"The league's gotten too much bad press lately, and he wants the focus to be on his winning team. Not on whatever trouble the players get into."

"This is bullshit."

"It's really not. It's a character issue." Coach headed to the door. "Training camp starts July twenty-seventh. From this moment on, we're not going to see anything but good press on you. I've talked to Tyler, and he's putting you on his foundation's Dreams Come True tour." At the door, he glanced back. "Get your ass to Calamity right now, because the tour begins the day after tomorrow."

"My camp starts on Monday. You know I can't miss it."

Coach turned fully and gave him a steely-eyed glare. "This trip's nonnegotiable. And it's only a week. After that, you can run your football camp. Are we clear?"

Obviously, Amie and Dean could handle camp in his absence. It just meant a lot to him to be there for the kids. He *wanted* to work with them. It was about so much more than football.

Anyways, what choice did he have? He didn't want to get traded, start all over with a new team. It took a hell of a lot of work to earn a team's respect. "We're clear."

"Now, I'm going to get back to my family." Coach opened the door. "I don't want to lose you, so you better make this team look proud over the next few weeks."

Chapter Three

HEADPHONES? *CHECK*. BOTTLED WATER? *CHECK*. Slippery elm lozenges? *Yep*. Licorice root...?

Wait. Crap. Had she forgotten it? As Gigi Cavanaugh dove into her tote bag, fishing through the mess, her mind went back to the last time she'd seen them. She remembered putting the dried sticks in the baggie...*AH.* She'd totally left it on the kitchen counter. *Dammit.*

It's okay. She could always order more. *Relax.*

But, of course, it wasn't the licorice root she was worried about. It was the contract. As if being a Lollipop wasn't a high enough hurdle to leap over when trying to reinvent herself in the music industry, now she might have to battle a bad reputation. Her bandmates had better behave themselves this month.

God knows I'm going to stay as far from trouble as humanly possible.

Settling into the comfortable leather seats of the foundation's jet, Gigi actually looked forward to the Dreams Come True tour. She'd done several of them since her first album had gone platinum. Nothing was more rewarding than seeing the children and their families smile, knowing she was offering them a respite from their troubles—however brief.

In sunglasses and a pink pashmina shawl wrapped around her shoulders, a middle-aged woman boarded the plane. Gigi startled when she realized it was Macy Guthrie, an Academy-Award winning actor.

"Morning," a crew member said to the movie star.

The actor nodded and made her way to a seat at the back of the plane. Gigi's parents had given her a heads-up about the actor. She'd come on these tours before, rarely interacting with the other talent but turning it on for the patients.

"So, this was a fun surprise, waking up to see your name added to the list." The man who ran the tour, Kevin, fell into the seat beside Gigi. "Hey, hon." He kissed her cheek. "Thought you were in the studio?"

"I was, but…we're taking a break to clear our heads." *Ha. Nice spin.*

"Well, our gain." Clean-cut, smelling fresh from a shower, Kevin was the most organized and amiable person she'd ever known. "First stop's St. Louis. The hospital's rented out a community center, and we're going to make a whole day out of it, so you're going to make a lot of kids happy tomorrow. I've got another surprise addition, too, so I'll be adjusting the whole schedule. This week's going to be great."

Grant Banner, one of the biggest country singers in the world, boarded, and Kevin popped out of his seat to greet the handsome man who wore his signature black jeans, cowboy boots, and a Stetson.

Her phone buzzed, and she checked the screen. *Lulu.*

She swiped to answer. "Hey. I'm on the plane so I can't really talk."

"Well, you can't leave a message like that and then not talk to me."

"I'm sorry. I was…I overreacted." Since leaving the studio the day before yesterday, Gigi had been freaking out. She'd called her sister, but Lulu lived in a different country, so it was hard to connect. "I'm okay now." *Liar.* "I'm just going to focus on this tour and hope my band-mates don't mess up again." *Please let me leave Clean Beatz on good terms.*

"It's not like you can control what other people do."

"No, I know. All I can do is make sure *I* don't get involved in any scandals. Which, obviously, I won't."

"I know it seems scary, but the thing you have to remember is that you've got real talent. Not just an amazing voice, but phenomenal stage presence. No matter what happens with your label, you're going to land on your feet."

As more people boarded, Gigi lowered her voice. "To the people in this industry, I'm a Lollipop. I crank out the songs I've been given, wear the costume assigned to my character—I'm part of a *package*. If I try to go out on my own now, no one will take me seriously."

And the worst part—what really scared her? She had no idea who she was. She'd dropped out of music school before she'd had a chance to discover her true style. Leaving behind Clean Beatz was scary, because the world saw her as a pop star, singing upbeat, silly songs.

The Lollipops might be an international pop sensation, but Gigi Cavanaugh on her own was nothing.

But she couldn't get into *that* with her sister, not when

Grant Banner had dropped onto the couch right near her. "I have to go. Talk later?"

"Call me when you settle into your hotel."

"I will." If she let them, the doubts would consume her. All she could do was forge ahead. Plan. Prepare. She had thirty days—*that's a good amount of time*. She'd fill it writing songs, finding her voice as an artist.

Feeling calmer, Gigi settled into her seat. Had everyone boarded? If so, she might try to catch up on the sleep she'd missed the last two nights.

Closing her eyes, she heard the low murmur of conversation and the high-pitched whine of the engines. Good. They'd be taking off soon.

A stir of excitement filled the cabin, but she kept her eyes closed, hoping to drift off. Between her dad, once considered the best quarterback in football, and her mom, a former model, Gigi and her three younger sisters had grown up with famous people. She didn't impress easily. Besides, she'd seen the list. No one on this tour rocked her world.

"Well, hell, man," she heard the country star say in his gravelly voice. "Look who's here. I didn't know you were on this tour." He laughed, and she heard some back thumping. "Can I get your autograph for my niece?"

"You bet." That voice.

A shock of adrenaline punched through her system.

"And, if you get me an address," America's favorite playboy said. "I'll send her a jersey."

Her eyelids popped open. Cassian Ellis stood in the aisle, surrounded by the crew—even the pilots had come out of the cockpit—the country star, and a few other guests, everyone so excited to see the nation's hottest quarterback.

For a moment, she forgot how to breathe. She wanted to sink lower in her seat. Disappear in a cloud of vapor. Her heart beat so fast it hurt.

He's on this plane? This tour? She could not *believe* she'd be with him every day for a week.

No. No. No. Her dad wouldn't do this to her. He wouldn't. The soft leather seat had turned into a bed of needles.

She dug into her tote bag and pulled out her phone, shooting off a group text to her parents.

Gigi: **Cassian Ellis is on this tour?????**

Mom: **Yes. He's a last minute addition, too**.

Dad: **Got a problem with that?**

Gigi: **You know I do.**

Dad: **Get over it. This is about the kids. Not you and Cassian and some decade-old feud.**

Feud? *Feud?*

For God's sake, he slept with my best friend *two seconds after I told him I wanted to be with him.*

She'd done everything she could to get over him. To forgive him. To let it all go. She'd gone to college on the opposite end of the country, dated, read self-help books… *you name it, I've tried it.* But, nine years later, the betrayal had barely diminished.

She didn't want to be this person who still hurt, whose heart still wrenched in pain every time she thought of him —of that night when he'd kissed her, then tossed her aside to hook up with someone else. He'd thrown away their friendship and the future she'd longed for.

Over the years, she'd seen him—hard to avoid when they lived in the same town, and he was close with her parents—but she always kept her distance. She had nothing to say to him.

And now the boy she'd loved so desperately had turned into a chiseled, gorgeous, elite athlete. His dark, glossy hair hit the collar of his T-shirt with a slight curl, and his biceps bulged with every handshake. Levis, nearly white with wear, molded over hard, sculpted thighs.

Like all celebrities, he intentionally didn't look around the cabin to see who else was on board. If he did, he'd have to acknowledge them, get into a conversation. Instead, he dropped into a seat at the front of the cabin, so she'd have to see his broad shoulders and fat head the whole flight.

So much for a nap. She was too wired to sleep now. Mostly, she wanted to throw her shoe at him, maybe trip him when he got up to go to the bathroom. Anything to wipe that cocky grin off his face.

But her parents were right. This tour wasn't the time or place to deal with her Cassian Ellis issues. The patients came first. She'd ignore the jerk—she was an expert at that. Besides, he'd probably be banging every nurse and oncologist he could get his hands on.

Her phone vibrated.

Dad: **You going to handle this the right way?**

Gigi: **Of course. I just don't know why you had—**

Ohhhhh. She deleted the last sentence. There could only be one reason why Cassian would join this tour at the last minute, especially considering the timing. At the start of every summer, the jerk ran a football camp in Calamity for underprivileged kids. He wouldn't miss it for anything.

Well, he'd miss it if he'd gotten into trouble. *Again.*

What'd he do now? She quickly typed his name in a search engine.

Hundreds of articles and images came up and…*there it is.* In the very first photograph at the top of the page, Cassian held a gorgeous, naked blonde in his arms. But he wasn't focused on her. He was talking quietly, intimately with Dean Maddox. She read the headline.

Has Ellis's Linebacker been Receiving More than a Football from his QB?

You're kidding me.

A threesome?

With Dean?

She tapped out a text to her parents.

Gigi: **I was really looking forward to this trip. I can't believe you'd let some guy with a PR crisis come on it.**

Dad: **Oh, hey there, pot.**

Gigi: **I'm not…**

Delete. Because, yes, she very well might have a crisis of her own. What were the odds her bandmates would stay out of trouble this month? *Low.* So, yeah, the Lollipops getting booted from their record label would be pretty scandalous.

Okay, well. Whatever. She was here because she loved singing for the patients. She'd just treat Cassian like the stranger he'd become. She closed her eyes, shutting out the conversation.

And there she was again, that seventeen year old girl who'd finally kissed the boy she'd loved so hard.

Come on. You know I don't see you like that.

The memory hit her body like a hard slap across the face. *God.*

You have to let it go. You had a crush on a guy, and he didn't feel the same way.

So what?

"Sorry, I'm late," a woman said.

Gigi's eyelids popped open to find a gorgeous woman carrying a Louis Vuitton tote on her arm. She looked vaguely familiar, and Gigi's mind scrambled to place her—actor? Singer? Model?

The woman flashed a bright, white smile to the crew. "I only found out I was coming along last night." Her flirty dress exposed toned thighs, and she'd clearly taken a lot of time on her long, blonde hair and make-up.

With a laugh in her eyes, she dropped into the seat beside Cassian. And then she snuggled up against him, whispering in his ear.

Gigi was gutted. Pure, raw jealousy burned through her. *That's the woman in the photo.* The blonde hair and big cleavage were the giveaways.

Over all these years, the press had caught Cassian in compromising poses with countless women, but she'd never known him to have a girlfriend. He seemed to be on a mission to have sex with every woman on the globe.

Except me, of course. He's not attracted to me.

As the flight attendants prepared the cabin for departure, Gigi couldn't take her eyes off the couple. Their intimacy was undeniable. They whispered quietly, smiling every now and then. The woman punched his shoulder lightly, reared back, and then burst out laughing.

"Hey, everybody." An older man with shaggy blonde hair stood in the aisle. "I'm Arnie, and I'm the tour's photographer. I'm going to get as many shots as I can, but I won't be publishing anything without your written permission."

"You can photograph me with the patients," the actor said. "But that's it."

"Got it. For now, everyone who doesn't mind a group shot, could you give me a cheesy smile?" He held up his camera. And just as Gigi started to lean in, she saw Cassian's girlfriend snake her arm behind his neck and rest her hand on his shoulder.

And that was the shot Arnie got.

The one with Gigi staring at the boy who'd hurt her in a way she couldn't come back from.

And the boy enjoying his fun, sexy girlfriend, as if Gigi had never existed.

An hour after checking into her hotel room, Gigi's phone rang. Wearing nothing but a robe, she dashed to answer it. *Mama Cav.* "Hey, Mom."

"Where are you, and why do you sound out of breath?"

"I'm having a spa night." She glanced at herself in the mirror over the dresser. A shiny green mask covered her face, and a white towel-turban sat on top of her head.

"Now? It's dinner time."

"I know. I'm just going to order in." *Am I avoiding seeing Cassian's sexy girlfriend run her hands all over him?*

You bet.

"Oh, no, you're not. You know how the first night goes. It's orientation."

"I can skip it. This ain't my first rodeo." She'd deal with everything tomorrow.

"Each tour is different—the *children* are different. You need to get down there and find out who you're going to be visiting. Besides, do you really want it to look like you get special treatment because you're our daughter?"

"No, but I do want one night to just relax."

"Yeah, okay, Diva, that's not how we roll. Now, get downstairs. They're waiting for you. Kevin said they're not going to start until everyone's at the table."

"Mom…"

"Sweetheart, I know it's not going to be easy to be around him."

"Understatement of the year." After the night he'd destroyed her, Gigi had completely fallen apart. She'd spent the first week in bed. *It's a wonder I graduated high school.* Her parents had reduced her feelings to nothing more than a crush on the hot, charming athlete—the same one every other girl—and woman—in town had. Only, intensified because he'd spent so much time at their house.

But they were wrong. She'd loved Cassian with all her heart. They'd spent every free moment together. Sometimes, when their schedules had been too full with sports and band practices, they'd cut classes just to be alone together. He'd told her things he didn't share with anyone. He came to her when he had big decisions to make.

She'd been so sure he'd loved her, too. That night, the way he'd looked at her—kissed her. God, that kiss. *I don't see you that way.* Those words had obliterated her heart.

Worse, he'd crushed her ability to trust her own instincts.

That moment when he'd lead Ashton up the stairs…to a bedroom…to have sex with her…It was imprinted on her soul.

A clammy sensation hit the back of her neck. The thought of seeing him made her sick to her stomach. She had to tell her mom the truth. "I don't think I can do it."

"You don't have a choice," her mom said gently. "We've already announced the new arrivals, so it's too late for you to cancel. And, to be honest, I've always wondered if your anger wasn't misplaced."

"What does that mean?"

"Sleeping with your friend…it wasn't something new. He'd pretty much gone through the female population of Calamity by that point."

"This doesn't make me feel better."

"I'm sorry, honey. But he is who he is. I just know *I* would've hated my best friend. Girl code, and all."

"Trust me, I did." She'd given Ashton a very large piece of her mind, and now Gigi barely had any residual feelings for her former friend.

Well, there you go. She'd not only confronted Ashton, but she'd cut her out of their group. Gigi had gotten closure. She hadn't done any of that with Cassian.

So maybe this trip…maybe she could pull him aside and just let it rip?

But with his girlfriend here? Yeah, no. That wouldn't work.

Besides, the focus needed to be on the patients.

"You have to show up for this tour, honey. You just do. The kids deserve the best you've got."

"You're right. You're absolutely right." She was being selfish. Petty. "I won't let my personal issues affect this tour. I'll get down there, and I'll act like he's just someone I knew in high school."

"Thank you, sweetheart. For whatever reason, things aligned, putting you two together. Maybe you can take advantage of that, find some sort of closure with him. Might set you free."

She smiled. "That's exactly what I was thinking. I love you, Mom."

"Love you, too, sweetie. I'm here if you need to talk."

After disconnecting, Gigi tossed her phone on the bed and went back into the bathroom to peel off the mask. Shaking out her wet hair, she ran her fingers through it. She didn't have time to dry it or put on make-up, so she just found a clean pair of shorts and a T-shirt, jammed her feet into her flip flops, and headed out of her room.

Dread pulsed with each step she took down the hallway. Cassian hadn't seen her yet, so he didn't know she was on the tour. When they'd landed at the St. Louis airport, a van had been waiting for them. She'd slid into the far back with the country star, happy to talk shop.

Okay, more like eager to show him she wasn't just a prop in a manufactured girl band.

And wasn't that part of her issue right there? Cassian was the real deal. Through talent, hard work, and drive, he'd become a great quarterback, whereas she'd become a Lollipop.

Stepping onto the elevator, she had to accept she was embarrassed. Whenever she fantasized about Cassian, it was always about him being in the audience when she performed at some big venue, like Madison Square Garden. Her favorite image, though, was of him with a beer belly and stained T-shirt as he sat on his couch and watched her win a Grammy.

She'd wanted him to eat his heart out. Instead, he was at the top of his career, while she was this platinum-haired robot who wore stupid plaid skirts and knee socks.

Whatever.

Shake it off.

You're here to bring people a moment of joy. Her embarrassment about being a Lollipop meant nothing in the context of this tour.

As soon as she entered the restaurant, the hostess took

her to a private room. There were only fifteen people in their group, but she walked into a buzz of conversation and laughter. Her focus went immediately to Cassian, who entertained the people seated around him. She'd bet they'd tripped over each other to score the chair next to him. He was the life of every party.

Beside him, his girlfriend beamed—her hair all tousled and sexy, her mouth bright red, and her cleavage bursting out of a skintight black dress.

A rush of mortification traveled up her spine and flared around her shoulders. In comparison, she looked plain and dull. Before she could bolt, though, she scurried toward the one empty seat left at the table, in a scramble to get there before he noticed her.

Why hadn't she spent an extra five minutes to put on a little make-up? Do something with her hair?

Fortunately, she got to sit next to the musician. "Hey."

"Looks like you got in a shower."

"Oh." Her hand went to her damp hair, and her cheeks went hot.

His smile flat-lined. "See, now, this is why I've got three divorces behind me. I always manage to step in it."

"No, it's…" She stuttered out a laugh. "I'm feeling insecure, because I came down here with wet hair and no make-up and…" She gestured to the blonde and the glamorous actor across the table.

"Can I tell you something—if you promise not to take this the wrong way?"

"Of course."

"I swear I'm not hittin' on you, but you're ten times more beautiful than both of them. There's something about a woman without her face all done up that makes her more real, more approachable. I mean, you're a

Lollipop, so I've seen you with make-up, but this...right here? They've got nothin' on you."

Her heart warmed with affection. "Thank you for saying that. I needed to hear it."

Someone howled with laughter, and Grant's attention went over to Cassian.

Cassian...God, the man just glowed. It was so much more than his handsome features or muscular body. It was his charisma. He gave off an aura of competence, of being the best in the world.

And everyone wanted to be around a winner.

A fierce longing howled through her. *I want to be a winner.*

"Oh, good you're here." Kevin swept by behind her, briefly cupping her shoulder. "We can get started."

"Sorry about that."

"No problem." He continued on to the head of the table.

Cassian still hadn't noticed her, so that meant she had a few moments to pull herself together. She appreciated what Grant said more than he'd ever know.

Mostly, she needed to remember she was on her own path, tending her own garden, and she wasn't going to get derailed by a man who lacked character. Regardless of his looks or charm or stats on the football field.

Exactly. 'Nuff said.

"Welcome, everyone," Kevin said. "I want to thank each and every one of you for taking time out of your schedules to work with the Dreams Come True Foundation. The families are so excited to see you, and I know we're going to have an amazing week. Why don't you go ahead and grab some food from the buffet? While you're eating, I'll go over the schedule."

While the rest of the table got up, Cassian's group lingered, riveted by his story, so she took the opportunity to grab a plate. Only when Grant came up beside her did she realize how panicked she felt. Because she'd run from the table like a freak.

You have to stop this.

You're giving him all your power.

And for what? Something that happened when you were seventeen?

She smiled at Grant. "I'm not shy when it comes to filling my belly."

He held up both hands, like *I'll get out of your way*, and laughed.

Under the bright orange heat lamps, she contemplated the chicken and something that looked like fish covered in brown sauce.

"Times like this, I stick with the vegetables." Grant tipped his chin to the other end of the table. "Salad, potatoes."

"Wise words from a man who's spent half his life on the road."

His grin cracked a well-lined face. "You've had a few of them yourself. I'm sure you learned your own lessons on food service."

"I learned you could demand pink llamas in your dressing room, and half the venues would oblige."

"You don't strike me as the kind to demand pink M&Ms, let alone llamas."

"No, I'm not too particular." They made their way down the line. "I've only been on two tours, and I can tell you they weren't anything like what I expected."

"They take it out of your hide, that's for sure." Grant helped himself to a pile of roasted vegetables.

Cassian and his entourage stood directly across from her. He said something quietly to the person next to him, and the guy's eyebrows shot up.

"Are you serious?" the man said.

Cassian's girlfriend rolled her eyes and said, "Don't get him started."

"No, tell me," the guy said. "I always wanted to know if that was real or not."

"Pretty much every story you've ever heard about DeBrowski's based on some kind of truth," Cassian said.

"But is that why they traded him?" someone asked.

Cassian's girlfriend leaned forward, her large breasts pressing on his arm. "You're going to have to get him a whole lot drunker, if you're going to get those kinds of answers."

"*Drunker?*" Cassian said. "I haven't even had a beer. Speaking of which, what do you want to drink? Wine, beer?"

"I'd love some wine," his girlfriend said.

"Hang on." Cassian stepped away from the table, looking around. When he spotted a server he said, "I'd like to buy some wine for the table."

Right. Always the big spender. Renting yachts and jets, buying two-hundred-thousand-dollar cars. He was such a cliché.

The server looked anxious to be in his presence, but whatever he said made her grin. Slowly, she relaxed until she was looking up at him as if he were the hottest boy in school who'd finally noticed her.

Anger rushed through her. "What kind of jerk flirts in front of his girlfriend?"

Oh, shit. She shouldn't have said that.

Grant chuckled. "Ah, don't be so hard on him. I used

to be the same way. Trust me, it's nothing more than a coping device."

Her whole body went on alert, desperate to learn more. The line moved forward, and she scooped some roasted potatoes onto her plate. "Is 'coping device' just a euphemism for infidelity?"

He laughed. "Nah. Social anxiety comes in many forms. We all wear masks. The one you put on depends on what you're trying to hide."

"And the callous boyfriend's a mask?"

"You've had your share of fame. You know what comes with it—a whole lot of attention. Lotta guys'll bed every woman in sight just because they can. Maybe they weren't hot stuff when they were younger and now, with money and fame, they are. And some do it…" He shrugged, color pinkening his cheeks. "Well, let's just say the amount of fame you crave is in direct proportion to how insecure you are."

Gripping the tongs, she snorted. "I don't think Cassian Ellis has confidence issues."

"Well, that's what I'm saying. Maybe he has a lot more than you realize, and that's how he covers it. There isn't just one way to deal with your issues, right? Sometimes, when you feel unworthy and the attention's comin' at you, you gobble it up. Even if it's the wrong kind."

She dropped some lettuce on her plate. "I think what you're telling me is to stop being so judgmental and look a little deeper."

He laughed. "Well, I'm just channeling my therapist here, but that sounds about right."

More people from the hotel staff gathered around Cassian. Someone took his plate so he could sign autographs. One of them tucked a cocktail napkin into the back pocket of his jeans.

She tried to see him from a different perspective. As a boy who'd lost his parents when he was fourteen. Who'd gone to live with a family he barely knew.

Even in high school, as captain of the football team, he still hadn't felt he'd belonged anywhere.

I belong with you.

Oh, God, just remembering those words, the way they'd curled through her, all sweet and creamy. They'd been laying on their backs in the tree house, feet braced against the plywood panels they'd crudely erected. He'd been telling her how his cousins had made him feel like an outsider. Griffin in particular, the oldest, had resented having to share a room.

They have their own way of talking to each other, games they play, jokes…I don't fit in.

She'd reminded him that he'd become the star of the football team, so at least he had that, and he'd said, "I took Landon's spot. The guys hate me for that." It had killed her that he didn't feel he belonged anywhere.

Until he'd reached for her hand and said, *I belong with you.*

It hurt. It hurt so much to remember the good times. He might act like a playboy, but she'd known a whole other side of him. A vulnerable, sensitive side.

That side's nowhere to be seen tonight. Cassian Ellis, the life of the party, commanded the attention of the staff who flocked around him. She wanted to ask his girlfriend why she'd stay with a guy who'd disrespect her so boldly.

Not my business.

A young woman held open his palm and wrote something on it.

"Cassian," his girlfriend called. "You want me to make you a plate?"

"Good idea," Gigi said. "He's going to need his energy if he's going to keep up with tonight's schedule." *Oh, dammit.*

His girlfriend looked up. "Right?" She shook her head. "He's a shameless flirt."

"What's that?" Cassian turned away from his flock, inserting himself back into the line.

His girlfriend tugged on his T-shirt, laughter dancing in her eyes. "You're making a scene. Grab your food, and let's sit down."

"A scene?" When he looked around to see what she was talking about, his gaze landed on Gigi.

The eye-to-eye connection exploded in her chest. A fireball of anxiety ripped along her nerves. Why the hell had she drawn his attention?

Surprisingly, the thing that brought her back into her own body was the hurt that flashed in his eyes. No, it wasn't hurt. It was...longing. But it disappeared so quickly she wondered if she'd imagined it.

"Well, if isn't a little Lollipop." He said it with a grin, like he was being cute.

Yep. Totally imagined it. Everyone stopped talking and stared at her. Shame burned a fiery path down her spine.

"What do you mean?" It took a moment for his girlfriend to make the connection. "Oh, my God, you're the lead singer of the Lollipops. I'm not used to seeing you without your get-up."

She hated Cassian Ellis. Hated him. "I am." The country star had made her feel legitimate, like she belonged. Leave it to Cassian to make her feel like a fraud.

"How fun." The woman's smile seemed genuine.

"Hope you brought your knee socks," Cassian said.

Fucker. "Why? Did you want to borrow them? A little role play with your girlfriend?"

"Oh, it's not—" the woman began.

Cassian snugged an arm around his girlfriend's shoulders, hauling her up hard against him. "You say that like it's a bad thing. Lollipops might be for kids, but we like our fun a little more grown up. Right, babe?"

The girlfriend rolled her eyes. "Okay, Casanova. Let me grab some salad, and then we can sit down." As she moved around him, he swatted her ass and said, "Sure, babe." But she just threw him a look over her shoulder. *Really?*

What was that? Gigi had no idea what was going on, but she'd obviously forgotten for a moment there that he was an elite athlete. He'd always go for the first down to win.

And sparring with him would only make her look naïve and young.

Why had she engaged with him? She wished she'd stayed in her room—or at least handled herself better. Because now he knew she was still hung up on the past.

When she turned to give Grant an apologetic smile, she found he'd already gone back to the table.

Her shoulders sagged in defeat.

Can I please have a do-over?

Chapter Four

As soon as she sat back down, Kevin began his speech. "Please go ahead and eat—don't let your food go cold—while I get you all up to speed. Let me just start out by telling you how awesome it was to let the hospitals know about our last-minute additions. Everyone loves the Mavericks, so Cassian, you're going to be quite popular this week. And we've got a couple kids who are going to love Gigi from the Lollipops."

Cassian hummed a few bars from "UpBeat," and people laughed.

Kevin shook his hips. "Hey, now, don't get me started. You're going to get the whole restaurant on their feet, dancing. Okay, so, first up, tomorrow the hospital's throwing a fair for the patients and their families at a community center, and you guys will provide the entertainment. This is going to be especially fun, because we've got a little boy who's obsessed with penguins. So…we've arranged a visit from the zoo."

A few people gasped and murmured, *No way, that's so cool.* Kevin smiled. "Right? We've also got a couple of diehard country fans, so Grant, you'll play for them in the main room." He smiled at the actor. "There's a reading nook inside, so if you want to read to the kids, that space is all yours."

Macy nodded. "Sounds good."

Kevin pointed at Cassian. "Your coach is overnighting some logo wear to the hotel, so as soon as it gets here, we'll race over there with it." He gave a faux-serious expression to the group. "Try not to stay out too late tomorrow night, because the next morning we leave at nine AM for Salina, Kansas. Now, there, we've got a seventeen-year-old boy with leukemia."

As Kevin continued to lay out the schedule for the next week, Gigi forced her attention on her dinner. Though she felt Cassian's eyes scraping over her skin like nettles, she refused to look at him.

Because if she did, he'd see so much more than anger. He'd see she hadn't forgotten the good, sweet memories.

I belong with you.

Every time she remembered the feel of her hand in his, the way he'd looked at her like she was the light drawing him out of the darkness, her heart just twisted.

That night at the party, yes, okay, she'd kissed *him*. But he'd kissed her back, and it had been real. *You can't fake a response like that.*

She should know. She'd never felt anything like it since.

When she couldn't take it anymore, she looked up, wanting to read his expression and see if he felt even an ounce of regret for having destroyed their friendship.

But he wasn't looking at her. He was smiling, as his girlfriend gazed up at him.

God, they made a gorgeous couple. So sexy and glamorous.

Rage rushed her, and she had to check the impulse to lob a roll at his head.

You are so stupid. Getting all worked up over a kiss from nine years ago?

Are you kidding me? He's had seven million kisses since then.

He'd forgotten her. Moved on.

When the presentation ended, everyone started chatting. She heard people talking about going to the bar after dinner, but she couldn't do it. She would give one hundred percent of herself on this tour—starting tomorrow. Tonight, she needed some time alone.

Kevin came up to her. "Can I talk to you for a second?"

"Yes, of course." She pushed her chair back and followed him a few feet away from the table. "What's up?"

"Is there going to be a problem between you and Cassian?"

"No, of course not." *Oh, God. How humiliating.*

"Okay, good. I thought I picked up some tension between you two. See, the thing is, we're really glad to have him with us, but he's got some bad press at the moment, and it's extremely important that it not impact the tour."

"Then why is he here?"

"Can you imagine what would happen if we didn't allow people on these tours who had something going on in the press?" Kevin asked with a smile. "That would get really complicated. So, our policy is to not give it any attention, keep the focus on the kids." He paused, his expression turning serious. "It just…it can't be on the Lollipop and the Bad Boy Quarterback."

The weight of embarrassment crushed her down to the size of a pebble. "I promise you there will be no problems. I'll be one hundred percent focused on this tour."

"Great. Just what I want to hear. We're actually adding a few more visits since you joined. There are a lot of kids who want to meet you."

"I can't wait to meet them." Honestly, they'd bring her as much joy as she brought them.

If she kept that in mind, it would be a great week.

———

Cassian swiped the bathroom mirror with a hand towel before he started shaving and looked into the face of an asshole.

Well, if it isn't a little Lollipop.

That was his first sentence to Gigi in nine years.

As regret scored his heart, he stopped scraping and closed his eyes. Jesus, he'd never get that image out of his brain, the proud jut of her chin, all while her eyes screamed hurt and humiliation.

I did that. I hurt her.

Again.

Okay, well. New day, fresh start. Tilting his head back, he shaved his neck. In his defense, he hadn't been expecting to see her. He'd choked, plain and simple.

Because she'd been looking at him with disgust.

That's because she thought you were flirting in front of your "girlfriend."

Who just happened to be the same woman he'd held

naked in his arms in a tabloid photograph. The same woman he'd supposedly had a threesome with.

Nice. Way to reinforce her shitty impression of him.

He turned on the faucet and rinsed the razor, before drawing it back over his jaw.

"Knock knock." Amie entered his room from the adjoining one. "Okay, I printed out the schedule, so now you have a physical copy. The guys get into Calamity tomorrow. I'll meet with them in the morning and get their groups worked out. Well, except for Dean. But he'll be there on opening day."

His friend had an opportunity to visit his new girl-friend—an actual princess—so he was grabbing the chance.

Finished shaving, Cassian peered out of the bathroom. "You confirm the teachers for the electives?"

"Yes." Amie read notes on her phone. "Let's see. Callie's committed to teaching art for all three sessions. Delilah can't do a daily class, but she's going to take the kids to the farmer's market Saturday mornings and then do a cooking class. And Meghan's psyched to do yoga—" She glanced up to find him heading for the luggage stand. Gawking, she immediately looked away. "Jesus, Cassian. Put some clothes on. There are some things a girl can't unsee."

He stood in nothing but his boxers. "You're the one who walked into my room without knocking."

"I knocked."

"You said the word, as you barged in. Now, turn around and let me get dressed." He grabbed his jeans off the top of his suitcase and stepped into them. While there, he glanced at his cell phone and saw a few text messages.

Tyler: **Need a favor**

There wasn't anything he wouldn't do for Gigi's dad.

Cassian: **Anything.**

Tyler: **10 year old kid's obsessed with penguins, so we're bringing in two from the zoo. Want to give him something he can take home. Got a car waiting for you at the valet desk. Get directions for toy stores and see if you can find a stuffed penguin.**

Cassian: **You got it.**

Tyler: **Thanks.**

"Everything okay?" Amie asked.

"Yeah. I've got to run an errand, though. Anything else we need to discuss before you head back to Calamity?"

"Just those money transfers, but let's wait until I pull all the receipts together for the new equipment we bought. I'll have it done by the time you get back to the hotel."

"I might not come back." Who knew how easy it would be to find a stuffed penguin? "Might have to head straight to the community center. Just send a PDF of the receipts to me."

"Or I can stop by the center. I checked, and it's on my way to the airport." When she saw his alarm, she said, "Would you chill out? I'll text you when I get there, and you can meet me in the car, so no one sees us together."

She'd come on the trip to go over last-minute camp business—but only on the condition that they not be seen together in front of fans or press. He didn't need to stir up more speculation about the nature of their relationship.

"Everyone's going to have their cameras out. Not going to risk it." Pulling on his jersey, he stepped into his running shoes and headed out the door. "Thanks for coming out here with me. I'll see you in a week."

"Hey, Cassian?"

Holding it open, he glanced back at her, wondering at the hesitation in her tone.

"Is there anything going on between you and the Lollipop?"

A shock of sensation ripped through him. The last thing he wanted was for anyone to make a connection between him and Gigi. "No, why?"

"Just…the way you two went after each other last night. I mean, you obviously have history."

"Her dad coached me in high school, so we've known each other a long time. But, as you can see, she can't stand me. And that's never going to change." *Not while there are headlines about me having threesomes.*

"She's not, like, the love of your life and you're secretly hoping to get back with her or something?"

Heat flooded his body, and it took a hell of a lot of self-discipline to remain disinterested.

"No." How the hell had she picked up on that? Was he that obvious? "Why're you asking?"

"Just the way you looked at each other. Sparks all over the place. But, okay, if you say so."

Yeah, they had sparks, all right. She could have ignited his clothing with all the sparks shooting out of her eye sockets. "See you later." He let the door fall shut behind him.

On his way down to the lobby, he texted Kevin, letting him know Tyler had sent him on an errand, so he wouldn't be taking the van. Once outside, he put on his sunglasses and hit the valet station. "Good morning. Tyler Cavanaugh told me there's a car waiting for me."

"Yes, sir. She's already in it."

"She?" He glanced over to find Gigi getting into the driver's side of a Chevy. "Hang on. There's only one car?"

"Yes, sir. As far as I know, only one car was rented for your group."

"Thanks." He strode over, but she'd already slipped inside and shut the door. He rapped on the window.

Ignoring him, she shifted into Drive.

"Hey." She was going to leave without him. He banged on the window. "*Hey.*"

When she gave him an impatient look, he made a circular motion with his hand. *Roll down the window.*

Pushing the button on her side panel, she cracked it. "What?"

"Your dad rented this car for *me*. I have an errand to run for him. But don't worry, I can bring you back your caramel macchiato with extra whipped cream."

She gave him a withering look. "I'm not hijacking your rental car to make a coffee run, you idiot. But, since I'm already running an errand for my mom, I'll talk to my dad and see what he needs, too. See ya."

He gripped the window frame. "Hang on. Your dad doesn't ask much of me, so you can bet your ass when he does, I'm going to do it."

"Aw, such loyalty. Shame it doesn't extend to your girl-friends." She checked her rearview mirror. "Look, you go back inside. I'm sure there's been a shift change with the staff, which gives you a whole new group of playmates. So, you do what you're good at, and I'll take care of business for my parents."

"Thanks for that hot tip, but—*shew*—those ladies wore me out last night. Guess I'm not as young as I used to be. Listen, you can drive away right now, but I think you know if you tell your dad you're going to do the errand for me, he's going to know we're not getting along.

Which means one of us is going to get pulled from this tour. Which one do you think it'll be?"

"Wow, you've really honed your assholery over the years. I'm impressed. Get in."

She popped the lock, and before she could change her mind, he opened the door and dropped onto the seat, reaching between his legs to shift it back as far as it went.

"Where to?" She idled under the portico.

And, oh, man, did she smell nice. Different than the teenager who'd carried the scent of lavender and vanilla in her clothing but familiar in a way that gave him a soul-deep wallop of recognition.

Mine.

"We need to get a stuffed penguin." He typed *Nearest Toy Stores to Me* into his phone. A few came up. "Penny Whistle's the closest."

"Do you know if they have them?"

"I'll find out." He hit Call. It felt so strange, sitting in a car beside her again after all these years, talking about penguins, like it was just a normal day.

But it wasn't normal. Because everything had changed.

She'd dyed her once-dark hair to platinum blonde, and her body had filled out, giving her a lush ripeness that, coupled with her take-no-shit spirit, was a real turn-on.

"Nice outfit, by the way." He noticed she'd replaced the ripped jeans, hoodies and Uggs of her high school days with knee socks and combat boots.

No, she didn't look much the same at all.

And yet…his soul stirred in recognition. He felt the pull deep down.

"Fuck off." She kept her focus on the oncoming traffic.

Which meant she didn't catch his grin.

"Penny Whistle," a man answered. "How can I help you?'

"Hey, I'm looking for a stuffed penguin."

"Nope. Sorry. That's one we don't have."

"Okay." But he wasn't showing up without one. "The thing is, we're visiting a boy at the Cancer Center this afternoon, and he's got a thing for penguins."

"Ah, okay. Gotcha. That's real nice. Let me think about that…" The man went quiet for a moment. "You know what your best bet's gonna be? The Maritime Center downtown."

"Excellent idea, thank you."

"You got it. Good luck."

Cassian disconnected. "He said to try the Maritime Center."

"Great idea. Well, I'm supposed to get cupcakes with penguins on them, so why don't you start calling bakeries and see if you can find someone who can do that for us? We can hit the Maritime Center while they're working on our cupcakes. If we're lucky, you'll get a woman on the line and you can work your charms on her."

He deserved everything she gave him, so he kept his mouth shut. Holding up his phone, he spoke into the mic. "Bakeries near me." A list came up, and he called the closest one.

"Good morning," a woman said. "Hanson's Bakery."

"Hey, we need about…" He glanced to Gigi.

"Three dozen?" she said quietly.

He nodded. "Three dozen cupcakes. Right now."

"I can do that." He could hear the smile in her voice.

"That's great…but can you do it with penguins on them?"

The woman laughed. "Ha. That's a good one. When do you need them by?"

"By noon."

"Nope, not a chance. Sorry."

"I understand." And he was pretty sure he'd hear the same answer from every bakery, so he needed a solution. "But we're delivering them to the Children's Cancer Center. There's a little boy obsessed with penguins, so any suggestion you have will be appreciated."

"Oh, man. You know how to get to a girl. Okay, well, unless you special order, I doubt you'll find a bakery who can pull it off for you, but there could be a compromise. There's a party store in the Cuperton Mall. You know the animated movie *Penguins*? I'll bet you can get plates and napkins and probably even something to put on top of the cupcakes from it."

"That's a great idea. We'll check it out. Hey, can you do me a favor and hang onto those cupcakes for me?"

"If you pay for them right now."

Cassian reached into his pocket and pulled out his wallet. He read the woman his credit card number. "We've got a few stops to make first, but we'll be there no later than eleven-thirty to pick them up."

"You own them now, so whenever you want to pick them is good by me."

He disconnected and gave Gigi a big grin. "Done." When she smiled back, her whole face lit up, and it struck like a clap of thunder. The connection was intense, powerful, and he'd felt nothing like it in nearly a decade. On a heady wave of hope, he raised a hand for a high five, but the smile flattened immediately.

"Let me tell you something, Cassian. What you did to me nine years ago changed me. I wish more than anything that I could tell you I'm over it, that I've moved on, but it's just not true. You broke me. We're stuck on this tour together, and I'll try to stop sniping at you." At the stoplight, she braked and turned to look at him. "But you and I will never be friends."

The community center turned out to be a sprawling ranch-style home on the outskirts of a nice, well-kept family neighborhood. A fenced yard took up one half of the lot.

The group gathered around Kevin in a yard filled with plastic toys, a few trees, a swing set, and a slide. With her arms full of cupcake boxes, Gigi stood close enough to Cassian to brush the warm skin of his arm.

It was electric, that touch. And it elicited a hot mess of emotion, because her mind hated her body's reaction to him.

But there was nothing she could do about it. She was attracted to him—just like everyone else in the damn world. He was so potently masculine, with his spectacularly fit body, handsome face, and that Pied Piper charisma that bewitched people into dropping what they were doing to follow him.

"So, here's the deal," Kevin said. "As soon as the zoo people get here, they're going to bring Cody and his family out, give him some special time with the penguins. Cassian, you'll go inside, and the director will take you to the dining room, where you'll hang out with a couple families." He nodded toward Gigi. "I'd love it if you could set up right there on that picnic table. After Cody gets some time alone with the penguins, we'll open up the yard to the festivities, and you can do your thing."

"That sounds great. Let me just drop off these…" She lifted her bakery boxes. "And then I'll grab my guitar from the car."

"Perfect. Just go in through the kitchen, which is back there." Kevin waited for her nod of acknowledgment before continuing to give out instructions.

Cassian, holding bags of supplies and a large stuffed penguin, walked with her across the springy grass.

With each step, her discomfort grew. She'd enjoyed their morning together a little too much, which meant she was susceptible. She didn't want to fall for his charm. "You want to hand that stuff to me? We don't both need to drop it off."

"I have to go inside anyhow."

An image hit—him surrounded by fawning hotel staff last night—and all that anxiety hardened into anger. "Right." She walked between two swings to distance herself from him. "There have to be, what, five or six women in this county who haven't had the pleasure of the Ellis Effect."

"You know, I never thought of it that way, but that makes a lot of sense. This tour gives me a chance to pour my honey across towns I might never have gotten a chance to visit."

Everything in her bristled at this tone. At his attitude. At his face. "Well, that's a super positive spin on the fact that your coach made you come because you're in the news more for your sexcapades than your playing." She gave him a faux-sorry look. "Sucks that my parents run the foundation, huh? I'm privy to all kinds of fun facts."

"You seem oddly fascinated with my 'sexcapades,' but

then you are a Lollipop, so you probably think French kisses are gross."

She bit her tongue to keep from smiling. "I'm more fascinated with the idea that a man who's won two Super Bowls still craves so much female attention. It's sad, really, the emptiness you feel inside."

"Oh, I don't know about that. Between playing on the Mavericks, partying with my teammates, and fucking every woman who happens to cross my path, I have a pretty full life."

"And yet…who are your real friends? If you took away the football, the superyachts, and the modeling gigs— who'd stick around? By the way, did they stick a cucumber in your boxers for that commercial?"

"This is your hardest?" he asked quietly.

She glanced over at him. "My what?"

"You said you'd try your hardest not to snipe at me."

"Oh, that. Well, I did make it through two hours in a car with you."

"True. I guess I need to lower my standards."

"Lower them? Is that even possible?" Just as she reached for the handle on the screen door, it flew open.

"Would you look who's here?" A woman in scrubs relieved her of the boxes. "In all my life, I never imagined I'd be face-to-face with two celebrities. Come on in. What'cha got there?"

They entered the warm kitchen that smelled of roasting meat with an undertone of pine-scented cleaning fluid. Several staff members surrounded them, peering into the boxes and pulling plates and napkins out of the bags.

"Oh, look at this." The woman held up the plastic

penguins that they'd stick into the cupcakes. "Aren't these adorable?"

"I love it," someone else said.

With a warm smile, Cassian shook hands with everyone. Effortlessly, he chatted, making them laugh, making each person feel special.

Gigi felt unsettled.

Because she'd said horrible things to him, and he'd been right to call her out. She was just so angry. She *wanted* to hurt him. She wanted to wipe that damn smile off his face, make him feel something real.

Regret. Remorse.

Was he really this shallow? Was everything just a joke?

She stood there, watching him win over everyone in the kitchen, and she finally got it.

He truly didn't care that he'd destroyed her.

No. That's not it. He didn't miss her. The friendship that had meant the world to her had meant nothing to him.

And that's what I can't stand.

She didn't know how she was going to do this, get through an entire week with him.

Quietly, she left the kitchen, filled her lungs with the warm, late spring air, and made her way back to the van to get her guitar.

I know exactly how I'll do it. She'd sing her heart out for the patients and their families. And then she'd go back to her hotel room and write songs.

Music had pulled her through before, and it would pull her through this week.

Chapter Five

"YOU READY TO MEET SOME KIDS?" THE NURSE ASKED with a cheerful expression.

"Sure am." Cassian had to force himself to be in the moment.

He couldn't get over Gigi's look of disdain as she'd watched him in the kitchen, as if he'd been some poseur. What did she expect from him?

I'm here to shake hands, take selfies, and sign autographs.

She was so damn angry with him.

"Actually, can you give me a minute? I'd like to see Cody's expression when he meets the penguins."

The nurse looked at him like he was the sweetest guy ever. *I'm not,* he wanted to say. *I hurt my best friend, and I continue to be a jerk to her, and I don't know why.*

Why can't I stop?

Why the fuck can't I just say I'm sorry?

"Of course." She tipped her head toward the door. "Come on. The zoo van's just pulling up." They headed out the sliding glass door. "We're so excited to have you guys here. You can't believe how many times we've applied to the foundation, and now…to be accepted when *Cassian Ellis* is on the tour? I just can't believe it."

Stepping outside, he headed toward the picnic table, because there was no one else he wanted to share the moment with other than Gigi. But she didn't even notice his approach. She was captivated by the sight of Cody. Surrounded by family, eyes wide and bright, the boy's excitement was palpable as he watched the handlers wheel the travel crate toward him.

Cassian felt the jerk inside him, a shifting of his perspective. Obviously, he worked his ass off—he'd earned his career—but he'd been given all the advantages, whereas this boy had spent his childhood in and out of hospitals. Sure, Cassian had lost his parents when he was fourteen, but he'd moved in with his uncle and aunt. He'd had Tyler Cavanaugh's guiding hand. He'd been born with a strong, healthy body.

And the worst thing that had ever happened to him— losing a piece of his soul—could be corrected, because Gigi was here right now, standing close enough for him to see the nick on her chin—the color of moonlight—from when she'd tripped on the trail and landed on a sharp-edged rock. He caught her looking at him, and he knew she got it, too.

What're we doing?

In the scheme of things, our issues are so petty.

A fierceness seized him. He couldn't take back what he'd done, but their paths had crossed again. It might only be for a week, but he'd grab the opportunity. First, he'd apologize. And then he'd do whatever she needed to help her heal.

The animal handler opened the door of the crate, and the black and white penguins waddled out. The boy's eyes flared with awe as the animals shook themselves like wet dogs, flapping their wings and shaking their heads.

The handler, a silver-haired woman, lifted one of them and set it on the boy's lap. His grin stretched across his face. Damn, if it didn't pinch Cassian's heart.

The family gathered around, as the boy gave a running commentary on what the penguins felt like, and how he couldn't believe he got to touch one.

Cassian didn't miss the father's eyes turning glassy, the way he blinked back tears.

"This is amazing," Gigi whispered.

"I'm glad I'm here."

"Me, too." She gave him a soft smile.

Energy roared through him. "I want you to know—"

She shook her head. *Not now.*

Kevin gave her a nod, and she picked up her guitar. Sitting down on a picnic table, she began playing.

Cassian stood transfixed, as her voice threw him back in time. To hot sun on his shoulders and cold lake water lapping onto a rocky shore, listening to her play for him on a summer's day. To the smell of wood burning, sparks snapping, while a bunch of them gathered around a bonfire and listened to her sing.

His pulse pounded in his ears, and he grew warm. *She's here.* And he had the chance to make things right.

He'd get her alone, talk to her. Do *something.* Anything was better than ignoring her and pretending his life hadn't been so damn empty without her.

Right then the sliding glass doors opened, and families and nurses came outside, gathering around the penguins. A few teenagers came straight for Gigi, who greeted them with her warmth and open spirit.

It was time for Cassian to go in, but he almost couldn't

bear being separated from her. He glanced back one more time at the woman who shared his soul...and caught Grant, the country singer, watching her.

Wait—*whoa*—was the older guy interested in her?

Of course he's fucking interested in her. Gigi was gorgeous, vibrant, talented. Her record label might've tried to sanitize the sexiness right out of her, but they couldn't. Because it came from within. She was artsy, sensual, earthy. No matter the platinum hair and trendy, youthful clothes, her essence shone through. Especially when she sang.

"Cassian?" Kevin called.

"Coming. Sorry. I just wanted to be here when Cody saw the penguins."

"It's a life-changer, isn't?" Kevin nodded.

"It is."

"Hey, so, listen. Good news. Your jerseys got here on time. We've got Sharpees and a bunch of kids who want some one-on-one time with you."

"You don't think...given my recent press, their parents might not want me around their kids?"

"They're besides themselves with the opportunity to meet you. Besides...can you think of a single celebrity who doesn't get thrown some shade in the media?" He tipped his chin to the country star. "He's been married three times, in and out of rehab...and this is his fourth tour with us. They love him, because he's got a big heart, and he loves meeting the families. So, just be your true self. You're here as the quarterback of the Mavericks, and in that capacity you're a role model to millions of people. When you're here, headlines don't exist."

Cassian didn't even know the tension he carried until it eased right then. "Thanks, man. I appreciate that."

With one last look at Gigi, he went inside. As he passed the nurse's station, one of them—a pretty young woman with short, spikey hair—swung around and clapped her hands over her mouth.

"Oh, my God, it's Cassian Ellis."

"Hey, there." He reached for her hand, reading her nametag. "Great to meet you, Heather."

She looked shellshocked. "I just can't believe it."

Wanting to set her at ease, he said, "You've got a great town here. And that's coming from someone who's driven from one end to the other on the quest for anything penguin."

"Oh, it's…I mean, I grew up here. It's all I know."

"Nicest people I've ever met."

"Oh…I…" She stood there wide-eyed and tongue-tied.

So, he gave a tug to the sleeve of her shirt. "Cute scrubs."

Her demeanor shifted. She went from excited fan to interested woman. Leaning over the desk, she pushed her butt high in the air, and reached for a pen. "Can you sign them?"

"Sure thing." He uncapped the pen, looking to her for guidance on where she wanted him to write his name.

"Here." She pulled on the hem of her top, as if he'd write across her chest.

But…no, he wasn't going to do that. Not here, in this context. *Not with Gigi on the other side of that wall.* So, he pulled her sleeve and scrawled, *You're an amazing person, Heather. Cassian Ellis* before closing the pen and handing it back.

"How long are you in town?" she asked.

"Just tonight. We head out in the morning."

"You guys need a place to eat? I could give you some recommendations."

"I think the guy who's running the tour's got us booked somewhere, but thanks." He couldn't even think about spending time with anyone else right now. Gigi was so close—like a scent rising off his skin, like a shadow flickering in his soul. Right there.

And she was everything.

"Well, if you can sneak away. I'll give you a personal tour of St. Louis."

"Yeah?" He saw the spark of hope, the way she turned seductive.

"Tell you what. I'll give you my number." She leaned over the counter again, snatching a Post-It off a stack, and wrote her digits. "I'm around tonight. So, any time you can slip away, just call me."

"Cassian?" Amie called.

He shot a look to the entrance. *Dammit. What's she doing here?* He'd told her he didn't want anyone to see them together.

Raising a hand, he waved the Post-It. "Thanks." And then headed over to his friend, who wore a baseball cap. Cupping her elbow, he led her right back out the door. "I asked you not to come here."

"I know, but I've got the receipts, and you know I like to make the transfers right in front of you. If anything goes wrong, I don't want to be blamed for it."

Once outside, he ushered her toward the waiting taxi. "I appreciate that you want things to be above-board, but right now it's more important that I don't wind up in the media with you."

He gestured for her to get back in the idling car.

"Well, hold on a second. I want to talk to you about

something." She grasped his wrist and led him to the bushes at the side of the building. "Look, we've been friends a long time."

Oh, Christ. "You're not quitting on me, are you?" Not now, when camp was just about to start.

"Of course not. Just listen. When I got kicked off the show, everyone patted me on the shoulder and said stuff like, 'You'll land on your feet.' But you didn't do that. You sat down and talked to me. Some of what you said hurt, but I really respected you for telling me the truth about why I'd gotten fired and what I needed to do to get back on the show."

That's not...what? He hadn't given her advice on how to get back on it. He'd asked what she wanted out of it, and then brainstormed other things she could do to get the same result.

"And now I want to be a good friend to you and tell you what I'm pretty sure everyone else is afraid to. Cassian, I don't know what Coach said to you, but if he flew all the way out to Colorado to talk to you, I know it wasn't good."

He looked around to see if anyone had spotted him. It didn't look like it but that didn't mean much.

"All I know is it wasn't because of a noise complaint." She gave him a pointed look. "He obviously doesn't like the kind of press you're always getting."

"Amie, we can talk about his later. I have to get back inside."

"Just hear me out. You know how some guys can fly under the radar? They do way worse stuff than you, but it never gets out?"

He did, actually. His backup quarterback was the perfect example.

"Well, it's because you invite that attention. You flirt, you charm. I mean, that nurse back there? She just wanted an autograph, you know? But you turned on all the charm, and now she thinks she has a chance with you." She scanned his features. "You're not even aware of it, are you?"

"I wasn't flirting. I was being *nice*." He knew what it felt like to meet someone he admired. He appreciated her excitement and wouldn't do anything to diminish it.

"Okay, let me put it this way. That nurse was super excited to meet Cassian Ellis, a Mavericks football player, but you turned it into the possibility of hooking up with Cassian, the Bad Boy Quarterback. Do you see what I'm saying?"

He wanted to argue with her, but he couldn't. That's exactly what had happened. In fact, he'd seen it. Like flipping a switch, she'd gone from fan to seducer.

This is what Coach is talking about. On this tour, Cassian was a representative of the team. Instead, he'd come off like a friend. Someone to grab a beer with. Or a potential hookup.

"So, okay, I just wanted to put it out there. I think it'll help keep you out of trouble."

"I hear what you're saying. Now, go on to Calamity and make this the best damn summer these kids have ever had. I'll see you soon."

After the group dinner, where Gigi completely ignored him by sitting at the opposite end of a long table, Cassian went to his room to make some calls. He checked in with the team's publicist to see what they were doing about the leaked photograph and with his manager to find out if he'd heard anything about being traded.

His manager was pretty sure they'd never trade their franchise quarterback, that it had just been a ploy to get Cassian to behave, but Cassian didn't believe it. Coach never said anything he didn't mean. Besides, the threat had come from the team's owner. And all Chuck Caswell cared about was football…and winning.

Which meant it was a very real possibility that Cassian would have to start all over again. The idea was…depressing. It took a lot of work to win people over.

There's nothing I can do about it now.

Tonight, though, there *was* something he could do. Apologize to Gigi. First, he needed to find her. Grabbing his keycard, he stuffed it in his back pocket and started for the door. His phone vibrated. *Dean.*

He wanted to ignore it, get to Gigi, but Dean was a man of few words. If he was calling, it mattered. "Yeah?"

"Turn on SportsNews."

Dammit. "What now?" He snatched the remote off the TV and turned it on. It took him a minute to find the station, but when he did, he found the sportscasters talking about a press conference. "What's this got to do with me?" *Oh, hang on.* In a smaller box, he recognized Zach Dimitri, his back-up quarterback sitting behind a microphone. "Is he making an announcement? Did he get *traded?*"

"Give it a second. They keep repeating the interview. Analyzing what he said."

Dean was right. A moment later the box widened to fill the screen.

"You excited to head to training camp in a few weeks, Zach?" someone asked.

"You bet." Zach sat at a long, rectangular table, alongside other players, facing a roomful of reporters. "We're all excited to get back on the field and win another championship." He motioned to someone else in the audience.

"Think you'll get some play time this season?" a reporter asked.

"You'll have to talk to Coach about that." He pointed at someone else.

The next guy asked, "What about Cassian?"

"What about him?" Zach looked almost menacing.

"Will his latest scandal impact his ability to lead the team?"

"As long as he's winning games, who cares what he does? He can have all the threesomes he wants."

The betrayal rocketed through him. Cassian didn't need to hear anything else. He punched the power button off. "Jesus." His own teammate had just confirmed tabloid gossip.

"Yeah. That's your backup. Nothing to do about it, but it's good to know who he is."

"He's full of shit. He was there. He knows it didn't happen."

"Of course he does, and that's the point. He's shown his true colors. None of us will forget it."

And with six simple words, Dean managed to snap everything back into perspective. His other teammates had his back. Always. "He thinks he's making me look bad, but no one likes a traitor. He really messed up."

"He's just trying to get onto the field."

"Even if he makes it, his teammates are going to hate him." Cassian didn't think the comment would do more damage, but it'd fan the flames. "Listen, thanks for the heads-up. I'm going to head downstairs, meet up with the others."

"You gonna be okay?"

"Yep. This week I'm all about the tour." *And Gigi.* "Talk to you later." Shoving the phone in his back pocket, he headed out of the room. There were a lot of things in his life right now he couldn't control, so he'd concentrate on what he could.

As he boarded the elevator, he recalled the others talking about hanging out in the bar, so he'd start there.

The minute he hit the lobby he heard the music. Two voices, a man and a woman. Hard not to recognize the deep baritone of Grant Banner and the powerful, clear-as-a-bell voice of Gigi Cavanaugh. His pulse quickened at the idea of being near her.

Being traded, his teammate's fuckery…all of his troubles evaporated just knowing she was right there.

Tonight, he'd talk to her. *Apologize.*

Explain.

The thought galvanized him.

Standing at the back of the packed, noisy bar, he saw a sea of glowing screens. Countless people held their phones up high to record the famous musicians. Wanting to stay unnoticed, he stood against the wall, off to the side, where he got an unobstructed view.

The yellow lights turned Gigi's hair gold, and the gentle slope of her bare shoulder made his fingertips tingle. Because he wanted to touch that smooth skin.

He wanted to kiss it, lick a path down to her cleavage.

Too bad she's staring into the eyes of another man. Someone who made her happy. The longer he watched, though, the more he got the impression they were writing a song together. Right then and there.

The advantage of living in Boston was that he didn't have to see Gigi with other men. As a Lollipop, her social media was the exact opposite of his. It was curated to show her doing wholesome things like shopping or getting gelato in Italy with her bandmates.

So, the idea of watching a relationship develop between her and the country star on this tour? A jealous beast reared up and exposed its fangs.

"Cassian Ellis, oh, my God." A petite woman came up to him. She was beautiful. Black hair, dark eyes. With a hand on his forearm for balance, she got up on her toes, shouting over the music. "I heard you were staying here, and I drove right over. Trust me, we never get this much excitement in our town."

His gaze flicked back to Gigi. He really wanted to hear her sing. "Yeah?"

"I can't believe you're standing here right now. Is this a dream? I want to pinch myself." She settled back down. "Can I buy you a drink?"

He felt it—the impulse to turn on the charm, chat her up—and he was damn glad Amie had pointed it out to him, because he didn't want to do that anymore.

"I was going to tell my friends to come with me tonight, but then I thought, Why would I do that, when I could spend time alone with you?"

He liked to think he was a good guy, only hooking up with women he'd never see again. Which meant women like this one, someone he met on the road or in a bar.

Since no one saw him with the same woman twice, people called him a playboy. But, really, he just didn't date. Not only because he didn't want to mislead anyone, but because he'd given his heart away long ago, and he knew to the bottom of his soul there was no other woman in the world for him.

Which consigned him to a life of partying and meaningless sexual encounters.

But, yeah, he got it. How he turned a friendly encounter into something that hinted of more. And it was time to cut it out. In this situation, he was representing the Mavericks—not looking to get laid.

It was time to start writing his own headlines, instead of letting the paparazzi do it for him.

"So, what do you say?" The perky woman had so much hope in her eyes. "Get a drink?"

He glanced at Gigi—*shit*. She'd clocked him. Some of her enthusiasm for the song had dimmed, and determination whipped through him.

Just like in high school, he wanted to be a better man for her. He *would* be. Starting right now. "That sounds like a nice idea, but I'm pretty beat. I just came down to check on tomorrow's itinerary."

"Oh, sure. I saw the pictures from today. The penguins? That was amazing." She caressed his bare forearm. "I think it's great that you take time out to do something like this. It means so much to the kids."

On another night, he'd have welcomed the invitation in her touch. He'd have hung out with her while she had a drink or two and then taken her upstairs for an hour of fun. But tonight…it wasn't going to happen. "It means a lot to me to spend time with them."

"I'm a nurse. Pediatric, so I know what it means to those kids to get a visit from someone special like you."

The music stopped, and while the crowd clapped and encouraged them to play another song, Gigi focused on fitting her guitar back into its case. From this angle, he could see her profile, see how unhappy she'd become.

I'm going to change that. "Hey, listen. It was nice to meet you." He gave a polite smile as Gigi made her way out of the bar.

And Cassian followed.

———

"Wait up."

Gigi ignored him. She'd tried. She really had. To ignore him at dinner, pretend he was a stranger. To be the mature woman her parents expected of her. To put the tour, the *patients,* first.

But watching Cassian flirt with every nurse, server, staffer…and now to witness him choosing his hookup for the night?

No. Just no.

She quickened her pace, hoping to catch the elevator before the doors closed.

I'm sorry, but I'm obviously not over him.

No, I'm not over what he did to me.

Except…the lines were blurred, and she couldn't see the difference between the two.

"Can you please hold the elevator?"

An older man's hand reached out, keeping the doors from shutting.

"Thank you." She slid inside, standing her guitar on end and nodding to the elderly couple who looked like they might not be speaking to each other.

Refusing to look into the lobby, she kept her eyes on the stickers that covered her case. Singapore, London, Istanbul. *This. This is what I should be focused on.*

Instead of being embarrassed at being a Lollipop, she needed to be grateful for the experiences and opportunities it had offered. She needed to—

"Hold up." Cassian's muscular arm sliced between the closing doors, and he leapt inside.

"Careful," the man said. "You don't want to risk that throwing arm."

"Some things are worth it." Cassian shot her a dimpled grin.

Screw you.

"You gonna make the Super Bowl next season?" the man asked.

"Or die trying," Cassian said.

"You know," the older man said. "As much as everyone loved Ben—and I'm a diehard Chargers fan, and even *I* loved him—he didn't win. You…" He wagged a finger at Cassian. "You're a winner."

"Yup," Gigi said. "He scores big on *and* off the field."

Oh, that's nice. A bitter Lollipop.

Can you just keep your mouth shut around him?

No one responded, and the tension between the two couples—although she and Cassian weren't an actual couple—was loud.

Cassian edged closer to her, and the older gentleman stood beside his rigid wife.

"You could have defended me," the woman whispered harshly. "You never defend me."

The gentleman, in a suit, watched the numbers light up on the panel over the doors.

More anger radiated out of his wife. "You should have said something."

Gigi glanced at Cassian, who gave her a look that said, *Uh oh.*

Bristling, the elegant woman looked at her husband, waiting for a response. When he didn't acknowledge her, she stepped away from him.

His arm looped around her waist, and he tugged her back. Into her ear, he said, "She's an old, bitter woman. I chose you forty years ago. I still choose you today." He nuzzled into her. "I will always choose you."

A shudder went through the woman's body.

The doors opened, and the couple walked out. As the woman turned to go down the hallway, the man reached for her hand, pulling her up against his body and—

The doors closed before Gigi could see the kiss. She lowered her gaze so Cassian couldn't see her smile.

"What's on your feet?" he asked.

"Slippers." She said it like, *Duh*.

"Those are the ugliest things I've ever seen."

"They're not *ugly*." She lifted her foot to show him all angles. "My mom had them made for all of us. They're Teddy."

"I can see that. But, objectively speaking, Teddy was ugly."

Their family dog had been a mutt with a tongue that flopped out of his mouth. Just like the little pink felt tongues sticking out of her slippers. "I don't mean to hurt your brain or anything, but some of us see beyond superficial beauty."

"Okay, but who wants to wear the dead family dog on her feet?"

"Oh, I can answer that." She used a fake cheerful voice. "I know it's a ridiculously hard concept for a cold-hearted asshole to understand, but we actually loved our dog. He was hilarious and loyal and snuggly and...literally the best dog ever." She pressed the button to their floor.

"That's not going to get us there faster."

"Yeah, but it's better than trying to explain the cuteness of these slippers to a man without a heart."

The elevator stopped, and Gigi reached for the handle of her guitar case. She walked out, tugged in two directions. She needed to get away from him as badly as she wanted more time with him.

Time to lash out at him, banter with him, yell at him, but this tour was not the right place for any of that. God, she hoped his room wasn't anywhere near hers.

But, of course, she could hear his footsteps right behind her.

"I have a heart."

"I know you're a jock, and you probably had tutors and fan girls doing most of your work in college, but if you do a quick search of the human anatomy, you'll see the heart and the penis are actually two different things."

He chuckled.

It was his laughter that did it, pushed her over the edge. She whirled around to face him. "Do you care about anything? I mean, other than winning a football game, do you actually care about anything? Or anyone?"

"Yes."

There was something in his tone that made her pay closer attention. And, even though they were in the hallway of the Marriott in St. Louis, it felt like being in their tree house all over again. It made her heart beat faster.

But it was all a lie. Cassian Ellis was a liar. She turned and continued her march to her room. "Goodnight. Don't forget to cover your stump before you hump." *Oh, God.*

Oh, my fucking God.

Dear Universe, please suck that last sentence into some kind of black hole.

"Tonight's hookup is hot, by the way." She kept her tone jovial in an attempt to cover her lame comment.

"I'm not hooking up with her."

"Oh." She shook her head with an expression that said, *I'm such a dummy.* "Of course. You'd already scheduled tonight's fun earlier in the day. Which nurse? Or is it a patient's Mom?" And then, feeling particularly mean, she said, "Or Dad. Whatever."

"Come on. You should know better than anyone not to believe what you read in the media."

"I don't care who you sleep with, my point—"

"You sure about that?" Whatever softness she'd seen a moment ago turned hard. "You seem very interested. Almost like you're keeping tabs."

At her door, she swiped her keycard. "You have a girlfriend, and I watched you flirt with women right in front of her. Sorry, but even if I didn't once know you, watching your blatant disrespect makes me a little ragey. Not that I feel sorry for your girlfriend, because it's her choice to stay with a philanderer, but you really should pull your head out of your ass and think about how it feels to her when you do it in front of everyone on this tour."

"I don't know, Gigi, rage is a pretty strong emotion. You sure there's not something else going on? *You* wouldn't have feelings for me, would you?"

Because that would just be sad, wouldn't it? To still be obsessed with the guy who'd treated her so cruelly? "Obviously I still have feelings. How could I not? I loved you, you jerk. And you knew it the whole time. You preyed on it." The truth rang like shattered glass, jarring her bones. "That's how you get off, isn't it? You turn on all that charm, lead women to believe they've got something special with you, and then let them know exactly how you really feel by messing around with someone else right under their nose. You *enjoy* hurting them. That's where you get your power. How did I never see it before? Wow. That's…you need help. I thought you were just careless, but you're sick."

Anger crackled off him like static electricity. "You don't know how wrong you are. But, maybe, instead of analyzing me, you might want to take a better look at yourself."

"What's that supposed to mean?"

He reached for a lock of her hair. "Who the fuck are you? Do you even know? The girl I knew wrote her own songs, had her own style. What happened to her?" He turned, heading back down the hall.

But he didn't get to walk away on that note. "I'll tell you exactly what happened to her." God, she was shouting at him in a hallway. But she didn't care. She was a ball of fury. "*You* happened to her. She trusted you with all her heart, and you betrayed her. How am I supposed to trust my own instincts anymore after what you did to me? I can't. So, no, I don't know who I am anymore, but I'm damn glad to have seen you in action, because I have a feeling my confidence is about to come roaring back."

His long legs ate up the carpet, and within seconds he was standing in front of her, too close, too intense. His eyes burned with anger, determination…and yet…underneath all that, she could have sworn she saw helplessness.

"I was seventeen." Intensity radiated off him. "I fucked up, but I was a kid. You have to let it go. You have to… you can't…*fuck*." He cupped her chin—and she felt the tremble in his fingers—and the fierceness in his gaze made her hot and restless and…and confused.

Because he might act like the cavalier playboy, but he felt like the boy she'd loved so completely.

Still watching her, he lowered his mouth, a tumult of emotion churning in his eyes. It all settled into a stark, desperate yearning that ripped through her body like a scream.

Because she knew what was coming.

One second later, he kissed her. Her heart kicked so hard it hurt. His mouth opened, as he licked inside, and he shifted closer. The heat of his body sank into her skin, and when his hands cupped her jaw, tilting her to deepen the kiss, she thought she would die.

Of pleasure and longing and…and…the sweetness of this moment, of finally closing the gap that had always existed between them.

Oh, God, she was just melting from his touch. The scent of him, the hunger in his kiss…everything just swirled around her, had her spinning, lifting, taking flight.

Until she remembered. *This is Cassian.* The careless playboy.

Kissing meant nothing to him.

She snapped out of it, tore her mouth away, and shoved him.

She wanted to burst into tears, but she wouldn't give him the satisfaction of letting him know he'd wrecked her.

"*That* will never happen again."

Chapter Six

CASSIAN PACED HIS HOTEL ROOM, WATCHING THE recording his friend had just sent. But it was hard to pay attention when desire still rocked his body.

And fear. What had he done?

Why would you kiss her?

She hates you.

That kiss sure as hell didn't taste like hate.

"You see it?" Dean's voice came through the speaker on his phone.

His friend had gotten the hotel to release security footage of the entire scene at the pool—from the moment Amie jumped onto the diving board and started peeling off her bikini, to him leaping onto it and blocking her, and then to Dean handing him a towel, saying something quietly. "Yeah, I see it."

"You don't sound happy."

Because I'm not. "No, it's good. Thank you. I appreciate it."

The way Gigi saw him—it made his stomach sick. He didn't prey on women, did he?

He flirted. He hooked up with women he met on the road. But neither of those could be considered *preying*. The whole point was to *not* hurt anyone.

"I sent it to Coach and Joan," Dean said. "They're going to release it. We need to show that you were being a good guy. That we were just partying as a team."

"No, they can't do that."

"What? Why not?"

"Because, in the photograph, you can't see that it's Amie Clover. Here, you can. And I don't want to jeopardize her job or her reputation."

"Fine. We'll blur her face, but you're not going to get traded over shit like this."

"Okay." He brought the phone back to his ear. "Do you think I prey on women?"

Dean went quiet, and Cassian breathed a little easier. He could trust his friend to take his question seriously and give him a thoughtful answer.

"I'm going to need some context here, because I've never known you to lie or mislead anyone."

"When I talk to a woman, am I nice? Or do I go into scoring mode?" He thought about the nurse, and how he'd talked to her. He hadn't been thinking about getting laid. He thought he'd been putting her at ease.

"First of all, you're allowed to have a sex life. It's okay to hook up with women who're looking for the same thing. That's hardly preying on them. And I'm not sure you treat women any differently than you do other people. Don't you turn on the charm when you talk to a reporter? A teammate? The person bagging your groceries?"

Relief loosened his shoulders. "Yeah. I do."

"Yeah, so, it's your personality. You're a fun guy. People

like you. A predator makes promises, manipulates… misleads. That's not you."

At the window, Cassian parted the curtains to look down at the pool. Underwater lights made it look a brilliant blue. At this late hour, he'd expected it to be empty. Instead, he saw two people.

Playing guitar.

Awareness shot through his body.

Gigi and Grant sat close together, strumming and singing.

"You want to tell me what got you thinking about this?" Dean asked.

He hadn't told Dean about Gigi being on the tour, but he needed to talk before he stormed down there and fucked things up permanently.

Because they're not already fucked up permanently?

She thinks I get off on hurting women.

And then I went and kissed her.

"Gigi's here."

"What—in your room?"

"No. On the tour."

"Oh." One word held a world of meaning. "That's…"

"Yeah."

"You talk to her?"

"We've been stripping off pieces of each other's skin."

Dean went quiet for a moment. "Well, cut it out. You've got seven days with her."

"Six. I wasted today." Actually, he'd made things worse.

"Doesn't matter how many days you wasted. All that matters is what you do with what's left. Let me ask you this, what's the best outcome you can think of for this week with her?"

I want her back.

His world bottomed out. All the bravado, the whole fucking foundation he stood on, collapsed. Jesus, he felt the loss of her like a huge, gaping hole right in the center of his heart.

He ached for her.

Ached for the friendship that had made him full. Complete. Safe.

Raw and broken, Cassian pressed his forehead to the glass. Would he ever stop hating himself for what he'd done?

She'd obviously gone swimming, because her damp hair had begun to dry in its usual gentle waves. She was laughing, totally relaxed with this guy she'd just met.

He couldn't have her back, so he at least wanted her forgiveness. "I want to fix what I did."

"You never told me the specifics. Just that her dad asked you to back off so she could reach her potential or some shit."

"I hooked up with her best friend." *Ah, fuck.* Every time he thought about it, it sliced open the same wound.

Dean exhaled.

"In front of her."

"Damn." His friend stretched that single syllable into three.

"Right after she told me she wanted to be with me."

There wasn't a day that went by that the memory didn't pass through him like a shiver. Some days, more like a violent twist. "I can't stand it."

"Okay, well, it's not too late to fix it. It's never too late."

Cassian felt a flicker of hope. Because Dean was a problem-solver. He'd help him see the situation clearly. "I don't know where to start. Every time we talk to each other, she winds up gutting me like a fish."

"Have you apologized?"

Cassian let out a bitter laugh. "No."

"Start there."

"I might've made things worse." He paused. "I kissed her."

"Before you apologized?"

"Yeah." Her scent had washed over him, erasing the hotel hallway, driving him back into the heart of *them*. That lush, sexy mouth, the vulnerability in her eyes… Jesus, she'd slayed him.

Because there was so much more than anger going on inside her. There was hurt…but there was also want. *It's still there.*

"Not your best move."

"Probably not." Cassian watched her foot stir the water, creating gentle waves that fractured the underwater lights.

"Look, it's not that complicated. Talk to her. Let her say everything she's stored up all these years."

"That's what I want to do."

"Well, quit kissing her and let her have her say. Think you can do that?"

"Yeah." He couldn't take back what he'd done, but he had six days left with her. Six days to fix things. "Sometimes, I think I'm going to go out of my mind without her. She's the only one I want to be with, to talk to. It's always been like that, from the moment I met her. And not having her in my life…" He was saying all this shit out loud, not something he normally did. But with Dean…with Dean he could.

95

"I've got Vivi now, so I get it. And I'm telling you, it's not too late. Quit fuckin' around and fix it."

With both hands full, Cassian kicked her door.

"Hang on a second," she called from inside.

He was determined, for sure, but also anxious. Gigi was a tough cookie. She wouldn't be won over easily.

If at all.

A moment later the door swung open, and he was gifted with her bright smile.

Her expression dulled when she saw him. Plucking a to-go coffee from his hand, she said, "Sweet. Thanks. I'll see you at breakfast." She let the door fall closed.

His boot kicked out, keeping it ajar.

"Nice reflexes. Not for nothing, all that training you do." She spun around on him. "I'm running late, so excuse me if I can't chat."

He pushed into her room, which smelled of a fresh shower and her expensive scent. "Joey Canton loves muscle cars and root beer floats. I found both."

She stood in front of her bathroom mirror, about to transform her face into a Lollipop—which meant heavy eyeliner, rosy cheeks, and bright red lipstick. "I didn't see that on the information sheet."

He liked her natural. With her creamy complexion and amber eyes framed with dark lashes, she was beautiful. "I did some research. Made some calls. Found a souped-up Mustang to rent for the day."

Lips parted, she applied mascara to her eyelashes. "He might not be able to leave the hospital."

"I checked with Kevin. We're good to go. You in?"

"Of course."

"Great. See you downstairs in fifteen minutes."

"I can't be ready that fast."

"You can't turn yourself into a Lollipop that fast, but you can be ready by then." As his hand closed around the doorknob, he heard, "I have to be a Lollipop, you ass. That's the only reason I'm on this tour."

"The rental place is two towns over. Fifteen minutes is all we have if we're going to make it to the hospital on time."

"Fine." She screwed the wand into the tube and tossed it into her make-up bag. "I'll get ready in the car. Let me just get dressed, and I'll meet you in the lobby."

Eighteen minutes later, Cassian was signing autographs, when he caught movement out the corner of his eye. He glanced over to find Gigi strutting towards him, wearing jean cut-offs, a Led Zeppelin T-shirt, and flip flops.

That woman had no idea how her beauty rang a bell throughout his body. Everything about her…

She's mine. She just is. Whether he got to be with her again or not, he knew—he'd always known—there was no one else for him.

Finished signing the last scrap of paper, he said, "Have a good day, guys."

He intercepted Gigi on her way to the door. Getting right up in her face, he felt the powerful charge between them. "You're late."

Her lips parted. "I'm…" She bit back a grin, nudging his arm. "Shut up. Let's go."

He led the way to the car idling under the portico. "What's in the bag?"

"I told you. I have to turn into a Lollipop by the time we get to the hospital, so I brought everything with me."

They made their way around the valets and guests coming in and out of the hotel. He reached the taxi first, holding the door open for her. As she ducked into her seat, he felt this terrible twist of longing—to be close to her again. He couldn't stand the huge, ugly divide.

He got in beside her and reached for his seat belt.

"Davis Rent-a-Car?" The driver peered at him in the rearview mirror.

"That's right."

The man scowled. "You understand it's in another county, right?"

"I do."

"It's at least a forty-five-minute drive."

"I know. It's cool."

"Okay." The driver pulled out of the portico and turned up the radio.

Gigi stared at her phone, but he had the sense she was using it to avoid conversation.

Say something. Anything.

Break the tension. "You like being a Lollipop?" He said it quietly so the driver wouldn't hear.

"Yep. Love it." She looked out her window. "My dream come true."

He placed his hand on the empty seat between them. "I know you always pictured a career more like Pink, but…" He checked to see if the driver was listening, but the guy's fingers tapped to a beat on the radio. "No matter how you look at it, you've achieved massive success. I don't know how much of it's your music, but it's your voice, your personality." He leaned closer. "You're a superstar."

For the first time she looked at him with something other than hate. "None of it's my music. They write and choreograph everything."

He figured, if she was talking civilly to him, then the subject mattered to her. Troubled her. And he felt like he finally had an opening. "Do you like doing it?"

He got a whiff of more than her shampoo and clean cotton scent. He got the essence of her—something sweet with a hint of cinnamon spice. Her toned legs were smooth, long, and it took everything he had to keep his hands to himself. Because he just wanted that contact so badly—to bridge the massive, Arctic gap.

And if I hadn't been so nasty, she might be talking to me right now.

So, fix it.

"Even if it's not your music, are you at least having fun doing it?"

She didn't answer, and he could see she was deciding whether she wanted to talk to him or tell him to fuck off.

But he'd gained an opening, and he wasn't about to let it close. It was time to get real. With a fingernail, he scratched at the stitching on the seat's upholstery. "When I saw you last night, it shocked the hell out of me. I was happy, but then I saw your expression, and...I didn't react well."

Her body relaxed the slightest bit. "I haven't been very nice."

"Do you think we can start over? I've missed you, Gigi. All these years, all the people I've met..." He swallowed. "It's never been the way it was with you. Not even close. I ruined us—I own that—and it's up to me to fix it, but I need you to give me a chance to make things right. Will you let me do that?"

"I don't know that you can make anything *right*, but... there's no point in us being so awful to each other."

Relief slammed him. "I'm sorry I made fun of you for

being a Lollipop. If I could kick my own ass, I would. I didn't mean any of it. I'm actually impressed by what you've accomplished."

He saw the moment she decided to let down her guard. "There are moments when I've loved it, but…" She drew in a breath and finally looked at him, the anger, the indecision cleared from her expression. "At first, I was insulted. I was nineteen, in my sophomore year at USC. I went to a karaoke bar with a bunch of friends, and I couldn't pick a song because they were all so lame, so I just started singing one of my songs. Afterwards, this really smart-looking woman came up to me and said she loved my voice and stage presence. And it was that moment of, *Oh, my God, I'm being discovered right here and now at Billy's Bar and Grill.*"

"I'm not surprised you were discovered. You've got a powerful voice."

She tilted her head. *Meh.* "But then she explained what she was doing—putting this girl band together—and my immediate reaction was, *No way.* It just felt like such a slap in the face." She played with the frayed threads of her shorts. "I didn't contact her for a few weeks. I talked to my parents and my sisters, my professors…I just needed advice, you know? And pretty much everyone said I'd be crazy to pass up the opportunity. Whatever I thought of a manufactured girl band, it would provide a platform that would take me years to build on my own."

"That makes sense."

"But I think…and I'm not trying to make you feel bad right now, because if you want to have a real conversation, this is the truth." She waited for his response.

"I want real."

She nodded. "I think, after the night you kissed

Ashton, I stopped trusting my own instincts. So, I've found myself going along with other people's advice." She twined a thread around her finger so tightly her skin went white. "I think I lost a part of myself when I signed that contract, because I'm not me anymore. I sing the words they write, wear the costumes they give me, and do the routines they choreograph for me on stage."

She'd moved on as though the first sentence hadn't carried any weight, but it had crushed him.

And he was stuck, hearing it on repeat.

I stopped trusting my own instincts.

And, then, the worst thing of all, *I lost a part of myself.*

He'd done that, carved out a piece of this vibrant, smart, independent, sexy, wildly talented woman. He'd known he'd hurt her, of course—he would never forget her expression that night—but he hadn't known the extent of the damage he'd caused.

Gutted, he couldn't say a word. He'd had this cocky notion that he could help her heal, but that was before he'd learned he'd fractured her sense of self.

"But..." Her whole demeanor changed, her vulnerability gone. "The good news is, once we turn in this last album, the world's my oyster."

She'd mistaken his silence for disinterest. And that was unacceptable. He didn't know how to heal her, but he had to start somewhere. "I'm sorry."

"What? No, I have a lot of options. And I have enough money that I can take some time to figure out—"

"For hurting you."

"Oh." Her legs shifted, and she glanced down at her finger. She must've noticed she'd cut off the circulation, because she unwound the thread.

"I should've told you long before now." He touched her chin, and she jerked. "But I never slept with Ashton."

She got riled up again, whispering harshly, "Fuck you, Cassian." She shot a look to the driver, but he was still listening to the music. "Don't you dare lie to me. I saw you go up the stairs with her."

"You know what I did when I got to the top of the stairs? I turned around and watched you leave the party. Then, I told Ashton I had to go home. Didn't she tell you?"

"She said she was sorry, that she was drunk, she didn't mean it… but I saw her. She *meant* it. And there's no doubt in my mind she'd have slept with you if you'd wanted."

"I didn't sleep with her. I didn't want to. I swear."

She held his gaze, her expression fraught with uncertainty. "What difference does it make? Whether you had sex with her or not, you wanted to hurt me…and you did."

The pain in her voice tore him to shreds. "There isn't a day that goes by that I don't hate myself for doing it."

"*Why,* Cassian? Why did you do it?"

He'd played out this conversation countless times in his head. Over the years, he'd wanted to write a letter, an email, a text, but he'd never followed through. There wasn't a damn thing he could say to make it better.

But she asked, and so he'd answer. "I did it to push you away."

"Ha. Well, you always were an over-achiever."

It hadn't taken long to leave the city limits. Cornfields surrounded them on either side of the two-lane road. He had one shot. He had to get it right. "You remember that afternoon your dad caught us in the treehouse?"

"I knew it." Her hand slapped the seat between them. "What did he say to you?"

"He came over to my uncle's that night. I was shitting my pants, because your dad...I mean, he'd given me so much, and I thought he was done with me."

"Done with you for what? For being my friend? We hadn't done anything. We were just friends." She let out a huff. "What did he say?"

"That he'd do whatever it took to get me recruited, drafted, the whole nine yards."

"If you stayed away from me." She tipped her head back. "I knew it. You changed after that. I knew he'd said something. Why didn't you tell me?"

"Hang on. Let me tell you the whole story. He said you and I were on different paths, that lots of people dreamed of being football players or rock stars or whatever, but that you and I had the raw talent to back it up. He said we could realize our dreams—as long as we didn't hold each other back. He asked me to give you a chance to fulfill your potential. And if I couldn't make that promise, he'd have to stop working with me."

"You should've told me. I would've talked to him. My parents—"

"He was right. That night, at the party, you said you'd go to Michigan."

"Yes, because it's a good program. We could have been together. I mean, obviously, you wanted to be free to have your fun. I'm sure I scared you...but you could've just told me the truth."

"You're damn right you scared me. Because that was the first time I realized you felt the same way about me. And that drove it home, what your dad was saying. The way we felt about each other...we would've made the wrong decisions. You needed to go to Julliard or Berklee. And, even though I wanted to be selfish and have you come with me, I couldn't let you do that."

"You wanted me to come with you? I figured you wanted to be free to hook up with every girl on campus."

"You couldn't be further from the truth." *You've got one shot here. Take it.* "I…honestly, I didn't think I'd survive without you. After…"

"After you slept with my best friend?"

He gave her a look that said, *Come on.* "I didn't sleep with her. But I was going to say, after I pushed you away, I thought about blowing off Michigan and just going wherever you went. And I'd have done it, too, but…what would that have accomplished? What, I'd follow you around the world as you wrote and played your music? You'd lose all respect for me. And I just didn't see a solution that worked."

"Well, kissing Ashton wasn't it."

"I know that. It wasn't planned." He cracked the window, just for some fresh air, because he was burning up. "I don't think you know how hard it was for me not to touch you. Every time we were together…it killed me. And then to finally kiss you…it messed me up."

"You've obviously recovered."

"I've never recovered."

"Really? Because it looks like you're having the time of your life."

"Well, I'm not." *Keep going.* "But you should also know that Amie's not my girlfriend."

"Oh, my God." She shook her head, looking disgusted. "You're obviously together. I saw you two all cozy on the plane. Not to mention the picture of you two that went viral."

"It hasn't gone live yet, but…wait, I've got the security footage right here." He swiped the screen of his phone and opened his email. When he found Dean's video, he handed it over.

Gigi sat quietly, watching the whole thing. It was only a few minutes—Amie doing a strip tease, him leaping onto the diving board, and then taking the towel from Dean. The video ended after Cassian handed her the shirt.

She handed the phone back. "So, no threesome?"

"No threesome."

"Because a Cassian and Dean sandwich…" She tried for humor, and he knew it meant she was relieved. Everything she'd believed had turned out to be untrue. "I'm just saying."

"There's nothing between me and Amie. She runs my football camp, that's it."

She didn't look convinced. "She touches you like you're her boyfriend."

"That's Amie. It's her personality. But if you pay attention, you'll see I'm not touching *her*." He wanted to spell it out. "I've never slept with her."

"Okay."

"Okay, you forgive me? Or okay, you don't give a shit?"

"Honestly? I don't know what I feel. Everything you said just now…you shook my world and…and now I have to see where all the pieces land."

Chapter Seven

Times like these, Gigi loved Lollipop songs. They were upbeat and positive, and no matter how silly the lyrics might be, every single person in this wing of the hospital was smiling, bopping their heads, and having a good time.

She scanned the faces of the kids, and a rush of happiness hit her so hard she stumbled over the next chords. Laughing, she got her focus back and continued on.

But right then, Cassian came around the corner, his hair tousled from the convertible Mustang. Those broad shoulders and bulging biceps, along with that easy grin… no wonder women stuffed their numbers into his pockets everywhere he went.

He looked happy, confident, like he was on top of the world.

She finished the song. "Well, that's it for me." The room burst into applause. A couple people whistled. "Thanks so much. I had a blast with you guys."

A young girl came rushing over, thrusting a T-shirt at her. "Can I please have your autograph?"

"You sure can. What's your name?"

"Marissa. I'm named after my gramma. I have a brother. He was born so I could be alive."

The world screeched to a stop. Gigi looked at this little girl who couldn't be more than ten, with her freckles and gangly arms and legs, just bursting with positive energy.

Emotion, rose, crested, and crashed over her. "Well, he's a very lucky boy."

"Why's *he* lucky?"

"Because he gets such a brave and strong older sister." She signed the shirt and handed it back. "Can I have a hug, Marissa?"

The girl threw herself into Gigi's arms. Cupping the back of her head, she said, "Thank you for making my day, Marissa."

She should be heading down to the van, but she couldn't resist watching Cassian hold court with his fans. As always, he was totally in the moment with them, looking each person in the eye, talking to them like they were old friends. He immersed himself in the experience.

A boy, who had to be around thirteen or fourteen, stood in front of him, talking a mile a minute. "I'm gonna play football, too. I'm trying out for the team when school starts, and I get to tell everyone I got to meet you. I'm going home tomorrow. I'm in remission."

"Proud of you, man." Cassian did some kind of fist bump handshake thing with him.

Another boy stepped forward, wearing Cassian's jersey. He was a little more reserved. "I never miss your games."

Cassian crouched to get eye-level with him. "Yeah? That's cool. Let me know your name, so I can shout out to you during the season."

"You'd do that?" The kid looked like he couldn't believe it.

"You bet."

"That would be the coolest thing ever. Thank you. It's Paul. Paul Thomas."

Out of nowhere, Cassian's gaze shot over to her. Cymbals crashed, reverberating throughout her body. Heat flooded her. Their conversation in the long car ride, revealing that he'd had real feelings for her, that Amie wasn't his girlfriend—it had changed things.

For so long, she'd held onto anger. Her victimhood.

And today he'd whisked it out from under her. All this time she'd thought he hadn't felt the same way. It meant everything to her that he had.

If only he'd told her back then what he'd explained today…

I'd have gone to Michigan.

And my life would've turned out so differently.

Everything must've played out across her features, because Cassian got up, all his energy focused on her. *It's still there.* They'd always been so connected—he could read her better than anybody.

Every cell in her body blossomed, opened…sang for him. She missed him, wanted him, *craved* him…

But her mind screamed, *Run.* She might understand things better, but that didn't mean she could trust him.

And, so, heart pounding, palms clammy, she turned and walked away.

As Gigi started to wash the green facial mask off her face with a warm washcloth, someone knocked on her door.

Seriously? She was not going to have any me-time on

this trip. "Coming." Snatching a towel off the rack, she dried her hands and peered through the peephole.

Expecting either Grant—maybe he wanted to jam—or Kevin—to talk about tomorrow's schedule—her heart flipped over at the sight of Cassian.

Without thinking, she opened the door. When his smile turned to surprise, she remembered the green mask. "Hey. What's up?"

Normally, he had this air about him, like he never broke stride because he knew doors opened automatically for him. But standing in the doorway, his shoulders tight with tension, that stride had faltered. "There's no group dinner tonight, so I thought we could go have some fun."

Part of her was like *hell, yes*. But another, louder voice, urged her to keep her distance. "Thanks, but I'm having a spa night."

"I see that." He shifted his weight onto the other foot. "Have you eaten dinner?"

"No. I thought I'd just order in."

"Yeah, that's probably a good idea. There's a kids' soccer team staying here, and you'd scare the crap out of them if you came down to the restaurant looking like that. So, sure, you stay in." He hitched a thumb over his shoulder. "I'm going to head out, then, to my homemade dinner. Mrs. Carson's got some brisket, mashed potatoes, and apple cobbler for me. I asked her to make it for two, but…" He patted his stomach. "I had a light lunch."

"Mrs. Carson? Is that a teammate's mom?"

"Nah. I looked up interesting things to do in this part of Kansas. Found some good stuff."

Crossing her arms over her stomach, she leaned against the door jam. "You know, you can just say it. You made plans for me."

"That's one approach."

"The direct one. Out of curiosity, what exactly do you think's going to happen if I go out with you?"

His unease flamed brighter. "I'm serious about fixing us. I want us to talk. I want you to talk to me."

She wanted that very much. "Then, it better not be in a restaurant or any other public place. Because, let me tell you, it could get loud."

"You say that as if I don't know you."

She was really curious now, but she wasn't about to let him know that. "You can't handle any more bad press, so another woman yelling at you…especially a Lollipop…?"

"It's in a field."

"You're feeding me dinner in a field?"

"Yes, a large one. And I'm going to make you earn it."

"Earn my dinner?" Oh, dammit all to hell, he was being charming and fun.

"That's right. Everything's better when it's earned."

"And what do I have to do to earn it?"

"You have to find your way through the second largest maze in the world."

Like she could say no to that. "And what if I can't find my way out?"

He lifted his hand, revealing a paper bag. "I've brought snacks." He opened the bag and tilted it toward her.

"Twizzlers? That's my dinner if I don't make it out of the maze?"

He pulled out a bag of peanut M&Ms. "Protein." He pulled out a box of fruit roll-ups. "I've covered the food groups, so if you fail, you won't die in the maze. Because that would be embarrassing. To both of us."

Charming, fun, and irresistible. *I'm in.* "Give me ten minutes."

. . .

As they drove along a country road, Gigi caught glimpses of farmers on tractors, cows swishing tails in fields of green grass, and endless rows of waist-high cornstalks. "How far is this place?" They'd been in the rental car for nearly forty minutes.

"It's the second largest maze in the *world*." Cassian cut her a look. "It takes some serious acreage to pull that off."

A big part of her wanted this—to feel like they were seventeen again. But another part didn't like it. He acted like telling her the truth had lasered away the pain he'd caused. Like now they had a clean slate.

She took another bite of her frosted Strawberry PopTart.

"You're not going to have room for dinner."

"The odds of me making it through a maze are low. The horse flies alone will drive me back to the parking lot. Besides, I didn't eat lunch."

"Yeah, I don't think we should let Kevin handle catering from now on. That meat…"

"Oh, is that what we're calling it?"

"It looked like a crusty brown pot holder."

She smiled. "That's exactly what it looked like. I hope dinner in a field is better."

"Trust me."

Two simple words hit her bloodstream like ice. "Yeah, don't hold your breath."

"No, I didn't mean…" Color spilled into his cheeks, and his lips sealed shut. A moment later, his hands flexed on the wheel. He looked stubbornly determined. "I'm well aware that I have a lot of work to do to earn your trust. I *will* do it."

What's the point? She wanted to ask. But she bit back the snarky come-back, because it meant the world that he cared enough to do it. She wiped her hands on a napkin. "This is weird. You and me in a car together." *Getting along.*

"It's nice."

"I'm gonna stick with weird. I never thought I'd talk to you again."

He went quiet for a moment, and she didn't know if she'd made him uncomfortable. Like, here he was trying to fix things, and she just kept smacking him down.

But then he said, "I've missed you every day." He kept his eyes on the road. "Every single day."

Oh, God. His tone was drenched in despair. She wanted to reach out, touch those fingers that clenched the wheel so tightly his knuckles had gone white.

But she wasn't going to comfort him. "Well." The car ate up endless miles of asphalt. Cornfields gave way to... sunflowers? Acres and acres of them loomed high on either side of the road. "I don't know what to do with that. I really don't. You say these things, but for nine years you've acted like you forgot all about me."

"You think I could forget you? You were everything to me."

"I honestly can't believe I'm hearing this. I never in a million years could have imagined driving down a country road with you in Kansas, hearing you tell me the things I wanted to hear when I was seventeen." She looked down at her hands. "I wish you'd told me back then. Everything would've been so different."

"I couldn't. I couldn't do that to you or your dad. But I wish like hell I'd handled it differently." He cut her a look. "I need you to hear me, Gigi. More than any other regret in my life, I wish I'd handled that moment differently."

I do, too. "I hear you." She said it softly, her voice thin. Because she heard his words, but they weren't sinking in. It was like a summer rain on hard-packed, dry earth.

That's me. Hard. Unforgiving.

Up ahead, a billboard advertised the world's biggest sunflower maze. Cassian flicked the turn signal and slowed, veering onto a smaller road.

"It's just…this is hard for me. When we're hurting each other, it fuels the anger, but when you're nice and telling me you missed me? It's really confusing."

Another, smaller billboard at the side of the road read, *World's Second Largest Maze Up Ahead!*

A mile later, Cassian turned into the empty parking lot of a farm stand. Tires crunched over gravel, until he came to a stop. He killed the engine but made no move to get out of the car. The engine ticked, and the air smelled both dusty and rich with earth.

"I'm sorry for the way I handled things. I hate myself for hurting you." He said it with a painful sincerity. "I never wanted to kiss anyone but you. I was…messed up. I wanted to be with you more than I wanted to play ball, but I knew your dad was right. That whether you followed me, or I followed you, whichever way it went down, you might never have realized your potential. And…I loved you too much to do that to you." He glanced across the street to a beautiful white farmhouse. "And I…went a little crazy."

He *loved* me. Tears blurred her vision, and she clasped her hands together so tightly her rings pinched her skin. "I know it sounds stupid, but I'm actually pissed at you for telling me this. I mean, you *loved* me?" She shifted toward him. "Why didn't you tell me back then? Do you know the hell I've been through? *God*." She blinked back the tears. "I wish I could be happy that you're finally telling me the things I've always wanted you to say. But I can't. I just…Hearing the words doesn't erase the experience, you know? And I just can't understand the choice you made."

"Which is exactly why I never tried to explain it to you. Because there's no excuse for what I did. There are no magic words to erase the pain I caused."

The door opened, and a woman stepped out onto her porch. She waved, coming down the stairs and hurrying toward them.

"We should go." She got out first, frustrated with herself. How long had she waited to have this conversation with him? And, now, she'd finally had it, but it hadn't cured her. It hadn't set her free.

"I can't believe this." The woman dashed across the street. "Cassian Ellis and Gigi Cavanagh on my farm. Oh, my goodness!"

The screen door popped open, and a dog flew out of the house. Barking like mad, his nails scrabbling on asphalt, he raced to catch up with his owner. Cassian dropped to a crouch, and the dog slammed into him.

"Beckett," a man hollered.

The dog pulled back as if someone had yanked his leash. He looked chastised and embarrassed.

"Ah, it's okay, sweetie." Gigi loved him up, while Cassian greeted the couple.

"We thought someone was pulling a prank," the wife said. "Bob's your biggest fan, so we thought one of his brothers was playing a joke."

"I'm grateful you took my last-minute request."

Cassian gestured to her. "I'd like you to meet Gigi Cavanaugh."

Gigi stood up, wiping her hands on her jeans. "Hello. It's nice to meet you."

"Oh, my gosh, my daughter's away at college right now, but she's going to die when she finds out you're right here on our property."

"Uh, honey?" the husband said. "He asked for our discretion."

"He did?" She turned to Cassian. "You did?"

"I'd appreciate it very much."

"Well, darnit. I was hoping to post it on social media and blow her mind."

The man shook his head. "*She's* the biggest prankster of them all." He gave his wife an affectionate grin.

Gigi was such a sap for this kind of love---the same kind her parents had.

Will I ever have it? She glanced at Cassian. How naïve had she been to think she'd found the love of her life at fourteen?

"All right, well, let's get you started," the wife said. "We've got to get back inside and finish dinner."

"Now, which one of you's the chef?" Gigi asked.

The woman slipped her arm through her husband's. "We're a team. You should see us in the kitchen."

"Team work," Cassian said. "I like that."

Gigi took in the endless sea of sunflowers, the heads so heavy with seeds they nodded in the faint breeze. "I've never seen anything like this."

"It brings us a lot of joy," the wife said. "Now, go on and have some fun."

As they headed back to their home, Mr. Carson called

out, "If you're not back in an hour, we're coming to get you."

"So little faith," Cassian said over his shoulder, as they headed into the maze.

The brilliant blue sky, the thick, green stalks…it was magnificent. "Oh, my God, look at all these butterflies." They fluttered all around them, the bright orange and black standing out against the broad, almost heart-shaped leaves of the sunflowers. "Cassian, this is amazing."

"I'm glad you like it," he said, quietly.

Surrounded by the towering flowers, they made their way along a hay-strewn path. The lowering sun cast long shadows, and the air smelled rich with earth. She probably shouldn't have been so happy to be here with him, but well…there it was. "I can't believe you arranged all this."

"I wasn't sure you'd come."

She eyed him sharply, surprised that, underneath all that cocky confidence, pulsed fear and worry. She'd been wrong. He hadn't assumed he could apologize and be done with the past.

His vulnerability softened her.

And that made her bristle. "On your mark…get set… go." She shot ahead of him. "See you on the other side."

"Hey." He laughed. "It's a *maze*, not an obstacle course."

She walked backwards. "Scared of a little competition, QB?"

"Have you *seen* me under pressure? But just remember…" Excitement glittered in his eyes. "I don't lose."

"Oh, sometimes you do. Like with the Tigers last season?" She cringed.

He laughed. "My tears dried up right about the time I

found out we were going to the Super Bowl. Again. And I know I didn't lose either of *those* games."

"You got pretty close last year."

"Right, but I came back from behind with eleven seconds on the clock." His long legs stalked her. Beneath his smile lay a hunger and determination that set her heart pounding. "Know why I win?"

"Well, it makes it easier to get laid, that's for sure." Exhilarated, she ducked around the next corner, aware of his footfalls not far behind.

"In the interest of full disclosure," he called. "I looked at a map of the maze this morning. It's online. Just in case you actually think you can beat me."

"How incredibly anal of you." Her skin flashed warm and cool as she stepped from one patch of sunlight to another band of shadow. "Why would you look at a map?"

"Because I wanted things to go well." From glimpses of his white T-shirt, she could tell he was right on the other side of a row of flowers.

That hard-packed earth? His unrelenting patter of sweet rain was beginning to soften it. And that scared the hell out of her.

She hurried down a path, dashing down the fork on the left.

His pace quickened, too. "It'd be a bust if we couldn't find our way out, and you got all sweaty and pissed off at me."

"I've been pissed at you for nine years. Why do you suddenly care?"

He went quiet, but she could hear the rustling of the leaves. "I never stopped caring."

Was he stepping through the stalks? She hurried along the path. *Go go.* "You're full of shit. If you missed me as much as you say you did, you wouldn't have hooked up with ten thousand women. Every picture of you, every interview, you looked happy. Like you were on top of the world. And now you want me to believe your woe-is-me story?" Tough words meant to cover the truth. Because she was beginning to believe him.

She cut down another path. This time she found herself in a clearing. A fountain burbled in the center, paths like flower petals radiating out in various directions. She could lose him now, for sure.

"What I want is your forgiveness. I didn't expect to see you on this tour, I don't have some plan, and frankly I don't know if I deserve it, but that's what I want. And the only way I know how to do it is to tell you my experience of us."

My experience of us. Dammit. Her soul knelt on the ground, head tilted back, and let the rain wash away the anger, the bitterness, the hurt.

She'd wanted this window into his thoughts for so long.

But softening led to trusting...and that...that she couldn't do. "Well, I appreciate it. Thank you." She'd had enough. "You're forgiven."

Okay, which path? Gazing up at the darkening sky, she tried to get her bearings. How could she find her way out if she didn't know where the farmhouse was?

"Don't humor me. You've lived with one perspective for a long time. Ask me questions, yell at me. Don't sweep it away. We have a chance to get it all out. Take it."

"So, you want more than forgiveness?"

He went quiet. And then, "I want my friend back."

God. The desolation in his voice. It hit the exact note strumming through her body. Because she was so lonely without him. Every minute of every day that tuned played in the background.

She chose a path, but her feet didn't take her down it. She wanted answers. "You could've had me back. If you'd told me what my dad said, if you'd talked to me freshman year, when we were away from my parents. You could've written a letter, an email….at any point since the night of that party, you could've reached out to me."

"I've thought about it. Pretty much every day in college, I drafted a letter to you in my head. But, whether you want to believe me or not, I knew your dad was right. I thought if I pursued you, I'd hold you back. I wanted…*shit.* So many times…I wanted to come and get you. To be with you. But I had your dad's voice in my head. Not only was he right but going after you would have been the worst kind of betrayal to the man who gave up so much for me."

The sudden chill in the air told her the sun had dipped below the horizon. She rubbed her arms.

"You still there?" he asked

"Yes. I'm…processing."

He went quiet, and she loved that about him, the way he respected her. Gave her the time and space she needed. Only…she didn't really want space. She wanted to see him, watch his reactions. "I guess I wish you'd wanted me more than you wanted to be loyal to my dad." She lifted up to touch the head of the flower, the dark center sticky with nectar. "I wanted you to want me more than anything."

"The first time I saw you, I was fourteen." It sounded like he was right on the other side of the row of flowers.

She couldn't see him, but her mind did. And, when she closed her eyes, she was right there in the tree house with him, lying by his side. God, she could almost smell the musty tarp, feel the pine planks under her back.

She felt the ghost of their initials carved into the wood on the tip of her finger.

"It was my third day of high school. My parents hadn't even been gone a month, and I was sharing a bedroom with a cousin I might've met once or twice before. I hated the world, but I swear when I saw you in the hallway, it felt like…you know when you're sleeping and you dream you're falling, and you get this zing through your whole body? It wakes you all the way up? That's what it felt like."

She knew exactly the moment he meant. The high school in Calamity Falls was small, so new kids got a lot of attention. Everyone talked about the city boy, tall, lean, cute, with shaggy hair and a chip on his shoulder. Cassian was the kid who strolled into class after the bell rang, never looked anyone in the eye, and acted like he was too good for their cowboy town.

But his attitude had disappeared the moment he'd laid eyes on her.

You bet I remember it. She recited the words to him. "'When I saw you I fell in love, and you smiled because you knew.'" A soft breeze ruffled her hair, making her skin break out in goosebumps.

"You remember that?" His tone held urgency.

He'd written that Arrigo Boito quote on the walls of their tree house. She'd read it so many times it was like he'd carved it on her soul.

When I saw you I fell in love, and you smiled because you knew.

120

It pissed her off that he thought she could forget something so monumental. "I remember everything, you idiot. Why do you think I'm such a mess? *When I saw you I fell in love?* You wrote that on the wall of our private place without any explanation—ever—and then you kissed my best friend and never talked to me again. Who does that? That's the whole reason I stopped trusting my instincts." She hadn't meant to shout, but dammit, he made her so angry.

Fuck it.

Fuck him.

Without even thinking, she chose a path and race-walked away. He couldn't possibly find her—not with eleven other options to choose from.

"Would you quit running and let me finish the story?"

She swore the breeze carried his scent to her, and it made her slow down.

"Anyhow, that first time I saw you, it rocked my world. But I was in a shitty place, and you were beautiful and popular and talented, so I didn't talk to you." His voice was right there, keeping up with her.

She stopped. She didn't want to miss a single word.

"But then your dad—of all people—showed up in detention and offered to teach me how to play ball. You want to hear something I've never told anybody before?"

"Yes."

"I didn't give two shits about football. The jocks at our school were entitled assholes. I didn't want anything to do with them. But I wanted to be around you, so I said yes."

"I never knew that."

"There's something else I never told you. Everyone

thinks it was your dad that turned my life around, but it wasn't. It was you. I only stopped getting into trouble, because I knew you wouldn't want anything to do with a fuck-up. The Cavanaugh girls were going somewhere, and I wanted to go with you. So, I might've had a natural talent for football, but I only took his offer so I could be with *you*."

Leaves rustled, and his running shoe emerged from between the stems and landed on the path. She took off before he came all the way through. Mostly because she felt the pull in her very core, that magnetic draw that both angered and excited her.

"I know I hurt you, but you need to know that I'd loved you from the moment I saw you, and that the worst day of my life was when your dad told me I couldn't have you."

Tears burned, and a knot formed in her throat. "Then you should've fought for me."

He rounded the bend, and he was right there. Walking toward her. "You think I didn't want to tell your dad to fuck off? You bet your ass I did, but how could I do that? I fucking *loved* you. I couldn't be the reason you didn't become the next Pink. Did I handle it well? Of course not, but I was a seventeen-year-old kid, Gigi. And I messed up. Messed up in a way I can't take back." He caught up to her, so fierce, so intense, so real.

The boy she'd loved had nothing on the man standing in front of her.

Still, she kept him at arm's length. "I never had a say in any of it. You took my choice—my power—away. I hate that you made the decision for me."

"You're right about that, and I'm sorry. All I can tell you is your dad sacrificed a lot for me. There wasn't a chance I could betray his trust when I knew how much he loved you, how sure he was that he was doing the right thing." He took one more step, closing the distance between them. "Losing you destroyed me. I haven't felt whole since that night." He scraped his hands through his hair. "I knew it when I was fourteen, and I know it today. Because nothing has ever felt as right as being with you."

And there it was again. He was singing the same tune playing in her heart. Emotion flooded her, and this time she didn't have the strength to hold it back. The distance no longer bearable, she threw herself at him.

He caught her, of course he did, and then he planted his mouth over hers.

The kiss was savage. That horrible clash of emotions she lived with every day of her life ignited into a flash fire of passion, and Cassian...

He was taking what he could get, while he could get it.

His kiss was possessive, hungry. *Desperate.* And, if his words weren't clear enough, his kiss told her exactly how he felt.

He licked into her mouth and coaxed her tongue into a dance of pure pleasure. Her senses lit up, making her feel everything acutely—the clutch of his fingers, the rasp of his beard on her chin. She drowned in his scent—the clean clothes and just-showered skin, and the essential *him* that emanated from his core.

She gorged on the sensuous sweep of his tongue, reveled in the big hands that clutched her, his grip so tight it was like he feared she'd slip away.

His hands slid down to her ass and gave a lusty squeeze. Everything about him was taut, ravenous, *wild.*

Her senses swept away, she let go completely. Sank into the kind of kiss that branded itself on a woman's soul.

I'm kissing Cassian. The boy I loved so fiercely. Clutching fistfuls of his hair, she ground against his rock-hard erection, restless for relief from all the building tension.

Shoving up her T-shirt, he pushed her breasts together, pressing a trail of kisses across the upper swells. She gripped the back of his head—*don't stop*—and he yanked the cups down, baring her breasts to the cool air. When his hot mouth covered her nipple, she arched her back and cried out.

That tongue—*God*—it swirled around the sensitive bead, taking deep, hungry pulls.

"Cassian." Her fingernails scraped across his scalp, that hair so thick and silky.

He stroked down her stomach, fingers popping the button of her shorts. Reaching into her panties, he caressed her slick heat. "Jesus Christ. I've wanted to touch you like this for half my life. You're so fucking wet for me."

Her hips rocked, begging for more. And he gave it to her. Two fingers slid inside her, his thumb circling her clit. Desire spiked, making her body tremble and her knees go weak.

Sensation inundated her—his hot mouth sucking, licking, pulling, his fingers stroking her to a state of bliss. His other hand clutched the small of her back, holding her in place.

But she couldn't be still. She arched into him, wanting more, closer, deeper. Her body went hot, electric, and she got up on her toes as the fuse he'd lit burst into flames.

"*Oh, my God.*" She tumulted through a galaxy of dazzling stars, and she never ever wanted this feeling to end. *So good.*

Slowly, she came back down to earth, to the smell of

rich earth, the breeze on her damp thighs, and the man gazing down at her in awe.

Her skin cooled. A fly dive-bombed her. The sunflower stalks rustled.

Reality hit. "Oh, boy." Righting her bra and lowering her T-shirt, she drew in a shaky breath. "I can't believe we did that."

He watched her, as though balancing a razor-thin line between hope and the bottom dropping out of his world.

Yeah, well, brace yourself, QB. "That..." She wagged a finger between them. "Was crazy." She wasn't embarrassed, exactly. More like...stunned, shaky, happy...*scared*.

Yeah, mostly just really scared that she'd opened herself up to him so completely. "I...um..." She had no words.

He reached for her. "Gigi—"

"No." She didn't want to hear any more of his magic words. Turning away, she buttoned her shorts. "Let's just go eat dinner, okay?"

Chapter Eight

Feet pounding on rubber, sweat dripping into his eyes, Cassian couldn't get the sensations out of his mind.

The hot tangle of their tongues, the grip she'd had on his hair—yanking it so hard the roots stung. The urgent rocking of her hips...and those sounds. Jesus Christ, whimpers had turned to gasps...until she'd cried out with a release that transformed her features into pure rapture.

The toe of his running shoe caught on the mat, jarring him. *Fuck it.* He had to get off the treadmill before he injured himself. He hit the red Stop button and stepped off.

An hour in the gym, and his body still vibrated with the thrill of kissing her.

Everything he'd ever believed about them had sprung to life the moment they'd touched. It was like plugging into a life force, their energies colliding with enough impact to birth a star.

Except...now what? For him, they'd finally blasted through the barrier keeping them apart.

They'd burned that motherfucker down.

But, for her…After they'd gotten back to the hotel, she'd gone to her room. When he'd tried to follow, to make sure they were okay, she'd said a crisp, "'Night."

Yeah, that's because she doesn't trust me. He'd thought he could tell her the truth, let her rip into him, get it all out and…then what? They'd be back to where they'd started?

He didn't want to go back. All the torment of wanting someone he couldn't have?

No, he *wanted* her.

Jesus fuck, did he want her. But he'd need a lot more than the four days left on this tour to get there.

Dammit. He couldn't miss his own football camp, and two weeks after the final session he headed to training camp for his sixth season with the Mavericks.

Grabbing a towel off the stack, he swiped his face.

What could he do? How did he fix the situation?

Fix yourself.

The first rays of hope slanted across his heart, warming him. He *did* have time. He had all the time in the world. First—*the easy stuff*—no more partying, flirting, and fucking around with women who meant nothing to him. That way he'd stay out of the tabloids.

That would build her trust right there. It would take time, but it'd be worth it.

And, then, he'd stay in touch with her. Text messages, emails. Those would lead to phone calls. He'd send her gifts from the road. Buckeyes from Cleveland, a Mardi Gras mask from New Orleans…yeah, he liked this idea a lot.

He tossed his sweaty towel in the laundry basket. Filling a cup with water, he downed it. He felt good, confident. He had a plan. It just…

It had to work. He needed her in his life. He glanced at himself in the mirror, acknowledging the truth he fought like hell to avoid.

I'm lonely.

Didn't matter how many people crowded into his apartment or filled the yachts he rented…the only person that made him feel happy, safe, settled…the only one who felt like *home*…was Gigi.

Pushing out of the gym, he headed down the long hallway toward the lobby. Soft splashing sounds grabbed his attention, and he peered through the long, rectangular window into the pool area.

Gigi. Just the sight of her hit like a shock to his heart.

Nice timing, since his plan to earn her trust started *right the fuck now*.

Someone dove into the pool, a sleek body cruising toward her like a missile under the water. A dark head of hair emerged right in front of her, and she laughed.

Grant Banner. What the hell was going on between them?

He stood there like a kid hiding on the staircase as his parents kissed in the living room. He should leave her alone. But, dammit, this was his only chance to spend real time with her.

Fuck it. He wasn't going to stand there and watch her relationship with Grant grow deeper. He flung the door open and headed in.

"Hey, man." Grant checked him out. "It's late for a work-out."

"Got to get it in at some point."

"Right." The man nodded, pleasant as could be. "Your season starts soon."

"Yep. Training starts the end of July." Neither looked

at him like he was intruding on a date, so he kicked off his running shoes, pulled his T-shirt over his head, and dove into the deep end. The water cooled his hot skin. When he popped up, he found the two of them standing by the rack of towels, drying off.

Now, he felt like shit for acting like a possessive caveman. "Don't leave on my account. I'm heading back to my room."

"Gotta head upstairs anyhow. Have to check in at home." Grant nodded to both of them, slung the damp towel around his neck, and walked out the door.

Gigi lingered, and he propped his arms on the edge of the pool, watching her. "Did you know him before the tour?"

"Yes, because all musicians know each other."

"Yeah? Ball players have a secret society, too."

She grinned. "No, we just met. He heard me working on a song, brought out his guitar and…turned it into a duet. It was pretty cool, actually."

"You're into country?"

"I didn't think I was, but Grant thinks I have the perfect voice for it."

Grant thinks…? "Yeah, but do you like country music?"

"I didn't used to, but he sent me a Playlist, and I couldn't believe how good some of the songs are. Really smart, emotional lyrics and powerful voices."

"Sounds like you."

"Maybe." She threw on her black cover-up. "All I know is it's really nice to work with someone talented. The girls in my band…well. Anyhow, it's late." She gestured to the door. "I'm going to go."

"The girls in your band what?"

"Nothing. We're just all very different. In a good way. That's what makes our music so strong." She leaned to the side, patting her hair with a towel.

"There's no paparazzi recording this conversation."

"With you around, you never know."

"You got me there." Hands braced on the rim of the pool, he hoisted himself out. Water coursing down his body, he came right up to her. "You should know, this ground we've gained the last few days? I'm building a house on it. A mansion. A fucking palace."

Excitement flared in her eyes.

He got so close he could smell the chlorine in her hair. Tipping her chin, he said, "Don't repeat this, but my coach said he'd trade me if I got caught in another compromising situation, but I'm telling you right now that's *nothing* compared to the incentive you gave me earlier tonight. Without you in my life, nothing outside of football matters to me. With even just the hope of having you back? You can bet your ass I'll do everything in my power to earn your trust. I'm going to show you just how important you are to me."

She swallowed, and her eyes gave away everything. How badly she wanted to believe him, but how far she was from being there. With a tentative nod, she said, "Okay. Well, goodnight." But she didn't go. "I know I already said it but thank you for tonight. It was a-maze-ing. Ha ha. See what I did there?"

He grinned. "Clever. And you're welcome."

"See you in the morning." Shoving her feet into her sparkly flip flops, she reached for the door.

He didn't want her to go. Wanted more of her. Always, relentlessly, more. "Truth or dare."

"*What?*" And then she smirked. "Okay, it's late, and

I'm not playing games with you." She picked up her phone and key card from a small table, before flashing a smile. "Dare."

Yes. "I dare you to get on the diving board, squawk like a chicken, and then cannonball into the pool."

She rolled her eyes. "That's ridiculous. I would never do that."

And then she surprised the hell out of him by breaking out in a grin. It was like she'd thrown off all the doubt and wariness, and standing before him was his Gigi. It was exhilarating.

She tossed her phone and keycard back onto the table, kicked off her shoes, lifted the dress, and sent it flying. She ran for the diving board and leapt onto it. Bouncing in place, she let out one loud, "Buck," before jumping high, drawing up her legs, and crashing into the water. When she broke the surface, she had a big smile on her face. "I can't believe I did that."

"I can't, either. You looked ridiculous."

She spit a mouthful of water at him, even though he stood at the side of the pool. "Truth or dare? And, by that, I mean brace yourself for your dare."

He cupped his hand, flicking it, in a gesture that said, *Bring it.*

"I *really* hope someone's got a hidden camera around here, because I dare you to sing a Lollipop song on the diving board before doing a belly flop. A real one. I mean, I want to see that six-pack crushed like a soda can and tears streaming out of your eyes."

"Funny, I never saw that evil streak in you before."

"Told you." She shrugged, treading water. "You changed me."

Ouch. "You know, some people become kinder after adversity."

"And others want to hear bellies slap against the surface of water. Now, get on that dare, Mr. Bad Boy Quarterback."

Without hesitation, he made his way over to the deep end.

"And if you don't know the lyrics to any of my songs, you have to at least hum one."

"What if I've never heard any of them?"

"Then, you can choose option number two, which is to deliver a room service tray to every single person on this tour...in nothing but a thong." She tipped her head. "Choose your poison."

"Tough choice, but since I don't own a thong, I guess I'm gonna have to wing it." Hopping onto the diving board, he started humming something tuneless.

"That doesn't count. I don't know if we wear the same size, but you're welcome to have a look in my underwear drawer."

He chuckled, playing it cool, but inside he was going out of his mind. This moment together—no anger, no betrayal—*just us.* His heart was full.

Diving under the water, she swam to the side of the pool. When she popped up, he was singing. "Let's do this, let's jam, let's take the chance while we can. Let's do this, let's fly, let's reach our hands to the sky."

As he did the dance moves, she covered her mouth with a hand, eyes wide in delight. "There's no way. *No way* you not only know the lyrics but the moves, too. Is this real life?"

But he just kept singing and dancing. "Get up, on

your feet, get up and move with the beat. Get up, and dance, let's make the most of this chance."

The joy glittering in her eyes, the delight in her smile...he hadn't felt this happy in nine long years. And he couldn't stand it. Sucking in a breath, he bounced high on the board and assumed the Superman flying pose, before landing flat on top of the water.

Holy shit. He might as well have fallen onto concrete. He stayed under for a minute, just to deal with the pain. Only when it began to subside did he come up for air.

She watched him with a remorseful expression. "I'm sorry. That was mean. I didn't think you'd actually do it." She grimaced. "It hurt so bad, didn't it?" She watched him climb out. "Oh, my God, you're bright red." She swam to the side and got out. "I'm so sorry."

"It's fine. I've had hits a lot worse." He lay down on a chaise and closed his eyes.

Sitting down next to him, hair dripping, she rested a hand on his thigh. "I'm done torturing you now."

He took in her concerned expression and the droplets of water he wanted to lick off her breasts. "And if you're not, I can take it." They went quiet for a moment. And then he said, "Truth or dare?"

"Truth."

"You and Grant...anything going on there?"

"Romantically? God, no. He's divorcing his third wife, and he really loves her. Unfortunately, it took her leaving for him to finally get clean." She glanced away, looking uncertain. "Life on the road is hard."

"Was it hard for you?"

"Oh, yeah. My bandmates and I..."

She hesitated, and he hoped like hell she'd open up to him.

"We don't get along. At all." She said it quietly. "But, also, it's a lot different than I thought."

He was so damn glad she was talking to him. "Different how?"

She got up and grabbed a towel, wiping her face, before wrapping it around that luscious body. Then, she sat back down. "My first tour, I was so excited. I was going to perform in the biggest venues around the world. What a launch, right? And there's this huge rush you get when you're on stage and look out into a sea of ecstatic faces. It's crazy, because the green room's filled with people who fawn all over you. You're never alone, and everyone caters to you."

He could relate to everything she was saying. "But…"

"But you're more alone than you've been in your whole life. Because no one cares about you, the person. They only want to touch a star. Like, at first, when they come up to you, talking to you like you hung the moon, you feel good, special. But then, they ask for a selfie, and you get it. You're nothing more than a spectacle, something to show their friends and family. Or a connection, someone who can help them jump the line and get a record contract. I feel stupid even saying this. Obviously, it's an amazing opportunity, and I'm so grateful for—"

"You don't have to play that game with me. I get it."

She smiled. "Of course you do. Everyone sees the happy-go-lucky playboy quarterback, but they don't see what goes on behind the scenes."

"They don't see you throwing up after training in hundred-degree heat. Or when your teammates turn on you." *Fucking Zach.* "The pressure's intense, and sometimes you just can't do anything right."

Her relief was palpable. "That's exactly right. And yet

you can't talk about the negatives or people think you're ungrateful. I think, for me, the joy is in performing. I love singing. Music has so much power, you know? It can change my mood like that." She snapped her fingers. "It puts me in touch with what's really going on inside me. Do you know what I mean? Sometimes I don't know what I'm feeling until the words pop out in a lyric."

He nodded, but he didn't have anything like that in his life. Except her. *She* connected him with his real emotions.

"On the road, there are screaming fans and sound engineers and managers and roadies…it's just pure noise and chaos—and yet, in the middle of that, there's no… heart. Until you're alone in your room, dredging up feelings, and turning them into lyrics. I don't know how to explain it. There's no—"

"Meaning. I get it. I'm surrounded by all the noise of reporters and interviews, constant travel and tabloids, but inside…" He patted his chest. "There's this big void. And, for me, the only real connection comes when I'm on the field. That moment when I target my receiver, let go of the ball, and wait for him to catch it. We're surrounded by chaos, half the guys on the field want to clobber us—but there's this one quiet moment of *I'm here. I got you.*"

Her smile was so…unburdened. "Honestly, I didn't think you'd get it because, in all the pictures of you, you're laughing, the life of the party. You've got women hanging all over you. You just look like you're living your best life."

He sat up, wanting her to hear him. "The women are strangers and being the life of the party takes a lot of work."

She looked more vulnerable than he'd ever seen her,

like she was right there with him, open and willing to give him a chance. "Truth or dare?"

He wouldn't blow it. "Truth."

"Have you ever been in love?"

"You know I have."

"No, I meant…" She looked embarrassed.

He cupped her chin. "I know kissing Ashton made you question your instincts about us, but they were right on. Everything you felt for me, I felt it, too. And it was torture, because I couldn't do a damn thing about it. And the minute I lost you I knew—down to my bones—that I'd lost a piece of myself. The piece that mattered most. And without that piece…" He gazed into those amber eyes, and all the words crashed into each other before they could leave his mouth.

She's here. My Gigi is right here.

"Finish what you were going to say. Without that piece what?"

He couldn't believe he had a chance to win her back. But to do that, he had to get very, very real. "I'm lost. The parties, the noise, I use it to fill in the gaps, but it doesn't work. Nothing works."

"I want to believe you. So much. But it's hard to let go of everything I've held onto for a decade."

"What you see in the press…a lot of it's true. I am partying that much. But…" How did he explain what he didn't entirely understand? "I guess I feel more like a host." Whoa—the truth clobbered him. But, yeah, that was exactly how he felt. "It's too hard to get back into shape once you let yourself go, so I've learned to maintain my habits year-round. That means I don't drink much. And you know I don't do drugs. I sure as hell don't stay up all night."

"Then why do you do throw all these parties? It doesn't make sense."

"Because I'm captain, and if my guys don't spend time together—don't bond—then we don't win. We have to be in sync."

She looked at him like what he'd said didn't make sense. But, then, she wasn't the quarterback of a professional football team.

"I don't remember my dad working so hard on bonding."

"Well, he had a wife and kids." Something clicked inside him, klieg lights blazing in a stadium. "You grew up in this perfect family, where everything revolved around you and your sisters. I didn't grow up like that. My parents...we lived in New Jersey, and they both commuted into New York City for work. They worked on Wall Street, and they were never home. I grew up with nannies, and when they had to get home to their families, I was dropped off at a friend's house. I don't think there was a day when I felt like anything other than a problem that needed to be dealt with. Every morning, my mom and dad had the same conversation. 'I have to work late, can you get Cassian from karate? No, I have to get out this proposal. You do it, no, you do it.'"

"And then you moved into Griffin's room, and he made your life a living hell." She watched him for a moment. "You never felt like you belonged anywhere."

"I belonged with you." *I still do.*

She looked away, her features wrenched with a mix of anguish and frustration. "You said those same words ten years ago. And then you kissed Ashton. Can you see how it's hard for me to trust you?"

"Yes, I can. But I'm a man now, and I'm trying to put us back together again."

"But you can't, Cassian. It's not about one thing you did, one choice you made. That night, yes, you were upset, it was an impossible situation, but your go-to response was to kiss my best friend. Right in front of me. You led her up those stairs. You *meant* to hurt me."

"I couldn't fucking take it anymore. I wasn't thinking."

"That's my point. It was your immediate reaction. All I know is, if I'd been in your shoes, I would *never* have kissed your friend. I don't know what I would've done, but I would never have carved your heart out and thrown it on the ground. I just don't know if I'll ever be able to trust you again." She got up, grabbing her phone and keycard. "But the real issue is I don't know how to believe in *myself* anymore."

"Hey, it's time to get going." Kevin approached the small group gathered outside the hospital's community room. "Why don't you guys head out to the van? We'll be right behind you."

"Sure thing." Cassian took one last look at the actor. Always the last to leave, Macy had turned out to have the softest heart of all of them. While she kept to herself, reading scripts on the plane and in the vans, never joining them for shared meals, she gave her whole self to the kids. She was warm, interested, and incredibly engaging.

The group of them left, giving final handshakes to the staff. Outside, freshly mown grass scented the Kentucky air, and the van's engine rumbled to life when the driver saw them coming out the doors.

When Gigi slid into the very back, Cassian shot ahead

of the others so he could sit next to her. Up on her knees, she had her back to him, as she fit her guitar case into the narrow trunk space. When she turned back around and saw him, she rolled her eyes. "Slick move."

"Gaining yardage is pretty much what I do for a living."

She settled in, reaching for the seat belt. "Are you telling me you tackled people just to sit next to me?"

He wanted to touch her very blonde hair, cup her cheek, and run a thumb along that plump bottom lip. "I'm telling you I have three days left, and I'm going to take every chance I have to be with you."

She dug through her black leather tote. "You should probably save your moves for training camp. After this tour, I go back to LA, and you go to Calamity. So…big waste of energy."

"Have you seen me on the field? I'm a boss at extending the play. I can take three days and turn them into a lifetime."

The stark yearning in her eyes gripped him hard.

She wants us to work out.

She wants me.

Grant slid into the seat in front of them, giving them both a chin nod.

"Or at least make them feel like a lifetime." She muttered it under her breath.

He chuckled. "No one does a better job of cutting me down to size."

"With your gigantic ego, it'd barely be noticeable."

"Well, aren't we saucy this afternoon?" He kind of liked it. Because this time her jabs lacked anger. Mostly, she sounded frustrated.

She quit fidgeting and looked him right in the eye. "I have a lot on my mind."

"Like?"

"Like my career is up in the air, and I'd really hoped to write some songs on this trip, and I haven't."

"That song you and Grant wrote's a good one."

"It is."

"You normally write more than one great song a week?"

She smiled. "No."

"Okay, then. Good job." He held up his hand for a high-five, but she just shook her head at him like he was being ridiculous.

Exhaust filtered in through the open side vents, so he closed his, then reached across to shut hers. He glanced down just in time to see her checking out his biceps. He flexed them. "You can touch it. Come on. You know you want to."

She laughed and pushed him away. "No wonder Elena screamed at you outside the Ivy. The whole world thinks it was about you ghosting her, but the truth is that you probably walked past her table and said, 'You can touch my hard, squat-sculpted ass. You know you want to.'" Her voice went low, her tone arrogant.

He barked out a laugh that had heads turning in the van. "That's a good line. Wish I'd thought of it." But, since she'd brought it up, he wouldn't mind addressing the situation. "You know better than to believe what you read in the tabloids. I met her at a club in Ibiza. I never thought I'd see her again."

"You were on a boat with her for an entire week and never thought you'd see her again?"

"Believe me, she never set foot on it. I met her in a

club in town, and I wound up spending a total of two hours with her."

Wearing her signature big, round sunglasses, the actor took the last seat. Slamming the door, Kevin sat beside the driver, and the van took off.

"Well, with the way you flirt with women, it's no wonder it meant more to her than it did to you. You're very convincing."

"I honestly don't think I'm flirting. I'm just being nice. Friendly."

"You want everyone to like you."

The truth hung in the air between them. He couldn't deny how deeply it resonated with him.

And it shamed him.

He'd never seen himself that way, as a guy who needed to be liked.

Fortunately, the chatter in the van grew loud enough to compensate for their lapse in conversation.

He wanted to talk about something lighter, something that didn't make him look so…weak. "Truth or dare?"

"Dare."

He grabbed her tote.

"Hey."

Reaching in for a paper bag from the coffee shop where they'd grabbed a bite to eat on their way out the door, he pulled out a napkin and balled it up. "I dare you to hit Macy in the head."

"She's one of the most famous actors in the world. I'm not hitting her in the head."

"That's a clear breach of the rules."

"I don't care about the rules of a stupid game, I'm not throwing something at an Academy Award-winning actor."

"Is it stupid, though? Truth or Dare is the ultimate test of courage. The unwillingness to face a challenge is the true test of character."

"Huh. I always thought the true test is what we do under pressure." She gave him a pointed look.

Ah, hell. She had him there. "Are you referring to something I did as a *child*? Well, today, right now, the pressure's on you, a fully formed adult. Let's see what you're made of." He held out the napkin.

She snatched it out of his hand. "She's going to think I'm crazy."

"*Or* she's going to be impressed with your courage."

She laughed. "You're nuts."

He tipped his chin. *Do it.*

"I can't believe I'm doing this." She hurled the napkin, and it landed between the actor and the retired baseball player next to her. Both of them jerked back, looking to see what had happened. Gigi fought back laughter.

Cassian pulled out another napkin. "Your target is literally ten feet in front of you. You can at least *try* to impress me."

She balled up the napkin and let it fly, hitting Macy in the back of the head.

The woman smoothed a hand down her hair and slowly turned. "For a second there, I thought I was on a road trip with my children."

"We're playing Truth or Dare," Gigi said. "And he's being an idiot."

The actor's gaze slid to Cassian. He was glad she wasn't his mother, because that expression would have him scrambling to rinse his dishes and put them in the dishwasher.

The others had gone rigid and silent, the tension high.

But, then, Macy said, "Truth or Dare?"

He nodded, giving her an easy grin.

"I'm in."

The others burst out laughing.

"Anything's better than reading yet another script where I'm the bitchy stepmother."

Chapter Nine

APPARENTLY, THROWING A NAPKIN AT MACY'S HEAD had knocked the stick out of her butt, because instead of going straight to her room, she gathered with the group in the lobby after check-in to discuss dinner plans.

Although, it could've had more to do with spending time with the patients. While there was nothing so satisfying as watching those faces light up with happiness, it was also emotionally draining. Behind their joyful smiles, Gigi knew the kids and their families were fighting the battle of their lives. Watching a mom blink back tears when her son, who'd spent half his life in the oncology wing, shook his idol's hand, well…it just put a lot of things into perspective.

And you need to talk about it. Their group had begun gathering in the evenings to share their experiences.

"Okay, the restaurant can't accommodate all of us at one table," Kevin said, returning from the hostess station. "So, I'm going to ask the manager about renting a banquet room."

"My suite's like an apartment," Cassian said. "Let's have it there."

"Yeah?" Kevin asked with a tone that said, *You sure?*

Cassian nodded.

"Great. Let me grab some menus and—"

"I'm cooking."

Everyone shot a look at the big, badass quarterback.

"Oh, you don't want to do that." Kevin seemed surprised at the suggestion. "There are fifteen of us."

"I got it." Cassian sounded confident.

"You cook?" Gigi asked.

"I'm single. Of course, I cook."

"I'm not eating any of those green smoothie things." The retired baseball player stuck out his tongue like it had a hair on it. "My days of eating veggies are done and gone."

"I got you," Cassian said. "Nothing green for you."

Gigi was still fixated on the fact that he made his own meals. "Don't you have a chef or something?"

"For just me? No. Besides, I like to cook. It gets my mind off a lousy play or the latest social media scandal about me."

"If only that worked for me," Grant said, and everyone smiled.

"If you're sure, then let me know what I can do to help," Kevin said.

"Just show up at seven for hors d'oeuvres and cocktails."

Gigi snorted. "Did the Bad Boy Quarterback just say *hors d'oeuvres*? Are you actually going to make them or are you opening bags of chips and pretzels?"

"You have so little faith in me." When he grinned like that, all cocky and playful, she got hot and restless.

To be honest, the whole party animal persona had lost its power. She saw him now, and he wasn't anything close to how the media depicted him.

She'd never fully trust him again, of course, but letting go of the hate…it was huge.

Cassian turned to Kevin. "My sous chef and I will have everything ready. All you have to do is provide the booze."

Kevin grinned. "I can do that." He clapped Cassian on the back. "Okay, I'll see everyone at seven."

She watched the group disperse, surprised that no one had offered to help. "You shouldn't have to cook for everyone all by yourself."

"I agree. That's why I've got a sous chef."

She stopped herself from making a crack about the woman behind the reception desk who'd been eyeing him since they'd checked in. It was time to kick that knee-jerk reaction to the curb. "And who would that be?"

He gave her a sexy grin and wrapped an arm around her shoulder, tugging her against him. "Only my most favorite person in the world."

They rolled the cart along the far wall of the store, past eggs, milk, cheese, and yogurt. Gigi couldn't believe the way everyone blatantly checked Cassian out. It was easy for her to go incognito—all she had to do was skip the costume and fix her hair a different way.

But Cassian? The worn baseball cap set low on his forehead might disguise the top half of his face, but it didn't make him invisible.

He strolled, eyeing every single thing in the refrigerated case but choosing nothing.

"What exactly are you cooking?"

"I'll know it when I see it."

That body—all tight, hard muscles and tan skin—made everyone doubletake on him. Dark brown hair curled out the back of the hat like a duck tail. Cassian projected potent masculinity, and once spotted, no one could take her eyes off him.

She was no different. No matter how much time she spent with him, that jittery sensation wouldn't ease. It was like the crush that wouldn't die. "Yeah, but we have to start somewhere. Are we making meat? Pasta? Oh, we could do lasagna. That's super easy."

"You can make lasagna if you want."

"You don't like lasagna?"

"I don't eat white flour, tomato sauce, or much dairy, so…no."

"What's wrong with tomato sauce?"

"Tomatoes are a nightshade vegetable, which means they're inflammatory."

"Right. Strict diet."

He stopped at the cheese section, tossing a wheel of brie in the cart. "I don't view it as strict. I just educate myself and use the ingredients that maximize my health and performance."

"That's a good attitude. So, what do you eat?"

"Mostly just vegetables, meat, whole grains, and legumes."

She hip-checked him and took over the cart.

"Hey. Where are you going?"

"You don't eat dairy."

"But other people do."

"You're cooking. It's your food. And I'm going to guess you cook as well as you play ball, so they'll love whatever you make." She turned down a random aisle. "If you were home tonight, what would you make?"

"It's Friday, so I'd eat leftovers."

"You're very annoying. Let's pretend it's—"

"Sunday. Because that's when I cook for the week."

"Okay, Sunday…wait, how did I not know this?"

"Because I didn't cook when I was seventeen?"

She stopped to face him. "No, I mean, how come you're all over the media for threesomes and models shrieking at you, but not for your football camp or your cooking skills?"

Passing a mom with two kids playing in her cart, they split up and met on the other side. "I'd like to keep my camp on the down-low for as long as possible. First, I don't want anyone to associate me with Calamity, but secondly, I don't want paparazzi hanging around, disturbing the kids and their families."

"I wonder how long that'll last."

"This is our third year, and it's worked so far."

She'd chosen the wrong aisle to cruise. They didn't need canned fruit or vegetables. "I think it's amazing that you do it. Those kids are lucky. How do you choose who gets to go?"

"We research community demographics, talk to rec centers and schools, looking for the kids we think will be a good fit for our program."

"Oh, so they don't just apply?"

"It wouldn't work very well if we did that. It's pretty intense physically, so we're looking for the right fit. When we find them, we offer scholarships." He lifted his cap, ran fingers through his hair, and set it back down, tugging until he got it where he wanted. "And why would I be in the news for cooking?"

"Because it's the opposite of your playboy persona. People should know things like that about you."

"They know what the press tells them."

"That's my point. Be a guest chef at a restaurant. Do a football clinic at the stadium over spring break. You don't have to be a victim to the press. Do things that showcase a whole other side of you. *Invite* them to see it." She pushed around the corner, turning up the next aisle. "Okay, so, it's Sunday night, what ingredients are you buying?"

"A big bag of quinoa, a pile of fresh vegetables. Some unsalted broth. Maybe some garbanzo beans. And lots of fresh herbs."

"Fresh herbs? The badass football player buys fresh herbs?"

"If he wants his food to taste good, he does."

"Fine. Then, that's what we're making, a big ole vat of quinoa and mixed veggies."

"Not sure Andy's going to like that."

She tossed a box of Ritz crackers into the cart for the retired ball player.

"Also, my suite doesn't have cookware, so we'll have to get those big aluminum pans."

"Great. You do the main meal, and I'll handle the appetizers." She snatched two more boxes of crackers off the shelf.

"We're putting Brie on those?"

"Of course not, silly." She pulled down a can of cheese. "We're putting this on them."

"That's disgusting."

"How would you know, Mr. My Body is My Temple? Have you ever tried it?"

"Will it make me run faster? Throw more precisely?"

"I'm down to put it to the test if you are."

"Training camp starts in six weeks, leave my temple alone."

Further up the aisle, they came upon cookies. "What were you thinking for dessert?"

"I'll get some berries, some fresh cream…"

"Yeah, okay. You've got enough on your plate with the main meal. I'll take care of appetizers and dessert." She snatched a package of frosted animal crackers.

"That's not…" He pulled the bag out of her hands and shoved it back. "Okay, *no*. We're not serving toddlers." He nudged her aside and took over the cart. "Jesus, no one would believe you're Tyler Cavanaugh and Joss Montalbano's daughter."

"I'll tell you what, when you grow up weighing portion sizes and finding raw broccoli in your lunch bag, you tend to go wild when you leave home."

"That was nine years ago. You haven't found some kind of balance by now?"

"Where's the fun in that?" She tossed a bag of Twizzlers into the cart.

He looked at them like they were poisonous snakes. "We're like night and day."

She scanned the gourmet chocolate bars. "Desert and ocean."

"Sweet and sour."

"Open and…wait." She looked up at him. "Which one of us is sweet and which is sour?"

"Well, I think your sniping speaks for itself."

"I only snipe around you." She smacked his arm. "Because you're a dick."

He watched her for a moment. And then he said, "But not anymore, right?"

She looked into those intense green eyes, took in his

handsome features, and saw the man no one else in the world got to see.

And this feeling swept in, water coursing over parched earth, sunlight hitting frosted glass…forgiveness healing a broken heart.

"No." She touched his arm. "Not anymore."

The suite smelled amazing. Gigi had only stepped out for ten minutes to take a call from her manager, but Cassian already had something baking—something with onion and garlic. *Yum.*

She took a moment to watch him at work. Wearing a long-sleeve navy blue Henley—the sleeves pushed up to his elbows—worn jeans, and bare feet, he looked like a domesticated bad boy.

He glanced at up her. "Everything okay?"

"It's only been four days, but so far everyone's behaving. Maybe there's hope for this third album after all."

As he chopped an array of colorful, fresh vegetables like a pro, his muscles flexed. Those broad shoulders and taut stomach, his strong jaw and sensuous mouth…

Good God, the man's gorgeous.

Stop staring. "Well, I guess I'll set up the hors d'oeuvres." She ripped open a sleeve of crackers, squirted some cheese onto one, and popped it in her mouth. "Mm." She prepared another one and brought it to his mouth.

"Get that thing away from me." Smiling, he twisted away.

As they worked easily together, she felt this rush of intimacy with him. She used to dream about moments like these. They'd be in their tree house, talking about any old thing, and she'd imagine them in their kitchen cooking together. Or her legs on his lap as they watched TV. Him shaving at the sink, while she showered...just being so comfortable together.

She never saw careers or kids or even what their house looked like. It was just random scenes with him. Easy, simple moments bursting with love. "Truth or Dare?"

"I'm going with truth since everyone'll be here in less than an hour."

She dumped the crackers onto a plate. "What's your proudest moment? In your whole life?"

He didn't even hesitate. "My first touchdown, freshman year."

That made sense, she supposed. Her dad had turned a delinquent kid into a quarterback in under a year. She peeled the plastic off the Brie. "You're prouder of that than being invited to play in the Pro Bowl? Making it to the Super Bowl? Being chosen MVP?"

He shoved the hair off his face with the back of a hand. "You remember the first thing I did when I crossed the line?"

Warmth spread through her. Of course, she did.

Chop chop chop. His fingers moved deftly. He didn't look up from his task. "I looked for *you*. You were on the sidelines with your dad. I wanted to know if you'd seen me do it."

"I did." She'd expected—like everyone else watching—for him to do some kind of victory dance or jump into a huddle with his excited teammates.

But he hadn't. He'd searched her out in the crowd—and when he'd found her, he'd looked almost startled, like *Did I just do that?* And then he'd given her a grin as shy as a little boy who'd just learned to tie his shoes. It had rocked her world, the way he'd shared that special moment with her. "But I mean your *proudest*. The one thing in life that—"

"I heard you, and that's my answer. Up until then, I'd been angry and…defiant. Pissed at the world. I'd made life hard on everyone. But then I met you, and I wanted to be better." He stopped chopping, shoving at his hair with the back of a hand. "It wasn't about football at first. I didn't know how to play, and the guys didn't want me joining the team after the season had already started, so it wasn't like it was *fun*. Most of the time, I felt embarrassed, because I kept screwing up. Coach didn't have time for a new guy who'd never touched a football before. He needed someone who'd hit the ground running. So, making that touchdown, it meant…" When his hair fell forward, he shook his head in frustration.

Gently, she tucked the errant lock behind his ear. His whole demeanor softened, and she recognized the want in his eyes.

"What did it mean?" she asked quietly.

"It meant your dad was right. He'd heard from the gym teachers that I was athletic, so he'd taken a chance on me, and I was glad to pay back his investment. But it also meant I wasn't a loser anymore, which gave me a shot at you. Gigi Cavanaugh wouldn't want anything to do with a kid in detention, but if I were a winner, you'd give me the time of day."

A week ago, she'd been a glacier. Now, this man's words were melting her so completely the ocean levels would surely rise. "You were always good enough for me. If only you'd felt it in here." She pressed her hand over his heart.

He dropped the knife to grasp it. "Your dad used to talk to me about being self-destructive. Said he was the same way before he met your mom, so he could see it in me. He said…" He looked away, clearly embarrassed. "He said he had it hard growing up, that his parents didn't have time for him, so he didn't have much self-worth. And he said, 'Neglect does that to a kid.' Until that moment, I'd never really seen myself that way. It made me think about my childhood, and…yeah, your dad was right."

"I think that's why he fell so hard for my mom. She takes care of people, and he needed that. I mean, right from the beginning, she was just so attentive to him. She dotes on him."

"Yeah, they're good together."

It struck her, what her dad had inadvertently done. "How ironic, though, right? My dad helped you gain self-esteem, and then he took it right out from under you."

"How's that?"

"By telling you to stay away, he was saying you weren't good enough for me. He might've said, *Let Gigi reach her potential*, but you heard, *Keep your dirty, self-destructive hands off her.*"

His features twisted into raw, unyielding pain. "I…" His jaw snapped shut. He swallowed. "Yeah. Guess I did." He picked up the knife and started chopping again. Only, this time, his movements weren't so smooth.

"You have to know he didn't mean it like that. He thinks the world of you." But her words couldn't reach that deeply ingrained belief. As she washed grapes and set them on a plate, she wished so badly her dad hadn't interfered. Who knows where they would've wound up?

Pulling a baguette out of its sleeve, she decided to tell him the truth. "I wanted your dirty hands on me. More than anything, I wanted all of you, and it killed me, because when I was alone with you, I was so sure you were mine, but then we'd leave our little cocoon, and you'd be with my dad, your coach, your teammates...or Melissa, Carrie, Jen...and you weren't mine at all. It was just so confusing." *Hurtful.*

"I'd have spent every minute with you, if I could have." Done chopping, he scooped a handful of vegetables and dumped them into the simmering quinoa pot. He wiped his hands on a kitchen towel and turned to face her. "I've missed you, and if you want the truth...the only time I don't feel alone is when I'm with you."

Tears burned, and she wanted to step into the shelter of his arms and say, *I feel that, too.* She wanted to forget the rest of the world and just be with him.

And she would, too. She could see herself selling her house in Los Angeles, moving in with him and sleeping beside him every night, running into his arms when he came home after practice.

They'd watch movies and snuggle and wander the farmer's market, have dinner parties with his teammates.

She could see them having all that...*if* he changed.

But she didn't believe he would. Whatever it was that had driven him to grab Ashton that night...it was still there.

It wasn't their past that blocked their way forward.

It was the damage life had done to him.

And that meant she couldn't trust him.

Because, inevitably, he'd hurt her again.

Lured by Gigi's powerful voice, Cassian hurried down the corridor. The oncology wing's community room, crowded with staff, family, and patients, throbbed with music and excitement.

He'd come too late, though. The song ended, and the audience burst into applause.

"Thank you." With her platinum braids, black shorts, polka dot tights, and combat boots, she waved. "You guys are the best."

"Encore," a man called, and others joined in enthusiastically.

"Kev," Gigi called. "Do we have time for one more?"

"We can absolutely squeeze in one more song." His eyes shone with happiness.

She scanned the room, breaking out in a big grin when she landed on Grant. "You want to hear a duet Grant Banner and I have been working on?"

The applause grew louder, a man in front whistling with two fingers in his mouth.

"Come on." Gigi gestured for him, and the country star lifted his guitar case and made his way to her. "This is a big moment, you guys. You're the very first people to hear the finished song."

"Woo hoo," a teenage girl called.

"Yeah," shouted a boy.

A doctor gave up her chair for Grant, and he sat down and opened his case.

"It doesn't have a title yet." Gigi had great stage presence. She talked like they were all good friends, gathered around a campfire. "So, after you hear it, we'd love your suggestions."

Over the shouts and applause, a little girl clapped and said, "We get to name a Lollipop song."

The duo launched into the music. Gigi looked so happy, so beautiful, and when she turned to Grant and whispered something in his ear, Cassian felt a stab of jealousy. He wanted that closeness with her.

And you'll get it. This tour had given him the chance he'd needed. He'd done the hard work, apologizing, explaining, which had enabled him to chip away at the wall she'd erected.

He hoped he'd helped her heal.

Sure, tomorrow, she'd be in Los Angeles, and he'd be busy with his football camp. *But this is a beginning.* He'd fly out to see her as soon as camp ended.

As Gigi sang, she closed her eyes.

A million years ago you owned my heart
Back when life was simpler
When all I did was think about you,
And wonder who you were with
and what you were doing with her
that you wouldn't do with me

When she opened her eyes, she looked right at him, and he felt a seismic shift in his bones.

If only you'd been a better man
If only you'd been worthy of my love
If only I'd seen the heart of you
If only…

A million years have passed, with you long gone
So how can you be standing in the place I last saw you
I thought you'd moved on and never looked back
But I was wrong, and now I don't know
If I'm looking at the man you've become
Or the man I wish you'd be

If only you'd been a better man
If only you hadn't twisted my heart
If only I could trust myself again
If only...

If only...
If only...
If only...

As the last note hung in the room, Gigi's held his gaze expectantly. He knew she wanted a response, but he couldn't give her one.

Because the song expressed exactly what he'd done to her, and it jammed his gears.

The roar in his ears drowned out the audience's applause. His skin went hot at the same time his blood ran cold.

Healed her? Fuck, he hadn't gained *any* traction. And that meant, when she went back to Los Angeles, she'd get swallowed up in her life as if this tour had never happened.

They'd be over.

And he'd have to live the rest of his life without her.

Slowly, he rose out of the fog, tuned into the clapping, the shouts and calls. Grant grinned like he knew he had a hit on his hands, but Gigi still watched Cassian carefully.

This is her moment. It's not about me. So, he lifted arms that felt like lead bars and clapped, forcing a smile.

When the room quieted down, she said, "Okay, hit me with your titles."

"A Million Years Ago," someone said.

"Worthy of My Love," someone else called.

A little girl whispered, and her mom leaned low to hear. When she straightened, the woman said, "'If Only.'"

Gigi gave the girl a warm smile. "Yeah, that's my pick, too." She nudged Grant. "What do you say? 'If Only?'"

"'If Only,' it is."

"We'll give a credit to you, Arianna, on our liner notes," Gigi said. "Would that be all right?"

Grinning, the girl nodded vigorously.

Kevin got up and murmured something to Grant and Gigi, before turning to the audience. "I know I speak for everyone when I say we've had a great time with you all. Thank you for welcoming us so warmly. Miss Dana has my contact information, so if you've been promised anything or just want to say hey, you can always reach me."

Movement all around Cassian prompted him to go, but he was stuck.

He had to face a hard truth. He'd never been good for her. Back in high school, he'd had her all twisted up. Confused. Because, when he was alone with her, no one else in the world existed, but when they were around others, he acted like she didn't matter.

He'd hurt her even while he'd loved her.

And now, as the Bad Boy Quarterback, he could damage her reputation. Her career.

"You coming?" Macy said.

"Yeah." He followed her out, resolve grabbing hold of him.

There was only one choice.

He had to be a better man.

Because a life without Gigi was unthinkable.

Chapter Ten

THAT NIGHT AFTER DINNER, A BUNCH OF THEM gathered in Cassian's suite. They'd borrowed a karaoke machine from the manager, and now they were taking turns.

After Gigi had kicked things off with Prince's "I would Die 4 U," she passed the microphone to Macy.

She was trying really hard to be in the moment, but she couldn't get Cassian's expression out of her mind. When she'd asked Grant to do the duet with her, she hadn't been thinking about the lyrics. She'd written that song at the beginning of the week, before they'd talked things through, when seeing him again had revitalized all the anger, and she'd needed to make sense of it all.

Every word was true, and she loved the song, but it had gutted him.

Yes, because he got it. Like, down to his bones, he understood what she'd gone through. *That's a good thing.*

Gigi looked over as Macy belted out a Pat Benatar song. It was hilarious. The closed-off introvert had become a funny, sarcastic woman who jumped right into the fun. *Nice to see.*

Gigi wished she could get into it, but tonight was her last night. Tomorrow she'd go home to LA, and she wouldn't see Cassian other than when they happened to cross paths in Calamity or at her parent's house.

And she wasn't ready to leave him.

Her phone vibrated, and she pulled it out of her pocket to see her manager's name on the screen.

Michelle: **Heard from Dale today. She's thrilled with the press you're getting.**

Gigi: **Glad to hear it.**

Though, she wasn't doing it for Dale.

Gigi: **My lovely bandmates still behaving?**

Michelle: **LOL. Dani was trying to lay low in Mexico but got caught by the paps drunk off her ass in a club, and Tanya had a blow-out fight with her boyfriend in public. But no one's heard from Jess in rehab, so that's a good sign.**

Fear sucker-punched her. How could they take risks like that when so much was at stake?

Gigi: **What does this mean for the band? Has Dale said anything?**

She really wanted to finish this album, leave Clean Beatz on good terms. She didn't want a ruined reputation.

Michelle: **Her usual rant, but I'm taking care of it.**

Nope. Gigi didn't work like that. She needed all the information.

Gigi: **Tell me what she said.**

Michelle: **That you girls are a commodity, easily replaced. If you don't perform per the contract's explicit guidelines, she can easily put together another band. You want me to go on?**

Gigi: **There's more?**

Michelle: **It's Dale. Of course there's more. Nothing I haven't handled a hundred times in my career.**

But Gigi already knew.

Gigi: **She's going to sue us for breach of contract.**

Michelle: **Correct.**

Gigi: **Will she win?**

Michelle: **Unlikely. Keep in mind it's less to do with actually recouping her losses and more to do with sending a message. She thinks it'll make the next set of girls fall in line. It really comes down to how much money she wants to bleed over this. In my experience, most people wave the contract around and stomp their feet, but their attorneys keep them from following through with litigation that could go on for years.**

The cost of a court battle could wipe her out financially—and keep her in the press.

Gigi: **How bad's my reputation going to be if we don't put out this third album?**

Michelle: **Let's talk about it when it happens**

She loved her manager, but Gigi didn't want anyone patting her on the head and treating her like a kid.

Gigi: **Just tell me. How bad?**

Michelle: **It's more than an album. It's a tour, merchandise, and marketing contracts. It's a big deal. But there's nothing you can do about it.**

She'd been noodling an idea. It seemed pretty farfetched, but it kind of excited her.

Gigi: **There might be one thing…**

Michelle: **what's cooking in that brain of yours?**

Gigi: **What if we pitched her a solo album? I've got a ton of songs.**

Unfinished, but she'd love to work on her own material.

Gigi: **I'm just thinking I could dissociate myself from the others if she signed me as a solo act.**

Michelle: **I can pitch it, but I think you know she's going for the girl band brand.**

Gigi: **This might save the label's reputation along with mine. I'd still be a Lollipop.**

When she thought of it like that, it lost some of its luster. *Ugh.* Did she really have it in her to write a whole album of super cheerful pop songs?

It's better than litigation and a damaged reputation.

Gigi: **Will you pitch the idea? I want to separate myself from the others.**

Michelle: **Sure, I can ask. Safe travels tomorrow.**

Cassian came up to her. "Everything okay?"

"My bandmates are screwing up. Pretty sure my label's going to drop us, which means…well, the owner's threatening a lawsuit."

"I've got a great entertainment lawyer—"

"I'm sure you do."

He gave her a smirk. "And if you're worried about expenses, most of these kinds of cases are settled out of court."

She leaned in to create a little more privacy. "I just pitched an idea to my agent." Her anxiety was high not because Dale would reject it—but because she might actually go for it. "I was thinking I could make a demo of Lollipop-type songs and see if Clean Beatz would sign me as a solo act. It'd save my reputation and give me a way to transition into the next phase of my career."

"You want to write those kinds of songs?"

"Ha. No, not at all. But I've got one more record on

this contract anyway, so instead of touring with my band, why not do it by myself? I want to be taken seriously in the industry, and this would be the first step."

"That song you played this afternoon…could you do that with Clean Beatz?"

"Not a chance."

"It's damn good. Maybe it's not a bad thing to lose this contract. If you walk away, you'll be able to write your own songs and work with a label that's a better fit. Memories are short in the entertainment industry, because the bottom line is always a product that will make money."

"I'm a Lollipop. No one will take me seriously until I reinvent myself."

"Let me ask you this. Putting aside your contract and all the obstacles, if your phone rang right now with the best news imaginable, what would it be?"

She knew the answer to that one. "That Irwin Ledger wants to sign me to Amoeba records."

"Have you ever sent him your material?"

"Oh, God, no. He doesn't do pop music. He's the best A&R rep in the industry. He only works with a couple bands at a time, and he turns them into superstars."

"That song you did with Grant…if you sent him that, he'd take you seriously."

"Cassian?" the baseball player called, holding out the microphone.

Cassian held up a finger. *Hang on.*

Grant shouted, "Come on, man, it's your turn."

He hesitated, like he wanted to finish the conversation.

"It's okay, I'm not changing the world tonight. Go on." Not wanting to draw attention to themselves, she headed for the karaoke machine. "I've got just the song for him." Kneeling, she flipped through the choices, stopping when she found the one she wanted. "Okay, look out guys. Cassian's pretty much expert level at this one."

She hit play, and when the first few notes of "UpBeat" came on, everyone burst out laughing. Cassian shook his head with a look that said, *I'll get you back for this.*

Being a good sport, he took the microphone and faced the group. "Why would I know a song like this? Isn't it for teenagers?" But then he started singing, not even looking at the lyrics scrolling across the screen, which just made everyone crack up even harder.

When he started dancing, the group lost it completely. An elite athlete, he moved with grace and pulled off the moves as well as any of the women in the band. He was hamming it up, belting out the lyrics, and her heart just squeezed.

How could she not fall back in love with this man?

Forget the picture the tabloids painted of him. This week, she'd seen him rent a Mustang for a seventeen-year-old boy, cradle the baby sister of one of the patients, and make dinner for the fifteen people on this tour.

He'd opened up his heart and shared some hard truths, and he'd stood there and taken everything she'd had to say. Even when it hurt.

She'd seen him vulnerable and funny, sensitive and strong. Kind, intelligent, charming…God, he was everything.

She knew all the reasons not to be with him, but Cassian was worth the risk, dammit.

When the song ended, everyone went nuts. She just felt so happy. Their group had become close this week. But, mostly, she felt so much…affection for Cassian.

Yeah, affection. That was as far as she was willing to go right now.

Cassian took a bow and handed the mic off to Grant. Then, locking eyes with her, he strode into the kitchen of his suite. Coming around the island, he stopped in front of her, lowering his mouth to her ear. "I won't stop, you know."

She could feel the heat of his body, and she had to press her elbows to her ribcage to keep her arms from lifting to touch his chest. "Stop what?"

"You can keep punishing me, and I'll take it. I'll take it until it sinks in that I'm never going to hurt you again."

Was that what she was doing? Punishing him?

She squeezed his forearm. "I don't mean to punish you." She let out a sharp breath. "I think I'm testing you."

"Good. Keep testing me, because when it comes to you, I will not fail. You hear me, Gigi? I won't fail you."

"I hear you." This was what she'd wanted back then, for him to want her so badly, that if she'd sliced him open, she'd see his love for her clean through to the bone.

"Come here." Grabbing her hand, he led her into the bedroom and closed the door.

Over the thundering of her heart, she could hear Grant singing "Fat Bottom Girls," the others laughing and singing along.

"You forgive me?" he asked.

She nodded. "I do."

Everything in him just melted, relief softening his features, his muscles, his bones. Cheeks stained with color, he closed his eyes and let out a breath. "Thank God." And then his eyelids popped open. "Because I forgive you, too."

"Me? What did I do?"

"Made me sing your Lollipop song in front of people

who once looked up to me. They're never going to ask for my autograph again."

She laughed. "This is the man I wanted back in high school. The man who knew what he wanted. And what he wanted was me."

He looked resolute, fierce. "I've always wanted you this much."

Emotion crashed over her. Grabbing the fabric of his T-shirt and hauling him toward her so hard he lost his footing. "I've missed you so much."

He looked bleak, stark. "You have no fucking idea."

"But I do. That hole you talked about? I have it, too. Most days, I go through the motions. I just feel restless and…"

"Incomplete. I know. Gigi, I *know*."

Cupping the back of his neck, she pulled him to her, covering his mouth, smothering his words. She needed him.

All of him.

She didn't have to wait. His hands slid down her back, pushing up the fabric of her dress and grabbing her ass. Lifting her, he pressed her against the wall and licked into her mouth, his hunger, his need, igniting every cell in her body.

No one had ever kissed her so deeply, so passionately. She clutched the hair at the back of his neck, her hips shifting against him, craving the kind of connection only he could satisfy.

He pulled his mouth off hers. "Fuck, Gigi. *Fuck*." He trailed kisses down her neck, his face burrowing into her cleavage. "You drive me wild. Your smell, the way you taste, move, talk. Jesus, everything about you is just… mine. You're mine."

He lowered her a little, so his cock aligned with her core, and when he pumped his hips, electricity tripped along her nerves.

She drew him back and kissed him, the connection so powerful it was like their fused mouths were the only thing keeping her body fixed to the earth. The insistent pulse between her legs demanded friction. Frantically, she yanked open the buttons on his jeans, reaching under the elastic band of his boxer briefs to grasp his hard, hot erection. "Oh, God, Cassian…" He drove her wild.

Shoving aside her panties, he slid a finger through her slickness and moaned. "Birth control?" His voice sounded rough as gravel.

"Yes." She said it frantically, breathlessly, desperate for him to fill her. "Are you—"

"Clean. Totally." He bent his knees, and then slammed up into her. Her head tipped back, her shoulders bracing her against the wall as she met his thrusts. Desire streamed, hot and wicked, and her legs clung to him.

His hips snapped powerfully, his back grew damp, and he groaned like he was drowning in pleasure. "Ah, Gigi, *dammit*. You feel so fucking good."

She swiveled her hips, trying to get closer, bearing down on him to take him deeper. "Harder." She cried out when he gave her what she wanted. "*Yes*. God."

His hands gripped her ass cheeks, spreading them, and he thrust deep and hard into her.

"Gigi. *Fuck*." He shifted at just the right angle for him to brush over her clit.

Succumbing to the rush of sensation sweeping over her, she closed her eyes. As her climax bore down on her, desire whipped into a whirlwind of lust. Tighter and tighter she twisted, the tension so good, until she burst into a state of pure, carnal bliss. She jerked forward, clinging to his neck, her ankles digging into his ass so he wouldn't stop. Never, ever stop.

Oh, my God.

He slammed into her, pinned her against the wall, as he bit down on her shoulder to stifle his cries. He released inside her with tight, quick punches of his hips.

They clung to each other, the only sound their ragged breaths.

Until…

"Where'd they go?" someone said.

She stiffened. "Shit," she whispered.

His forehead touched hers, and he let out a sigh of disappointment. Gently, he set her down, kissing the corner of her mouth. "I'll go." His movements dragged as he pulled up his boxers and buttoned his jeans.

"I'll be right behind you." She stood on shaky legs, watching him go. Her spirit was still in his arms, still kissing him. She could feel the fullness of his cock inside her.

Slipping into the bathroom, she faced herself in the mirror, taking in her swollen lips, disheveled hair, and pink cheeks.

Slowly, reality settled in. She'd had *sex* with Cassian.

With everyone on the other side of the door.

It felt naughty and wild. Before her mind could start processing, before she could start retreating…she shook it off. She had the rest of the night to stare at her ceiling and wonder what she'd done.

Though, she had a feeling she'd be smiling.

Because that was hot.

By the time she stepped out of his bedroom, the group had gathered at the door. "Well, I've made a big enough fool of myself for one night," Grant said before heading out.

"See y'all in the morning," the baseball player said.

Macy wrapped the cord around the karaoke machine and brought it to Cassian. "You want me to take this downstairs?"

"Nah. The manager told me to leave it in the room."

"Okay, great." She set it on the kitchen counter. "I'll see you both at breakfast."

The moment the door closed, Cassian came right up to her. "You regret it?"

"Regret? No, that's…I'm just a little overwhelmed."

"Gigi, I don't…" His eyes flickered closed in frustration. "I don't want it to end."

"The tour?"

"Us." He reached for her hand. "Come to Calamity. I've missed a week of my camp, so I have to go there. Otherwise, I'd go to LA with you."

"I can't do that." But even as she said the words her mind screamed, *Why not?* Her career was on hold. Either for another three weeks while Jess was in rehab or longer, if Dale dropped them. "I have to write songs, and you're going to be busy every day. Besides, I mean, we got our closure. We're good. It's not like we can be together. Our lives are so different." She was surprised how strongly she wanted him to convince her otherwise.

"I don't need *closure*. I want to bust the door wide open. You think I care how busy we are? That we live on opposite ends of the country? I want you, and if you think I can walk away after I finally got you back, you're out of your mind. I'm not going anywhere."

"But you *are* going somewhere. After camp, you start training. And then you're either playing football in Boston or on the road." It wouldn't work...right? "And if Dale doesn't tear up our contract, I'll be on a world tour in a couple of months. There's no chance for more."

Grabbing her shoulders, he turned her to face him. "I don't care if you're on the moon. That isn't going to change the way I feel about you. I've never wanted anyone else, and I never will. We have a chance here, and we'd be crazy not to take it. Let's do this Gigi. Let's do it right this time."

"I don't know." Of course she wanted to. She *longed* to. But... "This isn't high school, and we don't have the kinds of jobs that would keep us in the same town. I don't see how we can work." She had this crazy feeling, like she was pushing him to find the right words to keep them together.

"No one can see into the future. All we can do is try. I'm never going to be with anyone else. I knew that when I was fourteen, and I know it now. Give us a chance." He pulled her close.

The urgency in his grip, the perfection of his words... it was everything she wanted and yet... "I don't know. Just...let me think. I'll talk to you in the morning." She snagged her keycard and wallet off the counter and hurried out the door.

He followed her into the hallway. "I'm not giving up on us, Gigi. I did that once before, and I'll never make that mistake again."

Cassian stared into the darkness. Every time he'd start to drift off, he'd remember.

The tour had ended. In a few hours, they'd ride the

van to the airport together but then take different flights. She'd go to LA, and he'd go to Calamity on the Cavanaugh foundation's jet.

He wouldn't give up, of course. It'd just be damn hard with them so far apart and so busy.

And, of course, there'd be photos published. The press would make shit up, like they always did. Gigi would see them, and he'd have no way of convincing her of what really happened.

That's it. He was too wired to sleep. "Dammit." He threw off the covers and headed into the bathroom. *Might as well pack.* Turning on the shower, he waited for it to heat up before stepping inside. Lowering his head, he let the water saturate his scalp.

He thought of the studio in her parent's house. State of the art, because…Joss. She made sure her girls had everything they needed to realize their potential. Gigi's mom was a force of nature.

So, Gigi could work on her songs in Calamity.

Hope, that relentless bitch, came back swinging.

It's not even five. He still had time to convince her. He'd go to her room and try again.

He'd fucking never stop trying.

Twenty minutes later, packed and ready to check out, his body thrumming with energy, he knocked on her door. He didn't hear a blow dryer or shower or anything. With one hand he knocked again, and with the other he pulled his phone out of his jeans.

Cassian**: I'm here.**

That could mean anything. She might think he was in the lobby or in the restaurant getting breakfast.

Cassian: **Outside your door.**

Nothing. "Gigi?" He pounded. When he realized he was getting worked up, he took a step back. If she didn't want to talk to him, he couldn't force her.

She needed to do this at her own pace. *It's only going to work if we both want the same thing.* He had to cool his jets.

He just knew, though, in his gut, if he didn't get more time with her—in person—they'd drift apart.

And that was unacceptable.

He tried a different angle.

Cassian: **If you can't come to Calamity, I'll visit you in between sessions.**

His thumb tapped the screen as he waited for a response. Nothing. Not a single sound inside the room.

Cassian: **Are you on your way to the airport?**

Back off. Give her some space.

Fuck. Leaving her left him panicked.

But he had to do it.

He turned and headed for the elevator.

The van idled, ready to go.

Cassian stood outside, waiting. The early morning air had a chill to it.

"Everything okay?" Kevin asked.

He could only nod. Couldn't pry a single syllable out of his throat—because his heart was jammed in there. The van was full—everyone was ready to head to the airport. Except... "Where's Gigi?" His bones turned brittle, and his skin prickled. Tension strung him so tightly he thought he might crack.

"She took an earlier flight," Kevin said.

"Are you kidding me?" Macy leaned out the door with a fist full of paper napkins. "But I came prepared."

Everyone laughed, but Cassian's hope had crashed and burned.

Kevin climbed into the passenger seat, and Cassian sat beside the actor before shutting the door.

Gigi made her decision.

And it's not me.

As the van pulled away from the hotel, he sank into the loss.

Macy set her hand on his knee. "You okay?"

"Sure. Tired. Didn't sleep much last night."

She gave him a squeeze and picked up her book.

As they turned onto the boulevard, Cassian finally looked up, noticing a group of people gathered at a bus stop, some cars lined up in the McDonalds drive-through lane…life going on around him. Slowly, determination rolled in like the tide.

This is not over.

He'd visit her every chance he had—even if it was only one night between camp sessions.

It'll never be over.

Chapter Eleven

CASSIAN NODDED TO THE FLIGHT ATTENDANT.

"Welcome back." She gave him a big grin, as he pushed past her. If the jet had a gym, he'd be hitting the treadmill right now.

Anything to break through the tension. Instead, he fell into a seat apart from the others.

Dammit. If he hadn't already missed the first week of camp, he'd go straight to LA. He needed to see her. Find out what she was thinking.

"Can I get you something?" The attendant seemed concerned. She'd worked for the Cavanaughs for years. She was used to seeing him a lot friendlier. "Coffee? Juice?"

"I'm good. Thanks."

She gave a nod and moved on.

He pulled out his phone. No new messages since he'd arrived at the terminal twenty minutes ago. Restless, anxious, he needed a distraction. He'd brought a book but knew he couldn't concentrate. The words would fade, and he'd be right back in that hotel room, fucking Gigi against the wall. His spine tingled, and he shifted in his seat.

He glanced out the window. He needed to do something, so he scrolled through his social media sites, but nothing—*fucking nothing*—calmed him down.

Where is she right now?

What's she thinking?

He knocked out a text

Cassian: **Miss you.**

Then, he waited. Nothing. No response.

That's fine. He didn't need her to respond. Just needed her to know he was thinking about her.

"Hey, you guys." *That voice.*

Gigi.

Adrenaline crashed his system, making him jittery.

"Hey, girl," Grant called. "Thought you took an earlier plane?"

"And stay away from you guys? Where's the fun in that?" She kept walking, until she stopped right in front of Cassian. "That seat taken?"

Holy shit. She's here.

Wired, he patted the cushion next to him. "All yours."

She smiled and sat down, the energy between them electric.

"Change of plans?" he asked.

"Yep."

Happiness streaked across him. "Good. "

"It's Scraggles' tenth birthday. So, you know, double digits. It's a big one, so I can't miss it."

"You not only have the ugliest dogs but the worst names for them."

"Scraggles is a perfect name. He looks all scraggly."

"Okay, but maybe he'd like a more uplifting name, something that would inspire him to groom better."

Ridiculous conversation, he knew. But without it, he'd be grabbing her ass and hauling her onto his lap.

She's giving us a chance.

"You're a nut."

The flight attendant came by with a warm towel for Gigi. "Morning. How'd the tour go?"

"It was amazing." Gigi picked it up and shook it open. "Thank you."

He took the one offered to him. "Thanks."

As soon as she moved on, he leaned into Gigi, crowding her space, and said, "So, this is happening? You and me?"

A pink flush spread across her cheeks. "Yes."

He thought his heart might punch right out of his chest. He reached for her hand, turned it over, and pressed a kiss to her palm.

For one perfect moment, she held his gaze, and the connection was so powerful it crackled. He felt the joy of it, but also the relief. Finally, they were together.

But then she got this look of concern and pulled her hand away.

Oh, hell, no. "What was that?"

"Cassian, if we do this…it can't get out. I'm trying to save my career." She leaned closer. "And you are, too. The squeaky-clean pop singer can't hook up with the Bad Boy Quarterback. It'll ruin us."

Damn, she was right. Coach would lose his mind if he knew Cassian was debauching the lead singer of the Lollipops. "Okay." Especially after the threesome debacle. "We don't have much time until I leave for training camp, and you go back in the studio. So…I'm good with keeping this private, but I want this. I want all of you." He leaned in and gave her a soft kiss, but the heat coming off her skin, the scent of her, Jesus, it made him crazy, and a simple kiss turned wild.

Her hand came around the back of his neck, and she lifted to get closer to him. He loved it, loved the stroke of her tongue, the desperate sounds she made.

Abruptly, she pulled her mouth away, gripping his neck and pressing her forehead to his chin. "I'm afraid to see if they're watching us."

"We've been around them all week. They know, and they're not going to say anything." Everyone had shared personal struggles. No one would rat anyone out.

She settled back in her seat. "This isn't going to be easy, you know."

"What isn't?"

"Keeping your hands off me. And no dirty talking or looking at me with sex eyes in public."

"I can't *not* look at with you sex eyes, but…I promise, when we're in Calamity Joe's waiting for coffee, I won't wrap my arms around you from behind so you can feel how hard you make me. I won't tilt your chin up so I can kiss that hot mouth that makes me think very fucking dirty thoughts. And I definitely won't reach down to squeeze that perfect ass and slide my fingers between your legs just to get that shiver out of you that turns me on so much." He liked the way she squirmed, liked the desire churning in her eyes. *Oh, fuck yeah.*

Is this real? Am I really talking to Gigi Cavanaugh about grabbing her tight ass?

She shuddered and gazed out the window.

He leaned closer to her ear. "What about when we're hiking? If there's no one around, would it be cool if I put your hands on a tree trunk, pulled down your shorts and panties, and went down on you from behind—right there on the trail?"

She closed her eyes and bit down on her bottom lip.

He lowered his voice even more. "When my teammates go for beers at the Tavern, and you walk in with your friends…since you can't sit with me, can we at least agree on a hand signal, so we know when to meet in the bathroom and I can fuck you in one of the stalls? I'd really like to do that."

She whipped around to face him, looking grumpy. "How did you know I fantasized about all of that?"

"Because I did, too. Every single day."

"Did you?" She looked so serious, so intense. "Are you just saying that, or did you really fantasize about me that way?"

"I was so in love with you I couldn't see straight. All I did was fantasize about fucking you. You want to hear something funny? My first thought when your dad talked to me, told me to stay away from you, was, *Shit, he knows. He's seen all the filthy movies I've made in my head with his daughter.*"

She slipped her arm through his and whispered in his ear. "I wish we still had our tree house. I want to act out every one of those fantasies with you."

"I'll build a new one."

"It won't be the same."

"It'll be better."

She settled back in her seat, her hand caressing his forearm. "Truth or Dare?"

"Truth."

She shifted towards him. "Even if it hurts me, I want the truth. Can you give me that?"

Oh, shit. Please don't ask me about other women. "But I don't want to hurt you, ever again."

"Nothing hurts worse than what I make up in my head. The truth, I can live with."

"But I want to build, Gigi. I don't want the past to drag us back down."

"We can't build without truth."

"Okay." *Fuck.* Images flashed through his mind. The places he'd rented for his teammates over the years. The clubs, bars…the women waiting outside his hotel room. *Inside.* The truth of his life sickened him. It had all been so empty.

If he'd known he had a shot with her, he would never have touched anyone.

"Over all these years…did you think about me?"

"Of course…Jesus, Gigi, I never stopped thinking about you."

"No, I meant did you fantasize about me. You know, like when you were alone at night or in the shower, was it ever me that got you off?"

He barked out a laugh.

She smacked his leg. "Never mind, you jerk."

"No, I'm sorry. It's just…you don't get it. Yes, I fantasized about you. In fact, I've never fantasized about anyone but you."

"I'm the only currency in your spank bank?" She said it like she doubted him.

The flight attendant appeared with a tray of coffees, and they shook their heads with a quiet, *No, thanks.* After she moved on, he said, "I've only ever fantasized about you."

"Good." She faced forward, looking pleased with herself. "This is going to be fun."

"Are you saying the only reason you're coming to Calamity is to play out our sexual fantasies?"

"Are you saying there's something you'd rather do?"

His jaw snapped shut. "Nope. I'm good."

"To be completely transparent, the only fantasies I've had about you over the past nine years involved pain and humiliation, but luckily I have an extensive catalog from high school to refer to." She smiled. "We'll try to fit in as many as we can before you have to report to training camp."

"Tell me one of them."

"One of my sex fantasies?"

He nodded, shifting in his wide leather seat.

"Right now?" She leaned in, all flustered.

"Yeah, rock star. Right now."

"Well. Okay." She sat all prim and proper, which looked ridiculous with all that platinum blonde hair and those shorts with knee-high socks. "So, there were a *lot* that took place in school. Especially under the bleachers. I pictured you running off the field after practice, your hair tousled, your eyes all hot and hungry. You'd find me waiting there, lift me off the ground, and just…kiss me. It pretty much ended right there, because I didn't know what kissing led to back then." She gave him a sly grin. "But I do now."

"What else?" He motioned for her to hurry up. "And let's kick it up a notch."

Her eyes glittered with humor. "Hm, well, there was one about oral sex…"

"Go on."

"I'd be sitting in Algebra II, which you know was like Mandarin Chinese to me, and I'd imagine getting on my knees between your legs, unbuttoning your jeans, and pulling out your cock. Licking it like a lollipop."

"We're definitely recreating that one." He tipped his head back, closing his eyes. There was nothing he could do to stop the flood of fierce desire rushing through him. He wanted to see those amber eyes gazing up at him with heat and lust, wanted that hot tongue on his dick. Wanted to feel her swallow while she had him at the back of her throat. "Fuck."

"You okay there, QB?"

"I'm going to need a minute."

"I have lots of other scenarios. Should we make a list?"

"Yeah, that won't be necessary."

The moment the jet landed, Cassian growled in her ear, "Tonight. Nine o'clock."

"Sounds good. You coming to my house?"

"Fuck, no. I'm not chatting with your parents. Just be at my house at nine. And don't bother with underwear."

In the air strip's lobby, the group hugged and shook hands with promises of doing another tour together. The others were being treated to a night at the fancy spa in Owl Hoot, including dinner with the Cavanaughs.

Cassian needed to get to camp. "All right, I'm out of here." He hitched a thumb toward the exit. "Dean's waiting for me."

"Me, too," Gigi said. "My sister's here. Take care, you guys." She gave Grant one more hug, before following Cassian out.

"You probably shouldn't walk out with me." He didn't need the paps snagging a picture of them together and then making up some story.

"We just went on the same tour, so it's not a big deal to walk outside together."

He reached the door and held it open for her. "I want to skip camp and go home with you right now."

On the sidewalk, her steps faltered, and he nearly crashed into her. She stared at a car waiting at the curb. She cut a hard look at him, her expression one of betrayal and accusation. "What's she doing here?"

In her white shorts and platform shoes, big sunglasses and hair worthy of a Texas parade, Amie leaned against his car. "I have no idea." He'd specifically told her not to come.

Everything soft and easy in her turned hard. "Cassian, so help me God, if you're fucking with me." She broke away from him.

Heat blistered across his skin, making him break out in a sweat. "Hey, hey." He reached for her arm to pull her back. "Stop. You know I'm not."

"Don't touch me like this. There're people all over the place."

"Dean's supposed to pick me up. I don't know why Amie came instead."

"Listen to me very carefully. If that woman has feelings for you...you'd better figure that out right now. If we have a shot at anything here, you have to draw some lines."

"She doesn't have feelings for me." He leaned in. "There's only one line, and it's already been drawn. There's you, and there's the rest of the world. Period."

She searched his eyes before looking away. "We should go. Before someone takes a picture of us."

"I'll see you tonight." He watched her hustle toward a black Land Rover with tinted windows. The passenger side window rolled down, revealing her sister, a world-famous chocolatier. Coco gave him a hard look. *I'm watching you.*

Yeah, well, watch me all you want. He'd make no mistakes with Gigi.

Pissed, he headed toward Amie.

As he approached, she raised an eyebrow. "Did I nail that one or what?"

"What're you doing here? Dean's supposed to pick me up." Even in a tiny air strip in Calamity, there was no privacy. It was impossible to control the images that got uploaded onto social media.

"I know, but we've got a problem, and he's handling it. So, I get to fill you in on everything you've missed in the last twelve hours." She started around to the driver's side of his gleaming Porsche Panamera Turbo—which he only got to drive a couple months out of the year, since he lived in Boston and Calamity, two places with some of the worst weather in the country.

"You drove my Porsche?"

"Well, I wasn't about to pick up Cassian Ellis in my Kia."

"Keys." He held up a hand, and she tossed them to him. Before lowering into the seat, he glanced over to find the Land Rover pulling away from the curb. His heart ached in that familiar way—of wanting her but not being able to have her. Not completely.

He got into the car and turned the ignition. "I told you this in Kansas, and I'll tell you again. I don't want us to be seen together. If Dean can't pick me up, I'll take a cab or rent a car. But I'm not risking another shot of us going viral." As he headed out of the parking lot, Amie watched him.

"What?" He wanted to check in with Gigi, but he'd have to wait.

"I just knew it."

"Knew what?"

"You and Gigi."

"There's nothing going on. She's here to visit her family." He was absolutely not talking to anyone about Gigi. Especially someone who wanted to be on a reality TV show.

"Oh, come on. I just saw the two of you together. You're into her, and you did something to piss her off."

"I piss everyone off."

"Uh, no. Just the opposite, actually. You make people happy. You make the guys feel proud of themselves, and you make women feel like everything they say is important —you make them feel special. It's just what you do. One week with the Lollipop…you worked your magic on her."

He wanted to slam the brakes and make things very clear, but he needed to get to camp. "We knew each other in high school. Her dad coached me. End of story. Now, what's the problem? Is it the Walker kid?"

"Bingo."

Apparently, fourteen-year-old Walker Lovett had brought a bad attitude to camp. Worse, he had strong leadership abilities—only, he used them for evil. In this first week, he'd snuck out of the dorm in the middle of the night, broke into the kitchen while the other campers were in their afternoon elective, and got his table to boycott dinner two nights ago by streaking around the fire road, before climbing the fence and jumping into the pool.

In the three years of running this camp, they'd never had a problem. The kids were grateful to have been chosen and worked their asses off. Sure, there were personality conflicts. That, they could handle. But this kid? They had no clue how to deal with him. "What's the latest?"

"Andre caught him in the main office at one in the morning with three other guys watching porn on my computer."

"Jesus."

"I know, right? But Dean's talking to him right now."

"What am I missing here—why is Dean talking to him and not you?" He kept a very clear division between his coaches and the staff. Amie and his security team handled all off-field matters—including discipline—so the lines with coaches didn't blur.

"I've dealt with everything so far, just like you wanted. But…he said some offensive things."

"Offensive? How?"

She let out a sigh. "During lunch today, I leaned over to set the water pitcher on his table. After I moved on, I heard him say something about my 'knockers' and how he'd like to do me 'doggy-style.'"

Anger rose like a vicious beast. "He's going home."

She patted his arm. "I get where you're coming from, but the thing is, I'm pretty sure home is really bad."

Right. Which was the point of hosting the camp. "Everything else he's done, I get. He's rebellious." *I was, too.* "But I can't allow him to talk to you like that. If I don't kick him out, it'll set a precedent with the other kids."

"That's why Dean's talking to him. We're giving him a hard consequence, something the other kids will see."

"What's the consequence?"

"He's going to serve meals and clear tables for the next three days." She played with the hem of her shorts. "The thing that really sucks is that he's an amazing player.

Andre's been working with him and said he's never seen a kid with better instincts. Football could be his ticket to a better life."

It was moments like this that he appreciated Amie. She was a cheerleader and had been a cast member on NFL Cheerleader, so she got a lot of bad press for being shallow or vain. But they didn't see the way she ran his camp or treated the kids. She had a good heart and worked her ass off. "It sounds like you've already handled it, but if it happens under my watch, I won't be nearly as understanding. I have zero tolerance for that kind of disrespect." He cut a glance at her. "I'm sorry he treated you like that."

She smiled softly. "I almost didn't want to tell you." She patted his thigh. "You're a good guy, Cassian."

Funny, he'd had thousands of hands on him over the course of his life. Slaps on the back, handshakes, seductive and sexual touches…but he only realized in this moment how much he didn't like it. People seemed to think they had access to him—all of him.

I do that, though.

He'd never thought of it that way before. He invited that access by being so friendly and flirty. He shifted his leg away, and she withdrew her hand.

He needed to be aware of that.

And he needed to be honest. He might be the quarterback of the Mavericks but that didn't mean he was public property. It was up to him to draw those lines.

Even if it meant pissing people off.

Cassian pocketed his keys and headed across the lawn. "I'll catch up with you later."

Amie pulled open the door to the office. "Let me know how it goes."

He gave her a wave. The crew had cleaned up the field from morning drills, but they'd left out a blocking sled and a couple stepover dummies. He snagged a flag off the grass and tossed it toward the shed. He'd have to talk to the guys about that.

The kids learned more than football here. They learned respect and independence. His coaches needed to model the right behavior.

As he crossed the grass, he breathed in the clean mountain air, took in the snow-crested peaks of the Teton Mountain Range. Damn, he loved it here. Even as a four-teen-year-old kid from New Jersey, he'd been in awe of this Wild West town surrounded by intimidating mountains and the bison that wandered onto the road, not giving a single fuck about travelers.

When he'd bought this property, he hadn't thought about teaching kids how to play football. He just knew he needed a place where he could be anonymous. A place where he could relax.

A place that had Gigi Cavanaugh.

He'd purchased the land with an LLC, so his name wasn't associated with it. So far, his privacy hadn't been violated. Calamity had a permanent population of about ten thousand, though it swelled to over a million during the ski and hiking seasons. A good number of residents were successful entrepreneurs and celebrities who appreci-ated the healthy outdoor lifestyle and wanted to get away from it all in a magnificent setting. People left them alone.

He could get a coffee here, and no one asked for his autograph.

The idea for the camp came a few years later. He'd

invited his offensive line out for a preseason retreat so they could bond and get in some specialized drills. The Bowie brothers, four local extreme athletes, ran a training facility just down the road, and it had everything an athlete could ever need to get in top shape.

He'd bought his teammates mountain bikes, and they did long distance swimming in the lake, but given that they played football, he'd made some accommodations on his land. They couldn't run plays in a sage-filled meadow.

He and Dean had been sitting on his deck one night, drinking beers and gazing up at the stars, when the vision came to him. Together, they'd brainstormed their dream training facility. Not just for their teammates, but for kids. Specifically, kids who had the talent and drive but not the access.

The next day he'd contacted a landscaper about designing a football field and a contractor about building a facility where he could house and feed young athletes. He'd only been hosting the camp for three years, but he didn't think there was anything better he could do with his time in the off-season.

The kids had four hours of training each morning and an hour of rest after lunch. In the afternoons, they hit the gym to focus on exercises for explosiveness and athleticism. And then, from three to five, they attended a mandatory life skills class. Cassian didn't call it "life skills," of course, because he knew how that would go over, but he knew the kinds of homes these kids came from. He told them the classes had to do with being a better ball player. And it was true.

But it was so much more.

The cooking class didn't just teach how to cook—it taught nutrition. The art classes connected them to the greater world outside their small communities, opened their eyes and hearts, and fostered cognitive development.

Today, the kids were in yoga. They thought it was just another way to make their bodies more agile for football, to avoid injury, but for Cassian, it was a way for them to learn self-care, to meditate, to find peace in the chaos of their lives.

This afternoon it was held in a shady portion of the yard behind the rec center.

As he came around the building, he heard the quiet, calming voice of the yoga instructor.

He also heard snickering. Quietly, he peered around the wall to find a group of boys at the back.

The instructor was doing dolphin pose, and one of the kids, said, "I'd tap that ass."

Walker Lovett. He was sure of it. Cassian strode out there and said, "Come with me."

The boy's eyes went wide when he saw who it was. Immediately, though, his features settled into a smirk. "Can't. I'm doing *yoga.*"

This time his friends didn't laugh. Probably because Cassian looked like he was two seconds away from losing it. "Now."

The kid laughed. "Fine. I hate this pussy shit anyhow."

Cassian couldn't speak yet. He'd been a difficult kid, so he understood about acting out. But he didn't—wouldn't —tolerate sexual harassment.

He led the kid across the field. Anger made him feel dangerous.

Breathe. To be effective, he needed to calm down.

"Nice of you to show up." Walker's voice broke the silence. "Isn't this *your* camp? Aren't you the reason we come here?"

"I hope you came here to take advantage of this once-in-a-lifetime opportunity to learn everything you can from pro football players." *Keep it together.* "Not many kids get the chance to work with Andre Jordan, the fourth overall pick in the draft and the league's leading rusher last season."

"Yeah, but I want to be a quarterback. I want to live in a mansion and drive sick cars and bang hot chicks."

That was it. Cassian stopped in the middle of the field, the afternoon sun forcing him to shield his eyes with a hand. "There's one week left of camp. Do you want to stay here?"

"Hell, yeah. I saw your sweet ride. The lady with the big tits was in it, and I—"

"Stop. Shut your mouth right now." He marshaled every ounce of self-discipline he possessed to keep from flying off the handle. "If you want to stay here, then you're going to have to abide by the rules. The first rule listed in the contract you signed was to treat everyone with respect."

"Whatever."

"Oh, it's definitely not 'whatever.' Disrespecting anyone here is a deal-breaker." His dead-serious tone made the kid's eyes go wide. "Ms. Meghan runs a yoga studio in town. She volunteers her time here because she cares. It means something to her to teach you guys how to keep your bodies flexible—not just to give you a better chance of making your school's team, but so you can make it in the brutal world of football. So, for you to disrespect her?" He shook his head, drawing in a tight breath.

"She couldn't even hear me."

Cassian gave him a look that said, *So?* "First, it's unacceptable. But secondly? Man to man? I can't even wrap my head around why you'd talk about a woman like that. She's not an object. She's not put on this earth to be your plaything. She's a human being with a heart and a soul, and for you to degrade her reflects badly on *you*—not her."

"She's got a hot body. Nothing wrong with pointing it out."

"I know you think you're a real badass to the other guys, but you're wrong. Those boys who sneak out with you? Laugh when you degrade the director of this camp who was bringing a pitcher of water to your table? They're laughing because you make them uncomfortable. They join your little escapades because they don't want to be the object of your ridicule. They don't respect you, they don't want to be you, and the minute camp ends, they're going to be relieved not to be around someone as destructive as you. Do you know why?"

"Stop talking. You're boring me."

It took everything he had, but Cassian ignored him. "Because they want to be here. They feel damn lucky they get to train with the best athletes in the world, people that will help them achieve whatever they want in life. Maybe they come from shitty homes, maybe their parents don't pay attention to them, but this camp, this opportunity, gives them hope and a pathway for a better life. They *need* that pathway."

"Yeah, okay. I get it. I'm a worthless piece of shit."

Ah, hell. I suck at this.

He had to get it right.

Needing a new tactic, Cassian gazed down at the bright green turf, breathing in the scent of freshly mown grass. "You know how I came to be a quarterback? I was in detention when Tyler Cavanaugh pulled me out. He asked me what I thought my future looked like. Beyond that moment, freshman year of high school, when my home life sucked and I was getting into trouble all the time. He wanted me to think ahead a couple years. He said, 'Are you going to graduate high school? Go to college? Are you going to drop out and work at a gas station? Sell drugs? Are you going to get some girl pregnant, go to prison?'" It had been a life-changing moment. He'd been so angry about losing his parents and being dumped with a family he barely knew. "So, I'm going to ask you the same question. What's your future look like?"

"I already told you. I'm going to be you. With your fancy cars and your mansion and your hot chicks."

Nothing excused the way this boy talked about women, but every time he referred to them in a degrading way, in association with the life of a professional football player, Cassian felt a prick of guilt. Whether he wanted to be a role model or not, he was one.

And, if that's what my life looks like to this kid, I'm doing a shit job of representing it.

Offering this camp: good. Headlines about threesomes: bad.

"Okay, but *how* are you going to get to be me? Are you going to train every day? Eat right. Are you going to sacrifice partying with your friends? No drugs, no alcohol? Because that's what I did with the once-in-a-lifetime opportunity Tyler Cavanaugh gave me. I didn't want to make a single misstep, because I didn't want to be a high school dropout. I didn't want to wind up in prison or somebody's baby daddy. I wanted more. Mr. Cavanaugh had me set goals. The first was to get on the high school football team. Not easy, because we already had a quarterback, a kid who'd been waiting three years to start."

"You're boring me. I'd rather take a yoga class than listen to you. At least I'll get a view of tits and ass."

"Okay, we're done here." Cassian hustled toward the dormitory.

The kid kept up with him. "Thank you." His tone said, *That's what I'm saying.* "Can you get Amie to bring me some snacks? I'm going to be in the game room."

He held open the door. "I'll help you pack your bags."

The kid looked shocked. "My what?"

"Your bags. You're leaving."

"You can't kick me out. I didn't do anything wrong."

"You're disrespectful. That breaks the contract. Besides, you clearly don't want to be here, so it's time for you to go."

He didn't enter the building. "I'm not going home."

Looks like I found his vulnerability. "Look, I get it. I had a bad attitude, too. My parents died when I was fourteen, and I got tossed into a strange home. So, I get that you feel powerless. You come here and act like you're some badass. Though, hot tip, the other guys don't want to break into the office and watch porn. They can do that anywhere. They want to learn how to play ball so they can be a badass on the field. They'd rather get girls by being the jock than by having to force themselves on them."

"I didn't force myself on anyone."

He got up close, and in his most menacing voice said, "Let me tell you something. The next step after talking about them like they're objects is handling them like they are. I will not expose the women in my life to anyone who might be a threat." He pulled out his phone and hit Amie's speed dial.

She picked up on the first ring. "Hey, what's up?"

"Walker Lovett is leaving camp."

"Oh, shit. What happened?"

"I need you and Bill to meet us in his dorm room. I'll have his travel plans arranged by the time you get there."

"Are you sure? We've never sent anyone home before."

He held the kid's gaze as he answered. "It isn't fair to the other thirty-nine athletes who want to make the most out of their time here, and his behavior toward women is unacceptable, so yes, I'm sure."

Chapter Twelve

"Did Lulu tell you her good news?" Her mom set the platter of roasted vegetables on the table before sitting down.

"She did." Gigi helped herself to a piece of cod. "I'm excited for her." Her Cordon Bleu-educated sister had just been named executive chef of a famous restaurant on Maui.

With a foul look, her dad handed Gigi a bowl of feta cheese cubes in exchange for the Greek olives. "I'm not."

Her mom gave him an indulgent grin. "It's not that far."

"It's a six-hour flight." Her dad had retired when Gigi was fifteen, and he'd been very involved in their lives. He wasn't a huge fan of the empty nest.

"And Paris was a ten-hour flight." Joss Montalbano might no longer be a supermodel, but she still turned heads everywhere she went with her long legs, stunning beauty, and thick, healthy hair. Now, though only fifty-three, her dark hair had gone silver. She liked to say it was hereditary, but Gigi knew her mom had started graying after Stella left. They were a super close family, so the youngest daughter taking off like that…well, it had been traumatic. "We just gained four hours." She flicked an amused look to Gigi.

"You've got one kid nearby." Gigi tossed an olive at her younger sister.

"Thank God for my Coco," her dad said. "Did you bring me any chocolates?"

"Of course." Five years ago, Coco's life had taken a sharp turn. After discovering her college boyfriend's terrible deceit, she'd taken off for Vegas and had a crazy one-night stand that left her pregnant—and she'd never gotten the guy's name. Now, she was a single mother and running Coco's Chocolates, a popular store right in the center of town. "I brought you a sampler of some ideas I'm playing with."

"Like?" her dad asked.

"Like a black sesame passion-fruit truffle, which I painted to look like an Easter egg. I have a tangerine jam and thyme dark chocolate in the shape of a skull and painted silver. I've got one with honey caramel, bee's pollen, and egg custard cream in the center."

"Ah, crap." Her dad pushed back his chair and stalked into the kitchen. "I can't wait."

The women all grinned.

"So, what's your plan, sweetie?" her mom asked Gigi.

"Right now, I'm just going to play it by ear." She'd told her family she'd come to Calamity to spend time with them while waiting to hear from Clean Beatz. She didn't want to lie but seeing the bombshell cheerleader leaning against Cassian's car had rattled her. Which only served to expose an enormous fault line in their relationship.

She didn't trust him. Not all the way.

So, she didn't see the point in getting her family all riled up—not until she and Cassian knew what they were doing. Because truthfully? She really, really didn't want to go back to the emotional roller coaster of high school. This time around, she had much more at stake. *My career.*

"Well, I'm happy about that. I can book us a spa day. We can get in some good hikes. Hey, we've talked about renting a place on Whidbey Island. We could do that this week."

"Mom, no. I've got three weeks left before I find out if Dale's going to drop us or not. I'm going to use that time to write some songs."

Her dad came back into the dining room. "Unbelievable." He kissed Coco's temple. "You're a wizard." Before sitting down, he set a chocolate skull next to his wife's plate. "She made that."

Her mom picked it up, marveling at its glittery silver artistry. "It's fabulous, sweetheart. I can't wait to try it after dinner." She reached for her daughters' hands. "It's so good to have both of you here." This time, her smile was strained.

No one addressed the elephant in the room. What could they say? *Stella will be back one day? We'll be a whole family again?* There was no guarantee that would ever happen.

She couldn't stand to see her mom in so much pain, so she said, "I've decided not to sit around and wait for Dale to determine my fate, so I pitched a solo record to her."

"Good for you," Coco said. "That's awesome."

"I love that idea," her mom said. "What did she say?"

"I'm still waiting to hear back."

Her dad seemed distracted with constructing his dinner. Where he was a steak and potatoes kind of guy, her mom liked a little of this and a little of that. When she cooked, her dinners consisted of various interesting dishes that she liked to nibble.

Her dad didn't know what to do with it, so he constructed them into a meal he could understand.

"Give me that." Grabbing his plate, her mom made a bottom layer of roasted vegetables, added chunks of feta, tossed a couple olives on, and then rested a piece of cod on top. She handed it back.

"I'm grilling tomorrow night," her dad grumbled.

"So, you're making a demo?" her mom asked. "Do you have enough material?"

Gigi set down her fork. "I've got notebooks filled with half-written songs. Hopefully, there's something worthwhile in them."

"There is," Coco said.

"She's right," her mom said. "We've heard you composing and playing them over the years."

"I'd have to change the lyrics, though, since I'd still be a Lollipop." Their fans didn't want to hear about broken hearts and lost dreams. They wanted to feel happy. "But I think I can do it. I'd like to try."

"You think Dale will go for it?" Her mom popped an olive into her mouth.

"It could go either way. I'm hoping she'll see it as a way to save her label from the Lollipops blowing up, but she might just want to wash her hands of us and put together a new girl band. We'll see. In any event, that's what I'll be doing while I'm home. Writing new songs."

"You could do that in LA." Her mom gave her a knowing look. "Any reason in particular you're doing it here?"

Okay, so they already knew. "You obviously know why."

"We wondered," her mom said. "Now we know."

"So, how'd the tour go?" her dad asked.

Gigi cut a look to her sister. *Classic Dad. Avoiding the emotional stuff.* "It was the best one so far." She hadn't wanted to talk about it tonight, but since the truth was out, she might as well lay it all on the table. "Want to know why?"

Her dad looked up from his cod, interested. Totally oblivious.

Are you kidding me? She'd spent a week with Cassian, and her dad wasn't even slightly worried that she'd found out what had gone down in high school?

Her mom's uncomfortable—maybe even remorseful expression—said she sure was.

"Because I threw a balled-up napkin at Macy Guthrie's head."

"You what?" Her mom was not amused.

Coco raised a hand, and Gigi slapped it. "That woman's a stuck-up bitch."

"Coco," her mom said.

"Mom, she gives you these tight smiles, like somehow she's better than you because she won an award? You're an amazing photographer and interior designer, a kickass wife and mother, and you're a world-class philanthropist. She's got no business sticking her nose up at you."

Her mom got up, wrapped an arm around Coco's shoulder and kissed her cheek. "I love you, my fierce angel."

"I know why you'd say that, but she's actually pretty cool," Gigi said. "At first, she barely even acknowledged us."

"See?" Coco said.

"But as soon as I hit her in the head, she loosened up, and then we all had so much fun together. Kevin's absolutely amazing. He should get a raise. He works nonstop, and we hardly had any snafus." She didn't want to ruin dinner—she hadn't planned on bringing it up at all—but everyone at this table had to be wondering what had happened between her and Cassian.

She poked the tines of her fork into the fish. "And the kids and their families? Their spirits amaze me. You'd think there'd be self-pity and anger, you know? But they're all just warriors. I swear these tours are a reality check."

"Amen to that," her mom said.

"You guys have done a really good thing with Dreams Come True." As frustrated as she was at them, she needed to let them know that. "I'm really proud to have you as my parents."

"Aw, sweetheart," her mom said. "We're proud of you, too."

"How'd Cassian do?" her dad asked.

Oh, my God, are you serious? Throwing out his name like it doesn't land with a thousand tiny pin pricks? She looked at Coco with wide eyes and shook her head. The man was absolutely clueless.

"Cassian did great." She heard the bite in her words, but her dad didn't.

He remained focused on his dinner. "I figured he would. I don't normally send someone who's in the middle of all that tabloid attention, but I knew he'd take this tour seriously." He looked up with a smile. "And they love him. Everywhere he goes…they just love him."

Yeah, about that? Remember when I loved him, and you treated it like a stupid little crush?

How could her dad act like he'd played no part in their story?

Okay, calm down. You can talk to him later, privately.

"That seventeen-year-old from Salina? Cassian rented a convertible mustang for him. Don't tell anyone, but he let him drive it in an empty parking lot. And he was incredibly patient with everyone who wanted autographs. He ran out of jerseys on the third day, because he literally handed them out to everyone who approached him, and he had more overnighted."

Her dad's fork scraped across the plate. "Glad to hear it. He's a good kid. He just…"

"Needs a good woman," her mom said with a teasing grin. "Like you did?"

"Well, of course," Gigi said. "Cassian *had* a good woman." So much for not ruining a family dinner. "He had me."

Her dad's head jerked up, and he looked from his wife to his daughter.

"There he is," Coco said.

"In fact…" Gigi set her napkin on the table. She was done eating. "Cassian and I had some good conversations."

Her dad lowered his hands under the table and rubbed his thighs. "Okay." He faced her. "If you're looking for an apology, you won't get one. I don't regret what I did."

"Even after you saw how it ruined me?"

"I didn't expect that…reaction. And I almost changed my mind…but I—"

"We." Her mom reached for him, and they clasped hands on the table. "I know you want to keep me out of it, but we made the decisions together, so we take the hits together." She turned to Gigi. "Honey, it gutted us to see you devastated like that. I can't tell you how many nights we lay awake in bed and considered the problem from every angle."

"*The* problem? Mom, it was *my* problem. I was seventeen. Even if I made the wrong decision, it should've been mine to make."

Her mom looked tortured. "You would have gone to Michigan."

"I absolutely would have. Do I know for sure that Cassian and I would still be together? No, but we would've made our own way through life. You intervening...can't you see? It was just wrong."

"You could only see up until that moment, senior year of high school," her dad said. "But I had nearly three decades on you. And I knew college ball at that level. It's tough. It's serious. He wouldn't have been able to give you the time..." Her dad shook his head, like he'd gotten off-track. "The bottom line is that we believed you'd lose yourself in his career."

"Or maybe, instead of becoming a Lollipop," Coco said. "She'd be writing and performing her own music."

"High school relationships almost never work when they move onto college," her mom said. "They just don't. The twenties are for self-discovery. That's when you learn to live on your own."

"A lot of temptations, when you're the quarterback," her dad said.

"That's not...God, you're missing the point. He worshipped you, Dad. It wasn't about football—it was never about *football*. You were the first person to pay attention to him."

"Honey, he had a father until he was fourteen," her mom said.

"His dad worked on Wall Street. He hardly ever saw his parents. But *you* gave him attention. You taught him to be a man. And he felt like he owed you."

"Sweetheart—" her mom said.

She got up. "No. I get that you thought you were doing the right thing, but I'm telling you, you were wrong. You should've talked to me, told me your concerns."

"Gigi." Her mom got up, too.

But she was already halfway out of the room. She stopped, though, and got a hold of herself, because she had something to say. "You think the course of my life would've changed if I'd followed Cassian, but *you* changed the course of my life." The truth of it all weighed heavily. "I don't think you understand what you did to us."

She grabbed her purse. She needed to get out of the house.

She needed Cassian.

"You think I screwed up?" Cassian sat on a chaise by the resort's indoor pool.

All around him, his teammates partied. Some gathered around a table with booze and snacks, while others played around in the water.

"You've got to stop beating yourself up." Dean tipped back his beer. "The situation's not black or white. Don't you think you'd be just as worked up if you'd let him stay? Look, the kid's a distraction, and it's not fair to the others who want to take advantage of their time here. And, not a small point, we've got to have zero tolerance for sexual harassment." Dean let out a breath. "All that said, I obviously don't like that he's going home to the environment that created him."

"That's what's grinding through me. I got hot so fast… I should've at least tried to work with him."

Dean sat up, swinging his legs off his chaise and planting his feet on the ground. "You started this camp because you wanted to give kids hope, a way out of their shitty environments. Your goal isn't to rehabilitate them. Therapy isn't even in our wheelhouse."

That's true. And that made him feel better about his decision.

"Hey, you guys." Amie strode through the doors in a short, white coverup. "Whew."

"How'd it go?" She'd gone with Bill to get Walker checked in and settled at the hotel.

She dropped her purse and water bottle on a table and whipped off her dress, leaving her in a bright pink bikini. "It was one of the toughest things I've ever had to do." She headed straight for the Jacuzzi and turned on the jets.

Worried about the boy, Cassian got up. "Did he apologize?" Because if he had, Cassian would reconsider. Maybe give him another chance.

"Oh, God, no." Unscrewing the bottle, she tipped her head back and drank. The water rushed out, spilling down her chin. She laughed, arching her back, one hand brushing the droplets off her chest. "He talked about calling his lawyer. Spoiler alert: he doesn't have one." Sitting on the edge of the tub, she stirred the water with her legs. "He had some things to say about you."

"I don't need to hear them." Cassian pulled up a chair next to the Jacuzzi. "Did you feel threatened by him at all?"

"If you're looking to justify your decision, forget it."

She slid into the bubbling water. "He's been trouble since day one."

Dean came up beside him, phone in hand. "You gonna be okay?"

Cassian figured Dean wanted to check in with his girlfriend. "Yeah, sure. Thanks. I'll see you in the morning." Normally, Dean stayed with him at his house, but with Gigi coming over at nine, he'd gotten Dean a room at the hotel with the other guys.

Gigi. A zing of anticipation shot down his spine. He couldn't wait to see her.

Forty-six more minutes.

With a wave, Dean took off.

His teammates laughed and talked, oblivious to the situation with Walker. Cassian stared into the bubbling water. "I just don't know what he's going home to."

Amie patted the side of the tub. *Get in.*

Nope. He shook his head, not interested in being alone with her in a Jacuzzi.

Leaning forward, she tilted her head and pulled the hair away from her neck. A strand got caught in the ties, and she winced. "I think you have to stay in your lane. Your job is to run this camp, not save children. It isn't fair to the other campers, who're working their butts off, to have their one and only session with pro athletes ruined by Walker Lovett."

"I don't know his circumstances, but they can't be good."

"You've got one week left. That's not enough time to fix him." With a pained expression, she struggled to untie her bikini top. "Oh, forget it." She wiggled her fingers. "I got acrylic nails on my lunch hour, and I literally can't untie a bow. Can you do me a favor real quick? I just need to get my hair out."

"Yeah, sure." He stepped into the tub, resting a knee on the edge. The hot water felt good. "Lift as much of your hair as you can."

She tilted her head, gathering her hair. "If it helps, just know that he got a lot of support this week. From me, Andre, Dean. We all tried to talk to him, to help him, but he just wouldn't back down."

"I wish I hadn't lost my temper." Had he, though? He'd been pretty calm around the kid. Calm but intractable. "Or that I'd found the right words." He tugged on the tie, and then pulled the lock of hair free. "I feel like maybe I should talk to him one more time." What could it hurt to go over there and give him one more chance?

"I wish there was something I could say to make you feel better about this, but I can't. All I can say is you've got thirty-nine other kids who are here and ready to learn, and Walker's caused a lot of tension in the group. I'll bet anything, with him gone, the spirit of the whole camp will change." She glanced up at him with a soft smile.

"Maybe. I hope you're right."

Gigi: **I'm here**.

In her tank top, shorts, and cowboy boots, Gigi stood on Cassian's porch shivering. *Should've changed before I ran out of the house.* Living in LA, she'd forgotten how chilly it got in the mountains at night.

Gigi: **Open the door. I'm freezing!**

There wasn't a single light on in his house, and it was too dark to go exploring around back.

She checked the time on her phone. *8:20.* Forty minutes early. He wasn't home yet.

Gigi: **I know, I'm early!**

He said he liked to eat dinner and hang out with his guys, make sure they had everything they needed, be there to listen to complaints, so he was probably still at the hotel with them. She'd go there. She shot off a text.

Gigi: **Is it okay if I come to the hotel? LMK if that's not cool**.

How serious was she going to take this secrecy thing? She needed to hide their relationship from the public but from their friends and family? That would make it way too difficult. And they had enough obstacles.

Besides, if they were going to be together, she'd like to get to know his friends. It should be safe, since he'd booked the entire hotel for his guys.

Of course, he'd done that in Aspen and look what happened there.

So…what should I do? The frosty air made her breath come out in little white puffs, and she rubbed her arms. She could go home…but she wasn't ready to see her parents yet. And waiting in the car with the heater on didn't make sense, not for forty minutes.

You know what? She'd just go to the hotel. Meet the guys.

Yep. That's what I'll do.

Gigi entered the lobby of the Owl Hoot Spa and Resort, designed to recreate a hotel from a late eighteen-hundreds Wild West town. She stood there for a moment and took it all in. Gleaming brass banisters led the way up a grand staircase carpeted in red. Paneled walls in a rich, dark wood and bronze sconces gave the huge space a warm, cozy feeling.

The best part, though, was the costumed actors playing the roles of gunslingers, madams, and genteel guests. It was magical.

She texted Cassian again.

Gigi: **I'm here. Where are you?**

Since he'd booked the entire hotel, he could be anywhere. Heading for the reception desk, she stopped herself. If she asked for Cassian, the clerk would immediately associate the Lollipop with the Bad Boy Quarterback. *Yeah, that's a no-go.*

She should have thought about that before racing over here.

Okay, walk around and try to find him or go home?

When she thought of seeing her parents...that was a hard no.

Because her dad didn't care. She'd expected some kind of remorse, some...*guilt.* But no, he'd made his decision, and that was that. He'd washed his hands of the whole thing.

He just couldn't grasp that she and Cassian had a relationship just as deep and...and *essential* as what he and his wife had.

So what if we were a decade younger?

She needed to see Cassian. Talk to him. Because he was the only person in the world who could understand what she was feeling.

He'd likely be in a group area, so she'd start with the spa. It held a fitness center, sauna, and the pool. Following the brass plate signs, she made her way down a thickly carpeted hallway.

Wheels spun and pulleys rotated, so she peered into the gym, but no Cassian. She kept going toward the pool.

Tomorrow, she'd talk to her parents. Running out like that was juvenile. She would have a real and honest conversation with them, and then put the whole thing behind her once and for all.

The closer she got, the louder the splashing and shouting. Sounded like they were having a blast. Cassian was a good guy, making sure his teammates had fun while they volunteered for his camp.

God, she couldn't wait to see him. She felt ridiculously excited. She didn't know how she could stop herself from running into his arms and kissing him right there in front of everyone. Literally the only thing stopping her was the sharp reminder of the Aspen fiasco.

That could not happen to her. It would take just one questionable picture to hit the tabloids for Dale to drop her. And then what would she have?

A bad reputation.

Two very large men pushed open the door and came out of the pool area with towels around their waists, their big feet in rubber slides.

As one of them held the door open for her, he stared a little too long, before breaking into a huge grin. "You're the Lollipop."

"I am. Hi." She offered her hand. "Gigi Cavanaugh."

"Paul Krunkowski. But they call me Krunk. My sister loves you, man."

My sister. She was grateful for her audience, she truly was. But…oh, how she craved to be taken seriously as an artist. "I'd be happy to send her some swag, if you want to leave her contact information with Cassian."

"For real?" He laughed, like he'd just won the lottery. "That'd be awesome."

The other guy said, "You looking for someone?"

"Cassian, actually."

"He's in the Jacuzzi." They held the door open for her.

"Thanks, guys," she said, as she passed through. The air was humid and reeked of chlorine, but she didn't care. She just wanted to see him.

Where is he? He wasn't with the guys sitting around the table. He wasn't in the pool.

And then she heard low voices. Laughter.

In the corner of the room, she found a Jacuzzi. Two bodies. A woman in a bikini with her back to a man in board shorts.

Cassian.

And that blonde hair? The breasts spilling out of the skimpy top? Amie, for sure.

The shock of it sent her reeling.

Cassian, shirtless, knelt on the edge of the Jacuzzi, his hands on the back of Amie's neck. She was lifting her mass of blonde hair, the ends wet and clinging to her tan skin.

Anxiety had a grip so tight on her brain that she couldn't make sense of what was going on. Logic told her it wasn't bad. Cassian wouldn't cheat on her.

It was just…if there was nothing going on between them, why was he always so comfortable…so intimate with that woman?

Gigi moved closer, trying to overhear their conversation.

Was something going on between them? That would make Cassian a fucking liar.

Seeing her, Amie twisted around. "Hey, girl." There wasn't even a hint of cattiness in her voice. Not even the slightest sense the woman was trying to make her jealous. Nothing even possessive.

But Gigi only had eyes for Cassian.

He shot to his feet, as if she'd aimed a gun at him. "Gigi."

"All right, I'm out of here." Amie stood up, water cascading down her voluptuous body. She was every inch the sexy cheerleader. "I'll see you tomorrow." The woman didn't even cover herself with a towel, just grabbed a white cover up and slid her feet into leather sandals. As Amie passed her, she gave a little smile. "'Night."

Cassian climbed out of the Jacuzzi and reached for a towel. "Hey. Surprised to see you here."

"I'll bet."

He looked defeated. "It's not what it looked like."

"Do you always end your day in a Jacuzzi with Amie? Murmuring sweet little nothings in her ear?"

"No. Today, some shit went down at camp." He gestured to the door. "Dean left a minute ago." He had none of his usual confidence. "You can ask any of the guys."

"That would be a really crappy way to start a relationship, don't you think? Me checking your story with your friends?"

"Well, you're not trusting me right now."

"Would you trust me if you came to my parent's house and found me in the Jacuzzi with a hard-bodied dude that you'd already seen me snuggle with?"

"I've never snuggled with Amie, but yes, I'd trust you. That's not to say I'd like it."

"Well, I more than don't like it. Know why? Because

your explanation makes it a hundred times worse. You had a bad day, and it was *Amie* who comforted you? In a bikini?"

If it was possible to be patient and exasperated at the same time…Cassian nailed it. As much as he wanted to ease her concerns, he seemed one hundred percent convinced there was no problem. "She wasn't comforting me. I've been worried about a decision I made. She was part of it, so I was discussing it with her."

"In the Jacuzzi. Half-naked."

He drew in a deep breath, stroking his jaw. "I feel like shit, okay? I don't like that you walked in here and saw that, but you have to know there's nothing going on between me and Amie."

She took a step closer. "What I just saw? That *is* something going on."

"This afternoon, for the first time since I started this camp, I sent a kid home. I've been second-guessing myself ever since. Amie walked in not even ten minutes ago, and she wanted to chill out after a stressful day. Her hair got stuck in the ties behind her neck—"

"Oh, my God. Do you even hear yourself? You're making it worse. The problem isn't whether you and Amie were having a romantic moment, but the fact that you get caught in these moments with her at all. And not just her, but with other women. This isn't a one-off thing. How do you not see this?"

"My focus was on sending a kid back to a bad family situation. She asked me to help her out, so I did. I don't see the problem."

"You can't be this clueless. Trust me, she wants something from you. I can tell you from experience, because I have long hair, and it's gotten caught in my ties, too, but

I've never needed a big, strong man to help me fix it. You see what I mean?"

"I do." He gazed down at his bare feet. After a moment, he shook his head. "All I can tell you is I know when women are hitting on me, and Amie's never made a move."

"*That* was a move. Striking a pose against your car outside the air strip was a move. Snuggling with you on an airplane is a move. I'm a woman. I know."

"She has a boyfriend. They've been together a long time. He's one of the reasons she got kicked off the reality show. He's in IT, not a football player, so that made her less interesting."

"Okay." Hitching her purse higher on her shoulder, she turned to go. "Have a super great night." She strode away.

"No." He said it firmly.

She whipped around. "Excuse me?"

"I don't care how long it takes to make me understand where you're coming from, you don't walk away." He came up to her. "We only have a few weeks before life pulls us in separate directions, so every minute counts. How we fight, how we work things out, is going to determine whether we make it. Look, I'm not some boy with a crush who's going to ask 'how high' every time you tell me to jump." He looked exhausted but not defeated. "I'm a man with my own experiences and perspectives, but you never need to question my motivations when it comes to you. Do you understand that?"

She knew he didn't want Amie or anyone else. "I do. But this thing with Amie is not going to work for me."

"I understand, but you need to hear me when I say I don't see her like that, and I never will. If I'd never found you again, I still wouldn't have a sexual or romantic relationship with her. Okay?"

"Yeah, okay." She believed him, she did. And he really did seem down about sending a camper home. "As long as you hear *me*. I don't trust her intentions, and if you continue to be oblivious to them, that's going to be a deal-breaker." She dumped her purse on a nearby table. "You want to tell me what happened today?"

"Are we good?"

She pulled out a chair, its legs scraping on the concrete. "I'll be honest with you. I don't know what we are. I just think we've got enough issues going against us, we don't need to add Amie's shenanigans. There's a part of me that still wants to keep my distance."

"Yeah, I know that, and I'm working on it."

"I believe you, which is why I'm still here. For the *other* part, the one that feels like you're the one for me. The only one."

He sat across from her, gripping her thighs. "I am."

This man. She found his passion irresistible. Still... "Even if you are the only one for me, it doesn't mean we're going to be together."

They sat so close their knees touched. "Amie doesn't know about us. She thinks I'm single, so she's not worried about boundaries. If you want, I can tell her." He gave her a searching look. *Is that what you want?*

She shook her head. "I don't trust her."

"But you can trust me." He reached for her hands.

As much as she wanted to believe him, his words couldn't erase what she'd walked in on. Not tonight. "I'm tired. I think I'm just going to go home." She got up. "We'll talk tomorrow."

"Guys." His deep voice quieted the enormous room. "Thanks for a great day. I'll see you in the morning."

They waved and called out to him—the genuine smiles making it obvious how much they liked him—but he was already leading her out the door.

"You don't need to walk me to my car."

"I'm not." With his clothes balled in one hand, he followed her across the lobby. Outside, his skin immediately pebbled, but he didn't seem to notice. "We've only got a few weeks together, and I'm not wasting any of it. We don't have to talk about anything—you can watch a movie or go to sleep—whatever you want, but I want to be with you." They stepped out into the chilly evening. "Will you come home with me?"

She paused on the wooden planks of Owl Hoot's boardwalk and took in this strong, determined, incredibly sweet and generous man and knew without a shadow of a doubt that she had no choice but to be with him. "Yeah. I'll come home with you."

Chapter Thirteen

GIGI HAD NEVER BEEN INSIDE CASSIAN'S HOUSE before. Her parents had a gorgeous home, but they'd decorated it slowly, over time, with things they'd found on their travels. Light wood floors, bright and interesting textiles on the walls, comfortable furniture. The Cavanaugh home was comfortable, eclectic, and fascinating. Every single piece of furniture or art was unique with an interesting backstory.

Cassian's house...on the outside it looked like a mansion. But inside, it was like the world's most exclusive frat house. He had a massive pool table in the formal dining room, vintage pinball machines against the walls in the living room, and a bar that took up one whole wall.

"Is this your house or the Mavericks' game room?"

Turning on a lamp, he grinned. "I had about six guys with me the day I went house hunting. This was the last place we saw. Bought it on the spot."

"And furnished it with toys."

He leaned against a wall, arms folded across his stomach. "When I was a kid, we lived in a ranch-style house walking distance from the subway that took my parents across the river to Wall Street. It was a nice, clean, working-class neighborhood, but I went to school in the city—with the rich kids. When I'd go to their homes, I'd be in awe of their toys. I spent a lot of time alone, and I'd fantasize about having a house filled with cool stuff."

"And now that you have it, do you use any of it?"

He hunched a shoulder. "When the guys are here, I do." He pushed off the wall, moving toward her.

Excitement shot down her spine, as it always did. His potent masculinity, his confidence and powerful physique, his charm and genuinely caring spirit...she could fall so hard for this man.

And he could crush her.

He must've picked up on her hesitation, because his smile faltered. "Come with me. I want to change."

Dammit. What am I doing?

Finding them canoodling in the pool, right after seeing Amie leaning against his car that afternoon? All kinds of warning bells were going off in her head.

I should just go. I'm not ready for this.

But her feet didn't move. She watched him stride across the living room, all confidence and strength, and she wanted him. She just did.

He stopped. "You coming?"

His earnestness did her in. She *had* to give him a chance. "Yeah." Dropping her tote by the door, she followed him into the massive, gorgeous kitchen. "Wow. No wonder you like to cook." Rich cherry cabinets, terra cotta tile floors, gleaming expanses of black granite, and hanging copper pots gave the room a warm, inviting feeling. "My sisters would go nuts in here."

"How are they?"

"I don't know if you've heard, but Lulu's leaving her sous chef job in Paris to run her own kitchen in Maui, so that's amazing. And Coco just found out she's providing chocolate for the Oscar swag bags again. So, my sisters are still my heroes. My mom, of course, already has her only grandkid in some special sleep-over camp. It's always go-go-go in the Cavanaugh house." She liked that he knew enough not to ask about Stella.

Because she had no answers and wondered if she ever would.

In the laundry room, he untied his board shorts and jerked them down his hips. Kicking them up, he caught them and tossed them into the machine. With that tight, round, bare ass on display, he leaned over to pull clean clothes out of the dryer.

He was so hot. She wanted to get her hands on all those muscles, that firm, smooth skin. Wanted to squeeze those ass cheeks, sink her teeth into one.

She wanted to drop to her knees and lick him until he turned hard.

He stepped into pajama bottoms. "How'd it go with your parents?"

Way to kill the mood. She had to grin. If he only knew what she'd been thinking.

Throwing on a waffled Henley, he headed back into the kitchen. "Something to drink?"

"No, I'm good. It didn't go well. But, now that I've had some distance, I feel kind of bad. I may have over-reacted."

"Wait, what am I missing? What happened?" He filled a glass with water, took her hand, and led her into the living room.

"I told them I knew what they'd done to break us up,

and my dad couldn't have cared less. It was the most traumatic thing in my life, and he acted like it was nothing. Like…it happened, move on."

"Well, it's new information to you. He's had a decade to make peace with his choice."

Well, if that didn't just nail it. "You're exactly right."

"Your parents were in a tough spot, and they made a decision."

"That's the thing. It was *my* decision to make. I was eighteen."

"Technically, we were seventeen."

"But my dad *manipulated* you. He used your gratitude, your *loyalty*, to keep us apart." She sat on the couch, curling her legs under her. "I mean, if they'd showed the slightest regret or guilt, I might've been okay. But they were just so sure they'd done the right thing."

He set his water glass on a coaster on the table and sat down beside her. "If it helps, your dad said something to me once. We were talking about what happened after he turned his life around. He said he'd have these terrible moments when a memory would slam him. He couldn't escape it, until your mom reminded him that the past is dead and gone. It only exists if you keep it alive through shame and guilt. He said he'd decided right then that, if he was going to make this new life for himself, he had to let go of the choices he'd made before he met Joss. And I think when your dad makes a decision…"

"Yes, absolutely. That's part of his addictive nature. When he embraces something, he goes all-in. And you're exactly right. He made peace with his choice a long time ago. Still…" She knew she sounded petulant. "I just hate how they reduced my feelings to some stupid crush. Like, on a scale of one to ten, they decided my feelings for you hit a three. So, it was okay to break us up."

He moved closer and lifted her legs across his lap. "We were never together. We hid our feelings from *each other*, so how could they possibly know?"

He was right about that. "Um, because I didn't get out of bed for a week. I went through the motions for a solid three months. That should've been their first clue."

"Yeah, but that probably reinforced their decision, right? They figured, if you'd followed me to Michigan, and we'd broken up, you'd have dropped out."

"Would we have?"

"Broken up? Never."

She loved how he answered with such certainty. "I wish I'd known back then what you'd felt for me."

"I can't change the past, but I have you here with me right now." He stroked her skin. "And I'll do everything in my power to protect us." He cut her a look. "You never have to worry about me with other women. There's never going to be anyone else for me but you."

She didn't doubt that. She just wished he could see how Amie was playing him. Leaning forward, she scraped her fingers through his hair. He closed his eyes, the tension easing. "So, what happened today? You kicked out a camper?"

"We've got a difficult kid this session. The guys say he's a phenom. Really strong, great instincts. He's done some good work during the drills, but the rest of the time, he rebels. He's snuck out of the dorm in the middle of the night, broken into the kitchen, and watched porn in Amie's office."

"Sounds like he needs some guidance. Maybe you

could give him actual leadership roles. Turn it in a positive direction."

Color seeped into his cheeks. "That would've been a great idea."

She sensed his tension. "Except?"

"Except he's said some pretty scary things about women. At lunch the other day, Amie was setting a pitcher down on the table, and he talked about her knockers, about wanting to do her 'doggie-style.'"

She stiffened, the shock of it traveling through her. "Oh, my God. How old is he?"

"Fourteen."

"Do you know anything about his family?"

"See, the thing is, we have to choose the kids carefully. In order for everyone to get the most out of the program, we need kids who can meet the physical requirements, who have good grades, and who don't have a record of disciplinary problems. We're going into tough neighborhoods, the ones where kids don't have many opportunities, and so we meet the families before we offer scholarships."

"What were his parents like?"

"We met his aunt. She seemed genuinely invested in him. We didn't see any red flags, but now we're kicking ourselves for not digging deeper into the parents. The fact that they didn't come to the meeting, I guess that *was* a red flag."

"Maybe the aunt's raising him?"

"No, his parents are listed on the form." He tugged on the hem of her shorts. "In any event, I've notified his aunt and bought him a plane ticket."

"You don't seem sure you made the right choice."

"I'm not. Especially since you just gave me a great suggestion. Something I didn't even think of, since I was too busy lecturing him. What kid gets anything out of a damn lecture?"

"But we're talking about a boy who has no respect. Not to women, your program, or authority."

"That's exactly right."

"I mean, even if he's mimicking what he hears at home, he still can't talk about women or behave that way."

"No, he can't. But if I send him home…"

"He's going home in a week anyhow."

"Yeah. I know." But he didn't look comfortable with his decision.

She pulled back. "You want to go see him? Try to get through to him one more time?"

He seemed completely relieved to hear that suggestion. "Yeah. I do."

She crawled off his lap. "Then, let's do it." She held out her hand.

He took it and got up. "I don't know if it'll do any good, but I'd like him to hear what a woman thinks of the things he says." He paused. "You'll come with me?"

"I'm here, Cassian. I'm staying. So, yes, I'll go anywhere with you."

They stood in front of the door, the hotel hallway quiet and smelling of microwave popcorn. Gigi squeezed his hand. "You ready?"

Giving a curt nod, he seemed more determined than worried. Since he'd already informed his security guard they were coming, it only took a light tap for the door to swing open.

The very large man stepped back, letting them in. Gigi took in the nice, clean room. One bed was tightly made, while the other looked like a suitcase had exploded on it. The covers were kicked back, and a tall, skinny boy with surfer blonde hair sweeping across his forehead leaned against the headboard. Ear pods attached to his phone, Walker Lovett moved his head to the beat and typed rapidly.

Cassian strode right to the bed and yanked the cords out of his ears.

"*Hey.*" The kid tried to look pissed, but she could tell he was both relieved and a little scared to see the big, famous quarterback. "What do you want?" His gaze slid over to Gigi, and she could see the curiosity, but he turned his attention back to Cassian.

"I'm here to talk to you."

"Cool. Too bad I'm not interested."

Cassian stood there, uncharacteristically uncomfortable. He had a way of putting everyone at ease, of drawing shy people into the action and making them feel part of the group. Everybody loved him.

Except this belligerent teenager.

Okay, well. "Hi, I'm Gigi." She crossed the room and sat on the other bed, facing him.

"Yeah, so?"

"So, you had a pretty special opportunity here and you blew it."

The kid looked like he'd walked into a sliding glass door. He hadn't seen that coming.

She gestured to Cassian. "You were chosen out of, seriously, *thousands* of athletes, so why'd you apply if you don't want to be here?"

"I want to be here. He's just a dick."

"*Oh.* Well, there's always two sides to a story. I've only heard Cassian's. What'd he do?"

"He kicked me out for nothing. I didn't do *anything*."

Fortunately, she'd gotten a detailed list from Cassian on the car ride over. "You didn't break into the kitchen?"

He rolled his eyes. "It's camp. That's what you do."

"You didn't watch porn on the camp director's computer?"

His cheeks flushed deep red. "It wasn't that big a deal."

"Breaking and entering is against the law, so yeah, it's a big deal." She switched over to his bed, nudging his legs. "You're not really convincing me here. It sounds like you did do some things, you just don't think you should be kicked out because of them."

"This is a stupid conversation."

"I guess it's only stupid if you want to go home. If you want to stay, then the conversation's important, right?"

He watched her for a moment, his gaze sliding over to Cassian.

"You want to go home?" Cassian asked.

"Who cares what I want? You already bought my ticket."

"Okay, *this* is a stupid conversation," Gigi said. "Let's get back to the important stuff. *Why* you're being sent home. The issue is that Cassian can't trust you. He's responsible for forty kids, and to keep them safe he's got rules. If everyone were allowed to wander the campus whenever they felt like it, some would get lost, some would drown in the lake, and some would get gored by bison."

Walker looked at her like, *Are you serious right now?*

"So, to protect you and the staff, he has rules. You broke them. On top of that, you're insanely disrespectful. I mean, come on. Cassian flew you out here, gave you room and board and access to people at the top of their profession, and instead of being grateful, you tell him to stop talking?"

The boy kept his mouth shut. *Good.*

"Worse, you said some pretty offensive things about the director and the yoga instructor."

"Amie put her tits in my face. She was asking for it."

A chill shot through her. Now she understood why Cassian had jumped so quickly to his decision to send the boy home. "Asking for what, exactly?"

Was he just recycling words he heard at home? Or had they become part of his fabric?

"She put her tits in my face." The kid sounded far less sure of himself.

"Unfortunately, I heard you the first time. Did she look you in the eyes and say, I'm the director of this camp, here to serve all your personal needs? Please feel free to objectify me?" She didn't even wait for a response. "Because I don't care if she stripped naked and pranced around the dining hall. You keep your hands and your comments to yourself unless a woman invites you into her space."

She was shaking, her whole body in fight mode. She had to calm down so she could better understand the boy. "Let me ask you something. If you'd brought a pitcher of water to a table and reached between two guys to set it down, and one of them said they'd like to bend you over the table and have his way with you—right there, in front of everyone—how would you feel?"

"I'd knock him on his ass."

Now that she was paying attention, she noticed a lack of conviction in his tone. Almost like he was spitting out lines he'd memorized from a movie. "I didn't ask what you'd do. I asked how you'd feel."

He didn't answer, but she gave him a moment, because he had that focused but unseeing look in his eyes, like he was imagining the scenario.

And it clearly made him uneasy. She could be wrong, but she thought he was getting it.

"Are you kicking me out or not? If you want me—"

She cut him off. "This conversation isn't moving forward until you answer my question. How would you feel?"

He scratched his neck. Sat up a little straighter.

If there was any chance for him to stay, he needed to break. To show that he was more than a product of his home environment. He had to show that he was receptive to being a better human being. Otherwise—

"I wouldn't like it."

Oh, thank God. "Amie didn't either. She didn't deliver pitchers of water because she was looking for tips. She did it to check in on the campers, make sure they're doing all right. You know, keeping hydrated, eating good food, stuff like that. And then you talked about her like that, and it degraded her. Don't ever do it again. Not to her, not to anyone."

"You want to stay at camp or not?" Cassian asked.

She wanted to tell him to slow down, but then again, she'd said all she needed to say. *This isn't a therapy session and hammering him too hard will only make shut him down.*

"Who cares what I want?" the kid said.

Everything flipped for her in that moment. Her anger melted into heartache. Because that was it right there. He felt powerless. Sure, most kids did, but Cassian's security team had done a deep-dive into Walker's family and discovered mug shots for both his parents. They'd been in and out of jail for most of his life for using and selling drugs, which explained why his aunt had shown up for the interview.

"You already bought my ticket home." The challenge burned in his eyes. Mostly, it said, *Didn't you?*

"I know you're smart. Andre can't believe how quickly you size up the field and put the ball in the receiver's hands." She'd never talked to Andre, but she had no doubt he would say that. The running back had called Walker a phenom, after all. "So, when *Cassian Ellis* offers you one last chance to train with the Mavericks, you say, *Thank you, sir.* You say, *I'm sorry for being so difficult, and it won't happen again because I want to be here.* You say, *I'll do whatever it takes to earn your respect.*"

When the kid didn't say anything, she threw out one last line. "I'll tell you something. I could be wrong, but I think all this attitude and rebellion is just a front. I think you're playing a part. If I'm wrong about that, then go home, because we have zero tolerance for disrespect, but if I'm right...then drop the attitude right now and show us who you really are."

He looked at the blanket, totally out of his element. But he remained silent, and she didn't know if he had it in him to break free of the mold he'd been set in.

And that would be such a shame. Because not only did he have skills on the turf, but he had leadership potential. *If* he used his power for good.

When it looked like he couldn't do it, Gigi got up and gave him a sad smile. "Okay, well. Safe travels, Walker." She reached for Cassian's hand, ready to head toward the door.

"I want to stay."

Cassian lowered his head and let out a huff of breath. He faced the boy. "Look me in the eyes and tell you understand that women are not objects, and that you're not going to touch them or speak about them as if they are."

The boy looked painfully uncomfortable, scared even. But he found the strength to say, "I understand." His voice sounded soft and almost pleading.

"Good." Cassian's shoulders pushed back as if a weight had been lifted. "And, if you want to lead so badly, you'll do it on the field. Only."

Walker nodded, his eyebrows hitching in surprise.

Cassian held out his hand, and the boy looked at it for a few moments like, *You want to shake my hand?* And then he grasped it and they shook.

"You can come back now, or you can show up at breakfast," Cassian said. "Bill will drop your luggage in your room while everyone's eating."

"I'm not going back to that dump until I have to." The kid cracked a grin and nestled down into his stack of pillows. "I'm staying here. Might even order room service."

With his hand grasped firmly in hers, Cassian towed her out the door of the hotel. The cool air settled on his skin.

"Would you slow down?" She tried to wrench her hand free from his grip. "What is your rush?"

"My rush?" He gripped her wrist and yanked her right up against his chest. "Did you see yourself in there? I was crazy for you as a kid, but now? I'm out of my mind for you. You're fucking amazing, Gigi, and I want you. I want you right the fuck now." He hadn't even realized he was choking around the kid. It was only when Gigi took over that he could see how uncomfortable Walker made him.

The way Gigi had handled it…Damn. She just blew him away.

"Okay." She sighed, reaching up and pressing her palms to his chest. "That's a valid reason."

He laughed. "Gigi, I'm telling you, if you don't get your ass in my truck, you're going to be naked in the parking lot of the Roadside Inn."

She pushed away from him. "I'm going. But I'm wearing cowboy boots, not roller skates. Slow down."

"Can't." He bent his knees and lifted her into his arms. All that silky hair swished over his skin, and he breathed in her sweet, sexy scent.

"*Cassian*." She wrapped her arms around his neck, leaning in to nuzzle his neck. "You're crazy." She bit his earlobe. "Crazy hot."

Digging his keys out of his pocket, he hit the keypad to unlock his truck. Didn't even set her down, just opened the passenger side and dumped her onto the seat.

She quickly righted herself from the sprawl. "Are you serious right now?"

"As a heart attack." He swung around to his side, buckled in, and tore out of the parking lot. He was so fucking hard it hurt.

As he turned onto the highway, he reached for her hand and kissed the back of it. "Thank you." He had too much emotion bottled up to express any of it. If he even tried, he'd be tumbling her into the backseat and tearing off her panties.

"I'm glad you went back to see him." Her voice in the dark cab soothed like a down blanket and a crackling fire.

He set her hand on his thigh, wanting more of her, all of her. His heart pounded, his blood raced, and it was all he could do to keep focused on the road.

"Maybe in your next staff meeting, you can ask everyone to look for opportunities to give Walker a leadership role—"

"I can't talk about Walker. Not when my truck smells like you. When all I can think about is your mouth. I want it, Gigi. I want your legs wrapped around me, and your hands all over me. I *need* you."

Her thighs squeezed together. "You can have it. My mouth. You can have it anywhere you want it."

Chapter Fourteen

HE PULLED OFF THE ROAD AND DROVE INTO THE sage-covered meadow.

"What are you doing?"

Jerking the gearshift into Park, he killed the engine. "You want to know why I'm the Bad Boy Quarterback?"

She sat quietly, expectantly.

"Because there's nobody else for me but you. And, when I lost you, I knew in my gut I'd lost a part of me. The part that gave me my place in the world, the part that made me happy." He shrugged. "It means that, other than football—what I do, who I spend time with…nothing matters." He reached for her hair, twirling a lock around his finger. "What I'm saying is, there's no going slow for me. No seeing how things work out. I'm all-in. There's us, there's now, and for me, that's forever. So, I'll do whatever you want, but just know—"

Unbuckling her seatbelt, she lunged for him, her hands framing his face, her mouth covering his.

Yes. Oh, hell, yes.

She flung her arms around his neck, her tongue licking

inside and teasing his into play. Lust surged high and hard, and he wanted all of her at once.

Naked, open, *mine*.

He didn't understand how one person could make him feel so much. He met thousands of people every year, had good friends and close family, but no one set his soul on fire the way she did.

Her kiss turned hungry, and she grabbed fistfuls of his hair. Those moans…they spilled into the dry and barren holes that dimpled the landscape of his heart. He absorbed them, drank in her desire, her urgency, until the absolute relief of having her in his arms—his life—filled him to the brim.

And then…Jesus, and then the need grew too powerful. He tore his mouth off hers. "Get in back." He pressed the heel of his palm on his raging erection.

Watching him touch himself, Gigi's eyes flared, and after a moment's hesitation, she scrambled over the console and crashed onto the back seat. Even as he climbed over—and he was too damn big to have sex in a truck but like hell would he wait to get home—she was pulling those jean shorts down.

With a mischievous grin, she stuck her finger in a belt loop and swung them around. "Well, look at that. No panties, just like you asked."

Fuck, she was cute. And fun. And sexy. And every damn thing he could ever want.

Landing on the seat, half on top of her, he yanked the top of his jeans, popping the buttons open. He got them down to his ankles, when he remembered his damn boots.

Laughing, Gigi reached over him for the ties. Her hair tickled his bare skin, and her breath warmed his cheek. Her scent was like a direct hit to his pleasure center.

He couldn't take it anymore. "Get over here." Gripping under her arms, he pulled her on top of him.

She landed with a shriek and quickly fell onto her back, shoving the hair out of her eyes, revealing the joyful glitter in them. "You need to get naked, buddy. Chop, chop." She pulled herself into a sitting position, her bottom half naked, her top covered only in a lacy white bra. Her tits jiggled as she untied his boot, cupped the heel, and yanked it off.

He was so hard, and yet he wasn't ready to fuck her. He wanted this moment to last. Because it was them, laughing, just like in the treehouse, only this time they were really together. The promise of sex with Gigi was as exciting as the forbidden had once been.

She was having trouble with the other boot, so he batted her hands away and did it himself. "Take off that bra. I want your tits in my mouth."

Desire rose like a pink wave across her body, cresting over her cheeks. Eyes lusty, she flicked the clasp and pulled the straps down, dropping her bra to the floorboard.

As he kicked off his jeans, she reached for the hem of his T-shirt and pulled it up, her hot, wet mouth kissing a path from his belly to his pecs to the curve of his neck. "I can't believe I finally get to touch you."

Laying down, he shifted until he propped his head on the armrest. "Get on me." He wanted to see her hourglass shape rising over him, wanted to feel the ends of her hair fluttering across his chest. He wanted to watch those amber eyes turn soft and lusty.

Without hesitation, she straddled him, and he flicked the long hair off her shoulders so he could see her big, bouncy breasts. "My beautiful Gigi." He wanted to make sure she knew this was so much more than sex for him. "You're everything to me. You know that, right?"

Her smile was soft, a little shy. A lot naughty.

"If you never wanted to have sex with me again, I'd still die a happy man as long as I got to be with you."

"Oh, we're going to have sex, all right. Lots and lots of it." She shifted restlessly, and he clutched her ass, hauling her up his lap.

He moved her rhythmically over his cock, her slick heat lighting up his nerves. "Goddamn, you feel good."

Leaning forward, she clutched his shoulders, her hair falling like a curtain around their faces. Her hips moved sensuously over him—so sexy—eyes glazed with lust, brow furrowed in concentration. Each slide of his cock through her hot, slick folds struck his nerve center like a bolt of lightning. She gasped, so he knew he was stroking her clit.

He didn't think he could contain it, all this desire and want and need for her. Her fingernails dug into his skin. Their breaths mingled. He reached for her breasts, held their soft, heavy weight in his hands. Arching up, he sucked a nipple into his mouth, flicking his tongue over it, while his fingers teased the other one. "You ready for me?"

The little vixen gripped his cock. "Mm. God, yes." She lifted up on her knees and then sank down on him—nice and slow. Once seated, she swiveled her hips to take him deep. "You feel so good."

He couldn't even speak, the pleasure was so intense.

She fell forward, her cheek brushing his, as she rocked —letting him ease out and then slide back in—over and over—like she was savoring the erotic sensations. With each stroke, her nipples grazed his chest, and his body trembled with a need that threatened to break him.

"So good. I never want this to end." She gasped, tucking her face into his neck.

He cupped her jaw, forcing her to look into his eyes, the intimacy raw and pure. And then he pressed a soft, sweet kiss on her mouth.

She opened for him, licking inside. As the kiss deepened, turned wild, her hips moved faster. She sat up, tilting back, her hands braced on his thighs. He reached for those full, round breasts, pushing them together and feeling them bounce in his hands. *Oh, fuck, yes.* It was too much. Thumbs flicking over her nipples, he thrust up into her.

Her eyes closed, her lips parted, and a blush spread across her chest, rising up her neck and coloring her cheeks. A look of utter bliss captured her features, and if he wasn't so fucking close to coming, he'd freeze this moment in time and save it forever.

Jesus, he felt her everywhere, her hands gripping his thighs, his cock wrapped up in her tight, slick, velvety channel. *Gigi. She's mine.*

I love her.

I love her so fucking much.

It hit too fast, that roar of sensation down his spine, the tightening of his balls, so he reached between them, found her clit, so wet and swollen, and the moment he caressed it, her body flung forward, and she cried out.

She lost her rhythm. There was no turning back, his climax was right there, so he clutched her ass, jacking her furiously on his cock. She was out of her mind, swiveling her hips and slamming down on him.

And then she cried out, her body writhing, jerking. "*Cassian.*"

That voice drenched in ecstasy, calling out his name,

did him in. He came hard, his hips bucking off the seat. He held her ass tightly against him as he released, each explosion lighting him up, showering him with hot, fiery sparks.

He'd never felt anything like it.

She slumped on top of him, both of them breathing hard.

He felt whole, sated. His life had never been so perfect.

Finally, he had peace.

Everything would be all right.

Not once in his twenty-seven years had Cassian slept in the same bed with a woman.

Until today. Waking up with a warm, soft, curvy body tucked tightly against his, knowing it was Gigi…the rush of pleasure jolted him wide awake.

His arm slung around her waist, they held hands tightly, and his cheek rested on her silky hair.

If he hadn't already missed a week of camp, he'd stay just like this. But, no, he had to talk to the coaches about Walker. He'd messaged everyone last night, calling for a brief staff meeting. He needed to let them know the situation.

He knew the moment he released her hand, he'd wake her up, so he kissed her rosy cheek and gently let go.

"No." She tugged on him, rolling onto her back. "I'm not ready to get up."

"I am."

She looked shocked and maybe a little hurt.

But he just smiled. "Because the sooner I get going, the sooner I get back to you." He kissed her mouth. "I'll be thinking about you all day. But there's nothing new about that."

Her features melted, and she looked like she was about to tear up. Instead, she got all stern. "You're too charming." She sat up. "So help me God, Cassian Ellis, if you break my heart again, I'm going to—"

He grabbed her hand and kissed her knuckles. "Does that mean you've given it to me? Do I have your heart?"

She gazed up at him, pushing the hair back from his temples. She didn't say anything, but she didn't need to. The wariness in her eyes told him he had a lot of work to do to make her feel safe with him.

"I'm not going to break your heart, but I do need time to earn it." One more kiss, and he lifted off the bed. "I have to go. Got to get everyone up to date on Walker."

He headed into the bathroom, flicked on the lights and turned on the faucet. It had been the best night…but he was keenly aware that it could be his last.

However many steps he'd taken forward, seeing Amie leaning against his car and in the Jacuzzi had set him back. But it wouldn't happen again. He'd make sure of that.

He just…it wasn't about what *he* could do. Once the season started, he'd have no control over the press, the paparazzi, or the people who inserted themselves into his space.

He stepped into the shower, tipped his head, and let the hot water course over his body. With his eyes closed, he sank down into the way it had felt waking up with her in his arms. How happy she made him…how complete. And he'd use that. Every time he started to lose hope, he'd go back to those moments, use them to keep up the fight.

He *would* win her back.

She was his future.

His everything.

Eggs crackled in the skillet, and the scent of freshly brewed coffee filled his kitchen.

This moment, making breakfast with Gigi, after having her in his bed all night, spread through him like a blush. It seemed too good to be true. "What's your plan today?"

In one of his Mavericks T-shirts that ended mid-thigh, she stood at the island, one bare foot on top of the other, slicing strawberries for her fruit bowl. "First, I'm going to pull out my notebook and take a look at my songs, see if I've got anything that would work for Dale. But, then, I want to talk to Grant about recording that duet with me."

He poured coffee into a mug and handed it to her.

She shook her head. "Caffeine dries out my vocal folds."

"I didn't know that." But he was glad he did. He wanted to know every single one of those details about her. "What do you drink?"

"Tea with licorice root." She flashed him a grin. "Which you don't have. So, really, just room temperature water is good."

"You got it." He'd pick up some tea for her. "In fact, give me a list of everything you want. I'll run by the store on my way home from camp."

She got up on her toes, knife in one hand, strawberry in the other, and kissed his cheek. "Thank you." Getting back to work, she said, "I texted Grant yesterday, but I haven't heard back from him."

"You mean that song about me being an asshole?"

"It wasn't about *you*. It's about me. *My* experience of

us. But, yes, that one." She sounded particularly cheerful. And then the smile fell off her face. "Of course I haven't heard back from him. My phone's in my purse. Which I left in your truck." Shaking her head, she headed out of the room. "Is it unlocked?" she called.

"I wanted you naked. I'll be lucky if I thought to turn off the engine." He needed to check in with Amie, so he grabbed his phone from the charger. *Oh, shit.* When had all these messages come in?

Fuck, he'd turned the sound off during camp yesterday. He'd forgotten all about it. As he thumbed through them, his phone vibrated, and he quickly answered his manager's call. "Hey."

"How hard is it to stay out of trouble?"

"I haven't checked my phone since yesterday afternoon. Skip to the punchline."

"Just look at your social media pages. Pick one. It doesn't matter. It's everywhere."

"What's everywhere? I haven't done anything." He opened his newsfeed.

And there it was.

Two images side-by-side. On the left was a photograph of him in the Jacuzzi, untying Amie's bikini top. With her head tipped sideways, her long hair spilling over her breast, it looked like he was whispering sweet nothings in her ear.

The photograph on the right was of him carrying Gigi out to his truck. She was laughing, while he looked at her with pure, flagrant lust.

Is Cassian Ellis two-timing the hot cheerleader with a Lollipop?

"Dammit." *Gigi's contract.* This headline would kill any shot she had with Clean Beatz. "I'm not with Amie. I've never been with her. How do I fix this?"

"What about the Lollipop?" A seasoned sports manager, Ethan had dealt with these situations countless times.

"We just came back from doing the tour together." Which only fueled speculation that they'd hooked up. "We…" He was about to say, *We grew up in the same town,* but he didn't need to announce that kind of information. *Shit.* "What can I do?"

"Where's it taken? Is that your hotel? It looks like an indoor pool."

"It's the resort pool, why?"

"Well, that's a public space. And the one with the Lollipop? That looks like a parking lot."

"I'm not looking to *sue* anyone. I need to get it out there that I'm not with Amie, so I can't be cheating on her."

"You don't really think anyone cares about some formal statement you make, do you? Because they see what they want to see. Look, get me the direct line to Gigi's manager. We'll get on the same page before we approach your coach and her label. My number one priority is making sure you keep your job."

"Ethan, listen to me. That story's going to sink Gigi's career." *Fuck it.* Gigi wasn't his manager's job. "I have to call Joan." His publicist would understand. "Let me get off the phone."

"Get that number for me."

"I will." He disconnected, then took off to find Gigi. She hadn't come back into the house yet.

A horrible sense of foreboding had the hairs on his arm standing on end.

His phone vibrated again. *Bill.* He needed to check in with the head of his security, so he took the call. "Hey."

"All right, so I did hear back from them."

"Back up. I haven't looked at my messages this morning."

"Right. So, this story broke last night around eleven. I immediately contacted the hotel, requesting access to the security footage, and I've been waiting to hear back before briefing you. Fortunately, both properties—this one and the one in Aspen—are owned by locals, so it'll be easy to view what they've got. What I need from you is a time-frame. When were you in the Jacuzzi with Amie—"

"Around eight pm. And I went to the Roadside Inn about a half hour later. I was back home by ten, so that should make it damn easy to pinpoint."

"Excellent. I'm meeting with them this afternoon."

"Look, this guy's getting into my private parties. He's following me. I can't help but think it's Zach." Cassian wouldn't let some fuckstick ruin his life. "I want you to hire more security. Whatever we need. I'm done with this shit."

"You down to hire a PI firm?"

"Of course."

"Good. I'll make that call right now. Listen, Cassian, we'll get to the bottom of it, I guarantee it."

"We have to."

"I hear you. I'll let you know what we get from the footage."

He disconnected and looked out the living room

window to find Gigi pacing in front of his truck. *Fuck*. She was clearly upset, talking on the phone.

While he waited for her to finish her call, he skimmed the messages on his phone, freezing when he saw one from his coach.

Coach: **You're going to make me trade you, aren't you?**

Right before he could answer, Gigi ended her conversation. Hands on her hips, head lowered, she stomped a bare foot on his lawn.

Cassian threw open the door. "Is everything okay? Who was on the phone?"

"My manager." She sounded distracted.

"And?" Dammit, he couldn't believe this had happened.

"And I told her the truth. That we knew each other in high school, got reacquainted on the tour…"

"Did you tell her we're together?"

"Yes. I had to. She can't help me if I hide the truth from her."

"Okay. My manager said he's going to talk to yours. If you want to text me her contact info, I'll forward it. In the meantime, I'm hiring a private investigator." He couldn't be the reason she lost her contract. "I'm going to find out who's doing this."

She gave him an exasperated expression. "Why is your first thought not Amie Clover? You told me she wants to get back on *NFL Cheerleader*."

"First of all, she's caught up in this, too. As a cheerleader, she could lose her job if she's seen drunk and stripping for the football team. She's also got a serious boyfriend. But secondly, she's a friend, and she wouldn't do that to me."

"Does she know you might get traded?"

"Of course not. Outside my manager, only you and Dean know."

"Then she doesn't know how this could impact you. She's probably using this to get back on her reality TV show."

"It's a possibility, but she spent two nights on the tour with me and nothing was leaked. I think the common denominator's my backup quarterback. Right after Aspen, he gave an interview, basically confirming the threesome. It's no secret he's not my biggest fan. And he's the one who'd benefit if I got traded."

"Would he do something like this? In a time when it's so easy to find out who's behind these things?"

"People do stupid shit all the time."

"Wow, if he's behind it…" She softened. "What are you going to do?"

"The only thing I can do right now is wait to hear back from my security team. They're looking at the footage from both hotels and hiring a PI." He reached for her, but she didn't step into his arms. "Tell me how I can fix this for you. I'll do anything you need me to do."

"It's done. There's nothing I can say, no press release I can put out that will change peoples' perceptions. And, honestly, the only perception that matters is Dale's. If she decides she's done with me, then what do I have? She gave us one month to be in the press for only good things, and every single one of us is involved in some kind of scandal."

"Me carrying you is not a scandal."

"If Dean carried me it might not be. But it's you, the Bad Boy Quarterback." She looked exasperated. "It's not just this contract, Cassian. It's my career. My reputation. No label's going to want anything to do with me."

"In your field, real talent is a rare commodity. And you've got it, Gigi."

"Don't try to minimize this. It's no different for you. You're a great quarterback, but your backup's just waiting for you to screw up. Every year, new guys are drafted. We have to be very careful with our careers. We're too easily replaceable."

"I'm not minimizing anything. But you're telling me there's only one path, and that's not true. If there were only one path, there'd be a handful of successful people. Everyone hits walls, makes wrong turns…fucks up. That's when they blaze a new path and—"

"I don't want to blaze a new path, Cassian. I don't want to start all over again. If you get traded, you're still a starting quarterback. If I lose this contract, I not only go back to the bottom rung, but I've got a big mark against me." She shook her head. "Trust me, you wouldn't be getting in trouble if you knew that going to a new team meant starting from the beginning all over again."

"You're right about that."

"Yeah, I know I am. Look, I have to go. I've got to do some damage control."

"I don't want you to go like this. I want—"

"You have to get to camp anyway. We'll talk later."

He followed her back inside his house and watched her head up the stairs to get ready. Every step away from him raised his anxiety another notch. He didn't want her to leave.

It felt like she was slipping out of his grasp.

Later that afternoon, after the meeting with his security team, Cassian left his office and hurried along the hallway.

He needed to get back out there, see how Walker was doing in today's elective. Everyone on his staff would be watching, monitoring, the boy's behavior, but Cassian felt the greatest sense of responsibility.

As he passed Amie's office, he heard her voice. Hushed, urgent. *Upset.*

He'd been focused on himself. How the leaked photographs impacted his relationship with Gigi and his career. But, of course, Amie had a lot at stake, too.

Obviously, now wasn't the right time to check on her, but…it sounded like her boyfriend was giving her hell. *I could talk to him, let him know nothing's going on.*

Like he'd believe me—with my reputation?

For so many years, he'd skimmed by, not giving a shit about anything outside football, and now the consequences were hitting him fast and hard. His behavior was impacting other people. People who mattered.

He'd just let her know he was there for her. He cracked the door open.

"I don't know what more I can do." Her back to him, Amie had an arm tucked across her stomach, staring out the window onto the football field. "If this isn't enough, then…God, I just…of course I want this. You know I want it more than anything." She turned and saw him, giving him a plaintive look, and then said, "I have to go. Well, there's nothing I can do right now, and I have a camp to run, so let's just talk later." She disconnected and tossed her phone on the desk.

He gave her a chin nod. "Everything all right?"

"It's just…it's not fair. I have no control over anything."

"Steve's breaking up with you?"

She cocked her head. "Steve? Oh." She shook her head

dismissively. "I don't know. He's not speaking to me. Why would he? In the past two weeks, he's seen me all over social media with you. *That*…" She flicked a hand at the phone. "Was my agent. I didn't want to say anything, because you obviously have enough of your own stuff to deal with, but I might lose my job. They were already discussing whether being naked in your arms violated my morals clause, but now…this second time? It doesn't look good."

He'd wondered about that. "Is there anything I can do? You want me to talk to someone, make it clear we're not together?"

She shook her head. "I mean, it's not like cheerleading's a career. It's meant to be a stepping stone. Well, I'm almost thirty, and I don't have a next step. Which is why getting back on the show matters so much to me. I mean, I don't even know what I *can* be this late in life. It's too late for me to go into broadcasting, which was my major. I *need* to get back on the show, and I don't know how. And I just feel scared and hopeless…" She tipped her head back, blowing out a breath. "I'm a take-charge woman. I make things happen, but right now I have no control over anything."

He'd talked to her before about careers, and she'd made it clear she didn't want to coach cheer or be a fitness trainer. She didn't want to open a dance studio. Besides, he didn't think she'd want to discuss her career options right now. So, all he could do was reassure her that he was handling the photographer situation. "I get it. I'm feeling the same way about this guy who's following me around."

"This guy? You mean you know who's taking the pictures?"

"I just met with my security team, and they've gone

over the footage in both hotels. It's definitely the same person. In Aspen, the guy entering the room that overlooks the pool is wearing baggy jeans and a sweatshirt. The guy who caught the images last night came out of the bathroom. He was wearing cargo shorts and a baggy T-shirt. They're wearing different ball caps but carrying the same camera bag."

She seemed surprised. "Is he working alone?"

"It looks like it."

"So, how do we get him?"

He trusted Amie—she'd done a great job running his camp and helping him organize the parties he threw for the guys before and after, but he knew how badly she wanted to get on the TV show. How far would she go? If she were behind this, wouldn't she be freaking out that they were coming close to discovering the guy's identity? He watched her carefully, as he said, "We've also got footage of a rental car."

"Do you have the license plate? If you do, we can get the police involved. They can see which hotel he's staying in. He has to be staying somewhere in town."

Cassian couldn't believe the relief he felt. He didn't like accusing Amie, but he had to consider every possibility. "We can't get the police involved, because all the pictures were shot in public spaces. But we're going to see if a clerk at the rental agency's willing to help us out. I'm also hiring more security, because I'm done being stalked. This place…"

"I know. It's your sanctuary."

"It was bound to happen. I chose to run my camp where I live, but to the extent I can preserve its privacy, I'm going to. If I bring the paparazzi, I ruin things for a lot of people. I'd hate to have to shut down my camp."

She looked horrified. "That's not going to happen. I saw the shots. There's no indication which hotel or which parking lot. No one can figure out the details."

"It's not hard to figure out a location."

"Oh, God." She let out a shaky breath.

"What?" Did she know something?

"It's just...this camp is so good. We've worked so hard, and the kids get so much out of it. If the paparazzi start showing up, the guys might stop coming. One of the reasons we get so many players here is because of the anonymity. If that changes..." She gazed up at him, eyes glazed with tears. "I love working here."

"Hey, we're not closing our doors, and no one's bailing on me." *Yet.* "We've got a lot of people on this." Before he left, he wanted to address her boyfriend. "If you want, I can talk to Steve, reassure him we're not a thing."

She snatched a tissue out of the box. "He knows about your rule, you know? That you don't hook up with women you're going to see again. That's one of the reasons he's always been so comfortable with me working with you. But now this—two pictures in less than two weeks? He feels like a fool."

"I can talk to him, if you think it'll help."

"What about you? Are you in trouble for this? I didn't even ask."

"For being seen with two beautiful women?" He shrugged, faking a big smile. "Listen, I have to check on Walker, but we can talk about this some more, if you want. I'll let you know what we find out."

He started out the door, when she said, "Cassian? Is everything okay with Gigi? I mean, she's caught up in this, too."

"I can't imagine a Lollipop carousing with someone

like me's a good thing for her career, but…" He shrugged, like *Not my problem.*

"What were you doing with her last night? I mean, why were you carrying her?"

Fair question. "It was her idea to give Walker another chance. She came with me. I was just…really damn happy she'd gotten through to him."

"Are you sure there's nothing going on between you? Anyone can see the way you look at her." She came around the desk. "You can tell me, you know."

"There's nothing to tell. I know her through her dad— been friends a long time." He didn't like lying, but he had no choice. He'd done enough harm to Gigi.

He'd protect her at any cost.

Chapter Fifteen

CASSIAN STOOD ON THE SIDE OF THE FIELD, watching the running back drills. After a rough morning, the kids had asked if they could try again in the afternoon. He liked that. How much they cared.

"Foot back, shoulders squared." Andre had the kids working on stance. "You're leaning, Walker. What's bad about leaning?"

"It tells the other team where I'm going to run." Walker sounded bored. "But I'm not leaning."

Andre gave him a challenging look.

"I'm not." Walker straightened. "This isn't leaning."

Cassian noticed the other kids' frustration. Once again Walker was disrupting their session. "Walker." He flicked his fingers. *Come here.*

The boy's features pinched into a foul expression. "I didn't do anything wrong."

Cassian didn't waver. Letting out a huff of indignation, Walker started off toward him.

"Andre doesn't know what he's talking about," Walker said.

"Of course he knows. The guy averages eight yards per carry." He stopped and faced him. "But we've already talked about respect, and badmouthing the man who volunteers his time to help you learn your position is unacceptable."

He scowled. "Are you sending me home again? Jesus, make up your mind."

"Instead of asking me that question, which makes it all about you, I'd rather hear you tell me how generous Andre is to give up his very limited free time to help you out. I'm not sending you home, but I do want to talk to you about something."

"Talk later. This drill's almost over. Can I get back to my group now?"

Cassian pinned him with a hard look. It took a few seconds, but the boy finally relaxed his stance. "Yesterday, I asked you about your goals. You said you wanted to drive fancy cars and live in a mansion. But, today, I want a serious answer. Why are you here?"

At this point, he recognized the kid's facial expressions. He really hoped the boy had the courage to get real with him.

Walker dug the toe of his cleat into the grass. Without looking up, he said, "I like football. I want to play on my school's team."

Thank Christ. "That's a good reason. And we're here to help you get on the team. But, if that's your goal, why aren't you listening to what a professional player's telling you to do? You've got less than a week here. You could really up your game if you just paid attention, instead of fighting every step of the way."

"Whatever."

"I can promise you right now if your attitude is *what-*

ever, you're not going to make it to the next level. And, trust me, you've got a lot of levels to pass through to make it to Andre's."

"I have natural ability. Everyone says so."

"That and five bucks will get you a burger and fries. But it won't get you on a team. Look, think of it like this. You're at the bottom of a mountain. No one's allowed at this base camp unless they have natural ability. So, that's a given. That's your ticket in. Now, you've got to make it all the way to the top of the mountain. Ninety-nine percent of the guys standing beside you won't make it to the top. You know why? They're going to get distracted. They're going to want to party with their friends or blow off practice, or they're going to get sick of working so hard when it looks like they're getting nothing out of it. And there will be a lot of days when you think you're not getting better, will never get better. The only guys who make it to the top are the ones who push through those days and keep on working their asses off. You hear me?"

"Yeah." He stopped digging and looked Cassian right in the eye. "I hear you."

This is good. Really good. "When I was your age, I went to my first football camp. I came home thinking I was a badass. I was going to be a football god. But a week later, I got a letter in the mail. Turns out, coaches send the athletes evaluation forms. So, I'm reading mine, and of course I've got all tens for the drills. I kicked ass at them. Scored high for athleticism, agility, speed, *but* I got the lowest possible score for coachability. I didn't even know what that meant, so I ignored it. Until I applied for an elite camp in Florida a few months later and didn't get in. Couldn't believe it. I was the best, right? But guess what? Coaches won't work with kids with attitude. Why?

Because if you're not open to learning from them, then they can't help you. That was my wake-up call." Because he'd hated letting Tyler Cavanaugh down. "After that, I became the most coachable football player the world had ever seen." He grinned.

The kid looked down at his grass-stained shoes. "I want to make the elite team."

Well, hell. The kid was finally getting real with him. At the end of the season, Cassian hosted one last session. He and the coaches picked a total of twenty kids—the best athletes from the summer—and held an intensive one-week session. No more art or cooking. Just football. Watching tape, talking strategy…everything to get them on the right path.

"I wish I'd known that from the beginning." In fact, in the form the campers had to fill out about their dietary restrictions, allergies, and sleep issues, there was a box at the bottom that asked if they were able to attend the final session if invited.

Cassian couldn't remember if Walker had checked the box or not.

"If you really want that, you have to step it up. When Andre tells you what to do, you do it. You don't challenge him. You either say, Yes, sir, or ask him to clarify. In fact, the more you express an interest in learning, the more attention you'll get. Look, in a lot of situations you want to hold your cards close to your chest. Like, you have a crush on a girl, and you don't want her to know. But in football? The more interested you are, the more you get out of it. Does that make sense?"

Walker nodded.

He clapped him on the shoulder. "I'm really glad you told me about the elite team. Now, show Andre how much you want it." He held up his hand and ticked off a finger. "Be the first to show up at practice and help set up and break down." He ticked off another one. "Listen to your coach." And another. "Lead the others by helping them—not distracting them." And a fourth. "Keep your focus on making the elite team. When you get pissed off, when someone has the great idea to break into the director's office—remember what making the elite team means to you. Can you do that?"

His expression said, *I can do anything.* "Now, can I get back there?"

"And we're back to square one."

Walker grinned. "I got this. You'll see." He took off.

For the first time, Cassian felt hope for the kid. He was so glad he hadn't sent him home.

Thanks to Gigi.

Energy rolled in. Excitement spiked with the anxiety of not knowing how she was handling this morning's headline.

He needed to see her. Needed to make sure they were all right.

He'd skip dinner with the campers and go to her house.

"I just don't understand why you've changed your mind." Her mom's gaze flicked to the rearview mirror as she braked for a stoplight. "You said yourself you could work here just as well as your home studio."

"Grant's got a meeting in LA anyhow." On the one hand, she was thrilled the country star was down to record a duet with her. On the other…she was leaving Cassian.

And it broke her heart.

No, no, no. Not going to sink into the abyss. She had no choice.

"Where do things stand with the label?" her mom asked.

"Dale's disappointed. She 'expected better of me.'"

"That's just ridiculous. You did nothing wrong."

"I agree, and my manager says being carried by Cassian Ellis doesn't violate the morals clause, so they can't break the contract. But it doesn't matter what we think. Dale's the one with all the power."

"Maybe you should take this duet with Grant to a different label. Somewhere less restrictive." Her mom turned off I-191 and onto the two-lane road that led to the air strip.

"Mom. We've been over this. My best shot is to rein-vent myself through Clean Beatz. No one wants a demo from a damaged Lollipop. It's fine. Besides, I'll get more work done in LA."

Her mom was quiet for a moment. "You don't think Cassian cheated on you, do you?"

"No." She knew the strength of his feelings for her—his kisses didn't lie. "But he just refuses to see Amie's game. She's good, believe me. An amazing actress. But the fact that he can't see how hard she's coming onto him means it's just going to keep happening. He didn't have to untie Amie's bikini top. He could've told her to do it herself. He didn't have to sweep her off the diving board half-naked. Dad would never do those things."

"No, he wouldn't. But you don't doubt Cassian's love for you, do you?"

No. "It's hilarious that you're telling me to stay with a guy who's in the press for threesomes and infidelity." She shook her head. "After what you did to keep us apart, *now* you want me with him? When he's *actually* hurting my 'potential'? That's rich."

"I'm sorry, Gigi. I'm sorry that a choice we made caused you so much sorrow. You know how much we love you, right?"

"I do. Whatever. None of this matters anymore. I'm trying to build a future. And I can't do it with all of Cassian's drama."

"Well, I'm sad to see you go." Her mom glanced out the side mirror, concern creasing her forehead. "I don't like the empty nest."

"Mom, seriously?"

"What? Why do you say that?"

"You kept us constantly busy. We were never home."

"Of course you were home."

"Can you think of one time you let us just be lazy and watch TV all day?" *Or even for a few hours?*

"I was trying to help you find your passions. And it worked. You're a successful musician, Lulu's a Cordon Bleu chef, and Coco's making chocolates so special they go in Academy Award goody bags." That pained look in her mom's eyes made Gigi think about Stella.

It just felt wrong not to include her youngest sister in that sentence.

"We're all very grateful for the opportunities you gave us," she said gently.

"You don't sound grateful." With a worried expression, she checked the rearview mirror again.

"What's going on?"

"For the past couple of miles, I've been watching this guy on a motorcycle. I think he's following me."

Gigi slunk lower in her seat. "Oh, great."

"You think it's paparazzi?"

"Of course. My manager says I'm 'trending.'"

"He's coming up fast." Her mom's fingers flexed on the steering wheel. "Don't worry. It's not like he can take pictures while he's riding a motorcycle."

"He could have a GoPro on."

"Oh, come on," her mom said. "This isn't a James Bond movie. Besides, it doesn't even make sense—what kind of footage is he getting of me driving you to the airport? You don't think he'd try to cut us off, do you?" Determination set in, pulling her mouth into a tight line. "Well, we'll just see about that." Her mom accelerated, veering into the opposing lane. "I'm going to take the Old Preston Road. It'll drop us out a half mile past the air strip, but so what? If he's not from here, he won't know where we've gone. I just need to get ahead of that truck, so he won't see me turn off."

Smiling, Gigi sat up, not even caring if someone got a shot of her. She wasn't missing her mom's badassery, not for anything.

Joss Montalbano, the world's biggest supermodel of the Eighties, gripped the wheel, edging the Mustang into the other lane. Satisfied she could make it, she shot around the truck. The driver gave her the finger, and Gigi burst out laughing. She braced her hands on the dashboard to keep from flopping around like a rag doll, but she was no stranger to her mom's driving. She trusted her.

"Okay, big boy. Let me pass." Her mom pressed the pedal down, arms stretched taut, as she passed the flatbed truck piled with hay bales.

But it seemed like the driver in the oncoming lane wanted to play a game of chicken, because he accelerated, too. The distance grew smaller, and Gigi wasn't laughing anymore. "*Mom.* Oh, my God."

"Don't worry." As always, her mom seemed calm and collected. "I'm in a Mustang, and he's in a truck. I got this." Her mom floored it, easing ahead of the flatbed and dropping back into her lane with hardly any time to spare.

Gigi let out a breath. "You're insane."

"Maybe, but I've put some distance between us and the motorcycle, so I'm calling it a win." Her mom flicked the turn signal and headed down an unmarked road, surrounded on either side by an aspen colony. "Lost him." She slowed, since this little-used road was known for animal crossings.

Heart racing, Gigi said, "You literally just took ten years off my life."

"I just added to your emotion file."

"Sure, Mom, I'll jot it down." Her mom thought all artists should keep journals so they could write down their emotional experiences. She thought it would make Gigi's lyrics richer.

I have Cassian. Believe me, that's more than enough fodder.

After driving a few minutes in silence, her mom said, "So, you really think I was too hard on you girls?"

"I didn't say you were hard on us. I said you kept us busy. I remember coming home from Ariana's birthday party in sixth grade, and telling you how much fun I had dancing, and the next thing I knew, I was spending the summer in New York City in some famous dance academy. Or how about that time Coco took a picture and you made her spend a month apprenticing with that photographer?"

"I didn't *make* her. I encouraged her." She looked

pissed. "That was *nice* of me to provide you with those opportunities."

"It was. But sometimes we just wanted to hang out with our friends and with each other." She knew her mom had the best intentions, so she'd never told her any of this before. She hadn't meant to sound that worked up, but the conversation had really unearthed some old resentment.

Because she also believed Stella would never have betrayed Lulu like that if the focus had been more on hanging out as a family instead of chasing their individual passions.

"I can see that." Her mom looked upset. "I just wanted a different life for you girls. I guess I gave you the life I'd always wanted."

When a modeling scout discovered her in a mall, fifteen-year-old Jocelyn Montalbano had thought it was the coolest thing ever. She'd begged her parents to let her have this amazing opportunity.

"My parents...well, you know, life on a farm...they needed me. But I made such a fuss, and the agency made it sound like a year's wages could basically pay off the mortgage and debts, so they let me go. I was fifteen and living in New York." Her mom had a faraway look in her eyes. "I was eighteen and traveling the world. I was twenty-two and making more money than I could ever spend..." Resolve settled over her features. "You know what I remember? I came home for Christmas when I was twenty-two, and my friends were talking about boyfriends and frat parties and their dream jobs, and I just felt so lost. Like I'd missed out on finding out what I might be good at. I never did find that out." She flashed Gigi a smile filled with regret. "I didn't want you girls to miss out."

"You were—are—a great mom. We felt loved every

day of our lives. If the very worst thing you did was send me to LA to intern with a sports agent"—that was when Gigi had considered a job in sports management just to stay close to Cassian—"then I think you did all right."

The roar of a motorcycle interrupted the conversation. Gigi whipped around. "It's him. He found us."

"We'll just see about that." Her mom's grip tightened on the wheel.

"What does he want? Maybe we should stop and let him take a picture of me. I'm not *doing* anything."

"We don't know who he is, and he's in hot pursuit. I'm not stopping."

With a burst of speed, the guy caught up with them. He lifted a hand and pointed to the side of the road.

Recognition hit her. "It's Cassian."

"Are you sure? Be very sure."

With the helmet it was impossible to see much, but she would recognize those broad shoulders anywhere... and those muscular thighs. "I'm sure."

As her mom slowed and eased to the side of the road, the motorcycle pulled ahead of them and stopped, a boot heel smacking the kickstand. One long leg swung over the bike.

Cassian yanked off his helmet and shot her mom a furious look.

Body buzzing with excitement, Gigi got out of the car.

"What the hell were you thinking?" With his hair all tousled, he stalked toward her mom, who was just coming aroundine the front of the car. "You could've killed her." He'd never been anything but respectful to her parents, but now he was practically shaking with anger.

"I thought you were paparazzi coming after my daughter." Her mom spoke kindly but pointedly. *Which is your fault.*

"Jesus." He wrapped an arm around Gigi's back and hauled her toward him. She fell hard against his chest. "Are you okay?"

"I'm fine." Warning flares went off in her brain—*resist! Resist!* But, instead, she burrowed into the space between his arm and his ribcage. His T-shirt smelled fresh out of the dryer, and with that particular quality of Cassian— masculine, pine, and fresh mountain air—like a perfect day on the trails—she melted into him. *More.*

She always wanted more of him. It was never enough.

He pulled back so he could address her mom but kept one arm slung around her. "Where are you going? There's nothing along the Old Preston Road."

Gigi wasn't going to let her mom handle this one. She gave her a look that asked for some privacy. With a nod of understanding, her mom said, "I'll wait in the car." And left them alone.

The afternoon sun beat down on Gigi's head, not a single breeze stirring the leaves on the trees. "I'm going to the airport."

He took a step back. "Fuck."

"I'm sorry, Cassian. I need to get back to work."

"You can work here. I *will* protect you."

"I know you want to, but you're just not getting it. Last night proved it."

"Wait. Just hang on." Hope enlivened him. "I've hired a private investigator. My security team viewed the footage of both hotels, and we found the same rental car in both lots. I'm on this, Gigi. I've got this guy."

"It isn't about a guy, Cassian. It's about *you*. Your celebrity makes you a target, for sure. But you're the one who got on that diving board and carried Amie off. You're the one who got in the hot tub with her, not Dean, not Andre. *You.* You're not seeing what's right in front of your face."

"You keep talking about Amie like there's something there. There isn't. There never will be." He lowered his head, the tip of his boot kicking the asphalt in frustration. "We just found our way back to each other. Don't bail on me after one day."

"I'm not bailing. I'm going home to salvage my career. That's all. And, while I'm trying to get a contract from Dale, I need to keep my distance. I have to focus on the duet Grant and I are going to record and on the demo I'm making for Clean Beatz."

Emotion wrenched his features, and her heart twisted. But she had to stay strong. "I hate this as much as you do, but you have to let me go. Let me get my career on track."

"I want to deserve you." His shoulders pushed back in resolve. "I'm *going* to deserve you."

Unwinding from a long day, Cassian sat across from Dean in the Jacuzzi. The jets hit his lower back and burbled hot water around his feet.

The party in the pool area raged on, but for the first time in his life, Cassian couldn't do it. Couldn't pretend to be okay.

Because, no matter what she said, returning to LA meant she'd given up on him. They could stay in touch —*and you can bet your ass I will*—but his gut told him she was done.

Here he was, this powerfully built and mentally strong

man with tremendous discipline, and he felt listless and empty without his Gigi.

No surprise, really. She lived in his heart and ran through his bloodstream. With her, he felt whole. Without her, his entire body ached like it was gripped with the flu. "How do you do it, man? Live with Genevieve on another continent?"

The big, grumpy linebacker gave a soft grin. "Once she's done with these last two classes, she graduates, and then she's moving in with me in Boston." He shrugged. "We talk every day...couple times a day. Text. We stay connected." He reached for the water bottle and tipped it back, draining it. "It's not over with you two."

"I know her. She wouldn't have left if she hadn't made her mind up about us." *About me.* "But I'm not giving up."

"Oh, I know." Dean's toes popped out of the water, and he stared at them for a moment. "You want to know how I can stand the distance? Vivi's the only person I want to talk to. She's the only face I can't live without seeing. So, I deal with it." He cut Cassian a look. "And you will, too."

"Hey, you guys." Amie dropped her tote on a table, reached for the hem of her coverup, and whipped it over her head. "I'm beat." She got one foot in the water, before Cassian shot Dean a look.

I have to do this, don't I?

And Dean held his gaze. *You do.*

This is going to suck. He got out of the Jacuzzi. "I need to talk to you."

"Is everything all right?" She came up close. "What's up?"

"Can you please put your dress back on and come with me?"

"Of course." She picked up the dress but didn't put it on.

"We haven't identified the photographer, and neither of us needs more attention in the press." *And I won't have Gigi see one more picture of me and Amie.* "So, please put your dress on."

"I mean...okay. But, as long as we're not making out, there's nothing wrong with me wearing a bathing suit at the pool."

"There's nothing wrong...except I'm being targeted."

"Fine." She threw the dress on and gave him a look that said, *Happy?*

He ignored her and continued on. Holding the door open, he followed her into the hallway.

She swung around to him. "So, what's going on?"

He didn't know a nice way to do this, and no matter what he said, she was going to be upset. "We need to make some changes. From now on, I'm going to need you to work remotely."

She flinched as if he'd slapped her. "Remotely? What does that mean, exactly?"

"It means we can't work together. Both of our jobs are on the line right now, and neither of us can risk another photograph going viral."

He could see the struggle play across her features. She wanted to argue, but what could she say? He'd been there when she'd talked to her agent about losing her job.

After a tense moment, she looked resigned. "Where do you expect me to go?"

"Boston." He braced for her response.

Her eyes went wide. "I can't run camp from two thousand miles away."

"Amie, you just told me Steve's not speaking to you.

The Mavericks have their attorneys looking at your contract." He wasn't going to tell her his issues. "The only way to put an end to this crap is to stay away from each other."

"I have to be here. Are you going to handle food deliveries? Is Dean going to become the point of contact with the parents? We just had a major issue with Walker." She looked more than disappointed. Maybe even hurt. "Do you not like the way I handled it?"

"You've been great." Especially with Walker. Since he hadn't started performing until close to the end of his session, they couldn't invite him back for the elite week. Instead, after a last-minute cancellation—they'd let him stay on for the second session. It was Amie who'd thought to give Walker the spot. "I can't run this camp without you, but I also can't risk my career. That means we can't work at camp together."

"Then, I'll stay in a hotel or rent a place in town. But I have to be here for deliveries and all the other issues that pop up."

He needed her to understand the full implications. "As long as you understand that it means you can't hang out with the guys at night."

"Well, wait. If you think it's Zach, then kick *him* out. He doesn't get away scot-free, while I get banished."

"The fact is, I don't know who's behind it, but I can't fire my backup quarterback from his volunteer job. He's on my team, and I have to work with him every day. I'm sorry, but I don't have a choice."

"I don't like this at all." Looking defeated, she peered through the window. "This sucks. They're my guys."

"I know. But there's one more thing."

She tilted her head. *What now?*

"I'm cancelling the trip."

"Oh, come on. That's ridiculous. You can't cancel it. That's one of the reasons the guys volunteer here. For your outrageous trips."

"Yeah, I know." The guys would be pissed, and he was sorry to disappoint them. But he had to do it. He wasn't going to put a target on his back.

"So, what, they're just going home? You're not doing anything?"

"I'm going to invite them to stay in Calamity for a few more days. We'll plan some outings."

"They're going to hate this. I'll bet half of them won't even bother staying."

He shrugged. *That's their choice.*

Because my *choice is to win Gigi back.*

Chapter Sixteen

DURING THE BREAK, GIGI CHECKED HER PHONE again. In the week and a half since she'd left Cassian on the side of the road, he'd checked in with her every day. Mostly, just brief notes to say he hoped her day was going well or to show her a picture of the guys doing something funny.

Guilt pinched her heart. He'd tried to FaceTime, but she'd blown him off. If she saw him, she knew she'd fall right back into him. And she was doing really well. Not only was she recording, but she was *writing*. Something she hadn't done since becoming a Lollipop.

Four of the songs in her notebook were advanced enough to make a demo, but she'd found many more worth working on, which surprised her. She'd have thought songs written a decade ago would be too immature, but they were actually pretty good.

Besides, what kind of future did she and Cassian really have? Even if they'd made it through the summer, once he flew back to Boston for training camp, he'd get swept back into his world. And she knew herself. With them living so far apart, she'd be consumed with worry. Seeing him in the tabloids with women all the time, caught in questionable situations, would drive her nuts. She'd spend all her time wondering where he was and who he was with.

That's the thing about trust. Once lost, it's so damn hard to get back. She knew he had the best intentions, knew he cared about her, but doubt was a constant flickering light at the back of her mind.

And she didn't want to live like that.

Grant came back into the studio, setting her licorice root tea down.

"Thank you."

He put his headphones back on, picked up his guitar, and smiled at her. "Ready?"

She took a sip of the hot beverage and let the heat and honey soothe her throat. "Sure."

Grant eyed her phone but didn't say anything. He fiddled with the panel. And, then, when he was ready, he said quietly, "Use it."

The fact that he understood the unrelenting doubt that cycled through her, the agonizing conflict of loving a man who wasn't good for her, just made all the excuses she kept telling herself collapse. Why did she feel the need to keep validating her choice to leave him? She should just accept that she wanted him but couldn't have him. Not at this point in her life.

And she could channel all those complex emotions into music.

This time when she sang, she immersed herself in her loss. She believed they were connected in a unique and special way, but she also knew he couldn't stop trying to win people over. Like throwing these over-the-top parties for the guys and flirting with women…helping Amie untie a *knot. I mean, come on.* As long as he did things like that, they didn't stand a chance.

And drama was the one thing her career with Clean Beatz wouldn't allow.

Forget my record label. She didn't want that kind of drama. It was the same kind of madness she'd had with him in high school, always wondering who he was with, what he was doing. Always having to deal with the smug looks from the girls he took to dances.

She couldn't go back to that. It was the kind of distraction that sucked her creativity dry.

With the last note, Grant yanked off his headphones. "Damn." He grinned. "Nailed it."

"We've got a song."

He gave a deep nod. "We've got a *hit.*"

As they shut down the studio, she thought about her earlier conversation with her manager. "You know I can't do anything with it until my contract with Clean Beatz is over."

"Girl, this one's timeless." His guitar case snapped shut, he headed out of the studio, and she followed. "It's also got great crossover potential. So, when you're ready, we'll release it. I'm in no rush."

Grant was on a self-imposed hiatus from the industry. Not only did he want to be strong enough to stay sober on his next world tour, but he harbored a hope of reconciliation with his ex-wife.

"You want something to drink?" she asked, as they crossed the living room of her cottage.

"Nah, I'm going to head out."

"You're going to see her?" His ex lived in LA.

"I'm having dinner with some old friends. Jimmy Clutch, Bailey Havoc, Desiree Olander." He tipped his chin to the guitar she'd set on her kitchen table. "We're gonna jam, if you want to join us."

"That sounds like a lot of fun, but I'm not going to be good company tonight."

"Another time then."

She nodded. "Definitely."

At the door, he stopped and turned to her. "I'm the last person to give advice about relationships but let me just say one thing. After three marriages, I've learned that people get divorced because things get tough. They have some idea in their head about what love should look like, so when it turns ugly, when it gets hard, they want to quit." He scraped a hand through his scruff. "Thing is, you gotta do the work in all your relationships, even the best ones. And if you don't, if you go right to calling the lawyer, you miss out on the best stuff. The stuff on the other side of trouble. That's the stuff worth fighting for."

"It's just…I'm not sure I'm cut out for the kind of drama that comes with Cassian."

"What about the drama that comes with you? As long as you're in the spotlight, the press is gonna catch you out doing something. When you're on tour, you think it'll be easy for him? I guarantee it won't. You'll be in a bar, letting off steam, and some man will come up and put his hand on your butt, and the whole world will think you're cheating. Including the people who're supposed to trust you. The point I'm making, though, isn't about the particular kind of trouble. Because you walk away from this guy and pick up with someone else, you're going to have a whole new set of problems. My point is that if you find a love worth fighting for…then fight for it. Figure things out together."

"You're absolutely right." She gave the lean, rugged

man a hug and kissed his bristly cheek. "Thank you. For everything." He'd given her a lot to think about.

Grant opened the door, and they both reared back at the sight of large man sitting on the top step of her porch.

"Cassian." Grant slapped a hand on his shoulder. "Nice to see you, man."

"Hey." Cassian stood, but he only had eyes for her.

And in those eyes she saw hunger.

Grant headed down the steps and opened the back seat of his rental car. He slid the guitar case inside and shut the door. "I'll talk to you later."

A wild tumult of energy flowed between them, but neither said a word until Grant backed out the driveway and took off.

The ocean-scented air riffling his hair, Cassian swung around to her. "Hey." He looked haggard, like he'd had some rough nights.

"What're you doing here? Shouldn't you be at camp?"

"You need to know two things. One, I'm not fucking around with us. You come first—you'll always come first —and until we're right, nothing else matters. Secondly, I've made some changes."

His intensity thrilled her. "What...what kinds of changes?"

"I sent Amie away. She still runs the camp but from a condo I rented for her. She's not coming near me or the guys again. Also, I've changed the trip."

"Oh, brother." She ushered him inside her little cottage a block off the Venice Beach boardwalk.

He was such a huge presence, his charisma and strength, taking up all the space in her cozy living room. "The guys are welcome to stay in Calamity after camp ends. We'll set up some outings...white water rafting, heli skiing, things like that." He sounded matter-of-fact, like he didn't care what the guys thought of the new plans.

And that was...interesting.

"They're going to love that." But he didn't react to her sarcasm.

He shrugged. "I'm done. I'm not going another day without you in my life, so I'm doing everything in my power to be good for you. Even if that means quitting football."

Quitting...what? "Okay, hang on. This is not—"

"I have enough money, so I don't need the income. I can coach. I like coaching. And that means I can live wherever you are. I can coach anywhere."

She threw herself into his arms. "Oh, my God. Slow down." She kissed him, this man who truly couldn't live without her. She wasn't crazy—this feeling that she was missing some critical part of herself. He felt it, too. "You're not quitting. For god's sakes, you're the best quarterback in the league. You don't have to give anything up to be with me. We just have to figure things out. We need time."

"You can have all the time you need. I'm not going anywhere." He eyed her cautiously. "I just need to know that you'll give me another chance."

"Yeah." She threaded her fingers through his hair. "Of course I will." *This man.* To be loved like this...it was overwhelming and utterly beautiful.

"Thank Christ." He reached for her, and he just...held her. He tucked his face into her neck and breathed her in. Heat radiated off his body, and she felt a tremor in his arms. He turned slightly and kissed her jaw, and then pressed another kiss to the corner of her mouth.

But she couldn't take teasing. Not now.

Needing more, she met his lips in a hungry,

desperate kiss. He licked inside, and that first touch of tongues gave her a delicious shiver. His fingers curled into the flesh of her ass as he held her tightly against him.

She couldn't stop kissing him, couldn't get close enough. It was like she had to make up for all the hours they'd been apart, to ease the heartache that had nearly crushed her.

And that was when she knew she was a liar. All her big talk—*I'm fine without him, I have to focus on my career*—it was all baloney. The stark emptiness of life without Cassian versus *this?*

Forget it.

Grant was absolutely right. She needed to fight through the hard times. Talk through their issues. They needed to fight for each other.

So far, he'd been doing all the fighting.

Still kissing her, he backed her up against the wall. His familiar scent enveloped her, his powerful arms supported her, and the sweep of his tongue set off a shower of sparks.

Relief crashed through the flimsy walls she'd erected. She'd talked herself into believing she was better off without him—convinced herself she'd be just fine with half a life.

But a life without his deep, carnal kisses, his devotion, his *passion* meant existing. Not living.

She *had* to try to make it work. Had to.

"Bedroom." His voice was sexy growl.

On wobbly knees, she reached for his hand and led him down the cool hallway. She'd left the sliding glass door wide open in her room, and it ushered in a lemon-scented breeze. Quietly—urgently—she pulled her T-shirt over her head and peeled off her leggings.

Tension crackled between them, and he watched her with a hunger that thrilled her.

He unbuttoned his jeans, exposing tan, muscular thighs. When he lowered his boxers, he gave his thick, hard cock a squeeze. God, she wanted him in her mouth, but the pulsing between her legs demanded he fill her right now.

As soon as she kicked off her panties, he said, "Get on the bed."

She'd never heard that voice, commanding, sure, but also gentle, tender. Desire coursed through her, and she needed to get her hands on all that warm skin and hard muscle. Laying down, she rested her head on a pillow, so alive, so aware of him, she could barely stand it.

He came at her, all coiled strength and burning intensity. He was going to take her, and she wanted it—wanted him—with a fierceness that had her practically levitating off the mattress. Hovering over her, he gazed into her eyes with a look that somehow made her feel like the most precious woman in the world—and the sexiest.

Lifting the back of a knee, he hitched it over his hip and palmed her ass. "I love you, Gigi Cavanaugh. You're my heart, my soul, and I want to be good for you more than I want anything else." He lined his cock up at her opening. "You ready for me?"

Too lost in him, all she could do was nod. He pitched his hips forward and thrust deep. A current of electricity lit her up, making her tremble. All she could do was hang on, her arms around his neck, legs around his waist, as he drove into her.

Again and again, harder, faster.

Yes. God.

Beads of perspiration broke out on his forehead, and he never once took his eyes off her.

This feeling crashed over her—warmth, affection…love.

I love him.

I completely and totally love Cassian Ellis.

Tell him. But right then he reached between them, found her clit, and her hips shot off the bed. The jolt of sensation careening through her body had her crying out.

God, it was so good. So much pleasure. Her head tossed on the pillow, her hips thrust and twisted to get him deeper, and she dug her fingers into his back.

"Oh, fuck." He lost his rhythm, lost all finesse. The sounds he made—desperate, urgent, like he couldn't take one more second, yet needed it to last forever—inflamed her.

And then…her climax hit. She exploded into a shower of sparks and dazzling light. Desire crackled and flashed, a wildfire raging out of control. Back arching, fingers fisting in her comforter, she cried out.

His strokes grew tighter, more erratic. With a grunt he slammed into her, holding himself tight against her. With quick snaps of his hips, he shouted, "Fuck, Gigi. *Fuck.*"

And then…he collapsed on top of her, his breath hot at her ear. Rolling off, he wrapped an arm around her waist and cuddled up close.

Heart still pounding, she caressed his arm. "I'm so glad you came for me."

"I will always come for you."

"Grant told me to keep fighting. He said, if you love someone, you work through the tough times."

"He's a smart man."

Tell him.

She hesitated, because there was this small but vibrant piece of her that still wasn't sure.

He said he'd quit football to be with me. And he separated himself from Amie, for God's sake.

"So, what happened with Amie? You didn't find out she's behind the photographs, did you?"

"Hell, no. I'd have fired her if I had. We still don't know who it is."

"Then why move her into a condo? Don't you need her on-site?"

"What I need is to take control of my life. If I want to stay out of the tabloids, I have to stop feeding them. If I want you, I have to make changes. I don't give a shit about the trips or the parties."

Something didn't feel right, but Grant's voice in her head made her push past the doubt. They had issues to work on, but it was worth it. *He* was worth it, because… she loved him.

Say it. She knew she was holding back because she was afraid, if she said it now, tomorrow there'd be a new picture in the press of him with Amie.

She was afraid of being a fool.

But *he* needed to hear it in order to feel safe with her. And they didn't stand a chance if they didn't put their hearts on the line for each other.

Cupping, his jaw, she gazed up at him. "Cassian…I love you."

His body jolted. He looked startled at first, but then everything in him melted, softened. He let out a huff of breath. "That's the best—the *only* gift—I'll ever want."

He covered her mouth with his, a kiss full of passion and love and relief. "There's one more thing you should know. I'm building you a studio."

"You're only in town a few more weeks. That's not necessary." Let alone possible.

"I want you to move in with me."

Oh. She couldn't keep from smiling. *He's such a passionate man. I love that.* But... "I've got a meeting with Dale the day after tomorrow, so I can't come back to Calamity until after that. The thing is, once you leave for training camp, I'll be coming back here." She kissed him. "So, let's just take it one step at a time okay?"

He looked disappointed. "As long as you're still in this with him, anything's okay. We'll go at your pace." He drew her in even closer. "So, we're good?"

She pushed past the unease. "We're very good."

They'd get where they needed to be.

As Cassian stood on the field watching the quarterback drills, he felt better than he had in...well, ever.

All was right in the world. Best group of kids he'd ever had at camp—and that included Walker. And tonight, after team obligations, he'd catch up with Gigi.

She was giving him a chance, and he wouldn't screw it up.

Life is good.

The only negative was Zach. After camp ended, he'd confront him. Ask him directly if he was behind the leaked photos. They couldn't work together if his team-mate was trying to screw him over.

It just didn't add up, though. *That's not how you become the franchise quarterback for a team.* Hard to imagine he'd go to such weird lengths.

If you want to replace me, be better than me.

There were plenty of other possibilities, though. Could be just some paparazzo who'd followed him around or bribed hotel staff to get access to him.

This seems more planned, though. Targeted.

One of the kids lost his footing, and Cassian tapped his shoulder. "Remember you want to end up on your plant foot before you start your progressions."

"Walker." Zach's voice shot out across the field.

Cassian glanced over to find Walker running his own drill. One of his friends was thirty yards downfield, holding up a hula hoop, while another kid reached into a mesh bag full of footballs. He handed them off to Walker, who threw perfect spirals through the hoop.

Zach hadn't liked the idea of Walker switching into his group halfway through the session, but Cassian had seen something in the boy and wanted to try him out in this position.

He was disappointed to see Walker still pulling this crap.

"Get over here," Zach shouted. "Now."

From Walker's defiant stance, Cassian knew what was coming. To avoid an ugly confrontation in front of the campers, he said, "Hey, guys. Take a break. Go grab some water." And then he turned to Zach. "Can I talk to you a sec?"

Zach was in his face in a hot second. "Don't tell my kids what to do when I'm in the middle of a drill."

"Five of your kids are in the middle of a drill. Three of them are running around with no leadership."

The muscle in Zach's jaw worked aggressively. "Walker. Here. Now."

The look of hellfire in the kid's eyes fizzled out when

he saw Cassian standing there. He dropped the football and jogged over. "What?"

"You in my group?" Zach asked.

Walker gave him a look that said, *Duh.*

"Then why aren't you doing drills with the others?"

"Your drills are lame." He gestured to the field. "I just threw thirty perfect passes, while you're having them practice footwork."

"Through a hula hoop. A toddler could get it through a hole that size."

Cassian saw the flinch of embarrassment on Walker's face, and his protective instincts came out.

"I was doing the five-step drop." Walker lashed out. "Isn't that the point of the drills?'

Cassian had already talked to Zach—and all the other coaches—about Walker's home life, how they needed to find leadership opportunities for him.

"Walker," Cassian said. "Go get some water. When you're done, come see me."

Zach caught the kid's arm before he ran off. "After you get water, you're right back here for the next drill. And, if you're not doing *my* drills, then you're going to stay after and clean up the equipment."

Giving his coach one last hard look, Walker jogged off the field.

Zach turned to Cassian. "Don't ever undermine me in front of one of my players."

"You just told a troubled kid a toddler could do what he was doing."

"Did you miss the part where he blew off the drill? That, once again, he led the kids away from what they came here to do?"

"I saw it, and I'll address it, but not by making him feel bad about himself."

"Right, because you know all about leadership."

Well, it looked like they were going to have it out right then and there. "My leadership got us to the Super Bowl for the first time in twenty years. You got a problem with that?"

"My *problem* is that you're an embarrassment." He leaned in close, seething. "A fucking threesome with your linebacker?"

"You were at the party. You saw exactly what was happening."

"How come other quarterbacks don't get the kind of press you do? Huh? It's because you're a fucking joke. Your flashy cars, the trips you take us on."

"Rewarding my guys for a great season is a joke? And you seem to enjoy the trips." Everything in him hardened. "I might've fucked around, but *I* didn't have a wife or a girlfriend."

Zach's eyes flared, part embarrassment, part anger. He liked to come off as this good, moral guy, but everyone knew he fucked around on the road. "I don't embarrass the team."

"Oh, okay, so it's not the character of the man, it's his public perception? I've just learned something important about you. You want to take my spot? Well, the single most important quality in a leader is trust. And how's the team going to trust you when you're cheating on your wife? Believe me, a man who can cheat and cover it as well as you do, is operating at a scary level of deceit. At least I'm honest about my life, and I'm not hurting anyone. And if you dislike the trips so much, don't come on them. You won't be missed." He was done talking to the man.

Now that he knew what Zach thought of him, he wouldn't include him in his camp again.

He headed for Walker. "Come here."

The boy trotted alongside him. "I'm not cleaning up the field. That's bullshit. I didn't do anything wrong."

Far enough away from the other kids, Cassian stopped and placed his hands on Walker's shoulders. "Yes, you did. First, you drew the other athletes away from their one and only opportunity to learn from one of the best football players in the league. Secondly, you disrespected your coach. If you don't understand the purpose of his drills, you talk to him privately. You don't walk away and do your own thing." Holding Walker's gaze, he asked, "What's your goal?"

"To be rich like you so I can bang chicks."

He knew Walker was just messing with him, but he remained impassive. Because it stung. It confirmed Zach's assessment that Cassian was an embarrassment to the team, and it reminded him why Gigi didn't trust him all the way.

She loves me. It bloomed inside him, spreading heat and happiness throughout his body.

But, if he didn't gain control over his reputation, he could lose her.

He'd also lose his team. He'd worked his ass off to gain their respect and trust, and he dreaded starting over somewhere else.

And winning *them* over.

But I'm working on it. That's the best I can do.

After a moment, the mischief left Walker's eyes. "To play in the NFL."

Cassian didn't need to say anything. The kid was smart. He'd get there.

Walker let out a huff of exasperation. "To make my high school team."

"Anyone else in your school going to football camp this summer?"

"No."

"So, you have an advantage. That means you pay attention to your coaches. Trust that Zach knows the right drills—that's how he became the backup quarterback for the Mavericks. Think you can do that?"

"Yes."

"Good." Cassian started off. "And stop being so damn difficult." He got about ten feet away when he heard, "Coach?"

He turned.

"Watch your language," Walker said. "I'm an impressionable kid."

Cassian grinned, but mostly he felt like he'd done something really important.

He'd helped a kid get on the right path. *Paying it forward.*

And, once Gigi came back to town, he'd bring up moving in with him again. Living across the country from each other wouldn't work.

He'd build a studio in his penthouse.

Anything to make it work.

Chapter Seventeen

AFTER DINNER, GIGI CURLED UP ON THE COUCH with a glass of wine. "How'd it go with the guys?" She'd wedged the phone between her shoulder and a throw pillow.

"Not well," Cassian said. "I told them I needed to make some changes—for my career, sure, but also so I could start managing the story the press tells about me. Told told them about the plans Amie'd made with a local outfitter, but they just laughed. Thought it was a big joke. Why would they want to stand in a river for half the day when they could party in Monaco?"

"I'm sorry. That had to suck." She knew he didn't like disappointing them, when they'd done so much for him. "It's not too late. You can charter a new yacht."

"Hell, no. It might not be what I promised, but Amie will make it fun for the guys. She knows what they like."

"Are you sure about this? I mean, the press is still going to do what they do—they're going to look for moments to exploit."

"I don't *want* to go on the trip. I want to stay home with you and relax before the season starts."

She dragged the throw off the back of the couch and spread it over her, snuggling in. "The pressure's on. I better come up with some witty conversation, maybe buy some sexy lingerie."

He chuckled. "You don't need to do a damn thing to make hanging out with you more fun than hanging out with a bunch of my teammates. It might've been fun once, the parties, the constant travel, but it gets old. If I never hit up another club as long as I live, I won't miss it."

She played with the fringe on a pillow. "Is Zach coming?"

"I hope not. I don't want him around."

"I mean, I obviously don't know him as well as you, but would he really go to these extremes? Planning, plotting…hiring a photographer?"

"Zach fucks around as much as the other guys, and yet in the press he's known as the family man. Anyone who can pull that off? You bet. You know how they say you can always tell someone's cheating? That there are signs? Well, his wife has no clue. She's always got that smug look, like she's the lucky one. She scored the one player who's so in love with his wife that he'd never cheat. She doesn't know, because he's that discreet. So, yeah, I think it could be him."

"Or it could be just a random guy who happened to get the money shot in Aspen, and then wound up following you here."

"He's from LA."

"Wait, you got him?"

"We got a name. Heard from the private investigator on the way home tonight."

"Well, talk to me."

"It's Dustin Cade. He's got a photography studio in Studio City. Now, we have to find out if he's associated with Zach in any way."

"And Amie. You can't rule her out."

"I'm not ruling anyone out, but the truth is, catching this one guy isn't the answer. The only thing that's going to stop it from happening again is changing my behavior. And I'm doing that, so the guy's not going to be able to catch me in any more compromising positions. You can count on that."

Every night, after the campers hit the sack, the coaches gathered in the faculty room. It had Barcaloungers and a big screen TV, gaming consoles, a kitchen, and poker tables. The dorms had security, so someone was always watching the kids' activities.

Since it was the last night, Cassian had made dinner for the guys. His teammates had jumped on the food like a pack of coyotes. With the music blasting and everyone having a great time, he felt a little better about cancelling the big end-of-season trip.

The guys were being cool about it, but that didn't mean they'd show up next year when he put out the call for volunteers. He'd have to come up with another gift. Couldn't be something they'd buy for themselves, though.

In any event, he had a year to think about it.

"Can we talk to you a sec?"

In the middle of a poker game, Cassian looked over to see Dwayne, Andre, and Caleb. Glancing at his hand, he said, "Fold." He followed the guys out of the room.

"What's up?" If they were pissed about the cancellation, he wouldn't back down. They could just not come next year.

"Surprised to see you still around," Caleb said. "You're usually home by now."

"Talking to your girl," Dwayne said.

Cassian shot him a look of surprise. How'd they know? He thought he'd been so slick.

"Amie?" Caleb asked.

"No, the Lollipop." Dwayne elbowed him.

Caleb looked confused. "I thought he was with Amie."

"Hey. I'm not with Amie. Never have been." He saw from their expressions that he'd taken them off guard with his serious tone. "Sorry, but it's given me a lot of grief, and it pisses me off because I've never touched her."

"Besides, he's with the Lollipop." Andre gave him a chin nod. "We approve."

He grinned. "Thanks. I'll sleep better tonight." He wouldn't lie to them, but he did need their discretion. "But, listen, keep it to yourselves. It's not good for her career to be associated with the Bad Boy Quarterback."

"Ah, you're not so bad," Caleb said.

"So, how come you aren't with her right now?" Dwayne asked.

"She's still in LA for a few more days, and tonight she's putting the finishing touches on her demo." Tomorrow, Dale would hear it.

"Yeah, so anyhow, we wanted to let you know that we talked to Coach," Andre said.

Dread snaked through him. "About what?"

"We heard talk about him looking to trade you, and we're not down with that." Andre had his hands on his hips, looking stern. "He's got it all wrong, and we needed to set him straight."

"We've been there both times those pictures were taken," Dwayne said. "And you haven't done anything wrong."

"You're a good guy," Caleb said. "The best, and it's bullshit that he'd trade you over something you've got no control over."

Cassian was floored. "How'd you guys find out about the trade?"

"I heard you and Dean talking in the Jacuzzi first session," Caleb said.

"Listen, seriously, this can't go beyond us." He looked each guy in the eye.

"Course not," Andre said. "We talked to Dean last night, though. Told him what we were gonna do. He thought it was a good idea, so, this morning we called Coach. Told him we've been by your side for everything. We've done way more shit than you have, so why are *you* getting traded?"

Not one to hide from the truth, Cassian came right out and asked. "What'd he say?"

Caleb looked away.

Fuck. "Never mind. I already know. I talked to him a few days ago. He told me there's a balance between my value to the team and the damage I cause to its reputation. His star player caught in compromising positions with women is costing the business too much."

"He's trying to scare you," Andre said. "Because he didn't say anything like that to us. He said you're the anchor of this team, but you're setting a bad example. He wants you to be a better leader."

"You're a great leader," Caleb said. "And if Zach thinks his mean ass is going to be better, he can go fuck himself."

"I've been on this team my entire career," Andre said.

"And I can tell you this offense works better together than any one Coach has ever had. Which is clear because we *win*."

"We told him you're in the news because you're a good looking, rich, pro baller of a winning team," Dwayne said. "That if he really looks at it, you haven't done anything wrong. You just party a lot and look good while doing it."

"Yeah, okay. It's cool." But it wasn't cool. Cassian knew Coach did mean it. There were plenty of talented kids coming up behind him, ready to be the franchise quarterback for the Mavericks. "I appreciate you having my back." He gave them a chin nod, before heading down the hallway. He just wanted to go home.

Sometimes…it just got exhausting fighting for his place in the world.

———

Gold and platinum records lined Dale's Topanga Canyon home office. The scent of camelia trees wafted through the open windows of the sprawling, one-story house.

As Dale listened to the songs, nodding her head and closing her eyes, Gigi felt like she'd finally landed in her own skin. Forget the production quality, the songs were awesome. Really, surprisingly, strong.

She and Cassian were in a good place—and really, she wasn't sure she could stand more happiness than *that*—and she was finally making her own music. She was on the right track.

In her pale yellow sundress, Dale leaned forward and hit the Off button. "This is…Gigi, you're a gem. An absolute gem." She sat back, steepling her fingers. "You know, I'll never forget seeing you in that karaoke bar. I was completely focused on my daughter's birthday party, when this voice broke through. It was so...powerful, gutsy. It forced everyone, even the staff, to stop what they were doing and watch you. And your stage presence." With a slow shake of her head, she broke into a smile. "By that point, we must've gone through a thousand auditions and we were at the point of giving up. We just couldn't find someone who ticked all the boxes. And that night...I knew I'd found the focal point for our band."

All her joy flattened like a bad soufflé. *I'm a focal point.*

That *so* didn't sit right with Gigi. Here sat this prim woman, who looked like she should be in the front pew at church or organizing a philanthropic event with the Junior League, but for some reason, Dale didn't see her band members as human beings. She saw resources.

I'm a singer.

A songwriter.

An artist.

"I love this." Dale's smile faded. "But I can't sign you to my label if you're associated with that football player. Now, your manager swears you knew him growing up and reconnected on the tour, and that there's nothing going on between you two. And, if that's the case, then I'm very interested in moving forward with you. If you can tell me you're not seeing him, I'll present this demo to the team."

Oh, great. Draw a line, why don't you?

Give up Cassian, and I get a contract. I preserve my reputation in the music industry, record an album of my own work, and use Clean Beatz as a launching pad to the next level or...

Give up Clean Beatz, start over from the very beginning —only this time with a tarnished reputation—but I get to keep Cassian, the love of my life.

The love of my life. Joy glittered through her.

She'd held back for so long, so afraid of getting burned again. But, now that she'd told him how she felt, their bond had grown even deeper, stronger. Neither was holding back, and it was...well, it was something she wouldn't give up for anything.

"Dale, I've loved Cassian Ellis since I was fourteen years old. We found our way back to each other on this tour, and it's special. It's that once-in-a-lifetime kind of love. Asking me to give him up is like telling my heart to stop beating." Getting her thoughts together, she glanced away. "He's a good man and he loves me..." *No, that's not what I want to say.* "He said that when he lost me, nothing mattered anymore. And, now that he has me back, he's never going to let me go. He won't do anything to jeopardize our relationship." She smoothed her hands down her jeans-clad thighs. When she glanced up, she expected one of Dale's disapproving looks.

But her expression wasn't hard at all. Dale came around her desk, perching on the edge. "I like your demo. I'm not going forward with the third record in the Lollipop contract, so I like the idea of coming out with a solo project from the lead singer, but I need to be clear. If Clean Beatz produces your album, you'll be expected to adhere to our morality code."

"I understand. I haven't violated it, and I don't plan to." She held her ground on that point, because there was nothing immoral in Cassian carrying her.

And, really, all she wanted was for this album to give her legitimacy in the music industry. It was the only way she'd ever have the chance to approach a man like Irwin Ledger.

"Okay. Let me talk it over with the team." When Dale

stood up, that big grin was back in place. "I can't guarantee they're going to buy the Bad Boy Quarterback suddenly settling down. Maybe, if no more photos of him show up in the press, it'll prove your point."

"With the changes he's making in his life, there won't be." She stood up, too. "I'm really excited about this."

"Me, too. We can't use the duet with Grant, though. With his three divorces and rehab stint, that's a no-go. In fact, while you're under contract with us, you won't be able to release it. But you've got plenty of material here, and there's no question about your ability to write hits."

What the hell? "Grant's a really good guy. He spent the better part of ten years on the road. That's hard for anyone. But he's cleaned up his life. He's in a really good place. He's a success story, because he's healed."

"There's no discussion on this point, hon. If you're going to fight for that duet, then there's no deal here. Give it some thought and let me know. I won't pitch the demo until I know you're okay leaving off the duet."

She wanted to say, *Fuck you, and fuck your contract.* Grant was a good man, and she wouldn't let anyone condemn him because of his mistakes.

But, then, she reminded herself what he'd said. That their duet was timeless. After this contract ended, she'd put together a new demo for Irwin, and she'd include it. "No, it's fine. I don't even have his permission to put it on a solo album."

"Great. Then, we're on the same page. I'll get back to you soon, but I have a really good feeling about this."

Gigi wished she did, too.

. . .

As she pulled in front of her cottage, Gigi knew she couldn't spend one more night apart from him. Talking to Dale had crystallized everything.

She loved Cassian, and if they had a chance in hell of working, they needed to be in the same town together.

He was sincerely making changes to clean up his life for her.

Parking in her driveway, she hurried across the lawn and up her porch steps. Before unlocking the door, she pulled out her phone to text him.

Gigi: **Guess what? I'm coming home early!**

Her finger hovered over the Send button. *Wait a second.* Where was he right now? What was he doing?

Right. Camp had ended, and they'd started their vacation. Which meant the guys would be out on their adventures.

If she texted him, he'd insist on picking her up from the airport. He'd spend the night with her—not his teammates. And, since he was already letting them down by staying in Calamity, she didn't want to make it worse by taking him away from them.

Maybe she should stick to her travel plans?

No. If she got in tonight, she could see him in the morning, before he left for…actually, she wasn't sure what their plans were for tomorrow.

Which meant…ugh. She had to ask Amie about the schedule.

She canceled her text and started a new one.

Gigi: **Hey, girl. You figure out you're not getting in my man's pants yet?**

She chuckled, as she hit delete and then tried again.

Gigi: **How's it going? Can you keep a secret?**

Amie: **Of course! This better be good!**

Gigi: **I'm coming back to Calamity tonight, and I want to see Cassian, but I don't want to interrupt his time with the guys. What's the plan tomorrow?**

Wait, did she need to continue the ruse? Her family, his teammates, now Dale knew…did she still need to hide her relationship?

Nope. She was done with that. No more hiding from anybody.

Amie: **Knew you two were a thing! Awesome! And white water rafting starts at ten.**

Gigi: **Ah. So that's all day.**

Amie: **Yes, but you can come early. I've got a breakfast buffet scheduled in the suite for nine. Do you want to come by around eight?**

Gigi: **That sounds great.**

Amie: **Don't worry about waking the guys up. I promise, after tonight's party, they're going to be zombies in the morning. I'll have a key for you at the front desk. Just come on up. He'll be thrilled to see you!**

She wanted to ask if Cassian was partying that hard. He never seemed wasted when she talked to him. But she would never give Amie that kind of power.

Gigi: **Awesome, thanks!**

Amie: **Welcome!**

As she entered her cottage, an uncomfortable sensation tripped down her spine. With the guys partying like that, women would be involved.

They hadn't found the photographer yet, so he could find his way into the hotel.

Stop it. Don't borrow trouble.

Everything will be just fine.

Chapter Eighteen

A RAP ON THE DOOR STARTLED CASSIAN OUT OF A deep sleep. "Yeah?" Hitching up on an elbow, he checked his phone, a little disappointed he hadn't heard from Gigi last night.

The door opened, and Amie walked in.

Ah, hell. "What're you doing here?"

"Tito texted me last night." Her eyes were puffy and red. "They wanted cigars, so I brought them by. I wound up crashing on the couch. It was too late to go to my place." Tears streamed down her cheeks, and she held her phone against her stomach. "Steve dumped me. He's done." She stood in the doorway, fragile and overwrought.

He threw the covers off. "Let me get dressed. I'll meet you in the living room."

"Everyone's sleeping. Never mind." Her features crumpled in distress. "It's fine. I'll just go back to the condo." But her head lowered, her shoulders shook, and she swiped under her eyes with the back of her hand.

He didn't know if she was manipulating him, but he

knew nobody could fake tears like that. "What happened? I thought you guys were good."

"So did I." She sat down on the edge of his bed. Wracked with sobs, she hid her face in her hands.

Shit. Still groggy, Cassian set his feet on the floor. "Okay, what...what happened? You said moving into the condo was a good thing for your relationship, that you two had never been closer."

"Some of the guys posted pictures of the party last night. I wasn't doing anything. I was dancing with Andre and a few other guys, but there was nothing bad about it. I was dressed...I wasn't... I mean, I was wasted, but I wasn't gross." For a moment, she got too choked up to talk.

"He...he says he's a simple guy who wants a simple life, and I'm anything but simple."

"You've been dating him for two years. Isn't it a little late in the game for him to figure that out now?"

"Yes. It's so unfair." She fell against him, her forehead hot and damp on his bare shoulder, which meant...*shit.* He was shirtless, wearing nothing but boxers.

"He says...he says we want different things. He says I won't be happy being his wife, that I'll always want to be the center of attention, surrounded by fancy things. He said I'm too materialistic."

He wanted to say, *The guy's probably right.* She and Steve didn't sound like the best fit, especially if he was always threatening to break up with her. But he knew she needed to vent, not get a lecture, so he stayed quiet.

There might not be any cameras angled on them, but it still wasn't right to be comforting her in his bedroom... on his bed...in his boxers. Eyes on the jeans and T-shirt he'd slung across the chair, he started to get up.

"But he's wrong. I don't need all that." She tucked her

face into his pec, her body shaking. "I just feel like I've invested so much into this relationship and for him to throw me away? I can't…I…"

Shit. He hated to see her destroyed like this. *Not going to push her away right now.*

He'd give her a minute to calm down.

He was safe here in his bedroom.

"Good morning." Gigi smiled at the man behind the reception desk. "I'm Gigi Cavanaugh. I believe you have a key waiting for me. Cassian Ellis's suite."

His eyes went wide, but he worked hard to school his features. "We sure do. Let me grab that for you." He reached for a folio with her name scrawled across it. "Normally, I'd ask for ID. But you're….*gah*. I'm sorry. I'm supposed to play it cool with the guests." He leaned back, glancing into the office. Then, he whispered, "Could I please have your autograph? I'd tell you it's for my niece, but I'd be lying. My friends make fun of me, but I don't care. I *love* the Lollipops."

She grinned. "There's no shame in loving any kind of music. I literally have to pull the car over every time "Faithfully" comes on the radio, just so I can act it out like I did when I was a thirteen-year-old girl in my bedroom pretending to be on stage." She didn't let him see the way his reaction stung.

She got it a lot from people. They didn't even realize the insult behind the compliment. Hopefully, one day she'd be known for *her* music, and people wouldn't be embarrassed to like it.

"And you made it, playing arenas around the world.

Talk about realizing your dreams." He tore a sheet of paper off a notepad and handed her a pen. "Thank you so much. When does the next album drop, and is your tour coming anywhere near Calamity?"

"I wish I had answers for you, but nothing's confirmed yet." She wrote, *It was great to meet you, Arturo! Have a great day, Gigi.* And then handed it back. "Here you go."

Grinning, he flapped the note like he was trying to dry the ink. "Thank you so much." When she started to walk off, he called, "You'll need to swipe that key in the elevator to get to the top floor. And when the door opens, you're in it. It's like a huge apartment."

"Perfect, thank you." It seemed crazy, because she'd only been gone less than a week, but she already missed Cassian so badly. And she couldn't wait to tell him she was all-in.

The minute she saw him, she was going to jump into his arms.

Maybe she'd lock his bedroom door, so she could give him a proper wake-up call. Her whole body heated at the thought.

She hit the call button, aware of the eerie quiet of the lobby. Still, even though Cassian had booked the entire hotel, she didn't feel safe. They hadn't caught the photographer. He could be lurking anywhere.

She got a tingle at the back of her neck. The moment the elevator doors opened, she stepped inside, like she was fleeing from danger. She swiped the keycard for the penthouse.

Their time together was almost over, and it made her scared that they were going to live so far apart. Right when she'd decided she couldn't live without him, it was time for him to start training camp.

How would they survive three thousand miles apart?

Unless…what if she moved to Boston? For the short term, she could rent studio space. But, eventually, they could buy a place together. She could build a studio in it.

What does it matter where I live? I can literally do my business anywhere in the world.

The thrill of it swept through her. She was going to do it. She was going to move to Boston.

Excitement popped like champagne bubbles underneath her skin. She could make this album with Dale, live with Cassian…*God.* She hadn't fully believed they could truly be together. A part of her had held back, thinking they only had this summer.

But it had finally happened. After all this time, all the heartache, she and Cassian were together.

Forever.

Nothing felt more right. She'd never felt more complete.

The doors opened, and she nearly choked at the strong smell, a mix of booze, greasy food, and old gym bag. She stepped onto the marble-tiled floor into the huge living area.

Holy shit. Bodies were passed out everywhere. And were those…Jesus, used condoms on the floor?

Liquor bottles and pizza boxes littered the tables. A huge man lay curled up in the fetal position near the fireplace, and a couple women cuddled on the couch.

For a moment, all she could hear was the pounding of her heart.

If Cassian were here…what if the photographer had gotten pictures of him partying this hard? If he'd been this drunk, had he been dirty dancing with any of these women?

She felt sick.

What if Cassian had gotten so messed up, he'd passed out with some woman wrapped around him?

Stop it. Stop it right now. He said he's done with this lifestyle.

Every night while she was in LA, he'd gone home at nine so they could catch up with each other.

He loves me. She knew that. Down to her bones, she knew he loved her and would never jeopardize what they had. Which meant he wouldn't get so drunk he didn't know what he was doing.

She didn't bother looking to see if he was one of the guys in this room.

He wouldn't hurt us. He wouldn't.

So, which was Cassian's bedroom? She headed left, where she saw two closed doors along a dark hallway. She would guess the master bedroom would be off by itself, so she made her way across the living area, stepping around the refuse and sleeping bodies. She felt a little better, knowing—even if it was just logistically—that he was somehow separated from the decadence.

As she approached, her body tightened in fear of what she'd find behind that door.

Stop doubting him. You can't build a relationship on a shaky foundation.

I trust him. I do.

Except....she thought she heard murmuring.

The closer she got, the clearer the sound. Quiet conversation.

And, then, she was sure she heard a female voice.

Amie's.

No. It can't be. She's not staying here.

In the back of her mind, she was aware of noises—the

suite's door closing, sneaker soles squeaking on marble—but every cell in her body had gone on red alert, as she focused keenly on what was going on behind that crack in the door.

The rush of adrenaline was so strong she saw stars behind her eyes. Her heart hurt from beating too fast and hard. She peered inside to find Amie in nothing but a football jersey sitting on the bed, nestled within the shelter of Cassian's muscled arm.

The shock of it hit her system, stinging her nerves.

Cassian was naked, other than a pair of black boxer briefs. Amie, in a jersey—wait, was that Cassian's number? Yes, God, it was. With her bare legs, she was snuggled against him, and they were talking like lovers.

A sickening punch of betrayal shot through her. She looked to her boyfriend, the man who couldn't live without her, the man who'd rather retire from football than lose her. The volatile mix of rage and hurt spun, gathering velocity, turning into a whirlwind. "Cassian?" She smacked the door open and strode in. "What're you *doing*?"

He jumped off the bed, pointing at something just over her shoulder. "Turn that off."

It was only then that she felt the presence behind her. She swung around to find a man recording on his phone.

Cassian stalked around her. "Right the fuck now."

Chaos erupted, feet pounding, as some of the players came rushing in. Amie, in his jersey, stood there watching the scene unfold. Gigi didn't buy for a second her look of shock and upset.

Guys were shouting. Andre was wrestling the phone out of the man's hands.

Gigi went numb, sounds turned muffled, and right then she heard a crack inside her body.

She was done living like this. She was done with drama and heartache and pain and betrayal. She was just done.

"*Gigi.*" Cassian closed the gap between them, but her fight or flight instincts kicked in, and she shoved him hard. Hard enough that he—still moving toward her—lost his footing and had to sidestep, catching himself before he fell.

She bolted.

Oh, God, oh God, oh God, this isn't happening. Some of the guys were just getting up. She heard someone say, "What's going on?"

In the distance, she heard Amie cry, "You told me you're not together. You said you're not with her."

Cassian's bare feet slapped on the marble. "Get out of my way."

His voice was so scary, so fierce, she swung around to see who he'd talk to like that. She watched as he shoved the photographer aside.

Hands shaking, she hit the elevator button. The doors opened right away, and she stepped inside.

"Gigi, dammit. *Wait.*" Cassian sounded desperate, panicked.

She didn't care. She pressed the Close button, relieved when she blocked him out.

Because she was repulsed. She didn't want to see him. She didn't want him to touch her. And she didn't want to hear his pathetic, lying voice.

She was done.

She was never going to trust that bastard again.

Zach grabbed Cassian's arm and hauled him back. *What the fuck?* "Get off me."

The guy released him like his skin was covered in shit. "You're wearing *boxers*."

Cassian glanced down at his bare chest and legs, the briefs the only thing keeping him from nudity. "Fuck. I have to get her."

"You're not running through the lobby of a five-star hotel like this. There's staff all over the place." He looked disgusted. "You want to draw more attention to yourself?"

"I have to get Gigi back and explain."

"Explain what?" Zach lifted both arms in exasperation. "You had a woman in your bedroom. A woman you spend a lot of time with."

"Yeah, because her boyfriend broke up with her. She's upset."

"You think, if my wife lived in this town, that I'd let another woman into my bedroom? No. I would not."

He'd known that. He'd almost gotten dressed and brought Amie out to the living area. But he hadn't. "It was you. You set me up, you fucking asshole."

"*Me?* Why would I draw more attention to your drama?"

"You want to get me traded."

"I…*what?*" He looked genuinely confused. "I don't want you to get traded. I want you to stop being an embarrassment to this team. Is that what you've been thinking all this time?" He didn't wait for an answer. "You can't be this stupid. Everyone knows how much Amie wants to be on that TV show."

Panic flared inside him. He shot a look to the scuffle behind him, Amie, Andre, and the photographer.

Gigi was right. From the start, she'd told him, but he'd just kept defending his "friend."

Fuck.

Cassian barreled down the highway, fingers in a death grip on the steering wheel.

What have I done?

Why hadn't he gotten Amie out of his room? He'd known he needed to get dressed…

A clammy feeling crawled over his skin. The moment he'd started to pull away, she'd turned on the waterworks. Those wracking sobs had about killed him. He'd believed her.

And she'd been playing him. Using him.

Was there even a boyfriend?

How could his instincts have been so off about her?

He knew—even in this moment, when he was panicked and out of his mind—that Amie had never been hitting on him. He knew when a woman wanted to hook up.

But she *had* wanted to get on the show, and she'd used him to do it. She'd figured the press would be just more of the same for him.

Why hadn't he figured that out?

What was the matter with him?

Why did he keep fucking up?

The image of Gigi racing out of the suite—

Fuck, the suite. She'd seen people passed out, used condoms on the floor….

He might've cancelled the trip, but he hadn't stopped the party. He'd just thrown it in his hometown.

He'd fucked up. Badly.

Okay, okay. He'd talk to her. Explain.

Early morning summer traffic on I-191—campers and vans, tourists heading into the mountains—slowed him, when every second mattered. With every minute that ticked by, the distrust sank deeper, hardening from molten to rock. Veering across the divider line, he saw a car coming in the distance, so he floored it, accelerating past the RV in front of him.

The oncoming car laid on its horn, but he didn't care. He had to get to her.

And say what? He'd promised no more drama, and not only had she walked into his bedroom to find him in nothing but boxers consoling another woman, but the whole scene had been recorded for *NFL Cheerleader.* Andre might've gotten possession of the phone, but not before the photographer had emailed himself a copy of it.

Cassian had called his manager to see what legal recourse he had—because that shit was not going to air.

If it did, her shot at a solo album with Clean Beatz was dead.

And it's one hundred percent my fault.

Ten years ago, her dad had kept him away from her just so he wouldn't keep her from realizing her potential, and he'd gone and done it anyway.

He slammed his palm on the wheel. He'd trusted Amie with his camp, his kids. He'd talked her through countless crises…when she'd been dropped from her show, when her boyfriend had dumped her.

Why would she do this to him?

Why would she take advantage of his friendship like this?

It didn't matter. The only thing that mattered was what he'd done to Gigi.

And if she'd ever forgive him.

Pressing the intercom outside the Cavanaugh's security gate, Cassian's knee jackhammered. *Come on, come on.*

"Cassian?" Mrs. Cavanaugh said.

"Yes. Hello. I'm here to see Gigi. Can you let me in?"

"No. She doesn't want to see you and, frankly, I don't blame her."

The woman was fierce in general, but she'd go to the mat for her daughters.

"I did *not* cheat on her. I would never cheat on her. Let me in. I have to talk to her."

"Listen to me very carefully. *She doesn't want to see you.* You need to go away and leave her alone. Maybe one day, once you get your shit together, you can write her an apology on nice stationery. But there's nothing you can say that she'll ever need to see your face for."

The world went silent. The early morning air was scented with sage, and fog sat low to the ground. He pressed the buzzer again. He had no idea if anyone was listening, but he had to get through to someone. "I know I fucked up, but I didn't touch Amie. I don't want her. I don't want…I fucking love your daughter. I *love* her. I would never hurt her."

"And yet…you keep doing it. Again and again."

He lowered his head in despair.

A Jeep came around the bend in the driveway. From the breadth of those shoulders and the size of the man's head, Cassian knew it was security. He didn't care. He'd stay here until Gigi came out. She had to leave at some point.

The Jeep stopped on the other side of the iron gate. A big black boot hit the asphalt, and a behemoth of a man got out. Dressed in black jeans and a black T-shirt, the man approached Cassian with menace. "We can do this nicely, and you can leave on your own accord, or I can call the police and make your life even more messed up."

"I just need to talk to her."

"It ain't all about you, now is it? Gigi wants you to leave her the hell alone, so how much do you care about her? Enough to scat?"

Defeat smothered his lungs, making it impossible to take a full breath. "Yeah. That much." He jerked the gearshift into Reverse and backed out onto the road.

He'd had the miracle of a second chance, and he'd blown it all to hell.

Chapter Nineteen

"She's twenty-seven years old, and she's doing it again."

Gigi froze halfway down the staircase, her hand in a box of cookies. Her parents didn't know she'd left her bedroom.

"Last time she was seventeen." Her dad sounded calm, reasonable. "And, keep in mind, it all worked out. She went to USC, got discovered…she's strong. She'll pull through."

I'm strong, my ass. Gigi dug into the box and fished around for another cookie but came out with nothing but crumb-crusted fingertips. *Thanks for caring, Dad.*

"You're saying that because you don't want to deal with the guilt. We broke them up. Maybe Cassian wouldn't have become such a party animal if we hadn't interfered."

"Sweetheart, I pulled Cassian out of *detention*. He's always had a self-destructive streak. And, I'll tell you what, I stand by my decision to keep him away from my daughter at that time in her life. Besides, even If I hadn't warned him off her, he would've found another way to blow himself up."

"That's not true. He loves her. Anyone can see how much he loves her."

Three nights ago, wrapped up in a blanket, a box of tissue on her lap, Gigi had watched the footage of that night. It had been picked up by a gossip site and had gone viral. She'd gotten to see her expression as she'd raced out of the suite, and she'd gotten a close-up of Cassian who'd looked like he was witnessing a car crash.

She hadn't left the house since. What her dad didn't get was that this time she'd had all of him.

All of him.

And it had been almost perfect.

Losing him at seventeen…she'd lost the possibility of what they could be. This time? She'd lost her whole heart.

"He's damaged goods," her dad said.

That's one thing we can agree on. Gigi continued down the stairs, not appreciating their conversation.

"Well, you were, too," her mom said.

"And how long did it take me to get my shit together after I met you?"

"No time at all. You changed…" Her mom snapped her fingers. "Like that."

"Exactly. This time, he had her just like he always wanted, and he still blew it."

"Did he, though? I mean, you saw that woman. She was weeping. She was beside herself. How could anyone turn her away?"

"Nope. Not buying it. He was in his boxers."

"I know. I can't…" Her mom let out a weary exhalation. "I just don't want her falling apart like last time. That was really hard on me."

Breezing into the kitchen, Gigi tossed the cookie box on the island. "I won't."

Her mom startled. "Oh, honey. I didn't know you were listening."

"I was. Heard every single word. But don't worry. I'm done with cookies." She reached for the box, crushing it with her bare hands. "I'm also done with crying. I mean, whose fault is it, anyway? I'm the slow learner. Has he ever been different? No." *Not just no, but hell no.* "This is who he is." She was thirsty. She needed water. No, milk. Tea, maybe? She just…nothing really hit the spot. "Do we have lemonade? I'm craving it."

"I'll make you some." Her mom gestured weakly to the huge bowl of fruit on the counter.

"I can make it myself." She pulled a pitcher out from a cabinet and a knife from the drawer. "Stop looking at me like that. I'll bounce back. I always do."

Her parents exchanged concerned looks.

Wielding the knife, she said, "What? I do." She stood there in her pajamas and slippers, with cookie breath and unwashed hair. "I'm not giving Cassian Ellis another minute of my life. And do you know why? Because I get it now. Like you said, he's damaged goods. Maybe it's because his parents died in a car crash, and he had to go into foster care for a couple of weeks until his uncle showed up. Or because he was dumped into a whole new world with a family he barely knew. They put him in Griffin's room—like, really? Two teenage boys who were total strangers? And then he's dumped into a new school—a small one—with already established cliques. And *then* he gets plucked out of detention by the great Tyler Cavanaugh, and lo and behold he's on the fast track to becoming a football star."

Her mom took the knife and started slicing a lemon in half.

"I mean, his life's been nothing but drama from the time he was fourteen, and that's all he knows. Maybe all the drama keeps him from being alone with his thoughts, his feelings, from really facing the horrific loss of his parents. I mean, has he ever stopped moving long enough to really face that his parents *died*? He never talks about it, that life as he knew it flipped in the blink of an eye." Why were her parents looking at her like she was crazycakes? She was telling them she was fine. She touched the side of her head. "Don't worry. I'm washing my hair in the morning."

With a sad sigh, her dad reached out and pulled her into her arms. "I'm sorry he let you down again, sweetheart."

Gigi felt unstable, a little light-headed, her knees weak. Well, sure, she'd been living off cookies and chocolate milk.

And, then, she felt her mom's arms encircling her waist, fingers sifting through her hair, the same comforting gesture Gigi had grown up with. She felt like a little girl all over again.

There was nothing so familiar as her mom's scent. The same perfume she'd worn Gigi's whole life, mixed her dad's rugged, manly pine scent...it just made her feel safe and at home. "I just wish I understood why he keeps messing up. Why didn't he see what Amie was doing? Why didn't he kick her out of his room?"

"Because she's on his team," her dad said. "And the team's his family. And if you've never really had one, if you've never fit in anywhere, then you hold on pretty tightly to the one you cobble together. It's damn scary to be alone in the world."

Alarmed at the pain in his voice, Gigi stepped out of their embrace.

"His parents didn't have time for him," her dad said. "Griffin didn't want to share his bedroom with him, the high school team already had a quarterback. Even after he got drafted, Cassian replaced Ben Grady. He's just…never belonged anywhere."

Her mom reached for him, wrapping an arm around his waist.

Her dad hadn't belonged anywhere until he'd met Joss Montalbano. And once he found her, he'd burrowed in. Deeply and irrevocably. And her mom had given him all the love and nurturing he'd craved his whole life.

"He belonged with me." They looked at her, both of them reeking of pity. It reinforced what she'd already accepted. "I love him. I honestly don't think there's anyone else in the world I want to be with. But I can't have him." She took in a steadying breath. "When I look down the road, when I see myself making a family of my own, I see him. I can't imagine growing old with anyone else—but what kind of chaos and drama is he going to bring into our lives? He swore he wouldn't do anything to jeopardize us. He said he wanted to deserve me." The footage flashed in her mind, Amie wearing nothing but his jersey, sitting in the shelter of Cassian's arms. *God.* She'd never scrub that image. "I'm going back to LA."

Yep. It was time.

"I have to meet with Dale. She needs to know I'm not with Cassian, and there won't be any more drama from me." She looked at her parents, her heart just absolutely broken, and she wanted them to fix her. To give her the magic words that would make everything all right and enable her to be with Cassian.

"I'm sorry, baby." And the fact that her mom—the woman who never gave up, who always had a fresh idea and a new approach—had given up, just drove it all home.

It's truly over.

Strong arms banded around her, and the dam broke. Tears trickled down her cheeks. She felt their love and support like a powerful force streaming through her, giving her strength.

It broke her heart, but she would *not* fall apart like last time. She was stronger, better.

Cassian Ellis would not sink her.

On her way into the bathroom to grab her toiletry bag, Gigi's phone vibrated.

Her flight left in three hours, so she supposed it was time to talk to him. Setting down her towel, she went back to the nightstand. Sure enough, Cassian's name was on the screen.

She drew in a calming breath. "Hello?"

"Gigi." He sounded tormented.

"Yes." Her voice wavered. She didn't want to talk to him, because she didn't know if she could resist him.

"Thank Christ. It's been four days. I've been going out of my mind. You know I didn't touch her, right?"

And just like that, her temper flared. "Of course you touched her. I walked in on it, remember?" *No, no, no.* She couldn't let herself get all worked up over it. If she did, she'd get whisked right back into the drama. "Look, that's not even the point, and you know it. You just keep *doing* this, and I'm done."

"I know. Just…from my perspective, she came in crying, upset about a breakup I felt partially responsible for. I was going to get my clothes on and meet her in the living room, but she broke down. She was inconsolable."

"Cassian, in what world is it okay for a woman to come into your bedroom half-naked and expect to be comforted on your bed?"

He went quiet.

Exactly. She'd finally figured out the problem. "Think about that." *I know I will.* "Other than my sisters and my parents, no one would dream of taking the liberties with me that people take with you." There was no point in talking to him. As long as he didn't see his problems, he'd never change. "Listen, I only answered your call to let you know I'm going back to LA."

"What? No. Okay, I'm coming over."

"Don't bother. You won't get past the gate. I'm just letting you know that I'm done. I put up with the insta-bility of loving you in high school, but I won't do it as an adult."

"*Instability?* I love you. That's…I am devoted to you and you alone. There's not a shred of uncertainty in me about my feelings for you."

"I know that. I'm not afraid you'll cheat on me or fall out of love, but I'll never stop worrying what you're doing when you're away from me." The ache grew, forming a knot in her throat. "I do love you, you know. Very much. I just can't be with you."

"You can. Every couple has hurdles."

"That's true, but this is more than a hurdle. You're always going to break my heart, because you have no boundaries. You let people take advantage of you, and until you see that there's no chance for you to have a real relationship with anyone. But, most definitely, not with me."

"I fucking love you, Gigi. I love you down to my soul. You're part of me, and I can't live without you."

"Well, you're going to have to." Big words, tough voice. But underneath them lay a foundation as fractured as her heart.

"No, just listen. Listen to me."

The clouds had finally parted, and a light fell onto a glimmering truth. "It's funny, because everyone sees you as the life of the party. But think about it, Cassian. The people who trash your hotel, drive your fancy cars, drink all your booze…they don't respect you. And, as the captain of your football team, that's what you need most. Respect."

His silence made her believe he was really listening, and that gave her hope. *Dammit.*

"You had two jobs," she continued. "One was to lead your teammates, and the other was to take care of us. From what I saw in that suite, you weren't doing either. I love you, Cassian. I do. But I love you for the man you could be, and not the man who wants to belong so badly he lets people take advantage of him. Now, let me go. I have a plane to catch."

If Cassian were the type of man to accept defeat, he wouldn't have become the quarterback for one of the top teams in the country.

The sun filtered through an early morning haze, and he lowered his visor, watching his speed on the highway.

He didn't blame Gigi for leaving him. How many

times had she warned him about Amie, and he'd ignored her? No, what killed him was that she'd left because he hadn't protected her. *Them.* Even if Amie hadn't turned out to be a selfish, manipulating, self-serving…He drew a breath. *This isn't about Amie.* It never was.

This is about my lack of boundaries. Boundaries he'd never bothered with because, after losing Gigi in high school, nothing had mattered.

They very much fucking mattered now.

He flicked on his turn signal, and after a minivan sailed by, he turned into the driveway. He might've been inclined to give Gigi a little more time, but training camp started in one week and…

I miss her. Once, somewhere off the coast of Thailand, he'd gone scuba diving. Something had gone wrong with his tank, and he'd lost oxygen. The inability to breathe, the pressure on his chest—compounded by the weight of water—*that's what it feels like to be without her.*

So, here he was. Back at the Cavanaugh house. Idling outside the iron gate, he pushed the button on the security box.

"Again?" Joss sounded amused.

"Yes, ma'am. You going to let me in this time?" This was his third attempt at a visit. Each time they'd told him she'd gone back to LA, and there was nothing they could do for him.

"Are you here to talk about something other than my daughter?" she asked.

"No."

"Have a nice day."

"Wait. Can I please talk to Tyler?"

"He's not here."

"Okay. Thank you."

"That's it? You're giving up?"

"This is Gigi we're talking about." He glanced in the rearview mirror. No one behind him. "I'm going to wait for Tyler to come home."

"Cassian…you know there's nothing we can do, right? Gigi's moved on."

There it was again, that suffocating feeling. He jerked the gearshift into Park and got out, gulping in fresh mountain air.

I lost her. I fucking lost her.

"I'm not giving up, you know." He kicked a pebble, watched it skitter across the asphalt and land on the soft grass. "What happened with her contract? Did I ruin it for her?"

"Yes. It's over."

Shit. Fuck. "No solo album?"

"That's right."

"So, what's next?"

"She has no idea."

"Can't she get her demo to Irwin?"

A car raced by, trailing a country song. A hawk soared overhead. But Joss had gone silent.

"You still there?"

"Yes. I'm here. I'm just surprised you knew Irwin's name. You paid attention. It's nice."

"I love her."

"I know you do."

"So…Irwin?"

"She says she doesn't want to blow her one shot at getting his attention until she's a few steps removed from being a Lollipop."

And there it was. A way to make up for what he'd done. "Okay. Great." For the first time, he felt empowered. "Excellent." He had a plan. He'd make things right for her. He got back in his truck, slammed the gearshift into Reverse, and started to back up, when a Land Cruiser roared up behind him.

Tyler Cavanaugh.

The angry man drove right up to his fender, cut the engine, and swung out of the truck. "What the hell're you doing here, Ellis? You know she's not here."

It was hard to look his mentor in the eye, knowing what he'd done. What Tyler had seen on that recording. The look in his daughter's eyes, as she'd raced out of the bedroom.

Fuck. A thousand poisoned darts pierced his heart, and he couldn't escape the pain. He leaned into his truck, grabbed the waxed paper bag off the passenger seat, and handed it to him.

The big, muscular man scowled but opened the bakery bag anyway. When he saw his treat, he turned wide-eyed, like a kid getting a full-size candy bar on Halloween. He looked up. "Is it chocolate?"

"You save some of that babka for me, old man," his wife shouted from the speaker.

"I'm not going to eat the whole thing."

"No," his wife said. "But you'll hide it."

"Make some coffee. I'll get rid of Cassian, and be right in."

If his heart didn't hurt so fucking badly, he might've smiled at that. "I'm the one who brought it to you."

The man took a big bite out of the loaf of sweet, braided bread, closed his eyes, and moaned. "Damn, that's good." Then, he put the rest back in the bag and rolled it closed. "What do you want?"

"I want you to help me get Gigi back."

"No. Anything else?"

"If you'd messed up, and Joss had left you, would you have just let her go?

"*I didn't fuck up once I found her.*" The man rarely shouted, but his face had flushed with exasperation.

And, of course, he was right. The truth gutted him. That he'd finally won—earned—the love his life.

And then lost her.

Again.

The giant, sucking mass of loss threatened to yank him under, but fuck that. He wasn't giving up. Not ever. "I've loved your daughter since I was fourteen. I'm not giving up until I get her back."

"Well, how's that going to work if she doesn't want to be with you?"

"I…" He hadn't expected that question. "I'm going to prove to her that she can trust me."

"Been there, done that, fucked it up."

Fear clapped its steely jaws inside the cage beneath his feet. *Stay strong.* "I need your help."

Tyler shook his head. "You can't have it."

"You don't think I'm good for her?"

"*She* doesn't think you're good for her."

"I am. I will be."

"You'll be whatever she needs you to be, right?"

"Yes." *Okay, good. We're getting somewhere.* "Of course."

Tyler pointed a finger at him like it was loaded. "And *that's* why you can't have her."

Cassian felt more lost than ever. Panic made his blood pound. "I don't know what you're talking about. I just want you to help me."

"I'm not talking to you about my daughter." He reached into the bag and tore off a chunk of bread.

Sniffing it, he took one small bite. "Jesus, Mother of God." He closed his eyes, tension gripping his features. "How can anything taste this good? How?" When he opened his eyes, he must've picked up on Cassian's torment, because he turned compassionate. "Not gonna talk to you about my daughter, but I will talk to you about football."

"I don't need to talk about football."

"Okay." He closed up the bag and lifted it. "Thanks." And he started back to his truck.

Desperate, his ability to stay strong on its last thin thread, he blurted, "Coach is talking about trading me."

Tyler lowered his head and sighed. Slowly, he turned. "And what do you think of that?"

"I'm pissed." Which he hadn't even known—because, so far, he'd just been anxious. "I've got the best quarterback rating in the league."

"Don't bother reciting your stats to me. I know them. We all know them. You've got superior arm strength and pinpoint accuracy. You've got a sixth-sense connection with your receivers. That's why you're the captain of the winningest team in the league. Yup. Got it." He tipped his head, a challenge in his eyes. "But you're also in the news for threesomes and love triangles."

Shame spread through him hot and fast. It was one thing to experience that kind of exposure in the news and among his teammates. Another thing entirely hearing the sordidness from his mentor. "Nothing was how they represented it. I've never touched Amie."

"Thought we were talkin' about football?"

"I—" He was absolutely right. *And this is what Coach has been trying to tell you.* "Coach says I'm not a leader."

"Is he right?"

"I've led my team to two Super Bowls."

"Again, I know your accomplishments. I'm talking about qualities they don't track on the scoreboard. Leaders lead by example. What kind of example are you setting?"

"I'm the first one on the field, the first one to help set up. I live clean."

"Okay, so then Coach is going after you for no reason?"

"No. It's like you said. My celebrity overshadows football." *That's putting it nicely.*

"Cassian, you've been dancing a long damn time. You danced to get Griffin to like you, to get your aunt and uncle to keep you, to get your teammates to like you. Aren't you tired of it?"

He let that sink in. Experiences from a dozen years flipped through his mind, forcing him to admit the truth. "I'm exhausted."

"You want to play ball?"

"I do."

"You want to be captain?"

He didn't even have to think about it. "Yes. I do."

"Then quit trying to win the guys with vacations and blow-out parties and start earning their respect. Everything you do with them needs to be about ball. You can take them on retreats—hell, you're supposed to do that. But the focus has to be on bonding. Why do you and your receivers have that sixth sense for each other? Because you're good friends. You trust and respect each other. Believe me, when you're partying, there's no bonding going on. When you're drunk, you're not connecting on any level."

"The guys love those trips. It's the only reason they volunteer at my football camp."

Whatever he'd said twisted Tyler's features in pain.

"Ah, hell, son." He set the bakery bag on the hood of Cassian's truck and then came right up to him. He gripped his shoulders. "Cassian, listen to me. You're enough. Your talent, your leadership, your instincts…you're enough. I'm sorry nobody ever told you that."

Emotion hit like a wall of water, slamming him back. The knot in his throat felt sharp as razorblades, and he couldn't speak.

He was thrown back to his childhood, the little boy watching his dad—always watching. Waiting for him to notice him. Hang out with him. Talk to him.

That fucking *longing*.

And then his dad had died before he'd ever had a chance to know him. Know him as a man.

Tyler held his gaze with searing intensity. "You were always good enough for my daughter. I'm sorry if telling you to stay away from her sounded like you weren't. That was never my intention."

His chest—Jesus, it felt like a thousand pounds of defenders had piled on top of him—and he struggled to breathe.

"You've had to fight for your place every step of the way, but you've earned your spot on the team. So, from now on, lead by example. Be about football. It doesn't mean you're doing drills on these retreats. It means you're eating clean, working as a team to build a rope bridge across the Gallatin River or whatever ideas you can come up with. You don't need to provide top-shelf scotch. You need to help your teammates become the best damn players in the league. Do you understand me?"

"Yeah. I do."

"Good. Now, let me eat this while it's still warm."

Cassian watched him walk away, his lifeline to Gigi stretching so thin it was about to snap.

I'm about to snap.

He couldn't take it anymore. He just fucking couldn't live without her.

"But what about Gigi? What does any of this have to do with getting her back?"

"You can't connect the dots?"

"Not when I'm terrified I've lost her for good, no."

Tyler watched him carefully. "Son, you tell people how to treat you. You think any of my friends are going to come into my house for a party and leave used condoms on the floor?"

Of course not. He didn't even need to answer.

"Require the respect you deserve—and I guarantee all this noise will go away."

"What if it's too late? What if she moves on?"

"You think there's someone else for her?"

"No."

"There you go."

Chapter Twenty

THE RED LIGHT IN HER STUDIO FLASHED. GIGI pulled off her headphones and set her guitar down. Hurrying out of the soundproof room, she crossed her living room. *Who could be here?*

Grant was in town, but he wouldn't just show up, would he? He knew she was recording.

An ocean breeze swept through her cottage, ruffling the gauze curtains. She loved her little house. She really did, but it had never felt this empty. *She'd* never felt this empty.

Through the glass panels framing the old oak door, she saw a canary yellow delivery van double-parked on her narrow street. She opened it, and the young man handed her an envelope.

"Thank you." She signed for the package and closed the door. The shipping label had no return address, so she ripped it open to find two tickets for a Blue Fire show at the Staples Center, including two backstage passes.

She wracked her brain trying to think who would do this. It couldn't be random. Nobody would send her Blue

Fire tickets out of the blue. Only someone who knew Irwin Ledger was their A&R rep. And the only people who knew that Irwin was her brass ring were her parents...and Cassian.

Her phone chirped from the kitchen, and she hurried to answer. *Grant.* "Hello?"

"Hey. You lookin' for a plus one?"

"Okay, what's going on? Who sent me these tickets?"

"We can talk about it in the limo. Right now, you need to jump in the shower. I should be there in about an hour."

"It's tonight?" She held up the ticket. "Oh, for goodness' sake. I can't go to a concert tonight. I've been in the studio for four days. I haven't even washed my hair."

"Okay, well, how 'bout I swing by and take those tickets off your hands?"

She heard the amusement in his voice, but she wasn't smiling. "Did Cassian do this? Is that what's going on? Because he's crazy if he thinks I'm just going to hand my demo over to Irwin in the green room."

"You don't have to do anything but show up and enjoy the concert. Though, you might want to bring your Fender."

The line went dead.

Why would I bring my guitar to Blue Fire's concert?

What in the hell had Cassian arranged?

The audience screamed so loudly Gigi's ears hurt. Blue Fire, fronted by the hottest lead singer she'd ever seen, had just finished one of their older hits, "Get it, Boy," and the crowd went wild.

Grant tapped her on the shoulder and jerked his head. *Come on.*

"What are we doing?" she shouted, but of course he couldn't hear her.

He led the way through the mass of sweaty, shrieking bodies, and for the first time in five years she went unrecognized. Returning to her original brunette had done wonders for her anonymity.

"Thank you, LA," Slater said. "You're the best. Tonight—"

A collective "Ahh" sounded throughout the stadium. She glanced to the stage to see three kids—ages two, four, and six—come barreling toward him.

Cracking up, Slater dropped to a crouch, and all three climbed on him. He still held the microphone, so everyone heard the kids fighting.

"Mommy said it's my turn."

"No, she didn't. It's *my* turn."

"Daddy, I get to sleep on the bus tonight, right?"

And then the littlest one looked up at Slater and giggled. "Da da."

"Okay, tell you what." Slater stood with three kids clinging to him as if he were a jungle gym. "I gotta broker a deal with my kids here, but you need some tunes, right? Let me see what I can do about that." He turned to the side of the stage, where Gigi and Grant had just appeared. "Ah. Here we go. Just in the nick of time. Guys, you're in for a real treat. We've got Grant Banner and Gigi Cavanaugh here, and they're gonna rock your world."

Gigi reached the stage, just as a roadie handed her the Fender.

Oh, my God, I can't believe this is happening.

She threw the strap over her head and settled on a

stool. As she strummed, she reached for the mic, ready to introduce herself.

This is insane.

A couple of hours ago I was in my pajama pants, and now I'm performing in front of twenty thousand people.

When the first boo hit her ears, she froze. A few people clapped, but more boos followed. Soon, the stadium was filled with chaos.

"Aw, give a girl a chance." She said it with a smile, but she wanted to melt into a puddle and dribble down a drain. Lollipop shows were huge performances, complete with a full set of dancers and crazy pyrotechnics. On every tour in every city, the audience went wild for her.

Blue Fire's alternative rock fans weren't having it.

And she didn't blame them.

But I'm not playing Lollipop songs. I'm playing my song.

This is my chance to show the world what I've got, and I'm taking it.

Grant gave her a confident smile, as he set the mic in the stand. "Is that any way to welcome a Texas boy?" His voice settled the crowd down. "Gigi wrote the song. I'm just here to be her eye candy. Come on and give us a chance to knock your socks off." He mouthed, *A one, a two, a one two three four.*

And then they began strumming. Gigi blocked out the boos, closed her eyes to the haters, and filled the screen of her mind with her inspiration for this song. *Cassian.*

She loved him with all her heart and missed him in a way she knew would never go away. She poured that love, that loss, the constant ache of wanting someone she couldn't have, into the song.

Grant leaned in and harmonized with her, and she

knew in her bones they had a hit. It didn't happen all that often, but sometimes all the elements lined up.

Sometimes, you make magic.

With the last line, she grinned at him. Because, whether *this* crowd liked it or not, they'd knocked it out of the park.

She leaned back and gazed out over the audience. With the blaring lights, it was impossible to make out faces. *Is Cassian out there?* But, no, Grant had told her he'd started training camp.

And then someone clapped. A few more people joined in. And before she knew it, the stadium lit up with applause.

Gigi laughed. Looked like Blue Fire's massive audience liked her music.

Gigi's demo burned a hole in her purse.

The green room was crowded with reporters and friends of the band. She got a little thrill seeing some of the musicians she'd admired over the years—Lilly Raven was in the corner, chumming it up with Dash. Jimmy Blue had just tossed his head back in laughter.

And she, the former Lollipop, was still buzzing from her well-received performance in front of a sold-out audience at the Staples Center.

Because of Cassian.

The loss got a grip on her so fierce, she didn't think she could stand it. What was she going to do about him? Could she really live half a life?

"You just gonna stand here?" Grant gestured across the room with a water bottle. "That man over there? He'd love to hear the demo you've got in your hot little hands."

Irwin Ledger, tall and lean, with a mess of salt-and-pepper hair, was in deep conversation with Emmie Valencia Vaughn, Blue Fire's manager. His brow creased as he listened to the naturally beautiful woman who didn't look like she fit in with all these hard-partying rockers.

Her pulse quickened. "I can't interrupt them."

"Pretty sure he talks to Slater Vaughn's wife every day. Don't think she'd mind if you introduced yourself."

Reaching into her purse, she slid her hand into the side pocket and pulled out the USB stick. "I'll let them finish talking."

Oh, right. Good strategy. Wait until Irwin leaves. His elusiveness was a big joke in the industry. It was almost impossible to see him, let alone get time with him.

"Cassian opened the door for you. Walk on in, girl."

"You're a good friend, Grant, you know that?"

He nudged her. "Go on."

Why was she hesitating? She knew she had good material. And Irwin had seen the response she'd gotten tonight.

But, even though she'd dyed her hair, she was still a Lollipop in everyone's eyes. Her reputation had been tarnished. Irwin only worked with the finest artists in the world.

And he didn't work with troublemakers, no matter how talented. He was notorious for dropping bands who messed with drugs or didn't take the work seriously enough.

I'm talented, I don't do drugs, and I take my work seriously.

Sounds like a damn good fit.

Anticipation churned in her stomach.

Okay, what's the worst that can happen? He calls you out for being a vapid pop singer? A puppet for Clean Beatz?

Energy rolled in. And if he did, she'd tell him to listen to her songs. Because she was so much more than Dale had ever let her be.

And not signing her was Dale's loss.

She set off across the room, eyes on her target. He was such an intimidating man—so closed off and guarded. He'd reached a level in this industry where he could do anything. No one questioned or challenged him. They just let him do his thing—because every band he worked with went platinum many times over.

When she reached him, she felt a pulsing wall of energy around him.

Do Not Enter.

But she pushed through it. "Excuse me." She smiled and held her hand out. "I'm Gigi Cavanaugh."

Emmie grabbed it. "Oh, hey. I'm so glad to meet you. Your song was amazing. I'm Emmie Valencia Vaughn, and this is Irwin Ledger."

"Hello," she said to both of them. Then, she smiled at Emmie. "Your kids are adorable."

"Oh, sure. You have a flashy dance troupe on stage. We have toddlers."

"Yours are way cuter." Gigi felt the USB stick in the palm of her hand. "Irwin." She looked him right in the eyes. "I can't tell you nervous I am to meet you. You've always been my brass ring."

His gaze slid over to Emmie's with a subtle look that said, *Save me.*

Emmie jumped right in. "Irwin's not taking on any new clients at the moment, but—"

Gigi never broke eye contact. "I know you only work with musicians that blow your socks off." She handed him the stick. "So, it would mean the world to me if you'd give me a chance. Even if you only listen to the first song, that'll be enough to get a feel for my sound."

He looked at it like it had eight hairy legs.

Emmie reached for it. "Thank you. We look forward to listening."

"No, you don't, and I understand that. You see me as a Lollipop. Look, I got discovered in a karaoke bar when I was nineteen. I'd love to tell you that dropping out of USC and signing with Clean Beatz was a brilliant decision and that I have no regrets, but I can't do that. I did it because the boy I'd loved with all my heart broke up with me in the worst way possible, and from what I could see on social media, it looked like he'd moved on and was having the time of his life. I wanted him to see pictures of me as a superstar, living my best life." Her heart thundered, her palms went clammy, but she powered on. "I gave up the most essential part of me—my music—to stick it to a boy. But I'm back in my own skin now, and I'd like you to listen to my original songs."

Irwin watched her carefully, like she might rip off her facemask to reveal the clown underneath.

The ground beneath her feet turned to quicksand, and she wanted to hurry up and get sucked into it.

But, then, the legendary Irwin Ledger spoke to her in his English accent. "I don't listen to pop or country music, and while the song I heard tonight was lovely, it's more along the lines of a country-pop mash-up. If you're shopping a demo, I'd suggest committing to one style or the other as a starting point."

"I don't see myself as either."

"And yet, if I said I work with country artists—and your voice certainly lends itself to that sound—would you be willing to buy some cowboy boots and add a little twang to your voice?"

Okay, so he was going to make fun of her. She'd expected to be dismissed not ridiculed. "I already own cowboy boots, and I've just spent the last seven years being a puppet for a tyrannical record label. And, actually, I'm really glad I met you, because I'd turned you into this mythical creature in my mind, but I know this is a business and money is the bottom line, so I understand you're trying to fit me into a market that will bring your label money." A calm settled over her. "The thing is, I'm done fitting into someone else's idea of who I should be, and I think...I think I'm okay with spending some time building my own brand. So, the next time you're bored of hearing the same old same old, look for me on Song-Cloud. You might like what you hear." She turned to Emmie. "I appreciate everything my manager's done for me, but I don't think we're on the same page anymore. If you're looking to add another artist to your roster, I'd love to work with you." Then, to both of them, she smiled and said, "Thank you for your time. Goodnight."

Body bruised and aching, Cassian only had to get through one more repetition in the seven-on-seven passing drill. But, dammit, he needed to get this one right.

His rookie receiver flashed open on the right side, and Cassian released the ball. He knew the moment it left his hand that he'd fucked up. The angle was off. Didn't get the height.

So, when the assistant receivers coach lifted his paddle

to disrupt the throwing lanes and swatted the pass away, Cassian lost it.

Pulling his helmet off with both hands, he fired it to the ground.

The line coach jogged over, reaching for the ear pad that had popped out from the force. "Take a break, man."

"No, I'll do it again."

The guy turned his back to the field and lowered his voice. "Go home. Start fresh tomorrow." The compassion in his tone got Cassian's attention.

He was fucking things up for everybody. With a curt nod, he left the field. It was the end of the day, anyhow. He'd head home. Start fresh tomorrow.

Inside the cool locker room, he sat on the bench and untied his cleats, peeled off his uniform, and dropped it on the floor.

He needed to show up for his team. He needed to get his head in the game. Hell, he'd spent his entire career playing with half a heart. *Nothing new here.*

Heading to the showers, his legs felt stiff, like he'd forgotten how to walk, like the connection between his mind and body had been cut. He stood under the spray, tilting his chin down, and letting the hot water pour over him.

Eyes closed, alone in the locker room, he let it sack him.

I lost her.

I fucking lost her.

He didn't think he could stand going back to a life without her.

Squirting soap onto his palm, he lathered up and scrubbed the sweat off his body. As he rinsed, he reminded himself he wasn't going to win her back by turning into a sad sack of shit. His only hope was to clean up his reputation. Slamming his fist against the faucet, he stepped out and grabbed a towel, wrapping it around his waist.

Would she move on before he could put into action all the things he needed to do to make his world safe for her? She loved him. He knew that. He just...

I'm scared shitless I pushed her too far away this time.

He came back into the empty, dead-quiet locker room and put on his boxers, jeans, and a faded Lollipop T-shirt. Grabbing his sneakers, he turned to sit on the bench and found Dean, in his grass-stained practice pants, watching him.

Without a word, his closest friend opened his arms, and Cassian just fucking crashed. Dropping his shoes, he walked right up to him and leaned in. It didn't take more than a couple seconds for him to give Dean all his weight.

His mind went completely still for the first time in the three weeks since he'd lost her, leaving him nothing but pain and desolation. He languished in it. Tears burned, and he blinked furiously. "I want her back."

Dean grabbed his shoulders and held him at arm's length. "You can have her back...but not until you make a choice between her and us."

"What're you talking about?"

"Right now, you're dividing yourself between your teammates and Gigi—and she's come out the loser."

"That's bullshit. I would choose her over football any day. You know that."

He shook his head. "That's not the choice you need to make. Look, you can take your teammates on all the trips you want, buy them a new fancy watch every year, but if you're not winning, they're not going to like you. They'll consume you, but they won't *like* you. They need you as a leader." He dropped his arms. "Winning requires leadership—not weeklong parties where you're, essentially, babysitting them. You're George S. Patton, and they're the troops you're leading into battle. They need to believe on an emotional level that you're going to lead them to victory. If they do, they'll follow you anywhere. They'll take personal pride in being on your team. So, put your energy into being the best damn quarterback you can be, in energizing the guys on the field. When you do that, Gigi's not competing with the guys anymore, right? She's the priority of your personal life, and football's your career. You get me?"

He pulled his friend back in for another hug and slapped his back. "I do."

Before leaving the stadium, Cassian had one more stop to make. Up until now, he'd let management decide his fate, and he was done with that.

Coach's door was open, so Cassian leaned in. "You got a second?"

"Sure thing. Come on in." In his usual impatient manner, Coach flapped his hand. *Close the door.* "What's up?" The big man gestured to the empty chair facing his desk.

"I don't know how far along you've gotten in your discussions about trading me."

"Son, this is a conversation between me and your manager."

"He can't represent me the way I can."

"Fair enough."

"I've had a lot of time to think these last few weeks." He hadn't gone out with the guys. After training, he went home, made dinner, and crashed. And it wasn't about winning Gigi back. It was about figuring out his shit. And to do that he'd needed time alone.

"Yeah? Then I'm doing something wrong." He grinned but Cassian didn't play along. "I'm going to have to keep you busier tomorrow."

Cassian had something to say, and he didn't want to screw around. "I wouldn't be playing for you right now if it weren't for Tyler Cavanaugh. I don't know what he saw in me, but he chose to mentor me, and I've spent most of my life trying to make him proud. I didn't have that kind of relationship with…" He cleared his throat, unused to talking about these things. "It was different with my parents. They worked a lot, and I guess I wanted their attention. When asking for it didn't work, I tried to get it any way I could. But, with Tyler…I wanted him to be proud of me." He took a moment to get his thoughts together. *This is fucking hard.* "I don't think it was until the team made me captain that I stopped playing for Tyler Cavanaugh."

"You mean to make his investment in you worthwhile."

"Yes. And I think I was so busy getting my teammates to accept me as Ben's replacement that I didn't think about *your* investment in me. I'm thinking about that now."

Coach looked almost apologetic. "It's a cost-benefit analysis. On the field you're a natural leader and outstanding athlete, but the cost is that off the field you damage our brand. Football is family entertainment. What family wants to read about your threesomes?"

"I agree. A long time ago, Tyler asked me a question that turned my life around. He made me define my goals. If I could see myself as a professional athlete, he believed he could get me there. So, over the past couple of weeks, I've asked myself that same question."

Coach's gaze narrowed. He seemed very fucking interested, and that made Cassian feel like shit because his coach had worked so damn hard for him, and Cassian had let him down.

But I won't anymore. "My number one goal is to be worthy of Gigi Cavanaugh, which might not seem important to this conversation but bear with me. My number two goal is to marry Gigi Cavanaugh. Again, hang on. This is all leading to something that affects you."

Coach chuckled.

"And my number three goal is to beat every record ever set by a quarterback in the history of record-keeping."

His coach broke into a huge grin. "Yeah?"

"I hadn't really thought about it before, because I've been trying so hard to win over the guys. But I don't care about that anymore. I care about being the best damn player I can be, and to break records, I'm going to have to cut out anything that doesn't move me along that path."

"That's how to get it done."

"I don't know where you are in discussions about trading me, but I'd like to ask you to stop. I'd like you to give me a chance to see how my shift in perspective impacts my performance both on and off the field."

Coach's features softened. He had an almost paternal look. "Cassian, I'm not trading you. There are no discussions. I just wanted to give you a kick in the ass."

"Consider my ass kicked." Relieved, he got up and reached for Coach's hand. "Thank you, sir. I won't let you down."

"I know you won't."

Just as his hand grasped the doorknob, Coach said,

"Just so you know, Amie's been cut from the cheerleading squad."

"But she's back on that TV show. How can she be on it if she's not a cheerleader?"

Coach grinned. "She can't."

Cassian jumped into his truck. He wasn't much of a list maker, but he was damn glad to check off *Make amends with Coach.*

Next up? Drop to his knees and propose to Gigi.

But, since he couldn't do that, he'd hire a moving company to pack up her belongings and move her into his apartment in Boson.

Okay, can't do that, either.

Fine. Then, he'd like to get an ultrasound of his heart as proof it only beat for her.

Since he couldn't do any of those things, he'd do the only thing he could: he'd make his world a place she'd want to live in.

Prove through his actions that she'd be safe with him.

He picked up his phone and dictated all his plans.

For the first time, he could see the goal posts.

———

The cab barely crawled along Fifth Avenue during rush hour traffic. Fortunately, Amoeba Records was located near Central Park, so she had a great view of all the pretty storefronts. September in New York City meant colorful fall decorations.

Still buzzing from her unbelievable meeting with Irwin

Ledger, she reached for her phone. She needed to share the moment with…

Someone who isn't Cassian.

Right.

One day, she'd stop having the impulse to talk to him.

She'd done the right thing—breaking it off—she knew that. It just…it wasn't that simple. She'd be living the rest of her life missing a vital piece of herself.

What's the matter with him? Why won't he cut it out already?

Glancing out the window, she noticed the street perpendicular to Fifth ended in a large building. Grand Central Station.

An idea struck. "How far's Boston?" she asked the driver.

"Three and a half hours."

That's not bad. "Thank you." Her flight back to LA didn't take off until tomorrow afternoon.

Last time they'd ended things, she'd stewed for nine years. She'd never confronted him, never had her say. And hurt had hardened into bitterness and anger.

This time…she wasn't going to do that. She'd get it all out, purge all the anger.

And then she'd be free to really move on.

"Excuse me? Could you please drop me at the train station?"

The music was so loud *outside* his door, Gigi didn't think he could possibly hear her ringing the bell.

Unbelievable. Cassian's hosting a rave in the middle of training camp?

So, good, it only confirmed she'd been right to end the relationship. *He's never going to change.*

Pain got a grip on her heart and squeezed. *He had me back, and he still messed up.*

She pounded on the door.

What are you doing? He's having a party.

Screw it. I'm leaving.

Showing up at his door would only make him think she still had feelings for him.

And wouldn't that be embarrassing?

Right then, the elevator doors opened and out strode a bunch of men who absolutely had to be football players.

"Hey, girl," one of the guys said.

"Andre?"

He swallowed her up in his big arms. "What're you doin' in Boston?"

"I had a meeting in New York, and I thought I'd…" Stupidly, she'd imagined Cassian crapped out on the couch, drinking something green, and icing his shoulder. The last thing she'd expected was to find him partying. "I came to visit Cassian." *Like an idiot.*

His smile flattened into confusion. He motioned for the others to head into the apartment without him. When the door opened, music and conversation roared. It closed, and he asked, "When was the last time you talked to him?"

"I haven't seen him since I left Calamity a month ago."

"He forget to send you his new address?"

"His…what? Cassian doesn't live here anymore?"

"Nope. I do."

. . .

Confused, Gigi stood on the sidewalk, taking in the aged brick façade of a five-story townhome in an historic neighborhood in Boston. Quiet and elegant, the tree-canopied street, with its wrought iron streetlamps and cobbled sidewalks, was absolutely nothing like the party penthouse where Cassian used to live.

Why would he move to a family neighborhood?

It didn't make sense. *What's going on?*

On either side of the massive oak door, recessed platforms held planters spilling with brightly colored flowers and ferns. She rang the bell and heard, "Hang on a sec."

His voice hit her like a blast, rocketing through her body, and she was overcome with the impulse to run.

What the hell had she been thinking, coming to see him in person?

She wasn't ready for this. To see him, hear his voice… *it's too soon.*

I can't do it.

I miss him.

Her reaction told her the truth she hadn't wanted to admit.

She'd come because it was the only way to prove to herself that she was done with him. And she really, really needed to do that.

Because if she couldn't, she'd be doomed to repeat the last nine years.

That was not going to happen.

The door flew open, and Cassian stood there in his worn jeans, bare feet, and a white T-shirt. "Hey." He had a wallet in his hand. "Oh. I thought…Gigi?" And then he lunged for her, lifting her off the ground and hugging her to him so tightly she could scarcely breath. "You're here. Jesus. You're *here.*"

Tears splashed onto her cheeks. It was just so over-whelming to be back in his arms. The brush of his hair over her skin, the scent that spoke to the most primal part of her soul, the possessive hold that gave her roots.

Oh, dammit all to hell. She *wasn't* over him.

To hell with that. She pushed him away. "I'm here to tell you what I should have said ten years ago. You're a selfish bastard, Cassian Ellis. For weeks, you've been apolo-gizing, telling me how important I am to you, how you're going to *deserve* me."

He brought her into his foyer and shut the door behind him.

"But you *don't* deserve me. And I'm so hurt I can't even stand to live in my own skin. I can't sleep at night, I can't eat, and I can't stop this pain from eating me alive."

"I'm sorry, Gigi. I'm so—"

"No. I don't want to hear your stupid words. They mean nothing. Amie came into your bedroom wearing nothing but your jersey. You have a big heart, and I don't fault you for comforting a friend, but you had a choice to tell her to wait outside, and you didn't do it. You killed any hope of us with your stupid need to belong." She leaned in. "I'm angry. I'm angry, and I'm hurt, and I'm just so damn disappointed that you took away the only future I've ever been able to see for myself. The only future I want."

He grabbed her arms and hauled her up to him. "Oh, you're going to have that future, all right. Remember when I said I wouldn't stop fighting for us? Well, that means fighting *myself*, too. Yeah, I fucked up, but I love you enough to never stop working to become a better man. The best man I can be, because *that's* what you deserve."

She was helpless against the stirring of hope.

"It's taken me longer than I'd like to figure it all out, but I'm doing it. I see it now, in a way I never have before. That's why I moved."

"No, Cassian, you're not seeing it." She wrested out of his hold. "I don't need you to stay away from women or live in the damn suburbs. I don't need you to hide away from the world. I need you to have *boundaries*, so you're never caught in a compromising position again."

"I didn't buy this house because there are fewer temptations here. I bought it so that, when I get you back, you won't have to live in my party palace. I wanted a space where you could build a studio and we could grow a family, if it's something you wanted to do. Have your parents and sisters, my aunt and uncle and cousins come visit."

He'd managed to whisk the righteousness right out from under her. She stood transfixed at the man in front of her. He really had changed. No more excuses, no more indecision.

"I've actually been working on a lot of things," he said. "First of all, you should know, I talked to Coach and told him that I'm going to break every record ever set by a quarterback. That's going to take a lot of hard work and commitment, so I won't be hosting parties or trips any more. Secondly, I hired a professional manager to run my camp. Instead of bribing my guys to do me a favor, I'm going to hire football players and coaches, and they'll get paid for their time. Third—"

"You did all that?" Hope spread its wings and took flight. It was the most exhilarating experience in the world. Because, right there before her eyes, that future she'd wanted had dropped back into reach.

"I had it backwards. I thought I had to win them over in order to be on *their* team."

She couldn't believe it. He got it. He really did.

"I belong with you. I belong on the Mavericks. And with those priorities clear, the rest falls into place. I don't expect you to trust me right away. I'm willing to take all the time you need to prove that, from this moment on, I'm always going to put us first."

"I do believe you." She'd almost given up hope that he'd ever understand what his past had done to him, how it had twisted his perspective. But…God. She knew down to her bones that he did see it now. "Everything you've just said… every change you've made, *shows* me that." She couldn't bear the distance one more second, so she wrapped her arms around him. *Oh, my God*, he felt so good, so perfectly right. "I missed you. I missed you so much."

"I can't stand it without you."

She sighed in utter relief. "I feel the same way." She smoothed the hair off his forehead. "I love you so much, and I don't want to live a half-life. When we're together… there's just nothing better. The way you see me, believe in me…it's the best feeling in the world. You see *all* of me. I only saw the part that was embarrassed to be a Lollipop. You saw that I was—and always have been—so much more."

"I watched your show. You were amazing."

"You saw? Were you there?"

"No. I couldn't leave training camp. But I sent my manager, asked him to record it. I got to see it live."

"Well, you'll never believe this. I gave my demo to Irwin, and the craziest thing happened."

Bending his knees, he gripped her bottom and lifted

her off the floor, carrying her to the stairs. He lowered himself, and she straddled his lap. "Tell me."

"He asked if I'd be willing to go full-on country, and I told him to stuff it."

"You told Irwin Ledger to fuck off?"

"I did. Turns out, though, he was testing me. He only wants to work with authentic talent. He flew me out to New York to play a gig. That's why I'm here. He wanted to see how I did as a solo act, see if I could pull in a crowd."

"And once he saw that you could? That you brought the house down?"

She grinned. "He's going to get back to me in a few weeks."

"That's great."

"It is. But I'd rather do it with you by my side. Nothing feels right without you."

"I'm here. I'm not going anywhere. Scratch that. Actually, we are." He lifted her effortlessly, turned, and carried her up the stairs.

"Where are you taking me?"

"To our bedroom. Where we're going to stay for a long damn time."

"I'm going to need sustenance. I've been traveling all day."

"I'll give you anything you need. From this moment on, I will love you, honor you, protect you, and deserve you."

Grabbing a fistful of his hair, she kissed him. It was such a wild, wicked kiss that he had to stop at the top of the stairs and press her against the wall. "I love you, Cassian Ellis, and I'm so damn happy right now."

"Yeah? Well, trust me, it's only going to get better from here."

Epilogue

"I CAN'T FIND THE RING." CASSIAN SAID IT QUIETLY, his body strung tight with tension.

"You lost the *ring?*" Dean stood beside his girlfriend, her sister, and a few others from the royal family, as they talked near the massive Christmas tree that had replaced the driving arcade game. Holiday music played in the background, mostly drowned out by the conversation and laughter of a lively party.

Cassian should be making his guests comfortable, pouring drinks and chatting with them. Instead, he was freaking out.

Without waiting for an answer, Dean dragged him into the busy kitchen. "Where'd you last see it?"

He'd done most of the cooking himself, but they'd hired a caterer to serve and clean-up, so he moved to a quiet corner, out of the way. "In the attic. I went up there to make sure everything was perfect, but one string of lights wasn't working. I think I set the ring down, but I don't remember."

"You set it down or you put it in your pocket?"

He'd already patted himself down a dozen times, but he did it again, hoping like hell he'd feel that hard little object. *Nope. Dammit.* "I think I put it on the table, but then I heard her calling me. I didn't want her to come upstairs looking for me, so I left the room."

"So, it's still there. It's not like someone went in and took it. No one can even find the attic in this place."

"I just went back up. It's gone." Another wave of fear barreled through him. "I can't propose without the damn ring."

"All right, let's go—"

Will Bowie, a former Olympic freestyle skier, strode into the kitchen. "Hey, man. You got more ice?"

"Yeah, sure." Cassian headed for the refrigerator.

"Congrats on making the play-offs again. Great season."

"Thanks." Cassian pulled open the freezer door.

"We appreciate you and your brothers working with us," Dean said.

Last summer, he'd treated his teammates to sessions at the Bowie's training facility. The guys had loved it, since the brothers, all elite athletes, turned the Tetons into a training experience.

Staring at the cubes of ice, Cassian's mind went back to the attic. He remembered flipping the switch on, checking out the lightbulbs, screwing the faulty one in tighter, but...putting the ring down? That was the missing piece. What had he done with it? Had he set it on top of the table? In a drawer?

He wished like hell he'd left it in the velvet box. Just left it alone in that drawer in his closet until it was time to propose. But he'd wanted to show it to Dean, and he hadn't thought walking around with a velvet ring box would be too smart.

Will stood beside him. "I can do it."

Jarred out of his thoughts, Cassian took the metal bucket. "No, I got it." He scooped out some ice.

"You okay, man?" Will asked.

"Yeah, sure. Great. Thanks for coming to the party."

Dean chuckled. "He lost the ring."

Will's eyebrows shot up. "*The* ring? As in, *engagement* ring?"

Fear struck Cassian's heart. He nodded. "I'll find it. It couldn't have gone anywhere."

"Where's the last place you saw it?" Will asked.

His heart pounded. "The attic."

Will whipped out his phone and tapped out a text. Shoving it in his back pocket, he said, "Lead the way."

"To the attic?" Cassian asked.

Dean grabbed the bucket. "I'll bring the ice out there and meet you upstairs."

Just then, three more Bowie brothers hustled into the kitchen like they were on a mission. "Let's do this," Fin, the youngest, said.

"How the hell do you lose an engagement ring?" Brodie asked.

"Oh, that's nice," Gray said. "Let's make him feel worse."

"Let's go," Will said.

Heart pounding, Cassian climbed the stairs, reassured by the heavy drum of boots behind him. Together, they'd find it.

"You proposing tonight?" Fin asked.

"No. Soon. I don't know when." At the top of the stairs, he headed down a hallway.

"What're you waiting for?" Gray asked.

Cassian wanted everything to be perfect. "I only have a few days off before play-offs, and Gigi's been in the studio."

"Heard she's opening for Blue Fire," Will said quietly.

"Yeah." His girl had been busy. Irwin Ledger had signed her, and they were putting a band together. "I'm just waiting for the right time."

"Don't," Fin said.

The seriousness in his tone had Cassian nearly tripping on the runner.

"You lost nine years with her," Fin said. "You want perfect or you want to put a ring on it?"

His pulse quickened. "Yeah, I hear you." He picked up his pace.

"He *lost* the ring," Gray said. "Don't bring it up."

"It's an expression," Fin said.

"We'll find it." Will gestured to the door. *Let's go.*

Right. The moment Cassian opened it, a giant ball of fur came flying at him, knocking him back. A wet, sloppy tongue licked his face. "Get off, Rufus." He and Gigi had rescued the loveable mutt a year ago. He'd been scrawny, and a skin condition had cost him his coat, but with the right food and love, he'd turned into a small-size bear.

He pushed the dog off and found the Bowie brothers laughing their asses off.

"Guess we know what happened to the ring," Brodie said.

If he'd set it down on the table, that furiously wagging tail could easily have sent it flying.

In his panic, he'd forgotten that Rufus had been with him when he'd gone back into the attic. Rufus nosed him, begging for a rub-down. Cassian gave it to him. "I'm here. I'm here." *Calm down. Jesus.* "Sorry, buddy"

"You think he ate the ring?" Brodie asked.

"He didn't *eat* a ring," Gray said. "He's a *dog*. He's not stupid."

"No, he's pretty stupid." Cassian climbed a steep set of stairs, his dog's nails clicking on the wood as he followed. Once inside the attic, he stopped to take in the destruction.

Rufus had knocked the table over. "Ah, Rufus. I'm sorry I left you in here." The dog had knocked some of the framed photographs off the wall, messed up the bed covers, and tipped over a lamp.

"Holy shit," one of the brothers said, coming in behind him.

Dean came up the stairs, assessed the situation, and shot Cassian a look that said, *Really?* With a sigh, he said, "Come on, Rufus. Let's get a treat." The dog flew off the bed and galloped down the stairs.

"Okay, where'd you put the ring?" Will said.

"I'm not sure."

Fin righted the table, as the brothers dropped to a crouch. Gray turned on his phone's flashlight and scanned the hardwood floor.

Peering into the gap between the floor and wall, Will said, "Could've fallen down there."

Which would mean it was sitting on insulation.

On his knees, Cassian checked out the narrow slice of empty space. "Give me the flashlight." Gray handed it over. *Come on. Come on. Show me some glimmer.*

It wasn't just a ring. He'd taken a lot of care in designing it, wanted it to mean something more than a diamond he bought from a jeweler.

"Anything?" Gray asked.

"He'd tell you if he saw something," Fin said.

"I'm asking."

The band was etched to give the feel of tree bark—for their treehouse—and the setting cupped the stones like a flower's sepal, offering protection and support. The diamond in the center symbolized the love they'd forged out of enormous pressure and its indestructible nature. And the rubies on either side represented their passion.

Fuck. It wasn't here. He got back up. "I don't see it."

"That's okay. We just got here." Fin pushed past his brothers. "Let's open the drawers. Maybe it fell in."

Calm down. He didn't make touchdowns happen when he was frantic. The ring was in this room.

"When does Rufus shit?" Gray asked.

"What kind of question is that?" Brodie asked.

"In the morning," Cassian said. "But I'm not giving her a ring my dog shits out."

"What the fuck did you just say?" Dean came back into the room.

The Bowie brothers looked to each other, some weird silent communication thing, and then all four of them burst out laughing.

Cassian couldn't help it. He smiled at the image of his big, goofy dog shitting out Gigi's engagement ring.

"Hey, man," Dean said. "Gigi's asking for you. Blue Fire just showed up."

A couple years ago, the band had bought second homes not far away—in fact, right on the other side of Yellowstone. Since Gigi had opened for them a couple of times, she'd become close enough to invite them to their first annual holiday party.

"Yeah, okay. It's got to be here somewhere. I'll look

later."

"Here or in Rufus's colon," one of the brothers said.

As they headed for the staircase, Dean's gaze narrowed to something on the floor. "Pick up that picture."

Cassian lifted the framed photograph Rufus had knocked to the floor. Something glimmered in the soft yellow light. *The ring.*

He closed his eyes, peace settling over him.

Everything would be all right.

Now, all he needed was a *yes*.

And, in that moment, he realized he needed it now.

Cassian leaned against the wall, watching Gigi in her element.

They'd moved the pinball machines and game tables to the finished basement. Now, their huge living room had what Gigi called "furniture groupings." A leather couch, love seat, and club chairs faced the stone hearth. Around the blazing fire, a bunch of people had gathered to hear Gigi and Blue Fire singing and strumming their guitars. Ben, the drummer, beat out a tune on the coffee table.

Cassian loved seeing her so happy—so fulfilled—and he loved their life together. If they never married, he'd be fine. A rush of joy hit so hard it nearly took out his knees. Yeah, this life they were building together was enough.

In that exact moment, she looked up at him, her features softening. Love glowed in her eyes.

"When are you going to ask her?" Dean came up beside him, a beer in his hand.

"Right now." Because fine would never cut it. He wanted everything with this woman, and he wanted it now.

Dean grinned. "I'll leave you to it."

Song finished, she set down her guitar and made her way over to him. With a hand on his chest, she said, "Hi."

"Happy?"

"Never been happier in my life."

"Ever imagine you'd be singing songs with Blue Fire in our house?"

"Can't say that I have. But that's like an olive-size piece of my happiness."

"What's a Rufus-size piece?"

"You. Us." She gestured around. "This."

"It's pretty damn perfect." Grasping her hand, he led her to the stairs. "Come with me."

"He thinks we're having sex right in the middle of our holiday party," she muttered. "With Blue Fire right here."

"I mean, we can have sex if you want." At the top of the stairs, he took her down a long hallway. "But I really just want to give you your Christmas present."

"My presents are under the tree."

"Nah, that's just stuff for you to open." He opened the door to the attic. "This is your real present."

"I don't think I've ever been up here before. Can you turn on the light? I don't want to trip in this dress. Why does it smell so good? You'd think an attic would smell musty or stuffy or something. What is that—vanilla? Wait, cookies. It's like a cookie factory up here."

He let her steady stream of conversation wash over him, calming his nerves. At the top of the stairs, he stopped her. "You know what I love about you?"

"You mean there's only one thing? I'd better up my game."

He chuckled. "I love everything about you, but you know what I love about you right now, in this moment?"

"If I answer, do I get a cookie?"

His laughter shattered all his worries. "I love that, not once, did it occur to you to ask me where I was taking you. You just came with me."

He'd covered the skylight and windows, waiting for the big reveal, so he literally couldn't see her at all. He could smell her perfume and the shampoo scent in her hair. He could feel her heat, and the strong clasp of her hand. And he felt so much love it bubbled over.

"That's because I trust you. I'd follow you anywhere."

He flipped on the light switch. The A-frame space lit up with countless strings of lights. Some draped the walls, and others hung straight down from the ceiling. The walls were covered in photographs he'd collected from friends and family, chronicling both their lives. The bed in the center had a tall footboard, so they could brace their feet, when they lay on their backs and talked.

"It's our treehouse." Her voice was filled with awe. She turned towards him. "You recreated our treehouse."

"Only higher tech." He pressed a button and the visors covering the sunlight and windows retracted. The moon shone directly overhead.

She sucked in a breath. "This is magnificent. It's…Oh, my God." She found the framed photos and headed to the wall. She gasped when she saw the original plank of wood. Tracing her finger over the quote, she said, "You saved this?"

He nodded, warmed at her reaction.

And then she read it. "*When I saw you I fell in love, and you smiled because you knew.*" Tears spilling onto her cheeks, she caressed the words. "I can't believe you did this. It's the most amazing gift I've ever gotten. I love you so much." She turned to him to find him down on one knee, a ring in his hand. "Are you kidding me? You're *proposing*? Yes, of course yes. A thousand times yes." She rushed over to him, flinging herself into his arms.

She knocked him back on his ass and the ring went flying. Only this time, with her cupping his face and pressing kisses everywhere, he didn't worry about it. He just basked in all the love and joy pouring out of her.

"I love you so much, Cassian. Yes, I'll marry you. Yes, yes, yes."

He'd never felt fuller, more complete.

He belonged with this woman. And she belonged with him.

And he'd finally gotten it right.

Thank you for reading IT WAS ALWAYS YOU! If you love surprise baby romances, you're going to love CAN'T HELP FALLING IN LOVE, the story of Coco Cavanaugh, Beckett O'Neill, and a little blue-eyed project they made together that he didn't know anything about.

Do you subscribe to my newsletter? Get on that right now because I've got an EXCLUSIVE novella for my readers in 2022! You'll get 2 chapters a month of this super sexy, fun romance! #rockstarromance #whenyourcelebritycrushbe-comesyourboyfriend #teenidol

Need more Calamity Falls, where the people are wild at heart?

KEEP ON LOVING YOU
WE BELONG TOGETHER
THE VERY THOUGHT OF YOU
JUST THE WAY YOU ARE
IT WAS ALWAYS YOU
CAN'T HELP FALLING IN LOVE
COME AWAY WITH ME
WHOLE LOTTA LOVE
YOU'RE STILL THE ONE
THE DEEPER I FALL
LOVE ME LIKE YOU DO

Have you read the Rock Star Romance series? Come meet the sexy rockers of Blue Fire:

YOU REALLY GOT ME
I WANT YOU TO WANT ME
TAKE ME HOME TONIGHT
MORE THAN A FEELING

Look for LOVE ME LIKE YOU DO in September 2022! Grab a FREE copy of PLANES, TRAINS, AND HEAD OVER HEELS. And come hang out with me on Facebook, Twitter, Instagram, Goodreads, and Pinterest or in my private reader group.

Excerpt of Can't Help Falling in Love

Six Years Ago, Las Vegas

Coco Cavanaugh had never minded being unexceptional.

It came in handy during times like this, when she was surrounded by her sister's friends in a loud, frenzied club in Las Vegas. She could pretend to be having the time of her life, and none of these bright, shiny people would notice.

If she thought it wouldn't ruin her sister's night, she'd be back in their suite, heels kicked off, stripped of her too-tight dress, and butt-naked. She could almost feel the hot water saturating her scalp, as it washed away the make-up, perspiration, and bad choices.

Except, she was pretty sure she wouldn't make it to the shower. She'd walk in the door, collapse on the bed, heels dangling off her blistered feet, and bawl her eyes out.

Wake up in the morning with mascara streaks on the white pillowcase.

Nope, we're not doing that. It's Gigi's night. It had taken her older sister a long time to come back from a devastating high school heartbreak, but two years ago she'd grabbed hold of an opportunity that turned her into an international pop star. She was finally healed and kicking ass. Coco wouldn't do anything to bring her down.

At that exact moment, her sister, fresh from her sold-out concert, hiked herself up on a chair and lifted her lemon drop martini. "To *Colette,*"—Gigi used her real name as if to emphasize how mature Coco had become— "happy graduation and, more importantly, happy birthday. Finally, you're old enough to drink, old enough to—"

"Gamble," one of the women shouted over the insanely loud club music.

"Become a pilot," someone else shouted.

"Play with the big boys," a deep voice called.

All of them whipped around to find a group of men sauntering over. Where everyone else in the club dressed in suits and cocktail dresses, these guys wore T-shirts and jeans. With their overgrown hair, tan skin, and laidback attitudes, they could easily have been surfers.

Her sister's entourage broke out laughing, an invitation for the guys to join them.

Gigi, still on the chair, shouted, "She's already got a boyfriend, so there'll be none of that."

The words splashed cold water on her heart, giving her a shock, but her sister didn't need to know that. She'd catch Gigi up tomorrow. For now, Coco held her drink high and said a cheery, "Thanks, guys!" She sipped her martini, fighting back the roar of anxiety that threatened to pull her under.

I don't have a boyfriend.

I don't have a job.

She didn't have *anything*.

A moment later, Pitbull's "Timber" came on, and the whole group jumped up and dashed onto the dance floor, waving their arms and shaking their booties, leaving Coco blissfully alone. *Thank God.* She could finally relax her straining facial muscles.

When her sister motioned her over, Coco pulled off her stiletto and winced, using her aching feet as an excuse to stay put. Gigi blew her a kiss and lost herself in the wild crowd.

Coco could probably go now. No one would notice if she slipped out. She'd just text her sister, let her know.

A prick of awareness had her looking over to find one of the guys still sitting at the table. Watching her, he cocked his head. *You all right?*

She nodded. *Sure.* With his honey-blond chin-length hair and muscular build, he was undeniably hot, but Coco hadn't even been single twenty-four hours. *Too soon.* It really was time to leave. The flashing lights and pounding bass held her brain in a vise.

She finished off her drink, just for the snap of lemon and rush of sugar in her mouth, and then punched in the code to open her phone. She couldn't stop the leap of hope that she'd find something from her boyfriend—

Ex-boyfriend.

Face it. He ghosted you.

She could stop waiting for him. He wasn't going to magically appear, apologize for blowing off their appointment with the realtor, and tell her he was ready to build the future they'd planned.

Nope, she was on her own.

Fear knocked the air out of her lungs.

What am I going to do now? She'd banked everything on him.

A heavy body dropped onto the couch. Long, athletic legs spread out, as the surfer dude slouched beside her. "House music sucks."

Not expecting him to say that, she actually smiled. "Then, what're you doing here?"

"Jimmy…" He leaned in so their shoulders touched and pointed to a red-haired guy on the dance floor. "He's never been to Vegas. We promised him a survey tour."

"Gotcha. So…" She ticked off one finger. "Casinos."

"He already lost two grand."

"Yikes. That's not good." She touched the tip of the second finger. "David Copperfield or Celine Dion?"

"Worse. Everything was sold out. The only tickets we could get were for the fuckin' Lollipops, which is proof just how much I love that guy, since I'm willing to lose a piece of my soul for him."

Her grin grew wider. Her sister was the lead singer of that band, but she didn't see a reason to tell him. She didn't want to embarrass him as much as she didn't want to draw out the conversation.

"Now, that's a smile." He leaned forward, drawing his legs in. Elbows on his knees, he cut her a look. "And I'll bet that one doesn't hurt."

Heat rushed up her neck and fanned across her cheeks. "Please tell me it's not that obvious?"

He watched her for a moment—studying her expression, as if he actually cared.

And it just cracked the dam she'd worked so hard to build. All of it—the fear, the hurt, the *humiliation*—started slowly trickling in.

Oh, hell, no. I'm not breaking down in front of this guy.

She needed to go to her room and have a good, long cry. She needed to wallow. Just for a few hours, and then she'd be good as new. She'd make new plans.

A muscle in his jaw ticked. "Anyone gonna miss you if we take off?"

She glanced to the dance floor, so crowded she couldn't even see her sister. "I don't think so. I was about to head back to my room anyhow." With a jolt, she realized how that sounded. "By myself. That wasn't an invitation."

"Yeah, no worries. I'm not looking to get laid." He stood up and reached for her hand. "Come on."

As they chugged to the top of the incline, gravity nailed Coco to her seat and the cool night air washed over her skin. She thrilled in anticipation of the imminent fall.

She'd never been on a roller coaster at night, and certainly not in a city lit up in flashing neon lights. The wheels clacked, and she clutched the padded bar. "Oh, my God. I hate roller coasters. You have no idea."

Becks—that's what his friends had called him when he'd let them know they were taking off—covered her hand and gave it a squeeze. "I got you."

At the pinnacle, they paused, giving her a moment to take in the brilliant lights of Las Vegas, and then…it was on. The car plummeted, the dramatic descent whooshing the hair off her face.

Her stomach lurched, and her body smashed against the restraining bar. She laughed so hard tears streamed down her cheeks.

The moment the ride evened out, it twisted, flinging

her sideways and speeding along the track. The passengers behind them shrieked. Between the G-forces and her crazy laughter, Coco had to look like something in a fun house mirror.

When they rotated upside down, the blood rushed to her face.

Finally, the ride slowed, and they passed through a dark tunnel. Easing her grip, she released a breath she hadn't even known she'd been holding. The car jerked to a stop, the safety bar released, and Becks stepped out onto the platform, reaching back for her hand.

She clasped it and got out. "That was insane." She took a step, but her knee buckled.

He tugged her up against his hot, hard body, holding her gaze for a long, intense moment. One arm around her waist, the other lifted so he could smooth a lock of hair behind her ear. "Look at you, all wild and sexy."

"I feel wild." Did she feel sexy? Normally, no. But under his hot gaze, looking at her like he wanted to know what she tasted like…everywhere? *Hell, yeah.* "Thank you. That got me out of my head."

He nodded, releasing her slowly, as if he didn't want to let go. Reaching for her hand, he led her off the platform, his scent lingering—clean cotton and spicy shaving cream. Desire hummed, making her feel more alive than she had in ages.

Once out on the sidewalk, he said, "You want to go back to your hotel or do something else?"

She chanced a look into his icy blue eyes. It wasn't just his startling good looks that affected her; it was his kindness and concern. But what was the point in pursuing this attraction to a stranger? She had a future to figure out.

Then, again, she hadn't thought about her ex in a whole hour. "What else have you got in mind?"

As the spacious pod of the High Roller Observation Wheel ascended, Coco gaped at the view. Beyond the cluster of massive hotels and the glitter and sparkle of the Strip sat the vast blackness of the valley floor. "It's crazy to think they built all of this in the middle of a desert."

Though they were alone, Becks stood right beside her. Each time their arms brushed, it sent a flurry of sensation through her. She hadn't felt this butterflies-in-the-stomach, oh-my-God-he's-talking-to-me crush stuff since high school.

And she loved it.

"That's the club." He tipped his chin.

"Where?"

He came around behind her, boxing her in against the window. Extending his arm, he pointed. "That hotel right there." His warm breath at her ear sent a shiver down her spine. "The one with the weirdly shaped O spanning across the windows."

The moment felt dangerous. She could imagine turning in his arms, looping her hands around his neck, and pressing her body up against his. She could picture his hands grabbing her ass and lifting her against the window.

And she really, really wanted to feel his fingers push aside her panties and—

"You okay?" He perched his chin on her shoulder.

"Yes. Fine." But she didn't move—not a single twitch of a muscle or shuffle of a foot—because she wanted him to stay right where he was. She didn't want to lose these delicious sensations flowing through her. "You think they're still there?"

"Oh, yeah. My friends'll close it down."

"So will mine." Licking her bottom lip, she turned to look into his eyes. The connection sent a blast of excitement through her. "Why don't you want to be with them?" Was that her voice? All low and raspy, with the promise of a great blow job?

She should probably knock it off. She didn't want to give him the wrong impression. She wouldn't be going back to his room.

But...he hadn't shaved in several days, so he had a good amount of scruff. It accentuated the sexiest mouth she'd ever seen.

He's gorgeous.

And that hard, muscular body.

"I'm more of an outdoors guy. Clubs, loud music, shouting to have a conversation...it's not my thing." As the ride continued its descent, he stepped away. Reaching into his back pocket, he pulled out a small plastic bag. "Here."

Happiness danced on her heart. "You bought something for me?"

"Happy birthday and congratulations on graduating college." The contrast between his laidback attitude and gruff tone ignited something in her.

Sparked a hunger she'd never felt before. "I can't believe you got me a gift." Opening the bag, she pulled out a plastic Las Vegas sign jutting out of a black base. When she flicked the red switch, it lit up. She laughed. "I love this so much." In an impulsive move, she leaned in and kissed his cheek. His scruff tickled her lips, and she filled her lungs with his clean, masculine scent, as if she could bottle it and keep it forever. "Thank you."

"You're welcome."

Something about the intensity of his gaze had her staying right where she was, a whisper away from him. "This whole night…it's been perfect."

The pod landed. In a moment, the doors would open, and they'd get off.

But neither of them budged.

His big hand grasped the back of her neck, and the thrill of his possessive hold rocketed through her. "Know why I got it for you?"

She barely shook her head.

"Next time you have to fake a smile, I want you to look at this and remember to get out there and do something different. Shake things up."

"You got any other ideas for shaking things up?"

He gave her a devastating grin. "You know I do."

The waiter set a huge stack of buttermilk pancakes in front of her. A melting ball of butter sat on top. "What else can I get you?" he asked.

The table was loaded with syrup, a plate of bacon, a bowl of mixed fruit, two mugs of hot coffee, and two icy water glasses. "This is perfect." Coco smiled. "Thank you."

"You got it. Enjoy." He took off.

With the edge of her fork, Coco cut into a pancake and took a bite. Drenched in butter and maple syrup, it was the most amazing thing she'd ever tasted. She closed her eyes and savored it. "Oh, my God, this is unbelievable." She noticed him watching her instead of eating and grew self-conscious. "What? We can't all be mean, lean, fighting machines." She pointed to his vegetable-stuffed omelet. "No booze, no carbs...that hunky body. Professional surfer?"

He chuckled. "Not professional, no. But we did just fly in from Portugal. Ever hear of Ericeira?"

"No, but from the look in your eyes, I'm going to guess it was pretty awesome."

"It was insane."

"You travel a lot?"

"Used to, but not the good kind. The grind ended a couple months ago, though. From now on, I'm free as a bird and plan on staying that way the rest of my life." He drank some coffee.

"Good for you. I know all about the grind...and what does it get you? I mean, I've done everything I'm supposed to do. Studied hard, never skipped classes. Since I don't have a...you know, passion for anything in particular, I chose a business major. Can't go wrong with that, right?" Hearing herself get all ramped up, she set her fork down and washed the taste of syrup away with some milky coffee. Just thinking about all this made her stomach squeeze.

"You going to tell me how it all went sideways?"

Why not, right? It's better than bawling my eyes out alone in my hotel room. "I had a plan. A very good one. My boyfriend—" *You have to stop saying that.* "The guy I dated in college...okay, let me go back a little bit. Keith and I decided to take a class together, and we partnered on an assignment where we had to put together a business plan. We chose my hometown, because it has two really big tourist seasons. We did a bunch of research and figured out the one thing it needed was daycare. You know, you're on a family vacation, and Mom and

367

Dad want to go out to dinner without the kids, or maybe they want take a harder hike, go skydiving, whatever."

He nodded like, *Makes sense.*

She drank some more coffee to melt the knot of fear in her throat. "It was such a good idea that our professor asked if she could use it as an example in future classes. That got us thinking…why not really do this? So, while everyone else was applying for grad school and jobs and freaking out about their futures, we were busy starting a viable business."

His brow furrowed.

"Correct. This story has a bad ending. So, for the past two years, I've been taking jobs to save money, getting licenses and permits, lining up contractors and real estate agents." Now, the smell of food was making her sick. She pushed her plate away. "My boyfriend—" *Dammit.* "My *ex* went home after graduation. The plan was to work and live at home until we saved up enough money to launch our business. That was five months ago. Well, the perfect location became available, so I made an appointment with a realtor, and…" She hunched her shoulders in a gesture of helplessness.

Eyebrows raised, he sat back in his seat. "And?"

"And he didn't show." She still couldn't believe it. "I haven't heard a word from him since. Granted, he's been pulling away for a while, but I figured he was just partying with his friends, celebrating being done with school, whatever. But this? Not a single word of explanation? I mean, what kind of person just blows you off like that?"

"A fuckstick"

"That's exactly right. He's a fucking fuckstick." Anxiety rising, she swiveled around to check out the diner. "Does this place serve booze? I could go for another lemon drop. That was really good."

"They don't. But we can walk out that door and find all the booze we want." He held up his hand, gesturing for the bill. "You have any idea what he's doing? Maybe he got in an accident…?"

She let out a bitter laugh. "Unless he accidentally caught a flight to Hawaii with his high school girlfriend, then I don't think so. For three days, I've been reaching out to his friends, his parents, everyone I could think of. And then, out of total desperation, I checked out her social media pages. Get this, they're going to teach surfing. And the thing is, I can't even be angry about the fact that he's with her, because I'm too worried about my own future. I counted on opening this business, so I have no backup plan. Why would I? He was seriously in it all the way up until a few weeks ago. I have no idea what I'm going to do."

He reached across the table, turning his hand over. She set her palm on top of his, and his fingers closed around her in a warm, solid grasp. "You're going to shake things up."

The waiter appeared, scanning their full plates. "Everything all right?"

"Yep. Everything's great. We've just got somewhere to be." Becks handed over his credit card, and the waiter took off. He shifted out of the booth and slid in next to her, slinging an arm around her shoulders. "It's not over, you know." He picked up her hand, pressing his thumb over her finger. The simple gesture made her realize she'd been mutilating her cuticle. "You can still open this business. Find another partner, get some investors. You don't want a chickenshit for a business partner anyway."

She could do that. She'd thought about it. It was just…

"You don't want to do it?" he asked.

Warmth spread through her. She loved how easily he read her. "How do you do that? Read me so well?"

He brought the back of her hand to his mouth and kissed it. "It's all right there. You can't hide anything."

"Maybe, but I have a feeling it's your superpower."

He shifted. "I don't know about that."

Hm, she'd obviously tapped into something. "Oh, I do. All night, you've nailed me." She laughed. "Oh, my God, what is coming out of my mouth tonight? I swear I don't normally have such a dirty mind. Is there a portal? A wrinkle in the time-space continuum I could drop into?"

"Even if I knew of one, I wouldn't tell you about it." He made a face that said, *Forget about it.* "You're too much fun."

"And you're awesome at deflecting. You don't think you're good at reading people?" Had past girlfriends said he didn't pay enough attention to them?

He settled back in his seat, tapping his fingers on the table. "I know I'm good at it."

"But you don't want to tell me why?"

He glanced away. "I thought we were getting alcohol?"

"Do you even drink?"

"Not much, no."

"So…" She made a circular motion with her hand. *Go on and tell me.*

"Fine. Well, I lost my sister when I was twelve. She was six."

Oh, God. She rested her hand on his thigh.

He went quiet, emotions flickering across his features,

like shadows beneath a frozen lake. "Worst thing that ever happened to me." He stared at the syrup bottle.

"I'm sorry."

"I was there. Saw the whole thing." He plucked a sugar packet out of the plastic caddy. "Anyhow, it wrecked my family. And I guess I learned to watch my parents' expressions, so I could…I don't know…" He shrugged. "Fix things. I could tell when my mom was sinking into a depression, so I'd get upbeat, try to cheer her up. Or she'd be gunning for a fight, and I'd distract her."

"That's a tremendous amount of responsibility for a twelve-year-old to take on."

"People show up the first couple of months after a tragedy. After that, they go back to their lives. Maybe they think bad luck is contagious, or they just don't want to be pulled into the sadness. In any event, it was just me and my parents, and they didn't much like each other." He tapped the sugar packet on the table. "So, yeah, I'm pretty much expert level at reading expressions."

"That must get exhausting."

"Oh, I don't do it with everyone. In fact, I hardly ever do it."

"Really? Why me?"

"Here you go." The waiter dropped off the check. "Have a nice night."

"Thank you." Becks signed it and put his credit card back in his leather wallet. "Let's get out of here." He slid out of the booth and, once again, reached for her hand. Like before, he didn't back up to give her room, so when she stood, she was right up against him. He brushed the bangs off her forehead. "Because there's just something about you." His breath gusted over her, warm and scented with coffee. "I *like* you." He grabbed her hand and led her out of the diner.

Out on the street, the nightlife was electric.

"Want to walk?" he asked. "See what we find along the way?"

She loved the idea, mostly because it prolonged their time together. With each passing minute, she was aware of the clock running out. "Sure."

Even at one in the morning, cars jammed the boulevard, bass thumping. A limo went by with a woman poking out of the sunroof, her arms waving, the wind in her hair.

"You were trying so damn hard," Becks said quietly. "That's why I paid attention. You did a good job—I'm not sure anyone else noticed—but I did. You're different, Coco. Elegant, quiet, and yet you've got this funky look." He tipped his chin toward her deep purple satin bustier-style dress, the skin-tight skirt covered in a flare of dark lavender tulle. "You think no one notices you, but they do. You stand out. You're confident, strong, kind…"

"And funky?"

"Yeah, funky."

"My mom's a retired model, so I grew up with…let's just say an emphasis on hair, make-up, and fashion. My sisters rebelled in other ways—boys, booze, sneaking out…the usual—but I didn't care about any of that. I don't know why, but I just didn't."

"That's the confidence I was talking about."

She hadn't thought of it that way before. "The thing I did care about was my mom telling me how to dress. When we were little, she used to set our outfits on the bed the night before school, but I didn't like what she wanted me to wear. It wasn't that I was into fashion. I just had a preference. Things that I liked. I don't know about funky, but I knew my own taste." Self-consciously, she touched her hair. "I'm the only one with shorter hair."

"And, again, that's the confidence I'm talking about."

"I hated the ritual of blowing it out, adding product to make it all sleek. Just hated it. And when I looked in the mirror, I felt…I don't know. It just wasn't me. So, I cut if off." She didn't style it, either, so she always looked like she'd just come home after a day at the beach.

"I like it. I like your style. I like everything about you. And I really liked the way you held yourself together for the sake of your friends. No matter the shitty place you're in, you genuinely wanted to be present for them. I like that."

"You're a really nice guy, Becks." Affection…desire… just so much emotion crashed over her, and she tugged on his hand, making him stop. Standing up on her toes, she pressed a kiss on his cheek.

Only, he shifted at just the right moment for their mouths to meet. The brush of lips made him inhale sharply.

He smelled so delicious—a hint of salty ocean air, the remnants of a coconut sunscreen. She wanted her hands all over him. "Becks?"

"Yeah?"

"Do you have a minibar in your hotel room?"

A noise…a hum…no, a vibration. Coco fought to awaken.

My phone.

Too sluggish to move, she willed herself to rise through the levels of consciousness.

Where am I? Her dorm? No, her mattress didn't feel like this one. Her sheets didn't smell like these.

Wait, school's over.

I'm home.

Keith.

Yes. Finally. The dick. She was going to rip him a new one.

When her eyelids popped open, two things happened. One, a shaft of artificial light blinked from the gap between the curtains and, two, someone shanked her skull with a blade.

Her phone was still vibrating, though, so she reached for it. But it wasn't where she usually kept it.

To find it, she'd have to lift her head. *God, no. No, no, no.*

For a moment, she let herself wallow in the absolute torture of the worst hangover she'd ever experienced. Gazing at the ceiling, she blinked the sleep from her eyes.

Hang on a sec. This is a hotel.

Reality seeped in. Keith had ghosted her. She'd flown to Vegas for Gigi's concert.

Something bristled against her bare leg, and she jerked it away. *What the hell?* Slowly, so her brains wouldn't slosh around, she turned to find a man sprawled out beside her.

On top of the sheets.

Buck naked.

Tan skin, broad shoulders tapering to a trim waist, and round ass cheeks with matching, deep indents.

Holy shit!

She'd had sex.

With Becks.

Her eyelids fluttered shut. *Oh, for the love of God. What are you doing with your life?*

She'd never had a hookup in her life. Always the serious one, her dad liked to say.

But then…images started to roll in. Laughing so hard on the roller coaster tears had streamed down her cheeks. Making faces at the sharks in the glass tunnel of the aquarium.

Making out like high school kids in the elevator.

And, then, the dash down the long hallway to his hotel room. Him pushing her up against the wall. She could still feel the caress of his hand on her breast, the lusty squeeze. The way he'd groaned, like he couldn't stand one more minute of being separated by clothing.

Desire streamed through her body, making her hot.

Actually…she'd had the best sex of her life.

Oh, yes. That had literally been the best night ever.

Becks had held *nothing* back. Comfortable in his skin, he'd had zero inhibitions.

Had they done it *three* times?

She grinned. They sure had.

The throbbing in her head only got worse, and she knew she needed to hydrate, like, immediately.

She reached for her phone and saw Gigi's name. *Oh, shit.* When was the last time she'd checked in? Carefully, she peeled back the sheet, shifted her legs off the bed, and eased them onto the floor. In the bathroom, she answered the phone. "Hey," she whispered.

"Hey?" Her sister sounded outraged. "*Hey?* Where *are* you? The only text I have from you said you were leaving the club to go back to our suite. You're not here. It's *five in the morning.*"

"I'm sorry. I'm so sorry."

"Why are you whispering? Are you in the trunk of a car?"

"I'm—*what?* No. I'm totally fine. But I need to find my clothes right now and get out of here before this guy wakes up."

"This *guy?* My head just exploded. There are bits of brain matter all over the floor. Coco, my level-headed, smart sister went to a strange guy's hotel room?"

"Yes. And I loved it."

"I am seriously about one martini away from snatching you bald."

"Sorry not sorry? Let me get dressed so I can get out of here." She disconnected and crept back into the room.

Clothes. Where were they? She crossed the plush carpet to find her dress by the door, her heels kicked against the wall, and her bra on a table.

Where are my panties? She didn't see them. Maybe the bathroom?

Becks shifted, his head turning toward her. She froze. Held her breath.

She had no interest in small talk. Zero. Frankly, she might've had the best time ever, but it was time to get on with her life.

Because one thing had come out of her wild night— she was going to have an adventure. She'd followed the rules for her entire life, and what had it gotten her? It was time to go wild, have some fun.

She'd take some of the money she'd saved for the business and go somewhere amazing.

By myself.

Yes.

When Becks showed no signs of waking, she quickly dressed and grabbed her purse, the light-up Vegas sign sticking out of it.

Do something different. Shake things up.

She smiled. *That's exactly what I'm going to do.* She'd take this baby home, keep it front and center, so that every time she got too mired down in work, routine, the grind, she'd remember to take an adventure.

She took one more look around the room to make sure she hadn't left anything.

A bright spot of red peeked out of his jeans pocket.

My thong.

She smiled. *And that's his souvenir.*

About the Author

Award-winning author Erika Kelly writes sexy and emotional small town romance. Married to the love of her life and raising four children, she lives in the southwest, drinks a lot of tea, and is always waiting for her cats to get off her keyboard.

https://www.erikakellybooks.com/

facebook.com/erikakellybooks

twitter.com/ErikaKellyBooks

instagram.com/erikakellyauthor

goodreads.com/Erika_Kelly

pinterest.com/erikakellybooks

amazon.com/Erika-Kelly

bookbub.com/authors/erika-kelly

Printed in Great Britain
by Amazon